FORESTS OF STEEL

Modern City Combat From the War in Vietnam to the Battle for Iraq

EDITED BY

Colonel John Antal
U.S. Army (Ret.)
AND
Lieutenant Colonel
Bradley T. Gericke, U.S. Army

Published by Historical Explorations, LLC

ISBN: 978-1-934662-00-7

Additional editing by PJ Putnam (USAFA 1989)

Published in 2007 by Historical Explorations, LLC

for

EFW, Inc.
4700 Marine Creek Parkway
PO Box 136969
Fort Worth, TX 76136-6969

TABLE OF CONTENTS

AN ELBIT SYSTEMS OF AMERICA COMPANY

EFW is a full service electronics supplier, specializing in sophisticated hardware and software solutions for upgrade, integration and enhancement projects. EFW's defense programs cover fixed and rotary wing aircraft, ground vehicles, naval vessels, trainers and simulators as well as command, control and communication systems. EFW's other strengths include design, development, production and life cycle support for innovative electronic systems. EFW is also a fully accredited U.S. Department of Defense supplier currently producing high quality, cost effective, complex military electronics for General Dynamics, Boeing Helicopters Division, Boeing Military Aircraft and Missile Systems, Lockheed Martin, United Defense LP, and other U.S. and international defense contractors and governments. Every day, EFW's solutions are at work around the globe and a tangible result of an unwavering commitment to EFW's corporate mission: providing battle tested - and battle proven - solutions.

The views expressed in this book are solely those of the authors and do not reflect those of the Department of Defense or any government agency.

Cover Photo: *January 24, 2007 Pfc. MacDonald, from 5th Squadron, 73rd Cavalry Regiment radios information to Soldiers in his unit during a joint operation with the Iraqi Army to neutralize the insurgency in Balad Ruz, Iraq. Photo by Air Force Staff Sgt. DeNoris A. Mickle*

Special thanks to PJ Putnam, Tonya Gericke, and Alison Bettencourt for their expert assistance preparing this manuscript.

Dedication:

To the American Soldier, Sailor, Airman, and Marine. Our men and women in uniform give up much, so that others may live in freedom. They deserve our sincere gratitude and affection for putting themselves in harms way on our behalf.

FOREWORD

by Malcolm Quon

A few years ago, in early 2003, as American and allied forces prepared to assault Iraq, many pundits foresaw a bloody, house-to-house battle for Baghdad that would bleed U.S. forces to defeat. Instead, U.S. forces, utilizing advanced technologies and tactics honed by 3rd Generation Warfare advocates (precision destruction of enemy's centric infrastructure/power) pushed armored columns into the heart of the city, stormed through the Iraqi capital and toppled Saddam Hussein. However, the military victory over Saddam's forces and the capture of Bagdad did not end the war. New battles soon erupted with insurgent forces, sectarian militias and foreign terrorists in the cities of Iraq. Today, the control of Baghdad is the key issue in the war.

The fighting in Iraq underlines a long established fact: victory and defeat in modern war depends on the outcome of city combat. In the 21st Century, he who holds the cities holds a decisive advantage.

When you are in the middle of a fight, there is a tendency to forget the past. This is why you should read and study this book. Within the chapters of *Forests of Steel, Modern City Combat from the War in Vietnam to the Battle for Iraq,* you will discover the lessons learned that will shape wars to come. Whether you are a warfighter, politician, defense contractor, historian, educator or a concerned citizen, the nature of war and urban combat concerns you and your life in the years ahead.

Forests of Steel is a history of selected battles in cities from 1968 until today. The Editors, Colonel John Antal, U.S. Army (Retired) and Lieutenant Colonel Bradley T. Gericke, U.S. Army, are veteran Soldiers and respected authors. The authors assembled by the Editors are all experts in the field of military tactics in urban operations or dedicated students of the art of urban combat. Several of the authors are Soldiers who have been, or are now involved in urban combat operations. Together, these authors describe the last four decades of urban combat and explain how the tactics, techniques and procedures of city fighting are evolving.

A town in central Bosnia. Note the arterial urban construction oriented along the primary roads entering the town. Even relatively small cities such as this pose complex challenges for military units who must enter them. (US Army photo by Master Sgt. Kenneth Bell.)

Through the specific details of urban battles, the authors of *Forests of Steel* extract vital, hard-hitting lessons on the nature of urban combat. The pages of this book show that the battle history of the past forty years has been one of close combat in urban settings. The views of this book do not promote a vision of future land war dominated by the application of standoff precision weapons enabled by "information superiority." Urban terrain substantially negates many of America's technological advantages and standoff precision is of limited value when the enemy is next door. In addition, the close-in, three-dimensional urban battlespace is extremely complicated because tactics must be tempered by considerations of the civilian populace, the presence of noncombatants and nongovernmental agencies.

Because the urban battlespace mitigates U.S. advantages and because its complexities present U.S. warfighters with a set of multifaceted combat dilemmas, adversaries will attempt to draw American forces into the hostile environment of cities. The constricted confines of the urban battlefield compress the activities and decisions of military and political leaders. The chapters of this book highlight the finding that an intelligent enemy will often choose this low-tech, asymmetric option to avoid high-tech firepower and force a close battle in a forest of steel.

The world's urban forests of steel, concrete and glass are growing at an unprecedented rate. If cities in the past represented symbols and manifestations of strength and power, they do so with greater significance today. Today, cities are the military centers of gravity because they contain all of the essential elements of civilization that give governments and regimes their legitimacy. Armies, therefore, will continue to fight for cities in spite of the dangers and deadly challenges of urban combat.

The accounts of combat related in these pages serve to remind warfighters and interested citizens alike of the genuine and ongoing perils of urban combat. *Forests of Steel* also offers insights into the broader political, psychological, and ideological aspects that urban combat entails and how these fights can mold the organization and training of future forces and the development of weapons and technology.

EFW is sponsoring *Forests of Steel,* not only because we value this book, but because we (EFW) feel we have an obligation to be more than just a supplier but a partner to our armed forces. If this book can benefit any Soldier, Sailor, Airman or Marine – and especially the commanders in the field --then we feel have been faithful to our company's core value of supporting the warfighter.

Malcolm Quon
Vice President Marketing and Strategy, EFW

Malcolm Quon is a retired U.S. Army officer who served in both infantry & armored units throughout his military career. Injured on active duty, Malcolm entered the Aerospace & Defense Industry where he worked in both Program Management and Business Development positions within Honeywell and Fairchild Defense. Currently he is EFW's Vice President for Marketing and Strategy. EFW is a $400M Defense Electronics Company located in Fort Worth, Texas.

PREFACE

FIGHTING IN CITIES

THE MODERN EXPERIENCE

by Colonel John Antal, U.S. Army (Ret.)
and
Lieutenant Colonel Bradley T. Gericke

It is right to learn, even from the enemy.
Ovid, *Metamorphoses*, iv. c. 8 A.D.

This book is about the contemporary experience of urban combat. The epic struggles of World War II in Europe and Asia often occurred in cities. The memory of the devastation of Stalingrad, Warsaw Manila and Berlin, prompted policy makers, soldiers and civilians alike to recoil from the notion of urban warfare. A shared feeling emerged that cities should be placed off-limits to ground forces and that fast modern, fast moving mechanized armies should bypass cities whenever possible. Cities were considered obstacles too big and complex to conquer with conventional military arms and tactics and, when they did become battle-grounds, the suffering in cultural and human terms was too much to dare risk repeating.

The absence of major conventional war during the ensuing decades in Europe and the United States meant that Western armies, especially American, could turn away from urban warfare with little consequence. Depending on the time and the threat, military thinkers focused their attention on atomic weapons, counter-insurgency, or high-speed maneuver.

The problem with this self-induced amnesia is that cities remain the places where people around the world congregate to do business, to live, and to rule their societies. Cities do not only host sanctioned governments; they are also the place where terrorist organizations frequently assemble support and resources. In other words, cities have always been critically important, and they simply cannot be ignored.

Forests of Steel proposes that the urban battlefield is the battlefield of modern combat and not the exception. This book presents a series of essays that provide insights into the evolution of modern urban combat. They describe urban confrontations that occurred from 1968 to the ongoing war in Iraq. The authors, officers currently serving in the armed forces of the United States, some of them fresh from the battlefields of Iraq and Afghanistan, or civilians who work as Department of Defense analysts, are among the best and brightest military thinkers in our nation today. Each is a student of the art and science of war. Moreover, each reminds us that when our nation sends our young men and women into the world's cities to fight, we are asking them to prevail in a place that is extraordinarily perilous.

Can past city fights instruct us today? The authors believe that indeed they can. Urban combat remains with us, and future city fights likely will equal or exceed the scope of difficulties that armies already confront. As the world's population increases, the size, location, and density of urban areas around the globe grow as well.

Developing countries increase their urban populations by about 150,000 people each day. Some experts predict that by 2025, the number of people living in urban areas will double to more than 5 billion—between 60 and 80 percent of the world's population.[1] Moreover, it is in cities that people locate their governments, establish businesses, and travel to and from by means of ports, airfields, and highways. Cities contain vital communications and industrial facilities, harbor cultural attractions, and function as centers for housing. Armies that seek to control cities must come to the urban battlefield ready to engage their enemies ***and*** deal with populations. In developing countries, one or two cities may be the only decisive terrain, and hence be key objectives of military forces. The seizure of Panama City and Grozny are two examples of capital cities whose possession made the difference between victory and defeat.

An M1A2 Abrams main battle tank parked next to one of Saddam Hussein's palaces near the Tigris River in Baghdad. The Abrams tank again proved itself a dominant weapons platform in the confined battlespace of Baghdad. (Photo by Lt. Col. Odie Sheffield.)

The brief fight at Khafji, Iraq, during the Gulf

War and the lingering violence in Kabul, Afghanistan, serve as reminders that urban areas abound, even in places otherwise considered rural or lightly populated. And who envisioned the American deployment to Vietnam—a place boasting one of the world's most rugged and forbidding terrain—to be the scene of a violent city fight such as the one that occurred at Hue? Yet, as the authors of *Forests of Steel* are about to remind you that city fights should be expected features of every war that America fights in the future.

The topography of cities presents substantial physical contrasts to the "open terrain" customarily sought by military leaders practicing maneuver warfare. Beyond the "natural" characteristics inherent to any landscape, such as elevation and climate, a city contains a nearly infinite number of man-made constructs that in combination create virtually limitless micro-environments, each with a particular dynamic of visibility, special organization, and complexity. In other words, every building on every block of every city offers a unique problem for the Soldier who wishes to fight and survive in it.

As Soldiers move through the urban environment, they will encounter extraordinary variance. Soldiers moving along a street must be prepared to confront opponents who emerge from the subterranean networks of basements and sewers, while at the same time remaining cognizant of the threat posed by snipers perched in upper-story windows and on rooftops. Even during daylight hours, urban fighters must negotiate darkened alleyways and move through the interiors of buildings in which enemies may lurk in any room or behind any corner. In this highly restrictive terrain, "ordinary" military imperatives become excruciatingly challenging. Observation is blocked, artillery and aviation are hampered, direct fires have unintended consequences, civilians are typically present, resupply and evacuation is difficult, and communications is sporadic. The very complexity of cities makes them prime killing grounds and presents ideal opportunities for enemies for whom urban destruction operates to their advantage.

Cities provide opportunities for adversaries who fear U.S. technological supremacy. Seeking ways to mitigate American advances in precision firepower, high-speed maneuver, and networked command, control, and communications, opponents will occupy urban areas to attempt to fight U.S. troops in a "low-tech" battle. Potential enemies will try to lure U.S. forces into urban areas to hide from our precision weaponry and to inflict maximum casualties on our forces in order to erode American National will. Information operations by adversaries will feature allusions to Vietnam, Somalia, or the "Arab Street" to persuade the American public--and the international community--that a bloody battle in the streets of the city will not succeed. Running throughout these claims will be the reminder that cities contain large numbers of innocent civilians.

The presence of noncombatants contributes still another challenge to urban fighting. Military leaders have no choice but to weigh the humanitarian needs of the local population when planning and conducting military operations in urban terrain. Preventing food and water shortages, treating the effects of disease and epidemics, maintaining uninterrupted operation of utilities, and conducting direct relief efforts are unavoidable tasks. Once victorious, a military force will be required to administer the city, to deal effectively with the challenges of often-conflicting purposes of citizens, political leaders, and non-governmental organizations.

The city of Sarajevo, 2001. A sizeable urban center, Sarajevo was the scene of much fighting between 1992 and 1995. Utilities in many parts of the city remained intermittent for years after the end of the hostilities. The morning haze noticeable here is from wood smoke, as residents heat their homes and cook the first meal of the day over open fires. (Photo by Master Sgt. Kenneth Bell, U.S. Army.)

Today, many cities are vast in comparison to the size of urban areas only sixty years ago. Devastating a city in the fashion that occurred during WWII is the least likely option. Rather, armies will undertake city fighting to trap and eliminate the enemy and preserve the city itself. This is an ambitious undertaking and one that demands intricate coordination and flexibility on the part of the attacking force.

The need for mutually supportive civil and military objectives is obvious, but bears restating.[2]

The dictum that it is essential to fight the war with the nature of the peace in mind is vitally important in city fighting. Military objectives must often produce civil outcomes that help secure the peace. Planners, therefore, should anticipate a confluence of situations in city fights: humanitarian crisis, civil war, and insurrection may occur simultaneously. Armies should employ the destructive arsenals at their disposal in a manner that does not become counterproductive. It is no good to win the fight, create a wasteland and then lose the war. This multifaceted context requires military leaders to reconsider the assumptions by which they have been training and deploying their forces for most of the previous century.

As much as military leaders hope to dissuade enemies from defending urban areas, history predicts that fighting in cities will remain a feature of future war. Urban fights have been an enduring aspect of war, and they will remain so far into this new century. The ongoing conflict in Iraq is a case in point as it is essentially a contest for that nation's cities.

The stories that you are about to read reveal that urban combat is deadly, slow work. Armies entering cities venture onto a terrifying battlefield. To win, they must overcome remarkable adversity. For the men and women who will face the cauldron of city fighting tomorrow, today is the time to heed the history of earlier battles.

CHAPTER ONE

URBAN WARFARE: MONUMENTAL HEADACHES AND FUTURE WAR

by Lieutenant Colonel Lester W. Grau, U.S. Army (Ret.) and Jacob W. Kipp

Fortified towns are hard nuts to crack [when] your teeth are not accustomed to it... Benjamin Franklin, 1745

As the United States armed forces, especially the U.S. Army, restructure in the wake of the Cold War, their organization and footprint are undergoing a radical change from a forward deployed, division-centric force to CONUS-based, brigade combat teams. Much discussion in military circles correctly highlights the technological, doctrinal, and institutional effects that such a profound redirection will entail. However, what will not change and what is frequently overlooked by military observers is that regardless of how American forces deploy into a theater, Army and Marine Corps units will likely face what one contemporary author has called "combat in hell"—urban combat.[3] Although urban combat has been recurrent throughout history, its frequency and scale are likely to increase as emerging threats such as urban guerrillas, terrorists, and underdog armies seek refuge and resources in the cities.

The kinetic phase of urban combat requires large numbers of dismounted infantrymen, a significant amount of time, the application of combined arms, and the expenditure of astonishing quantities of ammunition. The assaulting force must run the risk of its own attrition by combat, insufficient supplies, and the threat of epidemic diseases where large concentrations of people co-exist and infrastructure is subject to destruction or damage. Assaults on cities have always resulted in heavy military and civilian casualties and left shattered the edifices and structures of cities. Modern urban combat has often destroyed operational tempo, drained logistics stockpiles and ruined the reputations of promising commanders. In addition, when the direct action subsides, occupying forces are left with responsibility for the city's infrastructure and occupants, and may still have to deal with insurgent forces as well.

Urban combat of the future will prove no easier and will present the commander with additional strategic and operational challenges – few of which are resolvable by "silver bullet" technology. Soldiers tend to think about combat in cities as just a matter of complex terrain, but it is not the local landscape, however central it may be to the solution of tactical problems, that poses the most daunting problems of urban combat. Rather, it is the nature of the city as a complex mix of man-made structures, networks, and systems that constitutes such an enormous challenge.

Welcome to Megalopolis

For most of man's recorded history, cities have represented the wealth and power of states and empires, constituting logical objectives in warfare. Cities were located on rivers, roads and seaports to facilitate commerce and trade and to control the countryside. Often they were constructed around forts and castles on militarily advantageous terrain. States fortified and garrisoned their cities in order to preserve their wealth, administrative control, and power. Although the bulk of the population was rural, early urban centers functioned as the hubs of political, economic, cultural, military, educational, and religious activity within the country. Wars began and ended with attacks or lengthy sieges against cities. The construction of city fortifications emerged as a dominant branch of military science. Its corollary, the conduct of successful sieges, also emerged as an equally rigorous area of scientific theory and practice. However, as Max Weber pointed out in his study of the evolution of the city, different civilizations developed very different cities.[4] Weber makes the point that in the Occidental city, ancient and medieval, the military qualities of the citizens were an inherent aspect of the city, and its self-defense was an indispensable part of city life.

This changed with the Thirty Years War. With the rise of the nation-states, standing armies, and the gunpowder revolution, cities ceased to enjoy military integrity and could no longer resist becoming a battleground. By the eighteenth century, the opposing national army, not the opposing nation's cities, became the immediate objective, and field commanders aspired to bring the enemy army to the one decisive battle in which victory would end the war. While this might be accomplished by maneuvering to threaten a capital or an economically important city, the cities themselves were no longer the objectives. Rather, the possession of intact, undamaged cities remained the ultimate political goal. During war, cities were often declared open, and battles were fought outside their walls in order to avoid the economic and social chaos that accompanied prolonged sieges and vicious urban combat. Military commanders, interested in maneuver warfare instead of attrition warfare, avoided fighting in cities when possible. Whenever cities had to be contested, the civilians were usually evacuated or encouraged to leave, and urban combat was conducted in largely "empty" cities. The burning of Moscow by its defenders and Atlanta by its attackers marked a shift in this policy, a hint of what Tolstoy called "people's war." Siege warfare in industrial cities, many already rife with class antagonisms, not only wrecked infrastructure, but also could become an incubator of social unrest and revolution, as was the case during the Prussian siege of Paris in 1870 and the subsequent Paris Commune in 1871.

The industrial revolution turned cities into the forges of national armies. In case of military failure, the city risked becoming a battleground. In the twentieth century, this was true with regard to both strategic bombardment and ground combat. At the beginning of World War II, there were only a few efforts to avoid urban destruction. The French declared Paris an "open city" to save it from destruction in June 1940. General Douglas MacArthur did the same for Manila during his withdrawal to the Bataan Peninsula in 1942. Nevertheless, these actions were the exception. Warsaw had the distinction of being an urban battleground on three occasions: September 1939, at the culmination of the Wehrmacht's lightning campaign; April 1943, at the time of the Uprising of the Jewish Ghetto and the Nazi's execution of the "final solution" against its population; and August-September, 1944, during the Armija Krajowa's general insurrection. In January 1945, when the Red Army finally took the city, Warsaw was utterly destroyed, with eighty-five percent of all buildings razed and its population gone—fled, killed, or carried off into captivity; and the Battle for Manila from 3 February to 3 March 1945, culminated in a terrible bloodbath, the total devastation of the city and the scene of the worst urban fighting in the Pacific theater. Prudent ground commanders tried to avoid urban combat, but circumstances often dictated otherwise. Strategic decisions by Hitler and Stalin turned Berlin and Stalingrad into their own hells on the Volga and the Spree. Horrendous civilian casualties were not necessarily the result of direct assault. By Hitler's orders, Von Leeb's Army Group North never mounted a prepared assault on Leningrad, opting instead to impose a 900-day siege that cost well over 400,000 civilian dead.[5]

In the post-war era, ground forces developed combat doctrines that advocated the avoidance of cities whenever possible and favored combat that circumvented population centers (Although the advent of strategic nuclear weapons threatened to turn urban devastation into a form of absolute war.) However, around the world since World War II, the percentage of rural population has dramatically shrunk while the percentage of urban population has skyrocketed. Thus cities have become too numerous and too large to ignore.

Describing the role of the city in the twenty-first century, Jacqueline Beaujeu-Garnier wrote, "The great metropolis is the symbol of our epoch."[6] The most rapid urbanization is taking place in Asia and Africa. United Nations' estimates project that by 2025, three-fifths of the world's population (five billion people) will live in urban areas.[7] Urban sprawl blocks many operational lines preventing military bypass (Korea's western corridor, the

German *Ruhr*, the Shanghai-Beijing approach, the Ganges valley, the Boston-Washington approach). Many cities are now too big to evacuate, and there is no place for displaced residents to go (for example Singapore, Hong Kong, Calcutta, Tokyo, Seoul, Lagos, Mexico City, Los Angeles). In short, cities are everywhere, and they are densely populated. Moreover, they will remain the battlegrounds of the future.

Spectrum of Urban Combat

Urban combat is waged at varying degrees of intensity and commitment. It can include the actions of an outside force intervening to rescue its citizens from a hazardous urban setting (U.S. Marine Corps non-combatant evacuations at Tirana, Kinshasa, Monrovia and Freetown), and it may include the actions of a peace enforcement force when local police have lost control and criminals or rival factions have seized control (Los Angeles riots, Mogadishu, Beirut, Rio de Janeiro).[8] Urban combat may be the result of armed insurrections (Budapest 1956, Monrovia, Herat 1979), and it certainly includes the actions in a city under martial law where urban guerrillas oppose the armed force and engage in terrorist acts (Kabul, Dublin, Kandahar, and Jerusalem).[9] City fighting between two distinct armed forces is the most obvious form of urban combat (Seoul, Hue, Panama City, Grozny, Sarajevo).[10] Strategic nuclear destruction of cities remains a possible, if irrational, form of urban combat. The likelihood of becoming involved in the lower end of the urban combat spectrum is more probable than the upper end. Thus, planners might spend more time considering how to fight criminal gangs, armed insurgents, and urban guerrillas than facing off against another conventional force in the city.

A well constructed by U.S. Soldiers in northern Bosnia. The fighting had destroyed the fresh water supplies for this village. When commanders took the initiative to dig the well, the bonds between local citizens and American Soldiers deepened. Military operations in cities have many dynamics that extend beyond traditional characteristics of maneuver warfare. (Photo by Master Sgt. Kenneth Bell.)

Operational Considerations and Consequences of Urban Combat

Not all cities are the same. Some are robust and resilient, while others are fragile and unable to cope with daily demands, let alone sustain the shock of military actions. Some cities, particularly in the developing world, are barely able to provide basic water, sewage, power, transport, garbage collection, and public health services to their citizens. Military actions in some cities, such as Hong Kong, New York, Frankfurt, Seoul, or Singapore, would endanger the economic stability of their parent nations–and the planet. Inevitably, military actions in cities will have greater political, economic, sociological, and commercial consequences than in the countryside. Consequently, the operational commander will probably be constrained by various political dictates, limitations, and rules of engagement. Political decisions, made far from the scene, may change the mission or cause civilian leaders to order other allied or government resources into the city.[11]

How does a military force seize a city? Traditional urban operations begin by surrounding the city. This may be the first obstacle. Shanghai and its surrounding environs contain over 125 million people and 2,383 square miles. Its police force approaches the size of the U.S. Marine Corps. Should the operational commander be faced with a city that he can physically encircle, the next question is how to reduce it. The traditional approach is to conduct a systematic sweep of the city, block-by-block, and clearing out opposing forces. Usually, the city is subdivided into small areas that can be controlled and reduced in-turn. This is a manpower intensive method, little changed from World War II, which consumes a great deal of time and logistics support.

One recent approach suggests that the commander can use urban penetration tactics to move on multiple axes to seize an important objective and then isolate and protect it from the enemy.[12] This was the initial technique applied by Russian forces in the first battle for Grozny. They moved along multiple axes to seize the presidential palace, railroad station, and radio/television center, traveling unopposed until they were deep in the city. The Chechen opposition learned not to construct permanent strongpoints that would draw a concentrated Russian attack.[13] Rather, the Chechens employed temporary strong points and a great deal of internal mobility to deploy and redeploy throughout the city.

Another recent tactic is that of urban raid, an assault on a narrow axis of advance in which the direction of the thrust is frequently changed to confuse the enemy.[14] The Russian forces' second advance into Grozny (during the first battle) was a variant of an urban raid, but due to the difficulties coordinating supporting fires and actions of adjacent units, they did not change the direction of their assault. Yet another recent tactic is that of urban swarm, in which small units patrolling assigned areas are on-call to respond to actions in neighboring sectors.[15] This is a tactic appropriate to a low-intensity battle not on the scale of Grozny.

A further method to seizing a city is to surround it and cut off food, water, power, and sanitation services while suppressing information sources. This is the classic siege. Civilians wishing to leave might be allowed to stay in a guarded and "controlled environment." However, such a decision rests with the commanders of both the attacking and defending forces, who may each have their reasons for keeping all or part of the civilian population in the city. Decisive points within the city might be hit from the air, but close, sustained combat is to be avoided. Rather the siege is maintained, the proponents argue, until the civilians remaining in the city have had enough and force their army to capitulate.[16] This approach mirrors Douhet's failed theory of strategic bombing in the 1930s and the Gulf War's premise that a defeated Iraq would rapidly overthrow Hussein. While civilians may lose heart and demand surrender, history has shown that civilians more often have as much determination as their military and prefer to have their own compatriots in charge instead of a foreign force. Starvation and disease can often strengthen their resolve. Civilians may even join with the military in the conduct of the battle rather than surrender as they did at Leningrad and Warsaw.[17] The Soviets managed to evacuate the children during the siege of Leningrad, and this further hardened the resolve of the remaining Leningrad civilians.

The Russians finally took Grozny using the World War II approach: they flattened it with artillery and aviation strikes and slowly pushed their way through the rubble. Two more battles for Grozny followed the first. In the second battle (August 1996), the Chechens conducted a thorough reconnaissance and then drove back the Russians who had failed to adequately garrison the city and maintain ready reserves or artillery, armor, and air support aircraft.[18] The Russians approached the third battle of Grozny (January 2000) methodically and avoided closing within range of the deadly RPGs and snipers of the Chechens. They brought a much larger force, surrounded the city and pounded it to ruins with artillery, tank fire, air strikes, and fuel-air explosives from the TOS-1 armored multiple rocket launchers. The destruction was even greater than during the first battle. Again, the Russians destroyed the city to deny it as a refuge for their enemy.[19]

Several years later, American Army and Marine forces faced the prospect of assaulting a major city across the desert of the Middle East. U.S. operational commanders pursued a battle plan that targeted Baghdad as the deep objective of a large, fast-paced and narrow strike. The leading American forces largely bypassed pockets of Iraqi resistance, and reached the capital city with just enough punch to prompt the Iraqi leadership to flee and Iraqi military organizations to accept defeat. Only months after conventional military operations ceased in a stunning victory for U.S. forces did an insurgency mature that caused enormous and persistent challenges for the occupying Americans.

While each urban fight is different in their particular circumstances, several lessons emerge that are widely applicable.

Considerations of Urban Combat

Even amidst combat, the military commander must be prepared to deal immediately with the physical needs of civilians. Resources must be prepared to restore or provide food, water, health care, public health services and public safety. This means that a greater than usual number of engineer, civil affairs, hospital, and military police units will need to deploy with the initial entry forces. It is possible that the bulk of logistics support will go to supporting the civilian population rather than the armed force. Urban combat traditionally consumes supplies at a much higher rate than maneuver warfare and the additional burden of supporting the civilian populace may seriously strain the logistics system.

The volume of both direct and indirect weapons fire will be constrained for political, economic, public relations, and humanitarian reasons. Attacks against cultural objects -- museums, ancient structures, monuments, temples and cathedrals -- will often be proscribed, regardless of enemy activity. This loss of indirect fire support will place the infantryman further in harm's way. Helicopter gunships will prove the most responsive and effective aerial support for urban combat. They are effective against snipers and enemy forces in upper floors. However, their use forward of friendly positions will probably be greatly constrained by enemy short-range air defenses. Loss of helicopters behind enemy lines in a city imposes the necessity of attempting recovery of downed crews under the most difficult circumstances.

The best sources of intelligence in urban combat are the local police force, city engineers, utility workers, hospital workers and shopkeepers–provided that they are on one's side. If not, enemy intelligence advantages will place attacking forces at great risk. Urban masking and access to communications traffic limit technical intelligence. Current maps in scale 1:12,500 are the most useful and frequently the hardest to find. All city maps are usually out of date and the UTM system is almost useless in a city. Information is provided by non-standard location systems ("the informant will meet you at the corner of *Kaiserdam* and *Einsiedlerhof*" or "there is an ammunition cache at 1512 *Cinco de Mayo* Street"). The precise location of underground metros and tunnels and conduits for electricity, gas, fiber-optic cable, steam, sewage, and emergency drainage will be essential items of information, and these passages may become key terrain.

The health of the expeditionary force must also be zealously guarded. Endemic disease as well as epidemics resulting from the collapse of civic services can infect and decimate the expeditionary force. The Russian force in Chechnya suffered from cholera, viral hepatitis, and other illnesses. During the cold weather months, up to fifteen percent of the Russian force was incapacitated by viral hepatitis.[20]

Psychiatric casualties are much higher in urban combat, necessitating an accelerated schedule of unit rotation for rest and recuperation, as well as integrating replacements and conducting training.

Force reconstitution will be a constant concern for the operational commander. Urban combat requires large numbers of soldiers, and battle casualties are typically higher in such combat. Units will have to be rotated regularly and in short intervals. Divisions will have to take responsibility for integrating replacements, retraining units and handling unit rotations. Such considerations will limit the available combat power and will force the commander to carefully manage his forces in sustained urban combat.

Communications within a city will prove a constant problem. If the local telephone system and cellular phone system are intact, they must be safeguarded, as they are necessary for the restoration of routine civil functions. Battle command will be threatened since FM radios work only sporadically in cities with tall buildings. Power lines, electric train and trolley lines, and industrial power lines interfere with radio transmissions. There are a limited number of frequencies, most in the lower bands, which work in cities, and consequently both sides will be trying to use the same part of the electromagnetic spectrum. Communications units will need to install redundant nets, directional antennas, and retransmission units.[21]

Some older technology is more applicable in urban combat than newer technology. For example, the .223 bullet common to most modern infantry weapons will not penetrate many walls–unlike the venerable .30-06 or .308 cartridges that chew through brick, wood, and adobe. Tanks are highly effective at ground level, but have limited utility among high-rises where the maximum elevation of the main gun and co-axial machine gun reduce the effectiveness of these systems. Self-propelled howitzers might provide better direct-fire support to the infantry, although collateral damage will be severe. In Grozny, the Russians found that the aging ZSU 23-4 armored, anti-aircraft quadruple machine gun was an excellent weapon against basements and upper floors.[22] The Soviets also employed the BM-21 multiple rocket launcher against guerrilla strong points and found artillery to very useful in providing smoke screens.[23]

A 6:1 advantage in the number of attacking to defending personnel is often necessary. Attacking forces soon realize that every building captured must be occupied or at least observed, or else an enemy can retake it. This level of requirement means that a combat battalion will expend its combat power within a few blocks advance.[24]

Urban combat will stress the logistics system, for city fighting expends huge quantities of ammunition, particularly hand grenades, smoke grenades, tear gas grenades, demolition charges, disposable one-shot antitank grenade launchers, artillery smoke rounds and artillery white phosphorus rounds. A supply of ropes with grappling hooks, lightweight ladders, pyrotechnics, and tank-mounted and dismounted searchlights are very valuable in urban combat.[25] Transporting these supplies forward to engaged forces is a problem, so armored supply vehicles are necessary.[26]

Company commanders, platoon leaders and squad leaders wage urban combat. Dismounted infantry contingents are the primary combatants, but these will require augmentations and reinforcements to their force structure. Fratricide will be a constant concern, particularly along unit boundaries.[27] Marking panels or other readily identifiable markers must be used to identify rooms and buildings captured to forces on the outside. Unit sectors need to be readily identifiable and avoid turns that could lead to one force moving in front of another friendly unit.

Conclusions

The overwhelming lesson for military forces contemplating urban combat is that cities must be approached as enormously complex systems that reflect tremendous human and environmental diversity. Fighting in cities is simply more grueling, more resource intensive, and more deadly, than any other form of warfare. Considerations of force structure, equipment design, logistics procedures, and deployment support must incorporate the necessity of urban combat missions. Only through exhaustive preparation can victory be achieved on the hellishly difficult battlefield of urban. Unfortunately, as the historical record of the past four decades reveals, such combat is unavoidable.

CHAPTER TWO

HUE, 1968

ARMOR IN HUE CITY

by Lieutenant Colonel Robert W. Lamont
U.S. Army (Ret.))

The NVA put fire over their heads; the grunts couldn't move. Christmas called up a tank for fire support. He unhooked the radio on the back of the tank, crouched down for cover, and directed its 90mm firepower. A B-40 suddenly blew on the front of the tank, spraying shrapnel. Another rocket burst against it. Christmas was unscratched. The tank kept firing.[28] *Keith Nolan, USMC, Battle for Hue*

Doctrinal Background

At the time of the battle for Hue City, the American military's Field Manual (FM) governing operations in cities was FM 31-50, *Combat in Fortified and Built-up Areas*, dated March 10, 1964. Despite the experience of the Korean War and the escalating conflict in Vietnam, the manual largely reflected the experiences of the U.S. Army in the European Theater of Operations (ETO) during World War II. Its text addressed operations against fortified positions followed by a discussion of the conduct of operations in built-up areas. The sequencing of these two topics reflected the Army's operational record as it breached the Siegfried Line and then conducted offensive operations through industrial Ruhr cities to defeat the German Army. Combat in cities and operations against fortified areas were linked because in the European experience many local towns along the Franco-

German border were directly integrated into the Nazi defensive scheme. However, FM 31-50 provided little guidance regarding combat against the irregular forces of Southeast Asia in urban areas, leaving Army and Marine forces with little doctrinal guidance.

Adhering to the Army's battlefield experience of 1944-45, the manual characterized three distinct kinds of built-up areas: outskirts, residential, and city center. In terms of offensive operations, FM 31-50 stated: "The ultimate mission of a unit attacking a built-up area is to seize and clear the entire area." It then presented a lock-step method consisting of three phases to accomplish such an attack. During the first phase the advancing force isolated the built-up area, setting the stage for what was described as the "the step-by-step capture of the objective." The second phase required the attacking force to advance to the edge of the built-up area and seize a foothold. The third phase demanded that the attacker advance through the built-up area and clear it. The manual also included discussion of control measures, fire support, and logistical support, consistently emphasizing centralized planning and decentralized execution.[29]

Finally, the doctrine provided some guidance on the employment of armor in the urban battle. It suggested that when enemy resistance was light an armor force should attempt to move rapidly through the built-up area with tanks leading. However, in the set-pace clearing operations FM 31-50 envisioned as the norm, tanks provided covering fire for assaulting infantry at the company level to form independent combined arms teams responsible for the reduction of block-size frontages.[30]

Unfortunately, for the Marines who would fight at Hue, FM 31-50 included only a short section on "counterguerrilla operations" that largely dismissed cities as likely arenas for insurgent activity:

> Since built-up areas are the most unfavorable terrain for an overt combat element of a guerilla force, such a force will not normally choose to fight in these areas until it has reached the later phases of its organizational development and has a strength and capability comparable to the conventional force.[31]

This approach differed markedly from that used by the North Vietnamese Army (NVA) in urban warfare. On a tactical level, the NVA used a technique known as the "Blooming Lotus," a method developed in 1952 during the assault on Phat Diem. Its key characteristic was that it avoided enemy positions on the perimeter of the town. The main striking columns were to move directly against the town center seeking out command and control centers. Only then were forces directed outward to systematically destroy the now leaderless units around the periphery of the town. This outward movement, like a flower in blossom, gave the tactic its name.[32]

In the case of Hue City, the NVA proved unable to drive to the center of the city, and, hence, they failed to destroy the command structure of the American defenders. Both the Army of the Republic of Vietnam (South Vietnam, or ARVN) 1st Division Headquarters and Military Assistance Command Vietnam (MACV) compound would remain operational throughout the battle.

The Urban Landscape

By the mid-1960s, Hue City contained a variety of urban development densities. The Palace of Peace was a citadel surrounded by large walls and served as the traditional center of Vietnamese culture and power.[33] The approach along Highway 1 was characterized by light building construction and rice patty fields. As the highway continued toward the Military Assistance Command Vietnam (MACV) compound, it entered more heavily built-up public building areas. The structures along Highway 1 south of the compound were medium one and two-story dwellings typical of residential construction found throughout Southeast Asia. The MACV compound contained stocks of military supplies, a nearby Helicopter Landing Zone, a boat ramp, and communications equipment. Routes leading away from the MACV compound included Le Loi Street, the Highway 1 Bridge, and the waterborne route formed by the Perfume River.

Le Loi Street was a wide avenue paralleling the Perfume River that typified French colonial design. With the exception of Le Loi Street, the street pattern on the south side of the river was a mixed bag of intersecting small avenues meeting at perpendicular and non-uniform angles. For the Marines this would complicate the clean division of labor as articulated in FM 31-50, in which each rifle company was assigned a city block. The buildings within this triangular section of Hue City were characterized by heavier construction than that found along the approaches of Highway 1. These larger structures included the central hospital, police bureau, a prison, and numerous schools. It was into this jumbled landscape that the Marines directed their initial efforts to clear Hue City.

The Battle for Hue City

North Vietnamese Army (NVA) forces, supported by the Viet Cong and local insurgent troops, were able to capture Hue City on the morning of January 30, 1968. By combining surprise with infiltration, the NVA seized the city with the exception of the MACV compound and the 1st Division, Army of Vietnam (ARVN) Headquarters. Early attempts to remove the attackers from the city failed.[34] This set the stage for the more deliberate counterattack that followed.

Lacking comprehensive doctrine and institutional training and preparation for urban combat in Vietnam, Marines on the ground were left to their own devices. From the Marines' perspective, the effort needed to clear the NVA from Hue City would require three elements. The first was the relief of the MACV compound and a build-up of forces for a clearing operation. The second phase was an effort to clear the south side of the Perfume River. The final phase revolved around attacks to secure sections of the Palace of Peace.

Company A, 1st Battalion, 1st Marine Regiment, under the command of Captain Batcheller, got the nod to lead the counterattack in the first phase of the battle. Batcheller took his platoons and mounted them in trucks for the march from Phu Bai Combat Base to Hue City. While moving north on Highway 1, he established contact with a platoon of tanks outside of the city. At this point, he shifted from the trucks to the tanks and continued to advance. As they moved through the city's outskirts, the convoy came under small arms fire from buildings adjacent to the road. The Marines of Company A returned fire and continued to press through the outskirts to a point at which the away ahead opened into a wide rice paddy. The column came under an increasing amount of direct fire augmented by mortars. In response, Captain Batcheller dismounted his Marines and prepared for a more deliberate approach to continue his relief mission.[35]

The tanks led the way down the road across the rice paddy; the infantry following in trace as the NVA placed a cross fire over the road from both sides. The volume and effectiveness of these fires was sufficient to force the infantry in the relief column to hit the ground. At the head of the column Lieutenant Colonel LaMontagne, the III MAF Embarkation Officer, took two tanks and a group of Marines and continued to press forward to the MACV compound. The tanks provided direct fire to suppress local threats, and the roles of the relief unit and those being relieved switched as friendly units helped break a roadblock ahead of the relief force. This action ended when Company A safely reached the compound.[36]

The first phase of the battle had ended and provided an opportunity for the U.S. side to assess its position. It was becoming clear to the MACV staff that a more force was needed to clear Hue City of its latest Tet New Year guests.

Clearing the Perfume River South Bank

By February 3, forces in and around the MACV compound had reached the equivalent of two understrength infantry battalions with supporting arms. Company A's higher headquarters had arrived, but the remaining line companies of the battalion had yet to reach the city, although 2nd Battalion, 5th Marines was able to muster three rifle companies. Additionally, Ontos antitank units, tanks, and 40mm quad truck-mounted guns were available for direct fire support.[37]

A Navy corpsman treats a wounded Marine during the battle for Hue on February 6, 1968. Enormous improvements in battlefield medicine increased the survival rate of U.S. servicemen in Vietnam. (USMC photo)

Colonel Stanley Hughes, the senior Marine commander of the operation, had assumed control of Marine forces on the south side of the Perfume River. The north side of the river and the area surrounding the citadel were the responsibility of the ARVN commander General Truong. Colonel Hughes' plan was for 2nd Battalion, 5th Marines to clear along the Le Loi Street as the main attack. A supporting attack providing flank security would be conducted in parallel to them by 1st Battalion, 1st Marines.[38]

The NVA's main body was positioned in a built-up area approximately 11 blocks across and nine blocks deep.[39] Line of sight in this congested area ranged from merely across the street, to several hundred meters between buildings; all within maximum range of NVA infantry weapons, including the B-40 antitank rocket, the AK-47 rifle, and light machineguns. The Marines knew very little about the specific disposition of NVA positions at the launch of the operation. They also continued to function under rules of engagement that restricted the use of artillery and air support during the early phases of the battle. The effect at the onset was that the two forces were relatively equal in terms of the weapons they brought to the field. Rifles, machineguns, and hand grenades were the primary tools of the trade for each side. The one advantage held by the Marines in the direct firefight was the presence of armor in their combined arms teams.

Friend and foe alike knew that the fire from tank main guns was decisive.[40] Many firefights followed a similar script: dismounted Marines held in check by withering small arms fire requested armor support. A tank was brought up to engage army strongholds at close range with 90mm cannon and .50 caliber machinegun fire. Forced from cover, the enemy fled into adjacent courtyards and fields were they became vulnerable to Marine small arms fire. Unable to counter this combined arms teamwork, the enemy died in place or fled.[41]

Given this kind of coordination of arms, the NVA commanders on the south side of the Perfume River began to lose their nerve and requested permission to withdraw across the river and into the citadel. NVA higher headquarters granted permission for this move, yet once begun, the order was reversed and NVA troops were sent back to face the Marines.[42]

Up to this point in the battle, the NVA had been fighting a delaying action, grudgingly trading space for time. From February 7, their forces on the south side of the Perfume River dug into strong positions and refused to withdraw. One of these strong points was the Quoc Hoc High School. The Marines referred to this structure as "Building 221." Its "U" shape and excellent fields of fire, as well as its solid masonry construction, shielded the defenders from the heavy fires of the advancing Marines. The ensuing battle was a hard fought affair in which the Marine direct fire weapons, consisting of recoilless rifles and tanks, ultimately provided the winning margin.

As the Marines learned more about the extent of the NVA position, they requested and received permission to relax the rules of engagement and use more lethal indirect fires. Within 48 hours, the Marines were able to secure the high school. Ironically, this school was the alma mater of senior North Vietnamese leaders, Ho Chi Minh and General Giap.[43]

The fight along the south side of the Perfume River was a tough house-to-house affair characteristic of many of the actions fought in the World War II. The Marines took advantage of their ability to use combined arms within this restricted battlefield, and thus dominated the battle. From the start of the action, they were able to select the point of attack and shift their effort when local resistance proved too strong to overcome. The ability to bring armor to bear on selected points provided the requisite firepower to dominate and reduce enemy resistance. These actions set the stage for the even more challenging fight that would follow on the north side of the Perfume River when the Marines assisted in the capture of the citadel.

A Marine crew of a 106mm recoilless rifle mans their weapon on February 3, 1968 in Hue. Heavy weapons support is essential for the protection of infantry fighting in cities. (USMC photo)

Capture of the Citadel

Initial ARVN efforts to secure the citadel came up short. In a series of back and forth actions, the NVA had been able to counter Marine efforts to recapture the citadel and other parts of Hue City on the river's north bank. The urban terrain on this side of the river was in some aspects more difficult for military operations than its south side counterpart because the density and number of manmade structures was far greater. The citadel itself was a fortress sited along the riverbank with defense in mind. These factors, coupled with extensive rubble from the previous ARVN efforts to clear this area, limited fields of fire to 25 meters. Finally, restrictive rules of engagement precluded the use of indirect supporting arms in some of the historic areas.

When 1st Battalion, 5th Marines, received orders to assault the citadel, it faced two essential sets of tasks.[44] The first involved pre-positioning units for the assault and the second was the attack itself. Hampering the Marines' mission was the fact that the bridges across the Perfume River were down. This meant that the battalion had to cross the river utilizing Navy small craft and helicopters. Consequently, it took several days for the battalion to gain starting positions along the citadel walls, and there was no lull in the fighting during this move. Another significant problem involved the Marines' handover of the battle area from local ARVN commanders. ARVN forces, upon learning that the Marines were taking over this part of the contest, simply moved to their new sector, leaving the Marines without any local intelligence regarding enemy dispositions.[45] This proved costly in terms of Marine loss of life. Further exacerbating the situation was the fact that low cloud ceilings nullified the possibility of close air support within an already complex battlefield. Once again, direct fire weapons had to fill the voids.

First Lieutenant Morrison, from 1st Tank Battalion, developed a new approach to providing the infantry with fire support. He paired a tank with an Ontos armored vehicle to form an armor section with dissimilar, but complementary capabilities. The tank, with its heavier armored protection, was able to lead the approach and provide direct fire support by the 90mm cannon and suppressive fire with the .50 caliber machinegun. Maneuvering behind the tank, the Ontos could gain a position from which it could fire all six of its 106mm recoilless rifles with canister shot across a street, thus preparing the way for the infantry to rush across.[46] These vehicle pairings were dubbed "killer teams." Their ability to provide the infantry with pinpoint firepower earned high marks from Marine infantrymen.[47] The level of teamwork demonstrated by tank-infantry teams continued to improve throughout the course of the battle. When restrictions on the use of air were lifted, Major Thompson, the operations officer, commented that the attack was a classic combined arms effort: infantry, armor, and air working in concert in the manner often pondered on the chalkboards at Quantico.[48]

It proved to be a bloody battle. Each side incurred losses representative of the brutal nature of urban combat, but strikingly, the NVA defenders experienced higher losses. Confirmed NVA casualties numbered 5,113 killed in action (KIA) and another 89 captured. Precise numbers of NVA wounded in action (WIA) are not known. On the Allied side, the ARVN lost 389 KIA and 1800 WIA. The Marines counted 147 KIA and 857 WIA. Within the Marine infantry units, half of those committed to the fight were lost as either KIA or WIA.[49]

Lessons Learned from the Tank Commander's Hatch

Lacking comprehensive doctrine for military operations in urban areas, the decisive aspect of the Battle of Hue City for Marines leaders was their decision to bring armor, in the form of tanks and then tank-Ontos teams, to the field of battle. The NVA's ability to counter this threat with anti-armor weapons fell short. Using a combined arms approach allowed local Marine commanders to tailor their forces to meet the unexpected opportunities and challenges of the urban battlefield.[50]

Hue suffered extensive damage during the fighting. City combat usually uproots the civilian population and destroys large swaths of any contested urban area. (USMC photo)

The tanks enhanced the mobility of the infantry by opening new routes within the urban landscape. Tank main cannons could open holes in the walls of defended buildings allowing the infantry alternate means of ingress that were lightly defended. Since tanks tended to draw attention, the infantry exploited maneuver opportunities away from the armor vehicles to obtain positions of advantage. Countering these dissimilar threats presented defenders with the need to repulse both an armored force operating in the streets and dismounted infiltration troops closing on his positions from within buildings and other concealed routes.

Furthermore, the tank had the ability to bring large amounts of firepower to the front lines of the urban battlefield. The tanks carried over 10,000 rounds of coaxial ammunition, which allowed them to suppress enemy positions for longer durations than the machineguns carried into combat by the infantry. The infantrymen could thus retain the majority of their basic load as they entered the assault, since their maneuver was shielded by accompanying armor forces.

In addition to the blast of the High Explosive Anti-Tank (HEAT) rounds, main gun rounds generated secondary fragments as the debris of buildings were propelled through the air. This resulted in behind-wall effects, which, while perhaps not visible to the attacker, were highly lethal to defenders.

Communications discipline, both on the intercom within the tank and on the radio outside the tank, was critical for maintaining control and providing effective support to the infantry. While the M-48 series tank included a tank-infantry phone mounted on the back of the vehicle, Marines found that after about a month in the field it was rarely operational. This forced tank commanders to use the radio as their primary means to establish communications with the infantry they supported. Controlling this net through effective radiotelephone procedures was a key attribute.[51]

The direct firepower of the tanks was crucial. Few structures on the urban landscape could provide the enemy cover from the primary and secondary effects of the tank main cannon. Once this realization settled in, the North Vietnamese wavered since the presence of tanks in the forward areas inspired shock and eliminated sanctuary for dismounted defenders. Even during the most intense fighting, the tanks could move from one squad in trouble to another and fire in direct support to silence any engaged NVA positions. The tanks were thus able to provide protection to dismounted infantry and evacuate wounded from even the tightest of tactical situations.[52] In turn, tankers knew that the infantry were their eyes and ears in the complex urban landscape.

As the fight for Hue City demonstrated, combat in built-up areas frequently sets the stage for a series of attrition-based battles that make urban warfare a costly undertaking. Approaches that exploit non-linear movement and disrupt the command centers of the opposition offer the potential to collapse defenses from the inside out. In this regard, the doctrinal approach of the NVA was very instructive, even if it proved unsuccessful in this case. However, if a defending opponent is willing to stick it out and fight, the prospects for an attacker remain grim. There is no other recourse but to undertake a high intensity urban battle.

At Hue, the North Vietnamese were indeed determined, which prompted the Marines to adopt innovative solutions. Ultimately, their adaptation of combined arms organizations that could successfully operate on the urban battlefield was significant. Their employment of armored firepower and mobility allowed them to set the pace of the battle. Close infantry support and interaction with armor in the urban battlefield offset the inherent weakness of each arm, setting the stage for a key advantage over an enemy unable to replicate this synergy. Ultimately, Hue proved to be a classic city fight: savage, close-range combat, widespread physical destruction, and high casualties.

CHAPTER THREE

AFGHANISTAN, 1979-1989

COMBAT IN AFGHANISTAN'S MAJOR CITIES DURING THE SOVIET-AFGHAN WAR

by Lieutenant Colonel Lester W. Grau, U.S. Army (Ret.) and Colonel Ali Ahmad Jalali

We were a very desperate people without much equipment or armaments, but we had the power of our faith, love for our homeland, love of freedom and reliance on the Almighty. We were fighting against very heavy odds. General Gulzarak Zadran[53]

When Soviet forces invaded Afghanistan in 1979, the landscape they encountered was not at all like the rolling plains of Eastern Europe with which they were familiar, but rather a mountain and desert expanse that contained some of the highest mountains and extreme temperatures in the world. The land was foreboding, the Soviets were clearly foreign invaders, and their plans, driven by communist ideology, were at odds with the core values of Afghan society; all these factors combined to make doubtful the prospect of Soviet strategic success.

A common image of urban combat is that of two conventional forces struggling for possession of a major city. However, urban combat often occurs in far more complex battlespace; often a mixture of conventional forces and guerrillas who fight in an ebb and flow of low intensity skirmishes to major battles. In Afghanistan, Soviet forces sometimes found themselves engaged with local Mujahideen (holy warriors) for possession of a town or village, but occasionally the Mujahideen would avoid the Soviets and instead try to seize a town or city from the Soviet puppet forces of the Democratic Republic of Afghanistan (DRA). Combat in the major cities of Kabul (population 1.1 million), Kandahar (225,000), Herat (177,000), Mazar-e Sharif (130,000) and Charikar (26,000) were typically contests between Soviet KHAD (the DRA equivalent of the Soviet KGB) and Tsarandoy (Internal Ministry Forces) troops and urban rebels.

The Soviet-Afghan War began as a Soviet *coup de main* when Soviet forces attempted to recreate the success of their Czechoslovakian invasion of 1968. Soviet paratroopers and Special Forces seized the Afghan capital city of Kabul and surrounding airports while ground forces crossed the border and moved to seize other major cities and to consolidate the bold usurpation of their southern neighbor. Soviet Special Forces killed the Afghan president and installed a more compliant Marxist president in the capital seat. There was little initial resistance and the Soviets felt that they controlled Afghanistan. Instead, the Soviets found that they had landed in the middle of a civil war between Afghan pseudo-Marxists and traditionally Islamic Afghans. The people rallied against the foreigners and the incumbent DRA government.

Despite the Soviet Union's best efforts, the Soviet and DRA forces were never able to secure more than fifteen percent of the country. Their area of control consisted only of the major cities and the roads connecting them. The opposing Mujahideen contested ownership of the cities and lines of communication between them. After a long, frustrating war, the Soviets withdrew, accepting a tactical stalemate and political defeat. Over a million Afghans were killed in the bloody struggle, and millions more were displaced. The Mujahideen guerrillas never wrested an Afghan city from the Soviets, yet the Soviets were never been able to fully control the cities either. Throughout, Mujahideen urban guerrillas fought a clandestine war to deny full control of urban areas to the Soviets and DRA.

The Mujahideen guerrillas waged their war by learning to survive in places tightly controlled by Soviet and DRA forces and infested with informers and party functionaries. Since the government could react much quicker to guerrilla actions in the city than in the countryside, Mujahideen urban guerrilla groups were usually small and limited their actions to short duration attacks. Small cells of urban guerrillas operated inside the city while larger bands of urban guerrillas lived and trained outside the city, entering only for specific missions. A major problem for the Afghan resistance operating in urban areas was maintaining its fighters in cohesive units.

Over the years, urban Mujahideen developed techniques that allowed them to function under severe limitations. Since all of the fighters lived underground, their bases were mostly located at the edges of the cities and sometimes in suburban villages. However, these places were also subject to regular searches conducted by the security forces. Consequently, urban guerrillas spent a lot of effort on the construction of individual and group hiding places.

Hideouts reflected many variations and their particulars were often kept secret within individual groups. The most common used false walls to create hidden rooms within houses and basements. These rooms contained hidden entrances that were usually covered with hay, firewood, or brush. The urban guerrillas created other shelters by building a parallel adobe wall around a house's orchard and then roofing it so it resembled a single, solid wall. The entrance into this hollow wall would be located at the point where an irrigation canal passed beneath. The guerrilla would enter the hideout by wading or swimming in the irrigation canal and then pushing aside a pre-fabricated floor covering to enter the hideout. The guerrillas also built hiding places by digging holes inside courtyards, which were then carefully roofed and camouflaged. These bunkers usually had circuitous entrances that began outside the house. Weapons were often hidden by wrapping them in plastic sheeting and placing them in sewers, water wells or camouflaged holes in the ground.

Security was a constant concern. Thus, communication was primarily by messenger. Messengers were usually students who possessed student identification cards and could move about the city, or old men and women who were often not subjected to search. Messengers sometimes carried information that was written on pieces of cloth and then sewn into the bearer's garments. Urban guerrillas maintained contacts within the government who aided their security measures. Undercover Mujahideen also worked in the army, police, KHAD, and party organizations. Besides providing vital intelligence, these contacts often doubled as messengers themselves. Some of these contacts were so well placed that they carried ammunition and explosives for the Mujahideen in their staff cars and army vehicles. In order to preserve operational security, combat orders were seldom given to more than a few fighters. Mostly, commanders issued fragmentary orders to avoid compromising an entire plan. In some cases, local commanders found it necessary to adjust base orders and issue separate instructions to their cells as events matured.[54]

Urban guerrillas organized themselves either in cells or in groups. The urban guerilla cells were the basic tactical units within the city, while groups were found among guerrillas who lived or trained beyond the city limits. Cells were limited to five to seven members–all longtime residents of the city who were close friends or relatives and who, as a rule, had grown up together and knew each other well. This prevented infiltration of the cell by government informers. Cells used a variety of safe houses to cover their activities. The houses usually belonged to members' families, school friends or work groups–who also provided lookouts and informants. To enhance security, there was little interaction between cells, and few cell members knew those in other cells. The cells were bound in a loose confederation headed by a leader who was usually located outside the city. The confederation was usually affiliated either with one of the seven major guerrilla factions headquartered in Pakistan or with one of the numerous guerrilla factions headquartered in Iran. Communications between the cell leader and the confederation leader was by dead-drop, messenger, or by face to face visits. Radio communications were seldom used, since most cells did not have radios and the DRA and

Soviet forces were able to pinpoint radio transmissions using direction finders and triangulation.

The cells were armed with an assortment of weapons, pistols, grenades, mines, and submachine guns, since members could readily conceal these types of arms. Cell members often moved around the city unarmed to avoid DRA and Soviet patrols that constantly checked people for weapons. Weapons training and proficiency presented particular difficulties because weapons firing could not be conducted in the city and it was difficult to move weapons back and forth between the city and country. Once weapons were inside the city, they had to be carefully concealed.

Cell tactics were usually limited in scope, and action was generally short; thus, the cells seldom had the time or opportunity to replenish their ammunition and weapons stocks from fallen enemies. Rather, old men and women often brought replacement ammunition and explosives through the checkpoints and into the city. In addition, guerrillas and their accomplices traded vodka, money, and hashish with Soviet soldiers for parts and ammunition.

Larger groups of urban guerrillas lived and trained outside the cities. The urban guerrilla group numbered up to 200 men. Group members were not as closely vetted as members of the cell, so other security measures were implemented to protect the group from government infiltration. Trusted members of these groups maintained overt occupations—such as traders, craftsmen, day laborers, deliverymen and drivers—allowing them frequent access to the city. This allowed them to carry messages, gather intelligence, and coordinate with accomplices in the city. The groups gathered their members from the outlying villages as well as sprawling suburbs, which sprang up around the cities during the war.[55]

Urban guerrilla groups maintained base camps separate from the villages and refugee camps, but members often lived in these villages and camps. Weapons and ammunition were kept, under guard, in the base camps. The groups received supplies and instructions from the faction headquarters located either in Pakistan or in Iran. Communications between the groups and the faction headquarters were normally by message, representative visits, and sometimes via radio. Some of the urban guerrilla groups also had short-range, handheld commercial radios to help coordinate their actions. Often urban groups from different factions would combine to create a bigger force for larger operations. They used weaponry similar to that used by the inner-city cells, though they also used larger arms—machine guns, antitank grenade launchers, recoilless rifles and mortars. The quality and frequency of training and weapons qualification varied among groups, but was usually higher than that of the urban guerrilla cells.[56]

In conjunction with the inner-city cells, guerrilla groups ran an extensive intelligence network through agents and accomplices in the city. Sometimes the group leader knew a cell leader from the same faction, and the leaders exchanged information. A great deal of the intelligence came from disaffected members of the DRA military or civilian government who cooperated with the Mujahideen. Both inner city cells and outer city groups of Mujahideen faced a daunting urban control system imposed by the Soviets and DRA.

This system focused its effort to intervention in cities rather than attempting to preempt the guerillas in remote sites located in the Afghan countryside. The key to the system was isolating urban enclosures. Soviets and DRA attempted this by establishing one or more rings of outposts around the cities.[57]

These outposts consisted of a series of bunkers and trenches surrounded by barbed wire and minefields. They were placed around the city walls within mutually supporting distances for direct fire weapons, well within the range of supporting artillery fires, and manned by a squad or platoon. The area between them was usually mined or patrolled. Roads leading in and out of the city were controlled by checkpoints where soldiers and police inspected passing cargo and personnel.[58]

Within a given city, security forces operated in both overt and covert ways to enforce security plans. Smaller police and military security outposts were situated at key intersections and outside important installations and buildings allowing security personnel to search people and cargo admitted through the checkpoints. Soldiers and police conducted mounted and dismounted patrols through the streets, demonstrating their control of the city. In addition, military rapid reaction forces, equipped with tanks and personnel carriers, were on standby in garrisons.

The streets were also under surveillance by informers and government spies. The KHAD, like its forerunner the KGB, had a countrywide web of informers and agents who were especially prevalent in the cities. Their reports often precipitated cordons and searches or raids by the police and military.

During the war, the cities were always under nighttime curfew. However, in the twisted adobe-walled alleys and streets of the bazaars, curfew was hard to enforce. The DRA and Soviets controlled the main thoroughfares, but after dark, the Mujahideen moved freely in the side streets and alleys. Soviet and DRA control varied by city, with Kabul being the focal point of their effort, and therefore the most secured of the country's urban areas. Kandahar and Herat were only partly under DRA control. In fact, Soviet artillery was often employed against parts of each city where other efforts at controlling the populace and its insurgents proved too tough. Two-thirds of the city of Herat was bombed to rubble by Soviet bombers, yet the Soviets never established complete authority.[59]

Mujahideen Urban Tactics

Urban guerrilla cell tactics included bombings, assassinations, kidnappings, and ambushes, whereas urban guerrilla group tactics included these as well as more sophisticated operations, to include raids and shelling attacks. Regardless of scale and whether undertaken by a cell or group, missions were well organized and carried out efficiently. Though not consistently guided by like operational goals, given that different cells and groups took their directions from differing affiliated sponsoring agencies beyond the country's borders, each proved effective.

Bombings

Mujahideen bombings were not random acts of terror, but strategic opportunities. They were carefully planned actions directed at specific targets which operatives discovered by careful surveillance and patient preparation. The urban guerrilla cell risked too much exposure to bomb widely and indiscriminately. While innocent bystanders might suffer from the bombings, limited Mujahideen bombing attacks caused far fewer civilian casualties than large-scale Soviet aerial bombing or artillery. Haji Mohammad Yakub, an Afghan fighter, described one of his bombing attacks:

> The Soviets lived in the eastern region of Kabul. We decided to attack the Soviets right where they were living. There was a bus stop in the area where the Soviets would wait for their buses to work. We checked the timing of the buses. There was a daily 0745 morning bus that drew the most Soviets. We needed to establish a pattern so that we could leave a bomb without drawing attention. We got a pushcart and loaded it with the best fruits and vegetables that we could get. The produce came from Parwan Province. We charged reasonable prices. The Soviets and local people got used to seeing us there and buying from us. We kept this up for several days. At night, we would work on the pushcart. We put in a false bottom in the cart so that we could put our bombs in the bottom of the cart and they would be undetected even if the cart were inspected. We attacked on the 2nd of October 1983. We loaded five bombs

> into the bottom of the cart. We inserted time pencil fuses in the bombs and set them for 0743. Then we put in the false bottom and loaded the cart with produce. Six Mujahideen carried out the attack. None of us carried weapons. We brought the cart to the bus stop as usual. Thirteen Soviets crowded around it to see what was on sale. We slipped away from the cart and mixed with the local people. The bombs went off at 0743 just before the bus arrived. The blast killed 13, wounded 12 and damaged a nearby store. The DRA searched the crowd but made no arrests from our group.[60]

Kidnappings

A kidnapping could result from random opportunity, but most—like bombings—were carefully planned and coordinated. Kidnap victims were taken for intelligence, future bargaining for the release of Mujahideen prisoners, or other concessions. Naturally, officers and government officials were better hostages than ordinary soldiers were, but there was greater inherent risk in such operations because they often required the cooperation of key individuals who were not members of the cell. Commander Shahabuddin described a successful kidnapping:

> We were in contact with an Afghan driver from Paktia Province who

drove for a civilian Soviet adviser. The adviser worked with the DRA mining industry. We wanted to kidnap the adviser. The driver had trained for a short time in the USSR and so the adviser trusted him. The driver agreed to help us, but we did not trust the driver and asked him to prove his loyalty. He stated, "I will bring my family to stay in a Mujahideen-controlled area as proof of my trustworthiness." The driver came to our camp with his wife and family. I sent his family to my village of Shewaki to stay while we captured the adviser.

One day the driver informed us that the adviser's wife was coming from the Soviet Union to join him. The driver would take the adviser to the airport to meet his wife. We gave the driver a small handheld radio and told him to contact us if there were any changes. We would contact with him within twenty minutes of his call. The driver called us one morning. He reported that the adviser's wife was arriving that day and that no one would accompany the adviser to the airport but the driver. We dressed one of our Mujahideen in a DRA military officer's uniform, put him in a car, and sent him to wait at the bridge over the Kabul River in East Kabul. He got out of the car and waited for the Soviet adviser's car. Soon, the Soviet adviser's car arrived. The driver pointed at our Mujahideen and told the adviser "That's my brother. He's going to the airport. Can we give him a ride?" The adviser agreed and they stopped to pick up "the officer". He got into the back seat behind the adviser and pulled out a pistol. He held the pistol to the adviser's back and ordered the driver to drive to Shewaki. Another car, carrying eight of our Mujahideen armed with pistols with silencers, followed the adviser's car. We had no trouble with the checkpoints since the guards saw the DRA officer's uniform, saluted and waived the car and its "security tail" right through.

We took the adviser to Shewaki and burned his car. The government launched a major search effort, so we moved the adviser again to the Abdara Valley. Government helicopters strafed Shewaki after we left and landed search detachments trying to find the adviser. We kept the adviser in the Abdara Valley near the Chakari monument (the Buddhist pinnacle) for two days. Then we moved him to Tezin, near Jalalabad, for a few more days. Finally, we

> took him across the border to Peshawar, Pakistan, where we turned him over to one of the factions. I do not know what happened to him.[61]

Ambushes

Urban ambushes were likewise well planned and patiently reconnoitered. The ambush was over in minutes, and the Mujahideen seldom had the opportunity to recover enemy equipment from the site. Some ambushes were done exclusively using remote controlled mines. Others ambushes used assault rifles, and, depending on the availability of larger munitions, machine guns and antitank weapons. Commander Asil Khan describes an ambush inside Kabul:

> On 28 May 1982, I led a group of four Mujahideen in an ambush at the very gates of the Soviet garrison in Kabul. At that time, elements of the Soviet 103d Airborne Division and some other units were based in Darulaman, about 10 kilometers south of downtown Kabul. The headquarters of the Soviet 40th Army was also located there in the Tajberg Palace. I was a small unit commander in my father's front. My father is Haji Dawlat and the Front's main base was at Morghgiran, 10 kilometers west of Darulaman.
>
> I selected the ambush site after we spent several days in reconnaissance

and surveillance of the Soviet traffic around Darulaman. During the reconnaissance, we detected a pattern in Soviet vehicular movement along the road from Kabul to the Soviet headquarters in the Tajberg palace. Just north of the Soviet Darulaman base is the small village of Afshar. It has a typical suburban bazaar with several grocery and fresh fruit stores and stalls. Soviet soldiers frequented this bazaar and would stop their vehicles there to buy cigarettes, food and imported vodka. Afshar looked like a good ambush site. Soviet soldiers felt secure there. There was room enough to set up an ambush, and an easy site entrance and exit. The path to and from the ambush was mostly concealed and we could easily reach Mujahideen bases and safe houses in the Chardehi District using this path.

We spent the day of the ambush in Qala-e Bakhtiar–a village six kilometers to the west of the ambush site. We had four AK-47s and a non-Soviet manufactured light antitank grenade launcher. In the early evening, we moved out toward Afshar. It was the Muslim month of Ramadan when Muslims fast during the entire day. Few people were out at sunset since this is the time to break the daily fast. Since our ambush site was in the immediate vicinity of the Soviet base, I decided to take prisoners if possible.

We moved through a narrow street of Afshar, which opened onto the main road north of the Darulaman palace. Around 1930 hours, as my leading riflemen reached the street intersection, a Soviet GAZ-66 truck approached from the east on its way to the military camp. The truck had five passengers–a driver, a soldier in the right front seat and three soldiers in the back. One of the soldiers had a backpacked radio. I told my antitank gunner to fire when the vehicle was in the kill zone. He fired, but he narrowly missed the truck. The truck came to a sudden halt and its occupants jumped out of the vehicle, took up positions and started firing at random.

During the brief firefight, we killed one Soviet soldier. Two soldiers ran away to the southwest toward their camp. One soldier crawled under the truck near the rear tires. The radioman rushed into an open grocery store and hid there. One of my Mujahideen was close to the shop behind a concrete electric pylon. I told him to follow the Soviet radioman into the front of the shop while I went into the shop's back door and introduced myself as a "friend". The Soviet soldier was flustered at first, but when he saw the foreign light antitank weapon in the hands of my Mujahideen, he uttered "dushman" [enemy]. He kept quiet as we bound his hands and led him out back. I recalled my team and we quickly left the area. The whole action lasted only a few minutes.

Fearing enemy retaliation, we moved out swiftly in the dark, heading to Qala-e Bakhtiar. From there, we went on to Qala-e Bahadur Khan, Qala-e Jabar Khan and Qala-e Qazi until we reached our Front's base at Morghgiran around 2200 hours. We kept our prisoner there for three days and then transferred him to NIFA headquarters in Peshawar, Pakistan. [62]

Raids

Raids required even more detailed reconnaissance and planning. Urban guerrilla cells did not have sufficient numbers to launch a raid, so raids were conducted by urban guerrilla groups based outside the city. Careful planning and coordination with accomplices was required to sneak the group into the city where raids were carried out in order to harass the enemy and inflict casualties. The raiding group used the same route to and from the objective, so route security required the bulk of the raiding forces. For additional protection, combatants were often briefed at the raid's objective, and the Mujahideen typically launched diversionary attacks to guard the attacking force. The raiding force also secured the flanks of the raid. Perhaps a maximum of fifteen percent of the raiding force might be involved in the actual raid. Once the raiding force was discovered, it had little time to finish its tasks before it had to withdraw. Commander Sarshar relates a raid in Charikar:

> Charikar, the capital of Parwan Province, has a compact city core, approximately one kilometer by one kilometer and a large suburb. The northern section of Charikar is called the "new jail" area. The headquarters of the DRA militia forces (self-defense units) was in the "new jail" area. Malek Shah was our contact inside that headquarters. In October 1983, he promised to get us inside the militia compound when the commander of the compound was asleep. I brought 65 Mujahideen from my base camp for this mission. We were armed with two Goryunov heavy machine guns, three PK medium machine guns, four RPG-7s, and Kalashnikov and Enfield rifles. I divided my force into three security groups and an assault group. One security group deployed near the road northeast of the headquarters; while the other deployed northwest of the headquarters to cover the other flank. These two security groups protected the assault group. The third

security group secured our withdrawal route north to Ofian-e Sharif.

We approached the target in the night at 0200 hours. At 0300 hours, we got a flashlight signal from the headquarters. I climbed the wall and the eight other Mujahideen in the assault group followed me. We were all inside the compound and Malek Shah was just starting to point out the three rooms of the compound building when one of the sleeping militia got up. He saw us and began shouting. We had no time, so we burst into the three rooms firing as we went. I led the group into the commander's room. We killed 20 and I lost one KIA and one WIA. We captured 16 Kalashnikovs and I got their commander's Makarov pistol. Since all the firing was inside the rooms, much of the noise was muffled and the other security outposts did not react. Apparently, the other security posts did not know that we had taken this post. We left the post before dawn. We went back to Ofian-e Sharif and the following night returned to our base camp in Ghorband.[63]

Shelling Attacks

Mujahideen shelling attacks on garrisons, outposts, airfields and cities were daily events.

These attacks usually employed mortars, rockets, and recoilless rifles. Sometimes they used mountain guns and howitzers. The usual objective was to harass their foes and destroy war material. Mujahideen gunners learned to construct multiple firing sites and to fire quickly and then displace immediately—before DRA or Soviet artillery or aviation could respond effectively. When possible, Mujahideen would keep water near their firing sites to dampen the ground behind the rocket or recoilless rifle. This would help curb the amount of telltale dust raised by the backblast of the ordnance. The Mujahideen fired from both fixed, surveyed sites as well as from mobile firing bases. The mobile firebase deployed in two phases. During the day, the firing survey party would move into the area, determine weapons positions, map locations, headings, intended positions for the aiming stakes, and firing data. At night, the firing party would arrive in a jeep, meet with the survey party, set up their weapons, conduct a quick shelling attack, and depart.

The Mujahideen also employed unmanned firing bases when firing positions were devoid of cover and concealment. As with mobile fire bases, points were surveyed in daylight and utilized for firing rockets on makeshift or disposable launchers at night. They would connect these rockets to time-delay firing devices. The Mujahideen would be well away from the area by the time Soviet or DRA forces launched a search for them. The Soviets and DRA tried to curb shelling attacks with counter-battery fires, rapid reaction forces, and ambushes.

Shelling attacks had mixed results. When launched against military airfields and garrisons, they occasionally destroyed military targets of value. Further, they prevented the DRA or Soviet forces from sleeping and depressed morale. However, when launched against cities, they frequently killed innocent civilians, costing the Mujahideen potential supporters. As some civilians expressed it, "the government suppresses us during the day; the Mujahideen oppress us at night."[64]

Mujahideen urban tactics in all their forms relied on effective intelligence gathering and patient preparation, even if the attack were a simple bombing. Thus, covert observers were of paramount importance. Citizen-insurgents within the cities carried out the tactics, though they were influenced and often directed by separate outside groups. The willingness of the urban cells or groups to carry them out was born of myriad motivations, from personal revenge for atrocities perpetrated by the occupying governments to simple hate of the occupiers themselves. In all cases, the victims of these attacks availed themselves to the urban attackers because they operated in established patterns, instead of varying their routines, and took risks in terms of their force protection measures, instead of ensuring that their activities were sufficiently secured and random.

The Final Tally

The Afghan urban guerrilla movement survived despite the best efforts of the Soviet and DRA forces. Guerrilla intelligence was excellent and had penetrated the intelligence service of the DRA. Though the population generally supported the Mujahideen, much of this support faltered due to the Mujahideen shelling attacks on the cities. Ten years is a long time to maintain a struggle and a particularly long time to maintain a covert fight inside a city against a determined foe. Some of the Afghan urban guerrilla experience is unique to the Soviet-Afghan War, but most shares a common heritage with other struggles by urban guerrillas.

Occupation of cities during wartime produces urban guerrillas (Paris, Warsaw, Beirut), when a portion of the population has a serious issue with the government (Algiers, Belfast, Jerusalem, Lima, Siringar), or when the central authority has collapsed or lost control (Mogadishu, Los Angeles, Rio de Janeiro). The authorities quickly classify urban guerrillas as criminals and deny them any legal protections, such as prisoner of war status. Acting alone, the urban guerrilla is usually an irritant and not a serious threat to the well-being of the occupying regime. Organized guerrilla movements that have strong outside support and are well received by the public, however, can grow to threaten the stability of the regime.

In Afghanistan, the inconsistent Soviet and DRA approach vacillated from draconian measures to attempts to placate the insurgents to various programs, which amounted to bribery. The Mujahideen urban guerrillas resisted all of these approaches and so lived to fight another day. Indeed, even after the Soviets left, the urban guerrilla cells both inside and outside the cities continued their covert war against the DRA government, finally collapsing it. The Mujahideen urban guerrillas triumphed, mainly due to the close-knit nature of their cell structure and their ability to endure.

CHAPTER FOUR

PANAMA, 1989

INSIDE A FIREFIGHT – URBAN COMBAT IN PANAMA

by Lieutenant Colonel Evan A. Huelfer

General Noriega's reckless threats and attacks upon Americans created an imminent danger to the 35,000 American citizens in Panama. As President, I have no higher obligation than to safeguard the lives of American citizens. And that is why I directed our armed forces to protect the lives of Americans citizens in Panama and to bring General Noriega to justice in the United States. ... President George Bush, December 20, 1989

(Editor's note: This essay is a firsthand account)

In the early morning hours of December 20, 1989, American military forces invaded the Republic of Panama in a lightning raid. Independent units simultaneously attacked isolated objectives in a brilliantly executed contingency plan. As the platoon leader of 3rd Platoon, Charlie Company, 4th Battalion, 17th Infantry Regiment, 7th Infantry Division (Light), I witnessed the ability of American Soldiers firsthand in Panama because during *Operation Just Cause*. This operation illustrates that conventional forces can operate successfully in an urban environment.

For several years preceding the invasion, Panamanian strongman General Manuel Noriega had subjected American citizens living in Panama to harassment. From early 1988 until May 1989, the U.S. Southern Command (SOUTHCOM) had attributed over 1,000 occurrences of harassment to the Panamanian Defense Forces (PDF). After a string of serious incidents in May 1989, including the abduction and beating of an American sailor and Noriega's interference with Panama's presidential election, President George Bush took action. On May 11, he recalled Ambassador Arthur Davis and dispatched nearly 2,000 soldiers to Panama. Bush warned that he "would not rule out further steps in the future."[65]

The United States exercised its rapid deployment capabilities by rushing two light infantry battalions from Fort Ord, California, a mechanized infantry battalion from Fort Polk, Louisiana, and a Marine company from Camp Lejeune, North Carolina, to Panama. As the situation stabilized, battalions from Fort Ord's 7th Infantry Division began to rotate in country for three-month tours. Their mission was to protect American lives and property and to exercise freedom of movement rights under the Panama Canal treaties. My battalion, 4-17 Infantry, began its rotation to Panama on October 29 after an intensive train-up period. This pre-deployment training focused on civil-military operations, rules of engagement, military operations in urban terrain, and gunnery, and included numerous live fire exercises. The high training tempo throughout 1989 would later yield huge dividends in combat.

Soon after arrival in Panama, the four companies dispersed to various points around the northern mouth of the Panama Canal. Charlie Company settled in at Coco Solo, a small community to the east of Colon, Panama's second largest city. The company established operations in an abandoned wing of Cristobal High School, a satellite school for American students in the area. From this base, the unit conducted security patrols in the surrounding areas to assure American residents of their safety, show American presence to the nearby PDF, and gather intelligence on the routines of these forces. The greatest potential threat in this area stemmed from the 8th PDF Naval Infantry Company located only 200 meters away. Their boats sat moored in a dockyard behind their headquarters building about the same distance away. For five weeks prior to the commencement of *Operation Just Cause*, Charlie Company co-existed within a stone's throw of its future adversary.

Panama City. The dense construction along the waterfront poses challenges for troops fighting in urban areas. Panama City's urban core is quite dense, and typical of modern cities. (U.S. Army photo by Maj. R. Wright.)

Following a botched attempt to topple Noriega's regime in October 1989, new SOUTHCOM

Commander General Maxwell Thurman developed OPLAN BLUE SPOON, a contingency plan to invade Panama and replace Noriega with democratically elected officials. Critical to BLUE SPOON's success was the neutralization of the PDF, Noriega's controlling arm and most effective tool for harassing Americans in Panama. Due to operational security precautions, the BLUE SPOON contingency plan was briefed only to the platoon leader level in 4-17 Infantry. However, with innovative and imaginative training, the junior leaders found ways to rehearse the mission without compromising security.

Charlie Company had a solid group of officers at its helm. The company spent the six months interim before *Operation Just Cause* on deployments or on training exercises, to include live fires. The commander, Captain Christopher Rizzo, a 1984 West Point graduate, had just taken command in June. The executive officer, First Lieutenant Chris Mahana, had prior enlisted experience in the Marines and had already been in Charlie Company for two years, the majority as a platoon leader. First Lieutenant Walter Burke, a 1986 Norwich graduate, had led first platoon for eighteen months. Second Lieutenant Daniel Kirk, a newly minted West Point graduate, had just arrived in September. Despite his inexperience, he would lead his second platoon into combat merely three months after taking charge of it. I had led third platoon for fourteen months and counting.

In mid-December, Rizzo began to up the ante with the PDF. He directed more aggressive surveillance, including platoon-sized patrols that came provocatively close to the PDF headquarters. Platoons would establish a position in the Southern

Housing Area directly across from the PDF building, and then continue with the patrol after a short time. On occasion, a 20mm Vulcan anti-aircraft gun would be towed into position and pointed at the PDF building to augment the infantry platoon's intimidating posture. At first, these demonstrations unsettled the PDF soldiers, but after several occurrences, it served to lull them into a false sense of security.

Captain Amadis Jimenez, commanding officer of the 8th PDF Naval Infantry Company, had only assumed command of his unit three days prior to *Just Cause*. When he took command, the menacing presence of the Vulcan in front of his headquarters alarmed him, but other PDF officers played down his fears. Not to worry -- they informed him -- Americans had been doing that every night for the past 15 to 20 days. This deception proved to be vitally successful once *Just Cause* commenced.[66]

On December 15, Noriega installed himself as head of the Panamanian government and declared himself as "Maximum Leader." On that date, he announced that Panama was in a "state of war" with the United States. The next night, PDF soldiers shot and killed an American Marine, First Lieutenant Robert Paz, at a roadblock. A Navy SEAL captain, innocently sitting with his wife in the next car, witnessed the murder. PDF soldiers on the scene detained the couple and hustled them to a secure location where they beat the officer and harassed his wife. They repeatedly kicked the officer in the head and groin and threatened him with death if he did not reveal details on his unit and assignment. Within hours of these two incidents, SOUTHCOM placed all units on alert.[67]

Charlie Company deployed to its BLUE SPOON assault positions as specified, but after several hours of tense waiting, all units eventually stood down and returned to normal operating procedures. Back in the nation's capital, top brass scrambled to brief options to the President. On December 17, General Colin Powell, the Chairman of the Joint Chiefs of Staff, had recommended firm action to the Secretary of Defense, Richard Cheney. After consultation with his top advisors, President Bush was convinced that an invasion was necessary. The formal order was issued the next day and established H-Hour for the invasion at 1:00 A.M. on the morning of December 20. Elements of the 82d Airborne Division at Fort Bragg, North Carolina and Ranger units from two locations in Georgia would parachute in at that synchronized jump-off time.[68]

Despite the killing of the Marine Corps officer and the harassment of the American couple, U.S. forces kept up the appearance of business as usual. Charlie Company resumed its routine schedule of patrols at Coco Solo. No one knew that other units in the United States had been alerted for an invasion of Panama. On December 19, the Brigade Tactical Operations Center told Rizzo to report for a briefing at 6:30 P.M. Immediately, he was briefed for the first time that his Soldiers would be going into combat that night.

Rizzo returned to Coco Solo two hours later and gathered the key leaders to review the mission. The air felt thick with tension; everyone in the room was a bit nervous, unsure of what the night's end might bring. Men displayed anxiety in many ways: some tried to add levity to the stressful situation, some offered up motivational aphorisms, while others merely sat in silence. At 9:00 P.M., the company assembled in the hallway for a final briefing. Since platoons had less than two hours before departing, little time remained to issue detailed operations orders. The platoons spent most of that precious time conducting backbriefs and final inspections.

Lieutenant Colonel Johnny Brooks, 4-17's battalion commander, stipulated five major concerns regarding operations at Coco Solo. First, he could not allow the boats to escape with their firepower intact. Second, he had to protect U.S. citizens in the area. Third, he had to minimize collateral damage to private property. Fourth, he had to prevent small groups of armed PDF soldiers from escaping the initial battle. Finally, he had to prevent the PDF from using their heavy machine guns to influence the fight.[69]

The PDF at Coco Solo had successfully concealed their strength and intentions. First Lieutenant Robert Murphy, 4-17's intelligence officer, estimated there were 100-115 soldiers in the 8th Naval Infantry Company, armed with a mixture of American and Soviet made weapons. The heavy machine guns on the boats accounted for their most potent threat. Docked at the naval yard were two Vosper patrol craft with 20mm chain guns, two Swift ships with .50 caliber machine guns, two PT boats with one .50 caliber machine gun, and several other boats hoisted in dry dock. These heavy weapons were potentially the greatest danger and, therefore, earned the most consideration in planning.[70]

Charlie Company had the mission to neutralize the 8th PDF Naval Infantry Company. To accomplish the mission, Captain Rizzo had a variety of units at his disposal. Besides his organic assets of three rifle platoons, a 60mm mortar section and an antitank section, he had control of an attached platoon from the 82nd Airborne Division, a platoon from the 549th Military Police Company, and two 20mm Vulcan anti-aircraft guns from the 2-62 Air Defense Artillery Battalion.[71]

The military police platoon was tasked to seal off access to Coco Solo via the main road to the east. Their vehicle-mounted M-60 machine guns would be ample firepower for the mission. The third platoon would block the PDF's possible escape to the south. First platoon would secure the PDF boats at the dock to prevent their escape to the west via water. The attached platoon from the 82nd Airborne would provide suppressive fires from the Southern Housing Area directly across from the PDF building. One of the Vulcans would also be placed at this location to augment the fires. The second platoon, the main effort, would enter the PDF building from the third floor of an adjacent building and clear it top to bottom. The other Vulcan would be positioned along the water's edge in the Northern Housing Area to destroy any boats that tried to escape out of Manzanillo Bay. The anti-tank section personnel reinforced the rifle platoons. The company 60mm mortar section, a key fire support asset, would move to a position where it could place indirect fire on the boats, if needed; however, the rules of engagement stipulated that indirect fires had to be approved by the brigade commander. Planners implemented this control measure to limit collateral damage to the surrounding area.[72] If Charlie Company needed additional fire support, an Air Force AC-130 Specter gunship was scheduled to be on station circling overhead and would be controlled by the company's fire support officer,

Second Lieutenant. David Kim. Unfortunately, the AC-130 was not on station when the company needed it and then came too late to be used.

As H-Hour approached, Soldiers went about their last minute preparations.[73] Each carried a basic load of 210 rounds in seven magazines for his individual weapon, plus two or more hand grenades. Some carried additional rounds for the machine guns, demolition material, or antitank rockets. Nobody seemed to mind toting extra firepower. Every Soldier wore a protective vest, Kevlar helmet, and carried at least four quarts of water. Leaders also had night vision devices, binoculars, radios, and flashlights. The typical combat load exceeded fifty pounds even without counting the rucksack.

To ensure that the attack would not be compromised, elements tried to deploy to their assault positions as routinely as they had done on prior nights. At 11:00 P.M., third platoon began its infiltration to the Southern Housing Area by squads. It began to evacuate all occupants from their homes and consolidated the residents at the house farthest from where the major action would be. Many of the evacuees were dependents whose spouse had already been alerted earlier to deploy somewhere else as part of the BLUE SPOON contingency. First platoon began its movement to its assault position at 11:30 P.M. Second Platoon assembled in the school's gymnasium at midnight.

Around that time, a U.S. counterintelligence unit intercepted a call to the PDF's Military Zone II Headquarters in nearby Colon. The caller said, "The party's on for one o'clock. Get out of the area." Shortly thereafter, Captain Jimenez received a call from his immediate supervisor, a PDF lieutenant colonel. Jimenez's superior instructed him to reinforce security around the complex because a U.S. operation "was about to go down." He recalled later that was all he had been told. He expected repercussions for the killing of the American officer, but not a full-scale invasion of the entire country. Lacking further guidance, Jimenez ordered one platoon to defend against U.S. forces from their sandbagged windows at the front of the building and another platoon to operate the boats out at the dock. He envisioned, if necessary, an escape to Colon, two nautical miles away.[74]

As these preparations were underway, an incident occurred that remains one of the night's most controversial and significant events. At H-minus-26, as platoons waited in their assault positions, Sergeant First Class Charlie Gray, the platoon sergeant for the military police platoon, spotted several men in the wood line near his blocking position. Gray claimed that the men were using a radio to report American positions. He relayed this information to his platoon leader and said he was ordered to "take that position and silence that radio at all costs."[75] Gray approached the group and demanded their surrender. He alleged that one of the men jumped him, and in the ensuing scuffle, he shot the assailant point-blank in the chest, killing him instantly. The other men he had spotted quickly came out of the woods and surrendered. Because the rules of engagement in the operations order authorized deadly force against an armed enemy after 12:30 A.M., and the shooting occurred at 12:34 A.M., Gray's actions fell within legal parameters. Due to the unclear circumstances surrounding the incident, the case was later referred to the Army's Criminal Investigation Command, but it was dropped due to a lack of evidence.[76]

However, justified Gray's actions might have been legally, he certainly jeopardized the operation tactically. His decision to fire a weapon before clearing it with the commander had monumental ramifications. Next to the slain victim, surprise became the second casualty of the night. At H-minus-26, synchronized or not, *Operation Just Cause* began for Charlie Company. For the most part, no one, except for Sergeant First Class Gray, knew what had happened. The sound of that single gunshot, reverberating with the rising tension, triggered an irreversible sequence of events.

Within minutes, PDF soldiers began scrambling out of the back of their building toward the boats. Lieutenant Mahana sat in a sandbagged bunker overwatching the street behind the PDF building. The bunker position protected two M-60 machine guns and an M-203 grenade launcher, placed there to seal off the escape route to the dock. To Mahana's dismay, as the enemy fled in strength, it was still long before H-Hour. He immediately radioed Rizzo and requested to open fire. Some of the boats started their engines at this time, so it seemed apparent that they were going to try to escape before the trap could be closed.[77] Rizzo notified battalion of the situation and requested to initiate early. Because of the relative proximity of the battalion's objectives, the gunfire would be heard at other locations. Brooks was concerned that his other companies might not yet be in place. During the planning process, this contingency had been addressed. The brigade commander had stated that early activity would not initiate H-Hour prematurely, especially since the operation depended upon the synchronized arrival of other units flying in from the United States. Yet, Brooks believed if the PDF escaped into the water with their firepower intact, it would spell disaster for other U.S. units in the vicinity. Contrary to his planning guidance, the brigade commander did not hesitate to grant approval to Brooks' spontaneous request for early initiation. Brooks immediately relayed the message to Charlie Company.[78]

After a surrender request delivered by bullhorn to the PDF drew no response, Rizzo ordered the Vulcan to commence firing on the building. The building shuddered as the initial barrage blasted the upper two floors. The Vulcan spewed out approximately 1100 rounds before jamming.[79] Simultaneously, the attached platoon launched some sixty antitank rockets (a mixture of both AT-4s and Light Anti-Tank Weapons (LAWs)) at the building. Third Platoon opened fire at designated targets within its sector. The cacophony of automatic weapons and rocket fire rose to a deafening crescendo. Mahana unleashed his two M-60 machine guns on the PDF guard shack protecting the dock's entrance and sprayed any PDF soldiers still making their way to the boats. If he had been able to fire earlier, he could have caused significantly more casualties. Because of the delay, many PDF soldiers had already made it safely to the boats across the 200 meters of open area on the docks. From there, they would be in an excellent position to spoil first platoon's mission of securing the boats, which should have been lightly defended, if at all.[80]

First platoon infiltrated toward their objective from the north along a seawall and then divided into two elements as they approached the dock. The smaller support element, led by the platoon sergeant, Staff Sergeant Arbues, was to penetrate and destroy a small barracks and boathouse on the dockyard, then support the assault element with suppressive fires from that position. The larger assault element had almost moved into position when some of the running PDF soldiers spotted it and brought it under fire. An intense exchange of gunfire opened up on the dockyard. A first platoon gunner pegged one PDF soldier in the head. Only his glasses and a large pool of blood remained after his comrades dragged him along onto a boat. As one of the boats made its way out into the water, Specialist Richards fired upon it with his Squad Automatic Weapon (SAW). Enemy fire converged on first platoon's men from almost every boat moored at the dock, effectively pinning down those at the front of the assault element.[81] The situation rapidly deteriorated into confusion.

Second platoon had been staging in the gymnasium in preparation to assault the PDF Headquarters building. If the PDF did not surrender, second platoon would enter the building on the third floor and clear it. The Vulcan's initiation at 12:43 A.M. was seventeen minutes before second Platoon had expected. As anti-aircraft, rocket, and small arms fire pummeled the PDF building, second platoon readied to go into action. It first had to traverse an open area 75 meters wide between buildings. Sergeant David Rainer, leading 1st Squad, tossed a smoke grenade into the clearing to conceal his squad's movement. Before the smoke had thickened, 1st Squad dashed across the gap to the front side of a Chinese restaurant, attached to the PDF building. The smoke grenade's initial flame silhouetted the moving soldiers against the night sky, which immediately drew PDF fire upon them. Although no one was hit, Rainer recalled tracers whistling by overhead and churning up the grass between his legs as he ran.[82] Once 1st Squad safely made the dash, the rest of second platoon crossed the gap under the concealment of the billowed up smoke.

Panama City. Punta Paitilla area with the airfield, seen from the southeast. The sprawling nature of large cities is evident. High-rise buildings extend for miles. If this type of area is defended, attacking troops could easily consume months trying to seize it. (U.S. Army photo by Maj. R. Wright.)

Without a diagram of the interior layout, they cautiously probed the darkness. Several wrong turns exacerbated their anxiety, especially since the Vulcan still hammered away at the adjacent building and its tracer rounds streamed visibly past the windows. Second platoon gathered seventeen civilians inside the building, including an old woman who fainted when two camouflaged soldiers unexpectedly surprised her. Several males, fearing that they would be shot, had to be coaxed out of hiding places. Second platoon soldiers safely escorted all of these civilians out of harm's way. With that time-consuming task completed, the platoon finally found the third floor door connecting to the PDF Headquarters.

Once the preparatory fires had ceased, second platoon received clearance to begin the assault. Only a locked door separated them from the PDF on the other side. Corporal Joseph Legaspi placed a 3-pound charge of C-4 explosives on the door with a time fuse. The blast jolted the door open, but also sparked a huge fire. The room they occupied happened to be a garment shop—with loose cloth spread everywhere. Once the cloth ignited, the fire immediately expanded. The smoke from both the fire and the explosion combined to produce noxious fumes, which made some of the Soldiers, including the platoon leader, vomit. Once inside the door, Kirk detached his 3d Squad to fight the fire. When the fire consumed the room, they had to exit the building the same way they entered. By accident, second platoon had lost a third of its firepower even before it began to confront the enemy at hand.

The two lead squads entered the PDF side of the doorway. To their amazement, the top floor housed an open basketball court. Second platoon's remaining two squads moved directly to the stairwell at the front of the building. It split down to the left and right and met again at a foyer on the second floor. Composed mainly of concrete interior walls and cinder block exterior walls, the building also had an open elevator shaft along its back wall. The bottom two floors contained a maze of rooms, offices, and partitioned sections.

As second platoon began clearing the second floor, it became apparent that the PDF had gathered on the first floor. The two squads methodically proceeded room-to-room using two-man buddy teams: one tossed in a grenade and the other followed the blast with a burst of rifle fire. The impenetrable darkness and incredible noise level created pandemonium inside the PDF Headquarters as two platoon-sized elements battled for survival. The pitch-black conditions rendered night vision devices inoperable and the building's cement-like composition made the explosions echo even louder. To add to the chaos, American and Panamanian soldiers screamed in both English and Spanish. No matter where they were that night at Coco Solo, most Soldiers in Charlie Company would attest that that was the loudest night they had ever experienced in their lifetime. When a group of second platoon Soldiers approached the elevator shaft on the second floor, a PDF soldier below bellowed up for the Americans to surrender because he had a weapon. Private First Class Michael Hardy ran toward the voice and began yelling obscenities. His partner, PFC Sidney Goffney, bowled a grenade by Hardy's feet and down the shaft and pulled Hardy out of the way.[83]

It was impossible for members of second platoon to ascertain the intentions of the PDF. Only as second platoon prepared for a final assault did Captain Jimenez inch his way toward the stairwell and called up his desires to surrender. Second Lieutenant Kirk vividly recalled the overwhelming confusion that ensued. He had finally cornered the enemy, but now faced the prospect of going down the stairs and negotiating with them face-to-face. His platoon had not taken any casualties yet, and the attack had gained momentum after its inauspicious and fiery beginning. This near the enemy, Kirk could not afford to make any mistakes, especially since he had already lost a squad to fire-fighting duties. His mind reduced the options to a simple calculation: Either kill or be killed. The bantering back and forth between his Soldiers and the PDF below was clearly audible, but neither he nor his lead squad leader, Sergeant Rainer, spoke Spanish. Kirk asked Specialist James Davis, a Spanish-speaking soldier, if he could understand what the PDF were saying. Davis replied that all he could make out was "something about weapons and surrender," but was unsure if the PDF were saying that they had weapons and wanted second platoon to surrender, or were willing to surrender themselves.

Fearing a trap and not willing to lose the momentum of his assault, Kirk ordered his squads to continue down the stairwell.[84] Rainer complied with the order by tossing a grenade down the stairwell. Jimenez later reported that the grenade injured three of his soldiers. He felt the grenade had been thrown intentionally despite his efforts to surrender. As second platoon narrowed the gap between forces, Davis finally maneuvered close enough to comprehend the PDF soldiers. Jimenez had continued his attempts to surrender, adding that he never heard the initial surrender requests made over the loudspeaker in front of his headquarters.[85] Although the grenade caused unfortunate injuries, it did serve to expedite the surrender process. More importantly, in accomplishing the company's most difficult mission, second platoon did not suffer a single casualty.[86]

Kirk and his Soldiers proceeded cautiously to the first floor. Through his translator, Davis, Kirk ordered the PDF men to crawl past him on all fours.

Second platoon Soldiers bound the prisoners in temporary flexi-cuffs and escorted them to a holding area on the school's tennis courts. Second platoon had taken fifteen prisoners out of the building by 2:09 A.M. and completely cleared the entire structure by 2:41 A.M.[87] The platoon found a fully locked and loaded .50 caliber machine gun on the bottom floor pointing out the window at the support by fire position, but fortunately, the weapon remained unmanned during the attack.[88]

From its blocking position in the Southern Housing Area, Soldiers from the third platoon fired at targets in their sector during the opening moments of the attack. One M-60 machine gun noisily belched away from the windowsill on the floor above my doorway position. As two entire platoons joined fires with the Vulcan, all firing from the Southern Housing Area, the noise level reached a deafening roar. The buildings we fired from shuddered from the violent vibration. Within sixty seconds, I ordered, "cease fire." I was sure that there were no more targets in our sector by that time and I was concerned about the many civilians who worked in factories to our front. With so much firing still going on all around us, especially from the Vulcan barely 100 meters to our right, it felt awkward *not* to be firing when everyone else still was. Yet, I was confident no enemy remained within our sector, so we waited for the other two platoons to accomplish their missions.

Sometime around 2:00 A.M., 2d Squad reported seeing sporadic sniper fire coming from the Lada car factory on our left flank. Corporal Robert Coulter, a 2nd Squad team leader, asked for permission to engage. Coulter fired an AT-4 rocket at the suspected sniper position, but because of the oblique angle from which it was fired, the rocket glanced off the concrete building and exploded across the street. The sniper fire stopped after that. At this particular point in the battle, I intently listened to the command net on the radio to ascertain the situation within the other platoons' sectors. The Chinese restaurant burned in brilliant flames that soon spread over to the PDF side of the building, eventually consuming the entire right side and collapsing the roof above the PDF. As we watched the fire blaze, we hoped for the safety of second platoon inside the building and first platoon on the other side of it. For more than an hour, grenade explosions and bursts of rifle fire continued as the building was cleared. We were quite surprised that gunfire persisted so long after H-Hour: resistance had been much stiffer than expected.

At 3:30 A.M., third platoon soldiers heard voices coming from the V-shaped factory building across the street to our front. Private First Class Francisco Lopez maneuvered directly in front of the location, dashing from tree to tree to where the sniper fire was spotted earlier. After several minutes, Lopez coaxed eleven frightened men out of the factory. They had been on the night shift when the H-Hour attack surprised them. After the power went out, several bullets had hit their building, and they had immediately dropped to the floor and had lain there in silence for several hours in the darkness. Third platoon soldiers searched, questioned, and evacuated the men to the company holding area, but Captain Rizzo waited until daylight to clear the rest of that building and the Lada car factory, enclosed by a cyclone fence. About 8:00 A.M., 2d Squad began to clear those two buildings. Inside the Lada compound, 2d Squad captured three PDF soldiers attempting to hide. They had donned civilian shirts over their uniforms. Although one possessed a pistol, they quickly surrendered and were taken to the holding facility for further questioning.

Meanwhile after a brief firefight on the dock, first platoon's support element had cleared its objectives. Initially they had to penetrate a cyclone fence around a small barracks. Once across, they tossed hand grenades into the structure but found it empty. Specialist Verlon Stokes rolled a grenade under a truck, killing two PDF soldiers hiding beneath it. Two more PDF soldiers burned to death when grenades thrown into the boathouse ignited a butane gas explosion.[89] First platoon's assault element faced stiffer resistance than expected. Prior reconnaissance indicated that there would only be about six enemy personnel at the boats, but the incident at H-minus-26 and the telephonic warning drastically altered the force ratio. Though the plan provided for a three-to-one advantage for the attacking force, first platoon attacked at almost even numbers. Sergeant Richard Mowatt led the 21-man assault element, which came under fire as it turned the corner around the seawall. At first sporadic, the volume of fire gradually increased as the element closed with the boats. Initially, Mowatt could only make out enemy muzzle flashes. As he crept closer to the objective, however, he began to distinguish actual enemy personnel. Although the attack occurred in the dead of night and in the open expanse of a boatyard, no one in first platoon used their PVS-7s to enhance their night vision capability.[90] This fact, coupled with the increased number of defenders, quickly put the Americans at a disadvantage.

The assault element soon found itself pinned, and Lieutenant Burke ordered the lead group to fire antitank rockets to reduce the incoming fires. Mowatt moved forward with one of his team leaders, Sergeant Joseph Hein. Sergeant James Daniel, the company's Anti-Tank Section Leader, also moved up with Private First Class Rudolf Ubersezig, forming two two-man firing teams. Alternating throughout the attack, one team would fire LAW rockets while the other covered them with machine gun fire. Daniel, firing a LAW from a kneeling position, knocked over a boat mast, but the blast illuminated his exposed position.[91] PDF fire rained in on him from two different directions as some 20 enemy soldiers fired on first platoon.[92] The hail of gunfire hit both Daniel and Ubersezig. Bullets ripped through the wrist and ankle of Ubersezig, a young soldier merely eighteen years of age. An AK-47 round struck Daniel above his knee, traveled along his femur through his upper leg, skipped off his hipbone, exiting through his buttocks. The bullet sent him spinning around and crashing to the pavement. Daniel screamed in pain, but Mowatt exhorted him to keep quiet so as not to draw additional fire to their position. Hein and PFC Hager administered aid to stop the bleeding and prevent the onset of shock. They did not even notice the entry wound in Daniel's leg. Private First Class Clifton, the platoon medic, arrived within minutes to continue treating Daniel. Daniel and Ubersezig, however, would have to remain in place until first platoon could get them out.[93]

Most of the assault element remained behind the cover of one of the boats in dry dock. Only Burke, Specialist Patrick DiBernardo (his radiotelephone operator (RTO)), the M60 machine gunner, and the two assault teams had ventured forward. Now two Soldiers from this small group were hit, and worse, enemy fire had them pinned down. The seven ducked for cover behind a large pile of scrap metal heaped on the dockyard's pavement. Hundreds of rounds blazed above and around them, audible as they cracked in the air overhead and visible as green tracers. Burke vividly recalled the fire-blue color of the bullets careening off the pavement as he lay pinned with one-third of his assault element, while the rest fired from the safety of the boat in dry dock.[94] To exacerbate their difficulties, they had lost communications with the commander when the RTO, diving for cover, loosened the antenna on his PRC-77. It took nearly fifteen minutes to re-establish communications with Rizzo, still at his original position in the Southern Housing Area.[95] When Burke reported that he had been pinned down and taken casualties, Rizzo dispatched the Vulcan from the Northern Housing Area to support first platoon's movement.

Burke realized that to gain fire superiority, he had to get his men out of the PDF's converging fires. They had to spread out and leave the safety of a covered and concealed position. The young enlisted Soldiers sought guidance, "We can't move. What do we do?" Several of the sergeants, demonstrating inspirational leadership, took the initiative and began to move forward, sparking the rest of the platoon to move again. The two casualties made this more difficult. Not only did the platoon have to secure their objective, but also had to evacuate their wounded buddies. The stark reality of their situation dawned on them: "They will kill us unless we kill them first."[96]

As Burke was making the decision to move, the second Vulcan took up a new support position behind the high school on ground that provided a commanding view of the dock area. Its crew began to shower rounds upon the PDF firing from the boats. The Vulcan gave the fire superiority edge to the American forces. First platoon could clearly observe the Vulcan's tracers streaking by them. Seeing this, Mowatt pressed forward. He fired four antitank rockets (AT-4s) that Soldiers passed up to him, suppressing the enemy and allowing the rest of the forward element to move. Mowatt's rockets connected with a couple of boats; he saw two of the enemy fall.[97] With the advantage in firepower, the assault element began moving forward again in earnest. Seeing the danger posed to the assault by the Vulcan's 20mm suppressive fires, Mahana personally ran over and ordered the crew to stop firing. The two M-60 machine guns at Mahana's position then shifted their fires onto the boats. The additional firepower had all but silenced resistance on the docks and allowed first platoon to close onto their objective.[98]The combined effects of the Vulcan, Mahana's M-60s, and Mowatt's heroic display of bravery encouraged the rest of the men to fire and maneuver. Mowatt earned the Bronze Star for valor for his actions that night on the dock. Lieutenant Burke received a grazing wound in the leg by a bullet, but did not notice it that night. No further casualties occurred, but the injuries suffered by Daniel and Ubersezig caused them both to be medically discharged from the Army.

In retrospect, it is possible that the company 60mm mortars could have been used to place suppressive fires on the boats. The Brigade Commander, Colonel Kellogg, retained the authority to allow indirect fires. However, Rizzo could have employed them if first platoon had been in grave danger.[99] The mortar section sergeant, Clarence Wolfe, expressed confidence that he could have safely hit the boats in the handheld direct fire mode.[100] Mowatt also believed that 60mm mortar fire would have effectively suppressed the enemy fire coming from the boats.[101] If necessary, Rizzo had planned for Burke to adjust in the rounds by first overshooting into the bay, then gradually dropping the distance onto the targets.[102] Rizzo and Burke, however, felt 1st Platoon was too exposed in the open area to safely employ them. Even without indirect fires, the assault element worked its way out of the temporary crisis. Once the platoon seized the first couple of boats and gained a foothold on the dock, the action quickly ended. Mowatt told Specialist Ruben Rodriguez, a Spanish speaker, to inform the PDF they had 30 seconds to surrender and to his relief, 12 PDF soldiers gave themselves up.[103] First platoon took several hours to find and capture the remaining enemy, who attempted to hide in the water and in the vehicles of the nearby Lada car factory.[104] After the battle, first platoon discovered that it had been opposed by about 25 enemy troops; about fourfold the number it had been told to expect.

In the darkness and confusion, it was difficult to determine if the assault had cut off retreat by boat. While first platoon was engaged on the dockyard, one of the Swift ships and Vosper patrol craft had, in fact, escaped out into the bay. The first report of boat movement came at 1:39 A.M. This initial report confirmed that one boat had definitely made it out into the open water, and possibly two. At 1:46 A.M., observers spotted two boats about 200 meters to the east of the Colon monument. At 3:41 A.M., an AC-130 gunship neutralized one of the boats. Ultimately, no boats escaped north out of the Manzanillo Bay.[105] Charlie Company had completely secured Coco Solo by 4:15 A.M.[106]

After the individual platoons secured their objectives, the company began to consolidate and reorganize.[107] Daniel and Ubersezig could not be extracted from the docks via helicopter until enemy fire had been completely suppressed. An aerial medevac, requested at 3:12 A.M., arrived at Coco Solo at 4:02 A.M.[108] Daniel eventually made it to a military hospital in San Antonio, Texas, the evacuation site for most of the serious *Just Cause* casualties. In addition to the two Soldiers in Charlie Company wounded by gunshots, two others from the attached 82nd Airborne platoon suffered backblast burns while firing antitank rockets in the prone position. Although no one took an official "body count" of the PDF at Coco Solo, rough estimates accounted for fifteen total casualties: ten killed and five wounded. Perhaps another dozen or more were presumed killed on the two boats that made it out into the water.[109] Importantly, there were no civilian casualties. The entire chain of command up to the Commander-in-Chief had emphasized that if civilians became casualties, "we might win the battle, but we would lose the war." Despite the proximity of civilians living and working in the area, none were injured. Charlie Company captured at least thirty enemy troops and detained 65 civilians that first night at Coco Solo. All civilians were released at noon the next day.[110]

Many factors contributed to Charlie Company's success at Coco Solo. Junior leadership was a clear strength. Lieutenant Colonel Brooks attributed the success to rehearsals and unit discipline.[111] Captain Rizzo echoed these observations and pinpointed teamwork and Soldier restraint as the keys to success.[112] Although none of the unit's Soldiers had been in combat previously, what they lacked in experience they made up for with ingenuity and innovation under fire. Victory was a testament of the quality of training undertaken by the all-volunteer force during the late 1980s.[113] As Burke noted retrospectively, "everything you do in combat is taught in the Officer's Basic Course."[114] Through numerous pre-deployment live fire exercises, U.S. tactical units believed in themselves and their leaders, a confidence with which they deployed to Panama.

In contrast, the PDF was simply not ready for a city fight of any intensity. Captain Jimenez had only assumed command a few days prior to the battle and did not have a thorough understanding of the forces arrayed against him nor of U.S. firepower capabilities.[115] Although the PDF possessed very lethal weapons systems, they did not take advantage of them. Nor did the PDF effectively use the extensive built-up areas available. In short, the PDF did not prepare for an urban battle, even to the point that many of their heavy machine guns remained in storage. The PDF soldiers were poorly trained, poorly led, unevenly motivated, and no match for their U.S. opponent. Fortunately, for American Soldiers, the battle for Panama proved to be a case in which a defender was simply unwilling to engage in sustained city combat.

CHAPTER FIVE

KHAFJI, 1991

THE BATTLE FOR KHAFJI

by Thomas Houlahan

It [Khafji]...gave the Arab forces an opportunity to gain a great victory. And it taught them too, that the Iraqis were not ten feet tall, that in fact that they could take them on and whip 'em.[116]
General Norman Schwarzkopf

In late January 1991, stung by the intensity and success of the American-led United Nations Coalition bombing offensive, Saddam Hussein ordered his army to launch an offensive.[117] Saddam reasoned that if his army could inflict even a small defeat on Coalition ground forces, he might reap benefits out of proportion to the size of the victory. Perhaps stung psychologically from an embarrassing defeat, Allied forces might think twice about launching an invasion of Kuwait or Iraq, and they would negotiate a settlement on Saddam's terms. Or, perhaps they would react to their humiliation by attempting to launch their invasion prematurely. Either way, Saddam would benefit. Even if the offensive failed, Saddam surmised, he might bag a few hundred prisoners to use as hostages. At least the army he had built and maintained at such vast expense would be doing something. It would be a city fight in one of the most barren of places, the Arabian Desert.

Contrary to the Iraqi dictator's intent his offensive, though showing promise at the beginning, failed miserably and yielded none of the benefits he had intended. Rather the opposite occurred: the series of engagements fought in and around the desert town of Khafji, collectively termed "The Battle of Khafji," convinced Central Command planners that the Iraqis might not fight well in the coming ground offensive. Coalition commanders began to sense that the impending ground war might not be as costly as they had anticipated. Gen. Norman Schwarzkopf would say later that Khafji was the moment when he really began to think, "We are going to kick this guy's tail," and that the Iraqi Army was "a lousy outfit."

The smoke from lit oil wells fill the Kuwaiti sky creating limited-visibility conditions in the middle of the day and creating uncertain health risks to American troops. (Photo by Lt. Col. Brad Gericke)

By the end of January 1991, though the air campaign was in full swing, the tactical situation on the ground was undeveloped. CENTCOM was in the process of repositioning its forces to set the stage for the coming ground offensive. On the far southeastern flank of the CENTCOM sector, U.S. Marines had not yet placed any major troop concentrations along the border of Kuwait; only a screening force was in position. CENTCOM established nine observation posts (OPs), numbered 1 through 9. Reconnaissance teams manned the OPs, and OPs 1 through 8 were backed by two battalions of mobile Marine light armored infantry. OP 9, outside the Marines' western boundary, was the U.S. Army's responsibility. The lightly defended OPs formed what was essentially an early warning system for the main force, still well to the south. OPs 4, 5, and 6 on the western end of the Marine line were the responsibility of the 1st Marine Division. OPs 1, 2, 3, 7 and 8 belonged to the 2d Marine Division. The men on the OPs were alerted to the possibility of a night attack when Iraqis attempted to jam their radios at dusk on the 29th.

Immediately thereafter, the Iraqis launched a series of probes across the Saudi-Kuwait border, about 45 kilometers west of Khafji and west of the cultivated area known as the "al-Wafra Forest." This area was defended by the 2nd Light Armored Infantry (LAI) Battalion. After losing one tank, the Iraqis withdrew. The rest of the night passed without incident; however, Iraqi activity in the area was a source of serious concern to the Marines. It appeared that the Iraqis might be preparing to raid or destroy the al-Kibrit logistics base, at which the Marines had been stockpiling supplies for the coming attack on Kuwait. To counter this course of action, the Coalition called for air strikes on the al-Wafra Forest.

View from of the city of Rafha in the Northern Province of Saudia Arabia as seen from the Trans-Arabian Pipeline Road. Dubbed the "Highway of Death" by U.S. Soldiers rushing up and down its length in the days preceding Operation Desert Storm, the highway was the primary route into the region. Although larger than Khafji, the congested, low-slung construction of the town of Rafha is typical of this remote area. (U.S. Army photograph by Sgt. Nathan Webster.)

Meanwhile, a company of tanks from the 1st (Tiger) Brigade of the Army's 2d Armored Division was sent to bolster the Coalition forces that barred the path to the al-Kibrit logistics base to the south. To the west, Task Force Shepherd, which consisted of two companies from the 1st LAI Battalion and two companies from the 3d LAI, destroyed 22 Iraqi tanks and another dozen armored personnel carriers (APCs). The Iraqis abandoned two other tanks intact, and sustained about 100 casualties. A few dozen soldiers were taken prisoner, one of whom was the force's commander. Over the next few days, several hundred more Iraqi foot soldiers made their way toward the Marines to surrender.

While the Marines were fighting in the west, an Iraqi mechanized infantry brigade crossed the border north of Khafji in the east. The area north of Khafji had been active since January 17th. About a mile south of the border stood OP 8 occupied by an Air-Naval Gunfire Liaison Company (ANGLICO) and Navy SEAL teams. South of the OP was a desalination plant manned by Navy SEALs, members of Marine Recon, and Green Berets from the 5th Special Forces Group. All totaled, between observers at OP 8 and the garrison of the desalination plant, there were 34 Americans north of Khafji, in addition to scouts from the 2d (King Abdul Aziz) Saudi Arabian National Guard (SANG) Brigade.

The 29th saw a marked increase in Iraqi ground activity in the coastal area. OP 8 noted a good deal of traffic along the coastal highway and on the east-west road, which ran into the al-Wafra Forest. When some two dozen heavy equipment transporters were destroyed by Harriers along the east-west road, Iraqi soldiers—rather than attempting to vacate the area—cleared the road under fire. The incidents along the road convinced Marine Lieutenant Colonel Richard Barry, the commander of the forward surveillance force, that the Iraqis would be mounting a major operation that night. The traffic along the road had been a hint, and the Iraqi soldiers' willingness to expose themselves to Marine ground attack aircraft while clearing the road demonstrated, at least to Barry, their pressing need to keep the road open.

At 8:00 P.M., the Iraqis further confirmed their objective by firing illumination rounds over the desalination plant, the first time they had done so. Barry had concluded that the al-Wafra attack would be a feint to the west, and the main Iraqi effort would be toward Khafji in the southeast. The illumination rounds were an indication to Barry that an all-out assault was about to begin and that it was time for him to get his men out. Barry led his force to a fallback position, a police station to the south.

Almost as soon as the force reached the police station, Iraqi tanks from a flanking force rumbled past in the distance. This armored force seemed to come out of nowhere. In an impressive display of tactical ability, the Khafji assault force had picked its way through the border outpost line, with no headlights and in almost total radio silence. It had then split, with one-half of the force making for Khafji down the coastal road and the other flanking the town to the west. The Marines, Green Berets, and SEALs made a hasty retreat as bullets and tank rounds flew over their heads.

The lack of coordination in the attack turned out to be a lucky break for the Iraqis. When their attack kicked off, it appeared to be an assault on the al-Kibrit logistics base, which led to the commission of air power elsewhere. Lieutenant General Walter Boomer, First Marine Expeditionary Force commander, diverted most of his fixed-wing air assets to the west, leaving very little air support available for the defense of Khafji when it was attacked later. The Air Force also read the attack on Khafji as a feint, and had most of its assets employed elsewhere, believing that the town was in little danger.

A Saudi resort town ten kilometers from the border, Khafji sits astride the main coastal highway running between Kuwait City and northeast Saudi Arabia. The town's 45,000 residents had been evacuated on January 17 to keep them out of Iraqi artillery range. Now without air support, the Saudis and Americans had no choice but to abandon the city.

The forces available in the area were four Saudi task forces of the Eastern Province Area Command (EPAC), which were also located south, out of Iraqi artillery range. Task Force Omar, the westernmost force, consisted of the 10th Royal Saudi Land Forces (RSLF) mechanized brigade and an Omani infantry battalion. It was stationed well inland, on the right flank of the Marines' screen line. To its right was Task Force Othman, made up of the 8th RSLF mechanized brigade with attached companies of Bahraini and Free Kuwaiti infantry. Guarding the coast was Task Force Abu Bakr, the 2nd Saudi Arabian National Guard (SANG) mechanized brigade and a Qatari mechanized infantry battalion. The coastal road south of Khafji was blocked by Task Force Tariq (two Saudi Marine battalions, a Moroccan infantry regiment, and two Senegalese infantry companies).[118] As Coalition special operators pulled back, these units began moving to establish a defense of the town, unaware that it had already been taken by the attackers from the north.

The Saudi forward commander, Major General Sultan 'Adi al-Mutairi, gathered an armored reconnaissance force, taking a tank company from Task Force Othman and a Qatari tank company and antitank missile platoon from Task Force Abu Bakr. The force, personally led by Major General al-Mutairi, might have been destroyed before it reached the town if not for the good judgment of a Marine Cobra squadron commander.

Lieutenant Colonel Mike Kurth, in a Huey outfitted with special night vision equipment, had arrived over the town with eight Cobras. In the confusion that characterized that night's activities, Marine air controllers, unaware of al-Mutairi's mission, had told Kurth that there were no friendly forces in Khafji, so his Cobras were cleared to fire on any formation they saw in or around the town. Looking for an extra measure of certainty before authorizing an attack, Kurth flew close enough to al-Mutairi's force to recognize that the tanks were American-made M-60s, which the Iraqis did not have.

Meanwhile, unaware that the Iraqis had taken Khafji, the Saudis and Qataris were headed straight for the town and a meeting engagement with Iraqi armor. Kurth was able to make contact with the force, and inform al-Mutairi that the Iraqis were in possession of Khafji. The commander adjusted his tactics accordingly: the reconnaissance force probed the northern approaches to the town just before dawn on the 30th; encountering a column of about a dozen armored vehicles. After four Iraqi tanks were destroyed in a six-minute exchange with the Qataris, 21 Iraqis abandoned their vehicles and surrendered. The Saudis were told that there were two Iraqi battalions in Khafji, one armored and one mechanized. What they did not know was that these units expected to be reinforced by additional advancing armor and mechanized infantry.

Shortly after the contact with the recon force, Kurth's Cobras attacked a column on the northwest approach to Khafji, destroying six vehicles. Realizing that his Cobras were not well equipped for night fighting and wishing to avoid unnecessary losses, Kurth discontinued gunship attacks for the night and handed the airspace over to fixed-wing aircraft, which then took over the battle. Throughout the day and night of January 30th, Coalition air power was active north of the border, dropping tons of anti-armor mines to slow the Iraqi armor. B-52s cruised high above the roads, looking for convoys to bomb.[119] Then, carrier-based aircraft dropped cluster and guided bombs. Close behind were Air Force jets firing Maverick missiles and dropping more cluster bombs. As a result of multiple air attacks, the follow-on Iraqi forces abandoned their attempt to reinforce Khafji, leaving the forces occupying the town cut off.

There on the ground, Khafji's occupiers were too busy looting the town to notice that they were being watched. Hidden in the upper floors of an apartment building were twelve Marine artillery spotters who had been trapped in Khafji. For the next day and a half, these men radioed information about Iraqi troop movements and, once indirect fire assets became available, called artillery strikes on Iraqi armor. When the Iraqis first took the town, the spotters had no artillery to call upon. Taken by surprise, most U.S. Marine units were too far south to respond immediately to the Iraqi attack. The nearest infantry unit, the 3rd Marine Regiment, was a dismounted unit and lacked the transportation support to move north immediately. The artillery unit supporting 3rd Marines did have transport, though, and with 5-ton trucks to tow its 155mm guns, the 1st Battalion, 12th Marine Regiment could move to within range of Khafji. The battalion's commander, Lieutenant Colonel Robert Rivers, immediately went forward to scout positions for his guns, and then ordered his unit north.

The first guns to arrive were those of Charlie Battery, commanded by Captain Stephen Morgan on the afternoon of January 30. Morgan's battery, after picking its way through retreating Saudi forces along the coastal highway, was directed by Rivers to position about four miles south of Khafji. There, it established radio contact with the trapped Marine spotters.

Simultaneously, Lieutenant General Prince Khaled bin Sultan, commander of the Saudi Armed Forces (as well as all other Arab forces in the Gulf War), also became aware of the plight of the two Marine teams on the afternoon of the 30th. He immediately directed Major General al-Mutairi to retrieve the spotters and retake the town. In this effort, most of the fighting would be done by the men of the 2nd (King Abdul Aziz) Brigade of the National Guard under Colonel Turki al-Firmi.

The Saudi National Guard differed significantly from that of the United States. Comprised of fulltime soldiers, the SANG was one of the two military establishments in Saudi Arabia, the other being the Ministry of Defense and Aviation, (MODA), of which the RSLF was the ground forces arm. The National Guard served primarily as an internal security force with a secondary combat mission. The national capital was garrisoned by National Guardsmen, as was every major industrial or oil installation in the country. Until Iraq invaded Kuwait, only SANG troops were stationed in the Eastern Province, where most of the kingdom's industry and oil resources were located. The National Guard accomplished its recruiting exclusively among the descendants of the nomadic

Bedouin, the kingdom's spiritual equivalent to the cowboys who roamed the American West. Therefore, National Guardsmen had more of a "rough rider" image than their RSLF counterparts.

For most of the kingdom's modern history, smugglers and internal nuisances have been more of a problem than the threat of invasion by a neighboring country. As a result, the National Guard has traditionally been the more important of the two ground establishments. With 56,000 men, it was also the larger of the two organizations. The RSLF's peacetime strength was about 35,000, though during the crisis it had grown to over 50,000. At an assigned strength of just over 5,000 men, brigades in the Saudi National Guard were relatively large. They contained four maneuver battalions instead of the three usually found in Western brigades. The 2d SANG Brigade was made up of the 5th, 6th, 7th and 8th battalions.

The SANG's basic combat vehicle was the Cadillac-Gage V-150 armored car, which came in twelve different variants, including TOW (tube launched, optically tracked, wire guided) missile launcher, 90mm gun and APC versions. These wheeled vehicles were fast, maneuverable and mechanically reliable. However, the V-150 was not particularly well armored, so it was not a vehicle to be used in armored charges. If casualties were to be kept down, V-150s had to be employed skillfully.

Just after 4:00 P.M. on the 30th, Lieutenant Colonel Hamid Moktar, commander of the 7th Battalion, 2d SANG, received orders to retake the town. Surrounding the town were a number of large sabkhas, areas of salt marsh that could not support vehicular traffic. The sabkhas limited the number of avenues by which the Saudis might attack the town, giving the Iraqi defenders the advantage. For the assault, two companies of Qatari tanks would reinforce Hamid's battalion. The attack plan called for two of Hamid's companies to attack along the road into the western part of town while his third company stood by in reserve. A company of Qatari tanks would support each of these companies.

At 11:00 P.M., Hamid's task force attacked. As the attacking forces approached the edge of town over open ground it was met by a hail of bullets, flattening the tires of several V-150s and stopping the advance in its tracks. The intensity of the Iraqi fire came as a complete surprise to Hamid's men. The Brigade's commander and staff officers were still under the impression that there was slightly more than a company of Iraqis in the town.

The RSLF had been aware since that morning that a significant Iraqi force had occupied Khafji, but in the confusion, that information had not been communicated. The two forces engaged in a violent firefight until 3:20 A.M. Because of the tremendous volume of ammunition it expended during the firefight, the task force was forced to break off the engagement and pull back for ammunition resupply. Hamid ordered his force to fall back to the SANG compound, which had been abandoned during the early weeks of the air war.

Unfortunately, the convoy carrying the ammunition missed its linkup point and wandered toward Khafji, prompting the Iraqis to engage it as soon as it came within range. Though the force miraculously escaped without sustaining any casualties, two vehicles carrying TOWs were destroyed, with the loss of over fifty missiles. The convoy reversed its direction and finally linked up with Hamid's task force. By this time, the Iraqi inhabitants of Khafji had consolidated, but their situation was becoming more and more tenuous. JSTARS (Joint Surveillance and Target Attack Radar System) had already reported the virtual cessation of Iraqi activity north of the border, telling the Marines and the Saudis that the Iraqis in Khafji were on their own. By dawn on the 31st, the Iraqis had also begun to realize that they were alone. All they could do at that point was await the next Allied assault.

Now aware that there was a significant Iraqi force in Khafji, Colonel Turki ordered the 6th and 8th battalions to assign one company each to the 7th Battalion. Further reinforced, Hamid's force was ordered to renew its attack on the morning of the 31st. The attack was to be coordinated with attacks by the 5th SANG Battalion to the north of the town, and an RSLF tank battalion, which was to drive into the town on Hamid's northern flank. Meanwhile, the 8th Battalion, 2d SANG, reinforced by a Qatari tank company and antitank missile platoon from the 6th SANG Battalion, drove northward, pushed into the town, and then took its place on the 7th Battalion's southern flank.

Allied support of the attack was limited to indirect fire and air support. Taking advantage of the observers who were still operating within the town itself, the attack would begin with a 15-minute Marine artillery barrage, and Marine attack helicopters would cover the assault. However, on the ground it would be an entirely Arab operation. Marine ground units were available to assist them, but the Saudis and Qataris considered the recapture of the town a matter of national honor, and insisted on retaking it themselves.

The assault started badly. Hamid had planned to attack with his own three companies and the attached Qatari armor, keeping the two attached companies from the 6th and 8th SANG battalions as a reserve. However, the RSLF tank battalion was not ready to attack when the assault force moved out. Hamid was forced to assign its mission to his reserve companies. At 10:00 P.M., the 5th Battalion hit a company-sized element of Iraqi armor on the coastal road north of Khafji. In the ensuing half-hour firefight, the Iraqis lost 13 armored vehicles, and the Saudis captured another six without sustaining a single casualty. Some of the tanks had been fitted with Iraqi-manufactured add-on armor. However, since the armor was nothing more than large, heavy blocks of steel, it did little more than weigh down the vehicles. TOW missiles were able to knock out these tanks with relative ease, despite the additional armor. When the Iraqis attempted to fall back and regroup, they were hammered by air and artillery strikes.

After sustaining heavy losses, including the loss of 116 soldiers who were captured by the attackers, the remainder of the force fled. Unfortunately, a handful of Saudi vehicles gave chase, and two men were killed and another five were wounded when they were accidentally bombed by a mixed package of U.S. and Qatari fighter-bombers. After rounding up its prisoners and evacuating its wounded, the 5th Battalion pulled back to positions north of the SANG compound.

The ultimate outcome of the battle was no longer in doubt. However, Iraqi soldiers still occupied most of Khafji, and National Guardsmen had to root them out. The Iraqis resisted fiercely as the attack turned into a series of confused, street-to-street and house-to-house firefights. Around noon, the Iraqis mounted a counterattack, which caught a National Guard company attempting to evacuate its wounded and destroyed two ambulances (one, a V-150 armored ambulance) before the Saudis and Marine Super Cobra helicopter gunships could counter it. The Saudis also lost a V-150 to friendly fire during the counterattack when it was accidentally hit by a TOW from a Cobra. The driver was killed, and the gunner, vehicle commander, and several infantrymen in the back were wounded. Two other V-150s were lost later in the battle.

The Iraqi forces were dispersed throughout the buildings in the town. One Saudi APC exploded after being hit by an RPG-7 fired by an Iraqi in a building. A V-150 was hit and burst into flames. The driver and commander survived the explosion, only because they were blown out of their open hatches and clear of the vehicle by the blast. The four soldiers riding in the back of the APC were killed. An American advisor ran to a nearby Saudi armored vehicle and banged on it with his helmet. When a crewman opened the hatch, the advisor pointed to the building and shouted: "TOW, TOW!" The crewman nodded, and a few seconds later, a TOW missile was on its way toward the building. After a large explosion, a stream of Iraqis left the building waving white cloth. Later, a V-150 equipped with a turret-mounted 90mm gun was hit by a 100mm round fired by an Iraqi tank. All four of the vehicle's crewmen were killed.

While the firefight was underway, a reinforced company of Iraqi Type 63 APCs was assembling on the street near the hotel where the Marine spotters were hiding. A volley from every gun in 1st Battalion, 12th Marine Regiment, directed by the spotters, destroyed seventeen of the APCs. Many of the vehicles, which were packed with ammunition, erupted in secondary explosions as the company's surviving dismounted infantry fled down the street. The spotters shifted the artillery fire, and another volley killed or wounded many of the fleeing Iraqi infantrymen.[120] Shortly afterward, the two Marine spotter teams, which had taken advantage of the confusion to make their way through the town, linked up with the attached company from the 8th Battalion and continued the fight with this unit, which was moving to join the attack with the 7th Battalion.

By 2:00 P.M., the 8th Battalion affected this link up. The attack continued, with the 8th Battalion on the southern flank and the 7th Battalion on the northern flank. As soon as the 7th Battalion reached the causeway across the sabkha, it was met by a wall of machine-gun fire from the other side. Seemingly oblivious to the Iraqi fire, Hamid's men raced across the causeway, gained a foothold, and unleashed their own wall of fire on the Iraqis. At 6:30 P.M., the attack was suspended because of darkness, with the 8th Battalion remaining in place and the 7th Battalion returning to the SANG compound to rearm.

The Saudis launched their final assault on the following morning at 7:30 A.M. At this point, there were about twenty Iraqi armored vehicles and 200 Iraqi soldiers in Khafji. The 7th and 8th battalions attacked on line at first, then split, with the 8th Battalion clearing the southern half of the town and the 7th Battalion driving northward, clearing the rest of the town, and ultimately retaking the desalination plant. During this final assault, the SANG battalions found that their foes were utterly dispirited. Most Iraqi soldiers surrendered as soon as they were engaged. Others were keen to avoid being engaged. Saudi TOWs and Marine Cobras destroyed several vehicles as they tried to escape to the north. By 3:00 P.M., the town and the desalination plant were in Saudi hands. In one final setback for the Iraqis, British aircraft spotted fifteen fast patrol boats attempting to land troops near Khafji. British naval attack helicopters sank two boats with missiles and drove the others off. Coalition aircraft gave chase, sinking or severely damaging 10 of the remaining 13 boats.

The Battle of Khafji was a lopsided affair, as a result of Iraqi confusion within the town itself and the fact that reinforcing armored units had been cut off by Allied airpower before they could arrive in the city. The Iraqi 5th Mechanized Division lost 23 tanks and 43 APCs, and another 9 tanks and 21 APCs were captured intact by the Saudis. Two self-propelled 122mm guns were also destroyed, as were about a half-dozen soft-skinned vehicles. Some 60 Iraqis were killed and 463 were taken prisoner (of which 35 were wounded). By contrast, the Saudis and Qataris lost only 40 soldiers, 8 killed and 32 wounded, two Qatari tanks (which were later repaired), and seven V-150s.

The fighting would undoubtedly have been more costly had the Iraqis been more organized. The Saudis would ultimately conclude that the Iraqi force had not been one distinct unit, but elements of three different battalions. Bringing the diverse clusters of armored vehicles under centralized control was made difficult by a lack of communications equipment. Because of the lack of a coherent command structure, the Iraqi defense of the town was uncoordinated. The fact that no one seems to have been in charge of the Iraqi force helps explain why the force's most effective weapons were never employed. Several Iraqi APCs were found with 82mm recoilless rifles inside them. Though not particularly effective against tanks, they would have been extremely effective against Saudi V-150s. A significant number of extremely dangerous French-made Milan missiles were also found inside Iraqi APCs. Though they would have been lethal to Saudi APCs and Qatari tanks, none of these were used either. Finally, though Marine attack helicopters savaged the Iraqi defenders, not one of the many available SA-14 shoulder-launched anti-aircraft missiles was fired.

Failure to use their weapons was not something of which the SANG could have been accused. The Saudis responded to every instance of Iraqi resistance with torrents of fire. More than 400 TOW missiles were fired during the fighting. One Iraqi T-55 was hit by ten TOWs. It was not unusual for heavily engaged units to finish a day's fighting with virtually no ammunition remaining. Indeed, the Saudis, who relied upon massed fire to retake Khafji, did most of the damage to the town. Though Saudi fire was often inaccurate, the sheer volume of it kept the Iraqi defenders off balance and pinned down, reducing Saudi casualties.

The Saudis also helped minimize their casualties by learning quickly from their mistakes. During the early fighting, SANG soldiers tended to stay in their armored vehicles. This meant that fewer infantrymen were out looking for Iraqis, and that increased the chances that unobserved Iraqis could get close-in RPG shots at the thinly armored V-150s. It also meant that if one of those shots hit the vehicle, it would make casualties of an entire squad, rather than just a driver and a gunner. After an entire infantry squad was killed in the back of a stricken V-150 early in the fighting, the Saudis learned to dismount and spread out in built-up areas.

In the wake of the ground campaign, oil wells were set afire by retreating Iraqis and military debris littered the Kuwaiti desert. (Photo by Lt. Col. Brad Gericke.)

The Saudis spent the next week combing the town, looking for Iraqis in hiding. About three dozen were captured. Though there was no resistance from the Iraqi stragglers, there were casualties. In a preview of a problem that would plague the Allies later in the war, over thirty Coalition soldiers were killed or wounded by unexploded bomblets in and around Khafji in the weeks following the town's recapture. However, the relative small number of casualties sustained during the fight, and, moreover, the victory itself, were the result of a formula for success found in many city fights—the use of combined arms, the ability to continue the fight in the face of many casualties, and the application of overwhelming force.

Ultimately, the fight at Khafji serves as a reminder that city combat can erupt in the most unlikely of environments. From an operational and strategic perspective, the sands of northern Saudi Arabia and western Kuwait are largely devoid of human civilization. It was reasonable for military planners, when preparing armed forces to deploy to this theater, to consider urban combat a low probability. Events indeed proved it infrequent – but when city combat did occur, it was decisive. The rule that wherever there are people, there are cities, once again was validated.

In the near term, this sharp battle validated the ability of the Saudis in combat. At the beginning of the battle, the Saudis were easily rattled, but as they became accustomed to combat conditions and gained confidence in their weapons, they settled down. After a few early mistakes, they began to show a solid grasp of tactics. They also experienced adversity and overcame it. Instead of becoming demoralized or overcome with fear, the Saudis kept the pressure on the Iraqis until Khafji was recaptured. Such battle savvy served notice to its Coalition partners that the Arab forces could hold their own. The Saudi performance at Khafji also served to convince the Saudi government that its army could fight. This was perhaps the most far-reaching consequence of the battle. Before Khafji, the Saudi government had planned to use its forces only to defend Saudi Arabia. Now it decided that its forces should take part in the coming offensive to liberate Kuwait.

CHAPTER SIX

SOMALIA, 1993

AN URBAN "PEACE" OPERATION GONE AWRY

by Lieutenant Colonel Bradley T. Gericke

United Nations Operations in Somalia, April 1992 – March 1995: Fatalities: 151 military personnel, 3 international civilian staff, 1 local staff. Cost: $1, 686,417,200. Department of Public Information, United Nations

An estimated 750,000 persons in Somalia lack sufficient food to meet minimum requirements. (as of spring, 2000), United Nations Somalia Report[121] *Islamist warlords have announced that they have taken control of Mogadishu.* June, 2006, London Times[122]

The advance and retreat of American troops deployed to Somalia between 1992 and 1994 reinforces to modern armies that urban conflict is something unique: a topsy-turvy kind of warfare that conflates the tactical and the strategic, the political with the military, the uniformed and the civilian. It creates a cauldron of conflict capable of unhinging the expectations of even the most well intentioned Soldiers and diplomats, and into which a nation must venture fully alert to the hazards. Certainly not revolutionary concepts and the U.S. Army knew these things institutionally in Mogadishu. Yet still, its Soldiers and their civilian leaders nonetheless found themselves astonished by how far astray their good intentions miscarried.

The well-publicized battle in October 1993 that pitted U.S. Army troops against Somali citizens and bandits in support of clan leader Mohamed Farrah Aidid was not exceptional in terms of the history of urban warfare. The by-now familiar characteristics of urban conflict were present: casualties rapidly inflicted and sustained, close-in fighting, spatial and situational confusion among participants, isolated small unit actions, and high expenditure of supplies and munitions. Nearly a decade after the agony of those hours in which American Soldiers fought for their lives and the honor of their nation, the memory remains raw. Americans, citizens and Soldiers alike, prefer outright victory whether they are facing opponents on athletic fields or battlefields. However, what happened in the dusty, hot streets of Mogadishu culminated in an outcome that lay somewhere in the twilight between victory and defeat.

Soldiers understand the risks they accept every time they don the uniform, and those assigned to Somalia were professionals. The casualties that they suffered from their eventual urban firefight, while significant, were not wholly unexpected by the troops. Soldiers recognize that their business is lethal and often unpredictable. Therefore, while the individual record of achievement from that time in Somalia adds luster to the record of American arms, a lingering acrimony, bound to the remembrance of Mogadishu, persists.

The mission was not supposed to end with Soldiers' bodies dragged through the dirt on worldwide television and another paraded as a prisoner, American will to provide humanitarian assistance in tatters, and U.S. forces in hasty retreat.

In a single afternoon, the military contest that played out in the twisted alleyways of a chaotic, third world state suddenly rent U.S. strategic policy. The heroism and pathos of that city fight foreshadow the perils that will repeatedly confront military decision-makers in the 21st century.

In Mogadishu, American Soldiers engaged in an urban gun battle due to a convergence of events that will likely recur. The setting of Somalia generally and Mogadishu specifically—a third world national capital embroiled in a humanitarian crisis, a civil war, and the subject of calls for a military-led response by the developed world—will reappear in other states and cities. This context requires military leaders to reconsider the assumptions under which they have trained and deployed their forces for most of the previous century.

The writing of nineteenth century Prussian theorist Karl von Clausewitz has long held sway over European and American military minds.[123] In an era that now posits increasingly ambitious military interventions to provide both humanitarian assistance and state building, the political ends of military engagement must be given ever more attention. A reemphasis of Clausewitz's dictate that the first purpose of a leader is to understand the nature of the conflict he undertakes is essential because one's understanding of war frames how one wages it. In the case of Somalia, American decision-makers prepared for the conflict they wished to fight rather than the one brewing in the turbulent, cacophonous streets of Mogadishu.

While Clausewitz wrote primarily from the perspective of the Napoleonic wars, what he described as the animating forces of war, a "trinity" of actors and their concomitant moral forces, explains war in all places and times. Violence, chance, and reason are war's universal characteristics.

Yet Clausewitz also recognized that the means of war could and did vary from epoch to epoch. Occupying a central place in his era was the European state with its formal distinction between government, the populace, and the army. Although not always following such delineation in practice, the ideal of officially sanctioned armed forces that are obedient to civil rule and supported by public opinion has been endorsed by generations of American military leaders, both civil and uniformed. What they overlooked in Somalia was the fact that societies cannot be compelled to organize violence to comply with American expectations.

Tribal societies, such as those functioning in Somalia, do not recognize clear distinctions between the army and the people. There are no standing armies with their extensive bureaucracies, formal training and equipment, and sanctioned authority. Rather, individuals constitute the fighting forces as they move in and out of various factions. Allegiance is local, not to a sovereign, central state. Along with the absence of legal civil authority is the lack of a notion of what constituted a legal use of force. Warlords and local strongmen wield violence to suit their needs. Thus, the security environment facing American Soldiers in Mogadishu was something about which they had little direct experience and preparation. American attempts to identify clearly the "enemy" were immediately frustrated, and U.S. ground forces found that a distinct boundary between friend and foe, and consequently peace and war, did not exist.

An American UH-1N ("Huey") helicopter flies over Mogadishu on a patrol mission to look for signs of hostilities. The widespread urban density of the city is clearly evident. (Photo Credit: USAF Photo by TSgt. Perry Heimer, 1st Combat Camera Squadron.)

The complex human environment of cities provides ideal battlegrounds for actors whose aim is not to achieve the overthrow of a state—because the formal trappings of state power barely exist—but rather sufficiently to obstruct opponents whose continued presence threatens to upset the traditional power structures. In Mogadishu, the greatest threat to the local power structure was the American force; hence, the U.S. troops became a prime target. The Somalis understood this fully, but the Americans, who did not see conventional armed forces opposing them, tended to underestimate their opponents' military capacity.[124]

Resultantly, U.S. forces strode confidently into a cultural and military situation in Somalia that they believed both comprehensible and malleable to their ends. However, contrary to their expectations, a "stability operation" escalated to a city fight within a short period.[125] The stabilization effort in

Mogadishu suddenly became a war, the place and time of which had not been sufficiently anticipated by either the political or military leaders who planned the deployment of U.S. forces. It was a dramatic wake-up call that signaled the arrival of the post-Cold War era in a newly tumultuous world.

The predicament that Somalia presented to the international community in the early 1990s was partly the result of natural disaster and partly the consequence of civil strife. Somalia is a crescent-shaped state located on the northeastern coast of Africa.[126] Its population was about 10,173,000 in the mid-1990s, most of it Somali, a Cushitic people. About 70 percent of the population is nomadic or semi nomadic. Islam is the state religion, and Somali and Arabic are the official languages.[127]

The land area of Somalia consists of nearly 650,000 square kilometers bounded by a 2,700 kilometer coastline on the north by the Gulf of Aden and to the East by the Indian Ocean. Northern Somalia is mountainous, while the south contains a plateau with two major rivers and a wide coastal plain. Somalia's climate is hot and dry.[128] Only about two percent of the land is considered arable. Farming techniques are primitive, and under the best of circumstances, the population in the countryside faces a precarious existence. The frequent droughts of the last several decades consumed what little agricultural productivity was available to the local population. Efforts to practice husbandry with small herds of cattle and goats had likewise proven futile.[129]

By the early 1990s, there was not enough for people to eat in the Somalian countryside, and the nation's infrastructure could not support the transport and distribution of foodstuffs in any case.

The vast majority of the road network remained unimproved at the time of U.N. and U.S. involvement. Distances between the main cities averaged hundreds of kilometers along lengthy dirt tracks.[130]

Mogadishu normally contained a population of about 900,000, but by the early 1990s, it had swollen to greater than 1.5 million due to refugees seeking succor from the drought. The city boasted an airport equipped with one of the country's seven paved airstrips, but its harbor facilities were in an advanced state of disrepair, and basic services such as telephones, plumbing, and electricity did not operate.[131] Manufacturing was in the early stages of development, with a cement factory, a cotton gin, a cannery, and a textile plant established and in operation. When not disrupted, exports included modest quantities of frankincense and myrrh.[132]

Disease from dietary inadequacies and lack of fundamental hygiene physically wrecked the populace. Somalia's population is young; 48 percent of Somalis are less than fifteen years old, and only three percent are older than 65 years of age. Life expectancy for males is only 55 years, and for females 56 years, each over fifteen years shorter than that of Western nations. Disillusionment and despair characterized the populace. Exacerbating these calamitous conditions was political strife that began in 1988 and escalated into open warfare with the toppling of the Siad Barre regime in January 1991.[133] Fighting between rival factions caused 40,000 casualties in 1991 and 1992, and by mid-1992 the civil war, drought, and banditry combined to produce a famine that threatened some 1.5 million people with starvation.

In July 1992, as fifteen clans and sub-clans vied for power, competing along tribal lines in multi-factional fighting, the U.N. secretary general declared Somalia to be a country without a government.[134] None of the clans could attain a decisive victory over its rivals. Seeking to buttress their individual positions, clan families resorted to the confiscation of relief supplies and the obstruction of foreign aid deliveries. The already precarious state of the Somali economy could not sustain such turmoil. Any remaining sense of order was swept away by the outbreak of widespread famine. This worsening quagmire sufficiently alarmed the international community to respond. In the event, the United Nations (and United States), would become deeply involved during the next several years.[135]

Between 1945 and 1987, the United Nations (UN) sponsored only thirteen peacekeeping operations. Between 1987 and 1992, the U.N. approved thirteen additional peacekeeping missions, excluding Somalia. The U.N. Charter authorizes such operations, although the term "peacekeeping" is not explicitly used. Rather, Chapter VI of the charger mentions such activities as the traditional roles of observing truces and monitoring boundaries in order to maintain stability between contesting sides. Chapter VII does contain the term "peace enforcement," and refers to other activities such as sanctions, blockades, and military intervention between states. Between these two concepts of "keeping" the peace and "enforcing" it lay a number of actions such as the restoration of order and commerce within a state or the forced distribution of humanitarian aid.[136] Somalia would prove to be a test case for the U.N.'s ability to address complex state crises.

As Somali shoppers watch, U.S. Marines march into Mogadishu's, Bakara Market to begin a sweep for arms and munitions as part of Operation Nutcracker. The crowded market was the hub of Mogadishu's small arms trade. Identifying friend or foe in this crowded area was nearly impossible. (Photo Credit: Combat Camera, PHCM Terry C. Mitchell, USN)

In April 1992, the United Nations Security Council approved Resolution #751 that established the United Nations Operation in Somalia (UNOSOM). The purpose of UNOSOM was to provide a peacekeeping force to monitor a cease-fire between warring factions. Fifty unarmed observers arrived in early July 1992, concurrent with the start of U.N. relief shipments. Their presence made little difference, so the U.N. requested additional support. President George Bush responded by authorizing Operation *Provide Relief.* Commanded by U.S. Marine Corps Brig. Gen. Frank Libutti, this operation, which began on

August 15, consisted of food shipments flown on military aircraft from Kenya to locations in southern Somalia for distribution by non-governmental organizations (NGO).[137]

As the security situation within Somalia continued to deteriorate, the U.N. Security Council approved in August an increase in strength of UNOSOM to four 750-man security detachments to safeguard humanitarian relief supplies and to ensure the continued operation of distribution centers throughout Somalia. By late November, several nations agreed to contribute observers, security personnel, and logistics support forces. Yet, even these efforts proved largely ineffective as looting, extortion, and running battles between clans continued unabated. Unrelenting theft and disruption frustrated U.N. relief efforts through the fall. When hostilities forced the withdrawal of a relief ship from Mogadishu's harbor, public exposure of the worsening state inside Somalia reached a new level.

On December 3, 1992, the U.N. Security Council passed a second Resolution, #794, which referred to Chapter VII of the U.N. Charter. This mandate allowed for both the provision of humanitarian assistance as well as the restoration of order in southern Somalia. The establishment of security for the distribution of relief supplies was a key component. On December 4, President Bush authorized Operation *Restore Hope* to implement the U.N. decision. U.S. forces under the command of Lieutenant General Robert B. Johnston, (USMC), would lead a multinational coalition to be known as the United Task Force (UNITAF). During the next six months, UNITAF would grow to a force of more than 38,000 Soldiers from more than twenty nations, of which approximately 28,000 were Americans.[138]

Several days later, American Marines entered Somalia under the glare of television cameras, news reporters, and floodlights in an early morning beach landing near Mogadishu. The Marines quickly moved to secure key terrain around the city and within hours could report that a measure of calm had been restored. On December 13, elements of the U.S. Army's 10th Mountain Division joined the Marines in the effort to secure distribution facilities and infrastructure. Between December and May, UNITAF troops worked aggressively to restore a measure of security by confiscating weapons from rival clans and convincing some Somali leaders to cooperate with U.N. efforts.

With the threat of widespread starvation largely at bay and in appreciation of the success of UNITAF under American leadership, U.N. Secretary-General Boutros-Ghali delayed the creation of a follow-on command. The Americans, however, were eager to pass their responsibilities to a successor U.N. force. Finally, Boutros-Ghali relented, and on March 26, 1993, the U.N. Security Council approved Resolution #814. This measure was significant because for the first time the Council explicitly mandated actions on its behalf under Chapter VII of the U.N. Charter. The command it created, UNOSOM II, was given an expansive list of objectives, to include the rehabilitation of Somali political institutions and economy, the disarmament of warring Somali clans, and the rebuilding of a secure environment throughout the nation.[139] To execute UNOSOM II, the U.N. established a robust peacekeeping architecture in Somalia. Retired U.S. Navy Adm.

Jonathan Howe assumed the position as Special Representative to the Secretary General, and Turkish Army Lt. Gen. Cevik Bir became the force commander of the multinational contingent. Reflecting the change in mission and the resumption of U.N. leadership, American forces soon thereafter began redeploying from Somalia.

Serving under the command of U.S. Army Maj. Gen. Thomas Montgomery, (USA), approximately 4,500 American Soldiers remained in the country in support of UNOSOM II. Of these, about 3,000 were logistical support personnel. Some 1,150 Soldiers from the 10th Mountain Division were assigned responsibility to provide a Quick Reaction Force (QRF) to assist UNOSOM II with military capabilities that might be required as events determined.[140]

However, under the new U.N. mandate, relations between U.S. forces and the Somali clans worsened. Faction leader Mohamed Farrah Aidid, who had overthrown the Somali government in 1991 agitated for greater power. Aidid's clan came under mounting pressure from the U.N. as the world body identified him as a chief obstacle to the reconstruction of Somalia. American troops responded by seizing arms, restricting movement within the city of Mogadishu, and inflicting Somali casualties.[141] Tensions grew higher in June when Aidid's militia killed two dozen Pakistani Soldiers returning from an inspection. The message for astute observers should have been that Aidid's forces had proven they could upset U.N. plans. They possessed numerous small arms, rocket propelled grenade launchers, and light mortars.

In mid-July, Admiral Howe declared Aidid himself to be a target and directed a raid against one of Aidid's headquarters buildings. Soon thereafter, Howe placed a $25,000 bounty on Aidid. The following month, a special operations unit, Task Force Ranger, commanded by Major General William Garrison, (USA), deployed to Mogadishu to capture Aidid and to dismantle his command hierarchy.[142] In the space of a year, American troops had gone from the airlift of relief supplies to the protection of distribution networks to a position of armed confrontation within a third world city of over a million residents. The stage had been set for a city fight.[143]

In physical terms, Mogadishu was a city like many others across the developing world.[144] Its streets and alleys were a product of centuries of local development and constituted a virtually indecipherable labyrinth to the visitor. Block after block of buildings existed as jumbled accretions—constructed, demolished, and reconstructed by residents—without the benefit of any broad plan other than to meet their immediate needs. Absent a sense of urban planning, and coming after years of drought, dislocation, and civil war, the city presented itself to American forces as a tangled maze and a forbidding place to have to fight. American troops could see with their own eyes the physical perils presented by Mogadishu, and though they were generally well trained and prepared to conduct conventional military operations, city fighting was another matter.[145] What they did not openly acknowledge, or perhaps did not recognize, was the fact that the vast professional edge that U.S. forces possessed—their technological capability, organization, firepower, and supply—could be neutralized easily by merely imposing the burden of urban combat upon the American Soldiers.

The Soldiers of Task Force Ranger understood that the prospect of urban warfare confronted them with difficulties. The risk of casualties was great, opportunities for confusion more than ordinary, and in the city, combat would be vicious, close-in, and rapidly dynamic. Leaders acknowledged that any combat within Mogadishu would require the height of their resourcefulness and tenacity in order to survive and to win. They knew the stories of Stalingrad, Warsaw, and a dozen other twentieth century battles. Nevertheless, missing from their preparations was the realization that the forces at hand were not suitable to achieve the broader operational and strategic objectives of U.S. diplomacy. They simply could not achieve the desired end state of stability and security for Mogadishu that had been devised for them in Washington, D.C. Moreover, when the city fight American troops did not explicitly seek, but imagined that they could handle, finally occurred on October 3 – 4, 1993, they were overwhelmed.[146]

The tension between Aidid and the U.S. officials had remained high throughout September. Soon, American intelligence sources indicated that two of Aidid's key subordinates were hiding near Mogadishu's Bakara Market District. The densely crowded district had become an area in which Aidid's militia could move and operate with relative impunity. U.S. human intelligence sources were unreliable, and Aidid left few electronic signatures that American hi-tech eavesdropping devices could detect. American officials knew, however, that Aidid's allies frequented the area and suspected that Aidid's men cached significant weapons and equipment nearby. Hoping to put further pressure on Aidid, Task Force Ranger developed a plan to snatch Aidid's lieutenants.

The concept of the intended operation was familiar to the Soldiers of Task Force Ranger since similar missions had already been carried out in Somalia.[147] The U.S. troops would use every technological advantage at their disposal to ensure the greatest opportunity for success. Four teams of Ranger infantrymen, about 75 men, were to rope down from four Blackhawk helicopters. Their mission was to isolate the building in which Aidid's men were hiding, preventing any unanticipated ingress or egress from the area, and to provide security while observing the local situation as the mission unfolded. A team of about forty Delta Force operators would descend from five of their specially equipped helicopters to assault the target building and to secure Aidid's men. A ground convoy consisting of twelve trucks and humvees was to hide behind the Olympic Hotel across the street from the target building. Their mission, once the Delta Force commandoes had Aidid's men secure, was to rush alongside the target building to transport the prisoners to captivity at the U.S. base at the Mogadishu airport. The U.S. command group was to be kept informed via an array of communications and intelligence platforms, including OH-58 observation helicopters, P-3 Orion spy planes, and remote sensors.

Around 3:30 P.M., Sunday, October 3, 1993, the main force of Rangers departed the U.S. base at Mogadishu airport aboard seventeen helicopters. A ground convoy followed. Initially, the operation unfolded according to plan, even though the ground elements began receiving ground fire. The troops emerged with prisoners and prepared to depart.

Unfortunately, for the Americans, Somali resistance quickly began to impose telling effects.

The U.S. troops on the ground and in the air had considered active Somali resistance as a possible reaction. The rules of engagement under which they had been operating, however, no longer made sense, and the difficulty they faced was that city fighting is immediately unforgiving, violent, and demanding. Because this was the first battle that many of the men had experienced and because it came as part of a "peacekeeping" deployment, Task Force Ranger had trouble retaking control of the situation as it deteriorated around them.

Like a flash-fire raging out of control, within minutes they were caught in a maelstrom that was impossible to contain. Mobs of Somalis—men, women and children—observed the Americans on the street corners and witnessed the hovering helicopters above; they quickly comprehended what was happening. They were already familiar with the American way of military operations in Mogadishu and were anticipating U.S. actions.

Suddenly, Blackhawk Super 61 was hit in the tail by a rocket-propelled grenade (RPG) and crashed several blocks from the hotel. Rangers closest to the crash site established a protective perimeter and attempted to aid the seven-man crew. Men from a search and rescue helicopter quickly roped into the site and extracted two injured Soldiers. Shots began to ring out from the surging crowd with such intensity that the Rangers and Delta Force members found it increasingly difficult to identify and separate combatants from witnesses among the hundreds and then thousands of agitated faces in the pressing throngs.

Furthermore, U.S. forces were confronting an ordeal made increasingly complex by problems within the force itself and exacerbated by unclear situational awareness. One Soldier had fallen prematurely from his fast rope and injured himself. There was confusion as to which helicopter had crashed and at what precise location. It was difficult to determine the welfare of the crash victims as communication nets were filled with frenetic reports from a variety of locations. The initial ground convoy, its vehicles and men alike riddled from the effects of gunfire, could not locate the crash site, so General Garrison ordered the vehicles, containing both Rangers and the prisoners, to return.

Somali gunmen were continuing to converge on the crashed helicopter, when at 4:40 P.M., a second Blackhawk crashed about three-quarters of a kilometer away from the first. Two Delta Force operators deployed nearby in an effort to protect the surviving crewmembers. They would be posthumously awarded the Medal of Honor for their heroism.[148]

At 6:30 P.M., a Quick Reaction Force (QRF) constituted around a company of the 2d Battalion, 14th Infantry Regiment (10th Mountain Division), departed the airfield with the intent of relieving the 90 Soldiers at the first crash site who remained pinned down and cut off.[149] However, the QRF immediately came under heavy fire and after a difficult fight returned, to base. Meanwhile, the Rangers on the ground continued to improve their defensive positions and aided their wounded as circumstances allowed. Gunfire attacks persisted in the faltering light, even as Little Bird helicopters attempted to suppress Somali gunmen. No living U.S. troops remained at the second crash site.

Another ground-borne relief column from 2-14 Infantry, numbering about seventy vehicles and this time augmented by Malaysian and Pakistani armored vehicles, finally departed at 11:23 P.M. and moved into the thicket of Mogadishu's streets. The column reached the Rangers' casualty collection point in the early morning hours of October 4. They began augmenting the defensive perimeter and loading wounded Soldiers onto the vehicles. Finally recovering the last body from the crashed helicopter at site one, they departed shortly before 6:00 A.M. Not all of the injured Soldiers could fit onto the personnel carriers, so some departed walking and running alongside the moving vehicles. Soon, additional humvees arrived and finally transported the troops to the relative safety of a nearby sports stadium.[150] From there helicopters transported the wounded to the airbase for medical attention.[151]

The cost of the fight was high. On the American side, eighteen had been killed, 79 injured, and one captured.[152] Numerous vehicles were damaged. Two helicopters were shot down, and three others sustained permanent damage that rendered them inoperable. Somali losses are difficult to quantify, but seem to be greater than 500 dead, and nearly 1,000 wounded.[153]

More importantly, the combat seared into the American conscience a fear that urban combat was such an ugly, bloody business that it could not be controlled, and perhaps not ever won. Haunted by the images and stories of roving, angry crowds, military and civilian decision makers turned away from the specter of city fighting. For at least a decade, the memory of Mogadishu would stalk U.S. national strategy and embolden America's enemies.

The Mogadishu Experience

Urban combat assumes many forms, from siege to assault to guerrilla warfare to terrorism; and like warfare in general, each city fight reflects to some extent the unique conditions of its place and time. Aspects of the American experience in Somalia have already reappeared in contemporary contests such as Iraq, and will occur in other places in the future. Hence, this chapter of American military history bears continued scrutiny.

Since city fighting is so difficult, it is virtually impossible for any army, including the most capable U.S. force, to fight in an urban setting without suffering casualties. Ordinary Americans, who expect to follow sweeping arrows illustrating the advances of their heroic forces as explained by television pundits, find it difficult to comprehend opponents who do not wear uniforms or fight by Western conventions. Americans cling to the assumption that war is made predominantly by the governments of states, and they maintain a strong cultural bias that prefers military figures to be well-groomed, uniformed gentlemen. Any other type of violence is viewed as lawless, to be remedied by a police or law enforcement operation. Westerners forget that the state is a recent, European invention, customarily dated in its modern form to the Peace of Westphalia in 1648 that concluded the Thirty Years' War. It was only at that point that nation states became the dominant form of political organization. Most Europeans, like Americans, accept war as an extreme form of political expression, but they still regard armed conflict as an interruption to the normal course of things. For a citizen of Europe and America, peace is the normal, routine state of affairs; war the exception. Peace marks progress and civilization; war is a regression.

Most non-European parts of the world underwent contrary experiences. In Africa and the Middle East, the exercise of power in the form of violence was, and is, conducted not by formal armed forces sponsored by state governments, but rather by informally constituted groups on the consensual behalf of local peoples. For these societies, the boundaries of conflict are indistinct. War often takes the form of an economic and social expression. The capture and possession of territory is less important than the achievement of other goals. In this kind of war, there is less separation of public and private property, and little distinction between combatant and noncombatant. Whether violence is an act of war or a crime cannot always be precisely resolved. It was this kind of volatile brew that greeted the U. S. Army in Somalia.

As American forces initially provided aid and succor to thousands, there seemed little cause for alarm. The surface waters of Somalian culture seemed calm enough. American civil and military leaders, accustomed to the demarcated, Western style of war, remained wedded to their conviction that this was a peacetime operation. The United States was not at war. Hence, the nation stayed comfortably on the peacetime side of the peace-war equation. In Somalia's capital, however, mobs of citizens believed differently. When they suddenly became fighters, they illustrated the innate fragility of partitions between the tactical and strategic levels of war.

After the fight in Mogadishu, U.S. policymakers recoiled from the carnage of the battle and the ensuing public examination in the mass media. The violence of the fighting and the images of American casualties desecrated in the city streets led to a drastic change of American policy governing the deployment of U.S. forces. Henceforth, the national commitment to operations in Somalia that prior to the fight had warranted significant American resources, dissipated.[154]

The United States withdrew its peacekeeping forces from Somalia in March 1994. When the last U.N. troops pulled out a year later, Mogadishu still had no functioning government, and separate armed factions controlled different parts of the country. Meanwhile, the suffering of the residents of the Horn of Africa continued unabated as drought conditions persisted and new fighting broke out in Ethiopia.[155]

In hindsight, it became clear that a classic rule of military planning needed to be reiterated within America's senior councils: military missions and their objectives must be clearly stated and resourced.

Amidst the reexamination of armed services' roles and missions after the Gulf War, that maxim had been lost. The troops in Mogadishu could not rely upon all of the tools available in the full arsenal of U.S. capabilities. They did not possess tanks or heavy artillery because such weapons were not considered politically appropriate. Nor did the troops mine, clear, or significantly fortify any part of Mogadishu prior to the battle. It hardly needs stating that they would have if they had been fighting through the streets of Fulda in a Cold War scenario or had Mogadishu been the setting for a war featuring another Western-style opponent in which the fate of the U.S. homeland was considered to be at stake. American leaders, both military and civilian, have shown no reluctance to commit whatever it takes when they consider the stakes high enough.

In a certain sense, the advent of warmaking at times and locations that do not directly threaten the nation is merely the return of so-called "limited" war, a concept practiced by fighting forces since the classical period but attributed most famously to the tactics of the eighteenth century. In fact, armies have long undertaken missions in which their intent was something other than the annihilation of an enemy. Often they sought not to kill so much as to capture a locality, secure a ransom, ensure access to provisions, or to intimidate an opponent into concessions. Diplomatic imperatives have always restricted the behaviors of the warriors undertaking such ventures.

During the nineteenth century, the British were particularly adept at the same business of policing, nation-building, and peacekeeping across Asia and Africa that the Americans attempted in Somalia. The U.S. Army and Marines also conducted "expeditionary" operations to China, the Philippines, Nicaragua, and Cuba. Hence, it is not so much that American armed forces were venturing into new territory, but rather that their journey tread a dimly remembered path. It is worth remembering that there is no silver bullet to the challenges presented by city fighting in a peacetime strategic context, although several meliorating measures avail themselves for consideration.

The need for civil and military objectives that are mutually supportive is critical, and bears restating.[156] Civil objectives must describe the desired endstates to be reached once hostilities have ended, and military objectives must be envisioned so that when achieved, they permit the transition to such a successful peace. Another obvious necessity is that in a situation like Somalia where the propensity exists for rapid escalation of a military conflict, forces on the ground must possess a full array of military weaponry, communications, and logistical capability. Finally, a clear enunciation of very flexible rules of engagement (ROE) that effectively link political, economic, and military goals may provide a partial solution.

Patrolling the streets of Mogadishu was always hazardous. Snipers and ambushes were a constant threat. Local residents observed the Americans up close, and learned how U.S. military forces operated in the city. (Photo Credit: TSgt Perry Heimer, USAF Combat Camera.)

The American servicemen in Mogadishu were caught in the limbo between the familiar doctrines and practices of declared war, which outline the methods and resources available to achieve victory, and the much more constraining limits imposed by the nature of "peacekeeping," which assumed no serious conflict, and thus no need for robust capability. To view the mission in Somalia as a success requires even the most optimistic observer to focus almost solely on the courageous actions of tactical unit leaders and to look beyond the lapses that occurred at the operational and strategic levels. American troops fought well – that is clear. Nevertheless, it is equally beyond question that they were placed in a perilous position that they could insufficiently influence on the ground. In addition, the potential for further such battles remains great.

On any given day in every year since the events in Mogadishu, tens of thousands of U.S. Army troops have been deployed to military hotspots around the world.[157] As of late 2005, nearly 180,000 were deployed overseas to about 120 different countries conducting a wide variety of missions. Meanwhile, the U.S.-led invasion and then occupation of Iraq has now provided fresh evidence for the complexity of urban operations.

As in Somalia, American troops entered the fight for Iraq's cities on unsure footing. Overall, the invading force lacked numbers to secure the ground they captured, possessed too few armored HMMWVs and trucks of all sorts, depended on inadequate radios and communications capability, and demonstrated poor individual and crew combat skills within support units. Army units could move rapidly and at great length operationally through the desert, but found the cities to be tough slogging.

The intervening years since the 2003 occupation of Baghdad have seen American efforts to pacify urban areas disrupted by small groups of fighters. Just as in Mogadishu, U.S. troops have proven extraordinarily proficient at killing opponents when they can be identified and located. Bringing all of the tools of American power to bear has proven difficult, and as of late 2006, only partially successful. When Army or Marine forces are concentrated in a city, enemy fighters are routed. As soon as military restrictions on the populace are loosened to allow the resumption of economic and social activity, however, the guerrillas reappear to conduct hit-and-run attacks. Although a combined arms approach is the surest way to apply decisive firepower against a fighting enemy, kinetic violence must be tempered with other non-lethal, informational, economic, and cultural assets if resistance turns to a low-grade insurgency. While the Iraqi guerrillas' methods are different from those undertaken by the Somali factions, it is the same complex stew of human and physical infrastructure that facilitates this kind of low-grade warfare. Once more, Soldiers and Marines are caught at the in-between point of using sufficient force to destroy an enemy, while at the same time minimizing damage to the city's buildings and fostering the support of residents to allow for the gradual return of peace.

Hence, the ongoing responsibility of military planners is to acknowledge the extraordinary demands placed on military units in an urban environment, and to structure ground forces to meet this challenge. This seems simple, yet in the complex negotiations between the armed services and among the branches of government that occur with each budget cycle and formulation of national strategy, competing demands inevitably crowd the picture. Yet the ability of American armed forces to operate in urban environments is frequently at stake.

For instance, during the last decade the Army's imagination in terms of force projection has been consumed in a debate between camps advocating either "light" or "heavy" forces. While the now fielded "medium-weight" Stryker vehicle bridges this capability, and the Army's Modular Brigade Combat Teams are inherently more organizationally flexible, the largely unchallenged and unspoken assumption in this discussion is that to be "expeditionary" Army formations must be readily air-deployable.

Yet, the U.S. Army has never lost a war, and seems to be at little risk of losing even a battle, for lack of the ability to move operational-level echelons by air. While it is definitely desirable to transport as many forces as quickly as possible both inter- and intra-theater, the priority given this ability seems out of balance with the benefits promised. Often lost is the fact that on the ground—where wars are won or lost—the characteristics of lethality and survivability reign supreme. "Aero-mechanization" is an intriguing theory that games well, and its proponents in the Army who conducted wargames during the 1990s are convinced it is a valid answer to situations like Mogadishu. It may prove to be a theory, however, that is difficult to translate into reality. In the final calculus of war, it more critical that ground forces be able to destroy an enemy and remain viable than merely to arrive expeditiously to the battlefield. The lesson of Custer, who galloped to his demise with tremendous alacrity, is one worth remembering. There are similarities between that disaster and the carnage of Mogadishu.

For the United States, the city fight in Mogadishu was the wrong battle in the wrong place at the wrong time. Images of its Soldiers beleaguered by impoverished mobs were broadcast around the world, emboldening terrorists and regimes hostile to the U.S. During the subsequent years Mogadishu became a rallying point and inspiration for those who found it convenient to cast the armies of the West as weak and vulnerable; a miscalculation for sure, but one containing strategic import for American security interests around the globe.

After the battle, one thing was certain. U.S. leaders—both military and civilian—had under-estimated the perilous conditions of "peace" in Somalia and ultimately achieved far less than they had hoped. For the Somalis, the suffering continues. As of 2006, an estimated 2.1 million people lack food and water. The United Nations recently asked the United States for assistance.[158]

CHAPTER SEVEN

GROZNY, 1995

THE SHAPE OF WARS TO COME

by Colonel John Antal, U.S. Army (Ret.)

Russian armored infantry move through the ruins of Grozny in 1995. (Russian Army photo)

An airborne battalion will settle the problem in a week.[159] *Russian Defense Minister Pavel Grachev*

Grozny, Chechnya, January 1, 1995: A Russian tank, its turret lying upside down near its tracks, smoldered in the desolate square near the city's railroad station. A terrific explosion shattered the cold, smoke-hazed afternoon and the reverberations from the blast of 152mm shells and 120mm rockets shook the ground. Chechen fighters scurried between the charred, burning armored vehicles as nervous television crews scanned the battlefield with their camcorders. The scattered bodies of Russian soldiers--many burned and disfigured beyond recognition--lay all around.

In the winter of 1995, the city of Grozny became a virtual meat grinder for the Russian Army. This army—the legacy of the great Kutuzov, whose forces stopped Napoleon, and the invincible Marshal Zhukov, whose armies defeated Hitler—was beaten and humbled by a people scorned in Moscow as "bandits" and "terrorists." For military professionals, the battle of Grozny is a stark precursor of war in the 21st century, for it was a war fueled by a toxic mixture of regionalism, ethnic hatred, and failed states.

The Russian government launched the Chechen war for myriad reasons, not the least of which was to preserve the "territorial integrity" of the Russian Federation. Chechnya was a vivid test of Boris Yeltsin's authority and political will and his ability to hold together a Russian federation of 89 ethnic republics and regions. Yeltsin feared that the Federation would split apart, as the Soviet Union had in 1991. For 21 months, from December 1994 to August 1996, Chechnya would also test the Russian Army's will to fight in the harshest conditions imaginable. Although the war was fought throughout Chechnya, and the Chechens raided Russia itself, the fight centered on the important industrial city of Grozny.

Background to the War

Chechnya is a country slightly larger than Connecticut—comprising approximately 6,000 square miles—Chechnya is bordered in the west by the Ingush Republic, in the south by the independent state of Georgia, in the east and northeast by Dagestan, and by the North Ossetin Republic to the northwest. The country's northern tier is mostly fertile plain, crossed by the Terek and

Sunzha Rivers. Southern Chechnya's wooded hills rise to the high slopes of the Caucasus Mountains.

The Chechens are a fiercely independent, predominantly Muslim people with a distinctive language that is neither Slavic, Turkish, nor Persian. Primarily herdsman and farmers who for the most part inhabit the country's mountainous regions, the Chechens have a long and bloody history of conflict with Russia that dates back to the 18th Century. Annexed by Tsarist Russia in 1859 after bitter fighting, Chechnya never fully assimilated into Russia's culture or succumbed to its political control. Resistance to Russian oppression and occupation is a source of much native pride. In 1832, Sergei Lermontov, one of the great 19th Century Russian poets, said of the Chechens, "their god is freedom, their law is war."

When Yeltsin took power from Gorbachev in 1991, dissident leaders in Chechnya took advantage of the turmoil in the central government to declare independence from Moscow. The rebels elected General Dzhokhar Dudayev—a former bomber pilot and Soviet Air Force general—by a ninety percent vote. Yeltsin refused to recognize the validity of the election and on November 7, 1991, declared a state of emergency in the Chechen-Ingush Republic. In response, the Chechens rallied behind Dudayev and 30,000 protesters demonstrated in Grozny. To inflame the crowds, Dudayev declared an Islamic Holy War on Russia.

The newly elected Chechen parliament immediately endowed Dudayev with special powers. When Russian troops soon after landed at Grozny airport, Chechen national guardsmen surrounded them. Unwilling to take drastic action, Yeltsin evacuated his soldiers after tense negotiations with the newly elected government. In exchange, Russian Defense Minister Pavel Grachev surrendered weapons and ammunition stored in Russian army depots and garrisons in Chechnya. Chechen forces thus amassed a considerable arsenal, which included 260 airplanes, 42 tanks, 48 armored vehicles, 44 lightly armored vehicles, 942 automobiles, 139 artillery pieces, 89 heavy antitank weapons, and 37,795 firearms.[160] Most ominously for the Russian army, they also procured thousands of rocket propelled grenade launchers [RPGs] – the lightweight, handheld antitank rocket launchers that would play such havoc in the close confines of Grozny.

The Chechen crisis continued to boil as Yeltsin insisted that "the territorial integrity of the Russian Federation must be sustained," while Dudayev retorted with cries for an independent Chechnya. Matters came to a head on November 26, 1994, when Russian forces made up primarily of "volunteers" recruited from the Russian Army failed to overthrow Dudayev in a direct assault on Grozny. An unknown number of soldiers were killed in the attack, and Dudayev's forces captured 21. On November 29, 1994, after the Chechens refused to negotiate the return of the captured Russian soldiers, Yeltsin issued a 48-hour deadline for all Chechen forces to surrender their weapons.

The Chechens had never been disarmed in their history, and it was preposterous to believe that they would do so on Russian orders, let alone in 48 hours. Dudayev contemptuously ignored the ultimatum, prompting Grachev to propose direct Russian military intervention. Yeltsin, who had even less regard for the Chechens than Grachev, agreed and ordered a "full force" option to commence in December 1994. Yeltsin, angry and humiliated, wanted Dudayev and his Chechen followers crushed by the weight of the Russian Army.

Preparation for Combat

In 1994, the Republic of Chechnya boasted a population of more than one million with 400,000 residing in Grozny, many of them ethnic Russians. Although most of the population lived in the densely populated cities, the high, snow-covered Caucasus Mountains were and still are the historical refuge and spiritual home of the Chechen people. The Russians knew that the first phase of their conquest of Chechnya had to include the capture of Grozny, Chechnya's capital and industrial and economic heart, followed by the seizure of its other major cities and villages in the plains. Once Russian forces controlled the urban areas, they intended to move into the mountains to finish the job.

Preparations for this war—at least on paper—had been going on in the Russian Army for some time. In September 1994, the North Caucasus Military District held war games that assumed Chechen resistance would be weak. In November, Grachev put Lieutenant General Anatoly Kvashnin in charge of the planning effort. Kvashnin assumed that a stand-up fight between Russian and Chechen forces was highly unlikely. He believed that Dudayev's forces were merely bandits and Mafia-types that would fall in a matter of days or weeks, once the Chechens saw the Russian Army on the move against them. Defense Minister Grachev agreed with this view and certified to Yeltsin that the North Caucasus Military District was "ready for combat."

In spite of Grachev's optimistic reports, some Russian generals opposed an invasion of Chechnya. Eleven flag officers, including the ground forces commander, Colonel-General V. Semenov, appealed to the State Duma, stating that contrary to the Defense Minister's claim, Russian forces were not prepared to attack and subdue the rebellious province. They objected on the grounds that their army had not conducted a single division level maneuver since 1992, that the ground forces were woefully undermanned, and that military equipment and morale was in sad shape.

In spite of this internal opposition, Yeltsin proceeded and the Russians attacked Chechnya on December 1, 1994. The Russian Air Force launched the first blow, destroying the weak Chechen air force on the ground without a single loss of aircraft. Unconcerned by the destruction of his fledgling air force, General Dudayev felt that the weight of history was on the side of his people and wrote: "We can see how the Soviet empire is collapsing, the Russian empire is next."[161] Dudayev went so far as to send a congratulatory letter to the Russian air force general who commanded the attack, telling him that the action would now be decided on the ground. The Russians did not take Dudayev's promise seriously. They should have.

The Approach March

In the first week of December, the Russian forces concentrated at Vladikavkaz, Beslan, and Mozdok. The forces were part of the newly reorganized immediate reaction force of the North Caucasus Military District, consisting of "an airborne and motorized rifle division, sub-units of two airborne assault divisions, several infantry brigades, two motorized rifle regiments, two battalions of naval infantry as well as Ministry of Internal Affairs (MVD) troops and border guards from all over Russia."[162] With the expectation that the Chechens would capitulate once they faced the Russian Army, the plan called for a rapid advance converging on Grozny to block reinforcement of the city. Then, as quickly as possible, the Russian Army was to transfer authority for establishing a new government to the MVD units.

On December 11, 1994—the first anniversary of the new Russian constitution—the Russian Army moved into Chechnya, invading from the north, east, and west. The next day, Federation Council Speaker Shumeyko announced that Russian forces would not fight the local population and that Grozny would not be stormed. Accordingly, and due to the large number of Russians living in Chechnya, the Russian Army's rules of engagement at this time were to shoot only if fired upon.

As the Russians rolled forward, Chechen resistance slowed the invaders on every route except in the north where native Chechen forces who opposed Dudayev moved in advance of the Russian column. Along the other routes, mobs of unarmed civilian protesters, mostly women and children, blocked the roads and slowed the advance. Residents of the settlement of Verkhniye Achaluki laid in the road, halting the 76th Airborne Division and the 21st Separate Airborne Brigade. In other areas, Chechen snipers fired at vehicle fuel tanks and wheels, avoiding direct fire at Russian soldiers, but harassing them nevertheless.

However, passive Chechen resistance soon transformed into active fighting as Russian commanders tried to bypass roadblocks or remove people who were blocking the streets. The 19th Motorized Infantry Division convoy, advancing and encountering opposition from civilians and Chechen snipers, had several vehicles set on fire and destroyed. A convoy of the 106th Airborne Division and the 56th Separate Airborne Brigade was attacked by multiple rocket launcher fire—a clear indication that the Chechens were well armed and knew how to fight. The casualties included six Russian soldiers killed and thirteen wounded; however, more important than the casualty numbers were the effects of these attacks on the emotional state of the already demoralized Russian conscripts.

The poor state of Russian Army discipline and training further delayed the deployment as the lessons learned from the bloody convoy battles in Afghanistan were forgotten. A few days into the advance, General Babichev, the commander of the western group of forces, refused to move any farther into Chechnya, citing his unwillingness to shoot mothers and children. In some areas, Russian troops fraternized openly with the civilian population while in other cases drunken Russians committed violent robberies and murders.

As problems with the advance mounted, General Eduard Vorobyov, First Deputy Commander of Russia's Ground Forces, was sent to Chechnya to assess the situation. On December 19, 1994, he arrived at the huge army base of Mozdok, located on the northwest border of Chechnya in Ingushetia. He reviewed the state of the army and quickly decided that the assault on Grozny, and perhaps the entire invasion, faced disaster.[163] Reporting to Moscow that whoever ordered the operation should be "investigated for criminal irresponsibility," Vorobyov promptly resigned on

December 22 rather than take command of an unpopular invasion that showed clear signs of imminent failure.[164]

By now, few Russians held the illusion that their advance to Grozny would achieve victory. General Kvashnin, who later became Russian Chief of the General Staff, expressed surprise at the organization and weaponry of the Chechen resistance, noting, "by December 21, 1994, a grouping of Dudayev's armed formations was concentrated in 40-45 strongholds protected by roadblocks, minefields, positions for firing from tanks, infantry combat vehicles, and artillery."[165]

As the Russian columns advanced towards Grozny, they met increasing resistance. It became clear that the Chechens would fight for their capital. Every turn in the road became an ambush against an enemy who would fire at the column and then fade away, rather than engage in open combat. Three Russian columns, totaling 40,000 men, finally neared Grozny on December 26 and took positions along the northern approaches. It had taken fifteen days to travel less than 120 kilometers. At their comfortable headquarters in Mozdok, Grachev and his officers were shocked at the lack of progress: "We never thought that on our own territory, anyone hiding behind women and children would shoot their own citizens in army uniform in the back."[166]

Frustrated and facing the promise of a protracted guerrilla war, Grachev decided that a show of force might cower the Chechens into submission. Based on this false hope he ordered a rapid assault to seize Grozny and capture Dudayev. The Russian plan to seize Grozny called for four "strike groups" to advance on the enemy's capital simultaneously: Group *Sever* (north), comprising the 8th Volgograd Corps, commanded by General Lev Rohklin; the division-sized Group *Zapad* (west), commanded by General Petruk; and Group *Vostok* (east), commanded by General Stas'ko; and a Spetsnaz group. Their orders were to advance to the center of the city, join forces, and destroy all enemy positions.[167] General Kvashnin describes the intent of the plan as follows:

> The operational concept at this stage provided for the assault detachments attacking from the northern, western, and eastern salients, entering the city and in collaboration with the MVD and FCS [Federal Counter-intelligence Service] special sub-units, seizing the "presidential palace," the government, television, and radio buildings, the railroad station, and other important establishments in the city center, and blocking the northern part of the city center and the "presidential palace" from the north.[168]

Though commanders were instructed to minimize civilian casualties, especially among the ethnic Russians in Grozny, the plan called for an artillery and air bombardment. The Battle for Grozny, planned as a surprise operation designed to seize the city in one fell swoop while the Chechens were celebrating the New Year, was about to begin.

The Chechens Decide to Defend Grozny

The Chechen fighters supporting Dudayev, in marked contrast to the invaders, faced the impending struggle confidently. With ample Russian weaponry and ammunition, and their spirits buoyed by folk stories of heroes who defied Russia's armies against terrible odds, the Chechens were mentally and spiritually prepared to fight.[169] "One thing I can tell you," said one determined 35-year-old fighter, Adi Ismailov, "whatever the cost, whatever our fate, even if we are driven into the mountains, we will not forgive them a single drop of Chechen blood."[170] Although internal Chechen politics were highly fractured, most Chechens opposed the external threat posed by the Russians -- not for vague political reasons, nor for Dudayev, but to defend their families and homeland from their historic oppressor.[171]

Although the Chechens lacked a formal standing army, many Chechen fighters had served in the Russian army. Enough former officers were present to form makeshift staffs, while most Chechen males were familiar with the use of small arms. Observers were struck by Chechen discipline, noting an absence of the accidental shootings and celebratory firing that characterized most tribal militias. Charismatic leaders like former Soviet Colonel Aslan Maskhadov, Chief of staff of the Chechen Army, and Shamil Basayev, a celebrated terrorist and guerrilla leader, provided dynamic and inspirational front-line leadership. About 6,000 Chechen fighters, armed principally with small arms, assembled to contest the Russian advance on Grozny, facing an equal number of Russian combat troops attacking with tanks, artillery and armored personnel carriers.

The city was a formidable obstacle, encompassing hundreds of square kilometers of sprawling urban expanse. By December 25, Grozny was blockaded by Russian troops from all directions except the south, a direction the Russian forces "deliberately left clear to provide a way out," but also a route from which Dudayev constantly received reinforcements.[172] To defend the city Maskhadov created three defense lines: an inner one with a radius of 1-1.5 kilometers around the Presidential Palace, a middle ring to a distance of up to one kilometer from the inner ring, and an outer ring up to 5 km from the city center. Taking the measure of their opponents, the Chechens did not set up obvious antitank traps and obstacles, which they knew would be blasted away at point-blank range by tank fire. Instead, they allowed the Russian columns to penetrate deeply into the city, where they could be attacked at close range by small teams.

Chechen resistance focused in the area near the Presidential Palace, where Maskhadov kept his headquarters. Here the buildings were strongly built, consisting of stone and reinforced concrete. The Chechens prepared the lower and upper floors of the structures for defense, creating firing platforms and openings for rifles, machine guns, and antitank weapons. Almost every rooftop had a 12.7mm anti-aircraft machine gun, courtesy of Grachev's deal to surrender the Russian Army's weapons in 1992. Prepared positions were created for direct artillery and tank fire along the main streets.

The middle defense line consisted of strongholds at highway entrances, in the residential areas, and at the bridges crossing the Sunzha River. Chechen fighters staged in a chemical plant, oil fields, and at the Lenin and Sheripov oil refineries also established strong points. The Chechens planned to set the chemical plant and oil refineries on fire if necessary. The outer defense line consisted of fortified positions on the Grozny-Mozdok and Dolinskiy-Katayama-Tashkala freeways, and in strongholds east and south of the city. In short, the Chechens had postured themselves effectively, and had planned their defensive response to wreak the greatest possible havoc on the imminent Russian advance.

The Russian Assault Begins

The attack began around noon on New Years Eve. Group *Sever* moved forward as scheduled with the 131st *Maikop* Brigade and a battalion of the 81st Motorized Rifle Regiment (MRR).[173] The group advanced along Mayakovskiy Street without encountering organized resistance, successfully reaching the railroad station. Another battalion of the 81st MRR headed to the Presidential Palace. The lead BMP (a thinly armored infantry vehicle) managed to drive right up to the Presidential Palace in the center of Grozny without a shot being fired. Puzzled at the empty streets and deserted square in front of the Presidential Palace, the battalion commander stopped the column and radioed for instructions. The lead vehicles bunched up in the square as the rest stretched at various intervals from the Presidential Palace to the jump off point. Inside their vehicles, many of the Russian conscripts were sleeping, exhausted after days of hard driving and hurry-up-and-wait operations.

The eastern group, *Group Zapad*, advanced three or four blocks, but was quickly stopped by several salvos and fire from firearms and grenade launchers. Group *Vostok*, for unknown reasons, moved only a few kilometers from its "forming up" position and halted. Elite Spetsnaz units were landed by helicopter in the mountains to support the mechanized drive, but became lost in the rugged terrain. One Spetsnaz group wandered around for three days and eventually surrendered to the Chechen fighters. With all but one of the Russian columns blocked, Group Sever found itself in the center of Grozny without support.

As the battalion of the 81st MRR idled in front of the Presidential Palace, the Chechens made their move. Their tactics were rudimentary but effective. They destroyed the lead vehicles, then the rear vehicles, blocking the route, and finally, at their leisure, smashed the remainder of the entire column. With no idea what to do, the Russian soldiers panicked. A free-for-all ensued, as BMPs and tanks tried to flee the killing zone.

Russian infantrymen huddled in their vehicles, unwilling to dismount. One Chechen fighter explained, "The Russian infantry wouldn't get out of their BMPs to fight, so their tanks had no infantry support. We just stood on the balconies and dropped grenades on them as they drove by underneath."[174]

With their tracks becoming coffins, many Russians eventually tried to flee on foot. As one observer described the situation: "There was a crazy game of hide and seek, with Russian soldiers hiding in apartments, bunkers, and even toilets, and the Chechens hunting them with swords, knives and pistols." [175] The commander of the 81st was killed, and more than half his men either killed or wounded. The commander of the 131st Motorized Rifle Brigade was also killed. Only a few Russians escaped uninjured.

Chechen hunter-killer teams then went on a spree of destruction. The typical Chechen team consisted of three men: An RPG gunner, a light machine gunner, and a rifleman/sniper. Teams went from vehicle to vehicle, blasting BMP infantry fighting vehicles and T-72 tanks with volleys of RPGs. Unwilling and unprepared to conduct a combined arms defense, the Russians were easy prey for the Chechen fighters. One Russian soldier, Private Sergeyev, a BMP gunner in the *Maikop* brigade expressed the horror of the debacle:

> [O]n Dec. 31, they ordered us into our BMPs, and we set off. We did not know where we were going, but the next morning we found ourselves by the railway station in Grozny -- then all hell broke loose. There were 260 of us there. Our commander was killed right away. We lost a lot of officers. We did not know what to do. Our armor was burning. We gathered some wounded and tried to take them out, but the tank transporting them was destroyed too. I escaped and tried to hide in the basement of a bakery, but the wall collapsed. . . I don't know how many Russian soldiers died in that slaughter.[176]

Group *Zapad*, whose mission was to back up Group *Sever*, failed to move to the northern group's aid, even when the sounds of gunfire clearly indicated that *Sever* was in serious trouble. The *Maikop* brigade lost 20 out of 26 tanks, 102 of 120 infantry fighting vehicles, and all six *Tungas* self-propelled anti-aircraft vehicles. Only ten men and one officer survived, a decimation that resulted from ineffectual leadership, a lack of combined arms tactics, and the inability or refusal of reinforcing units to carry out their missions.

On January 1, two airborne battalions from the 106th and 76th Airborne Divisions were told to break through to the railroad station to rescue the survivors of the 131st Brigade and 81st MRR. By 5:40 P.M., the airborne troops reached Grozny-Tovarnaya station, engaging the guerrillas about a kilometer from the station. Nevertheless, as General Kvashnin reported, "it soon became known that the units which the airborne troops were coming to assist had already left the region of the railroad station."[177] In fact, these units had disintegrated, their commanders were dead, and the survivors had scattered randomly about the city center. International television reporters arrived on the scene and captured the carnage with their cameras. Dozens of smoldering Russian armored vehicles and groups of dead Russian soldiers littered the streets of central and southwestern Grozny. Meanwhile, in the background, the sound of battle continued in the northwest and east.

General Kvashnin blamed the disaster on "the lack of resolve of some commanders and the inadequate moral and psychological preparation of the personnel." As a result, many leaders were replaced the next day, including Major General V. Petruk, the commander of the ill-fated Group *Zapad*, who had failed to come to Group *Sever's* aid.[178] Others blamed Grachev, Kvashnin, and the Mozdok officers who ordered the attack. One officer placed responsibility for the failure of the New Years Eve assault squarely on the Russian high command and particularly on General Kvashnin:

> Those who fought in Grozny believe that Kvashnin and Shevtsov are mostly to blame for the faulty organization of the operation. When the troops entered the city, they had to protect themselves. What these generals created in Grozny is what the troops describe as a "meat combine." There are mountains of wrecked equipment in Grozny.[179]

The Russians Change Tactics

In spite of this setback, the Russians regrouped, refusing to accept defeat. While Russian leaders realized that fighting in cities consisted of much more than small units clearing rooms and driving tanks down broad avenues, their forces lacked the training to achieve the tactical and operational ideal the leadership envisioned. The first few weeks of the Chechen War saw failures by virtually "every arm of the Russian armed forces."[180] The initial assault pitted lightly armed, untrained troops against a determined enemy in complex urban terrain, and it proved a grisly business. The Russians knew that trained, disciplined, and rehearsed combined arms forces were needed. Though none were on hand for the first phase of the battle, Russia was not without other resources.

From January 2 through 5, General Rohklin and Babichev's forces were reinforced with tanks, motorized infantry, naval infantry, artillery, and Spetsnaz units. On January 6, they attacked Grozny again, this time with a vengeance and with slight regard for the civilian population. To overcome the glaring lack of training that their units had heretofore exhibited, the Russians resorted to sheer firepower. Russian General Rohklin introduced a new tactic called the "carrousel of fire." In essence, unleash a hurricane of direct, aimed fire to suppress and then disintegrate Chechen strongholds.

A T-72 tank would first move into range of a building or block controlled by the enemy, then fire all twenty 125mm rounds in the tank's automatic loader as fast as possible. The two other tanks in the three-tank platoon would move forward in turn and do the same as the first tank reloaded. The rate of fire was staggering and continued without interruption on the focal structure until its defenders were either killed or they fled. For a long time the veteran Chechen fighters could not understand how there could be such fire from one point.[181]

The Russians abandoned all restraint, throwing every available gun into the battle to smash not only their enemy, but the city of Grozny itself. The battle quickly degenerated into a "no quarter asked, none given" situation.[182] Under new commanders, the Russians began to take the city block by block, pounding the enemy into submission with heavy firepower. These heavy-handed tactics alienated the civilian population and prompted many Chechens to join Dudayev's fighters. Soon the heavy bombardment from artillery and aircraft reduced more than half the buildings in Grozny to rubble, forcing many of the surviving residents to either flee for safety or cower for weeks in dark, cold basements.

Recognizing the Russian advantage in firepower, the Chechens adopted "hugging tactics" to force the Russians into close combat. A complex ambush was their standard technique, often organized into three tiers: in basements, on the ground floor and on rooftops. This tactic, coupled with an indomitable spirit, kept the Chechens in the fight. "We have stood for two months against this onslaught," Aslan Maskhadov said proudly. "The world has never seen anything like this. If you compare the size of our army and theirs, you'd never believe we could do it."[183] All the while, Russian casualties mounted. The Russian supply system, already strained to the limit, proved unfit for the task of providing ammunition, food, and clean drinking water. The general lack of supplies and of water in particular, exacerbated the drain on Russian combat capabilities.

However, the Chechens could not hold on forever against the focused effort of the Russians, and although the Chechens controlled most streets and buildings, the Russians enjoyed complete control of the air. Indiscriminate bombing of suspected enemy centers of resistance became commonplace. After hammering a few important buildings, Russian air power was redirected to indiscriminate attacks on civilians. Chechen forces managed to shoot down two Russian helicopters, executing their crews, but the Chechen air defense capability was rudimentary and ineffective against the dominant Russian Air Force. Based only a few minutes flying time away in North Ossetia, Russian Sukhoi-25 fighter-bombers plastered Grozny with impunity. As a result, the battle for Grozny began to look like a medieval siege conducted with modern weapons.

Eventually, the Russian Army adapted, regrouped and fought on—a historic characteristic of Russian armies that should not be forgotten. At length, Russian columns surrounded the center of the city while those Chechens trapped inside fought a desperate battle, refusing to yield even as massive Russian firepower took its toll on the surrounded defenders. At one point in the battle, a reporter counted 4,000 artillery detonations per hour.[184] In the end, Russian firepower blasted the city to rubble and forced the Chechen militia to flee to the countryside. The Presidential Palace was never stormed; after a relentless bombardment, special air-delivered munitions were used to penetrate to the basement, driving out the die-hard defenders there.

The Russian Army finally took control of the charred, bombed-out remains of Grozny in mid-February 1995. Shootings, beatings, rapes, and other crimes against the remaining civilian population broke out sporadically.[185] Even after the Russian flag finally waved over the smoking rubble of the Palace at Grozny, the killing had not stopped. On March 21, the Russian Army launched a major offensive to capture all the cities and towns in the open plain south of Grozny. At the same time, Russian forces advanced across Chechnya and into the mountains.

By April 1995, many of the key cities in Chechnya were under Russian control, but a hatred for all things Russian, fueled by the Russian army's unrestricted firepower tactics, united the Chechens in a frenzy of defiance. Unable to oppose the Russian juggernaut with conventional forces, the Chechens girded themselves to fight a protracted guerrilla war. One reporter, close to a Chechen fighting group, put it this way: "The Chechens are prepared to make a very, very long war. They have time, they know that there aren't enough Russians to control everything . . . it may not be a well-organized guerrilla campaign, but nearly every village will oppose the Russians."[186]

The Aftermath

In a February 27, 1995, interview, General Alexander Lebed, Russia's Security Council chief, remarked that the assault on Grozny was "launched by either dilettantes or madmen."[187] Although the Russian Army captured the broken ruins of Grozny and several other villages, they could neither stop the fighting nor break the Chechens. In a dramatic sequel in June 1995, Shamil Basayev seized 2,000 hostages in the Russian town of Budennovsk. Russian special operations forces attempted to storm the hospital that Basayev was holding, killing 100 hostages in the ensuing battle. The botched Russian rescue ended in the negotiated release of Basayev and his fighters to Chechnya and a victory for the Chechen cause. In January 1996, the Chechens seized more hostages in neighboring Dagestan, and then moved them to the village of Pervomaiskoye, just outside Chechnya. Again, the rebels escaped, but many of the hostages were killed in the fighting.

The Russians, frustrated that the war would never end, finally gained a victory when they ambushed Dudayev. On April 21, 1996, in a gully near the village of Gekhi-Chu, a precision-guided bomb, fired from a Russian fighter homed in on Dudayev's cellular phone. In retaliation that same month, Chechen gunmen ambushed a Russian army convoy in the village of Khurikau in Ingushetia, a restive region bordering Chechnya, killing a Russian general and five soldiers. The violence continued back and forth, protracted by the fact that despite their gains, Russian forces could never gain a decisive victory.

In spite of Dudayev's death, the war in Chechnya labored on as Russian morale sagged ever lower and Maskhadov planned a climactic counterstroke. On August 6, 1996—approximately three days before Yeltsin's inauguration for a second term as President—1,500 Chechen fighters infiltrated Grozny and retook key positions in the city in a mater of hours. The Russians garrisoned Grozny with 12,000 troops supported with tanks and artillery. By midday, every Russian unit in the city was under fire and pinned down as more Chechens moved into the city. Russian units radioed frantically for support and ammunition resupply. Russian relief columns, comprised of tanks and BMPs using the same bad tactics as they had in January 1995, tried to fight their way to the isolated Russian units but were ambushed and destroyed by Chechen hunter-killer teams. Russian helicopters and artillery pummeled the city but air-to-ground coordination was poor. Russian bodies lay everywhere as burning tanks and burning buildings filled the sky with thick black smoke. It was the New Year's Eve debacle all over again, though the roles of attacker and attacked were reversed as the Chechen fighters went on the offensive.

With little fighting spirit left, the Russians, in spite of their superior numbers and firepower, fought a losing battle with the Chechens. Yeltsin ordered General Lebed to travel to Chechnya. Faced with the collapse of the Russian Army in Grozny, Lebed met with Maskhadov and brokered a cease-fire. The negotiated settlement of August 1996 led to the complete withdrawal of Russian security forces from Chechnya.

The Battle for Grozny was the worst defeat at the hands of an irregular force in Russian military history. The fighting in Grozny clearly required the use of "infantry with armored support, a tactic clearly described in Soviet Army manuals."[188] Despite this, a lack of training prevented its employment and resulted in disaster for the Russian attackers. Of the 6,000 combat troops that initially went into Grozny on New Year's Eve 1994, virtually all became casualties, precipitating a national trauma that continues today. In the August 1996, siege of Grozny the Russian Army lost nearly 500 killed, 1407 wounded and 182 missing.[189] The once-proud Russian Army, the powerful Russian bear that had made the world tremble since 1945, was bloodied and beaten by an army of Chechen wolves seemingly more suited to clan warfare of the 13th Century than high-tech war at the dawn of the 21st.

City fighting is always – always—brutal, deadly and unforgiving. Despite their history of success while fighting in cities during the unspeakably tough battles of Stalingrad, Budapest, and Berlin during World War II, the Russians had few units prepared for urban combat. In fact, only their marine battalions were well trained in city fighting.[190] The haste with which the initial attack on Grozny was planned and executed, the shoddy state of the Russian Army units sent in to do the fighting, and the tactical savvy and fighting spirit these units lacked all combined to result in nothing less than a nightmare of senseless death.

The casualty figures in this 21-month war speak to the scale of the horrific fighting. During the fighting for Chechnya, Russian casualties were 2,805 killed in action, 10,319 wounded in action, and 393 missing in action. Russian forces claimed 13,000 Chechen fighters killed and civilian casualties numbering approximately 30,000. Russian losses included 250 tanks and armored personnel carriers, 24 aircraft and 3 helicopters. Chechen losses in equipment were 99 tanks and armored personnel carriers, 108 artillery and mortar systems, 219 aircraft and 2 helicopters.[191] High casualties ultimately broke the already low morale of the Russian Army. Current assessments of the Russian military suggest that the majority of Russian officers disapprove of fighting separatism—and some will actually choose to disobey orders rather than fight another war like Chechnya.

Lessons to Remember

What are the tactical lessons of the Battle for Grozny? The obvious one is that hastily assembled and ill-prepared conscripts cannot take a city held by determined fighters defending their homes. Urban combat requires quality forces—forces with an advantage in organization, training, technology, political preparation, and timing (tempo).

Most importantly, fighting in cities takes combined arms, a lesson that has been lost on many an untrained eye from journalists to military theorists. The idea that the fight in an urban area is best won by hordes of light infantrymen is nonsense, as Robert R. Leonhard, writing in *The Principles of War for the Information Age*, makes clear: "Nothing could be further from the truth. The force of choice for most future urban scenarios will be armored, mechanized forces."[192] While perhaps the most terrible aspect of such scenarios, the systematic clearing of rooms and buildings is not the centerpiece of urban combat; it is merely a subset. Balanced, combined arms forces are required to win combat in urban areas with minimal friendly casualties. Specially trained units are required to handle civilians and gain the human intelligence necessary to secure an information advantage in urban combat. The Russian failure in Grozny was more a matter of poor preparation, badly trained troops, low morale, and poor leadership than the misuse of tanks and infantry fighting vehicles in narrow city streets.

Lastly, the Battle for Grozny is a cautionary tale that foreshadows conflicts to come. Professional soldiers and anyone interested in warfare in the 21st Century should study the Chechen War and the fight in the forests of steel and concrete of Grozny. The story of this battle shows that the warfighting functions--movement and maneuver, intelligence, fires, sustainment, command and control, and protection—are very difficult to employ on the urban battlefield. This battle indicates that, in the end, firepower can devastate a city, but firepower cannot conquer a people if employed with any intent short of genocide. It also graphically portrays the horror of war waged with modern weapons in close fight of the urban battlefield. Moreover, the battle for Grozny is further proof that the urban battlefield is the battlefield of modern combat and not the exception.

CHAPTER EIGHT

GROZNY, 1994-1996

INTELLIGENCE SUPPORT TO MILITARY OPERATIONS

by Brigadier General Brian A. Keller

The pale light of Russian flares or burning buildings revealed ghostly figures of [Chechen] fighters in white smocks and green Islamic headbands; obscure piles of branches disguised a machine-gun post, its ammunition belt glinting against the snow; barricaded into the upper floors of apartment buildings, ambushers waited with their RPGs for the Russian armor to roll into the wide streets below. Sebastian Smith[193]

The previous chapter outlines the events during the Battle of Grozny and analyzes, from the tactical, operational, and strategic perspectives, the causal factors in the initial Russian defeat—mainly deficient preparation, the lack of combined arms, and passive leadership at many levels. Clearly, the Russian Army that attacked Grozny in January 1995 was not the same professional, well-led, well-equipped, and well-trained force that faced the North Atlantic Treaty Organization during the Cold War. By 1995, low morale reflected by the growing number of desertions, budget tightening brought about by the floundering Russian economy, and the legacy of Afghanistan plagued the Russian Army. Infrequent field training exercises combined with the lack of command post drills above battalion level further degraded military effectiveness, and without the skills to apply combined arms under fire, the largely conscripted soldiers of the Russian force found it easier to simply abandon the fight than to continue to attack into the teeth of Chechen defenses.

Certainly, the Grozny operation provides a useful case study for those interested in better understanding modern urban warfare. Clearly, the lack of training was not the only factor in the initial Russian defeat. The failure began with the collapse of the intelligence estimate, a fact made clear and distinct by the expectation, from Moscow especially, that a show of force would lead to swift culmination of the defenders. This was not the only intelligence failure. Indeed, an analysis of the battle offers many relevant lessons about the complexities of intelligence as an imperative in future city fighting.

The Battle of Grozny: Intelligence Lessons

Reduced to its simplest terms, Russian mistakes in the analysis of Chechen capabilities and intentions was one major reason for the debacle in Grozny. More to the point, Russian intelligence staffs—and their commanders—failed to adequately *define the urban battlespace environment and describe its effects*, and *evaluate the Chechen threat.* As such, Russian commanders viewed their operational plan through an intelligence lens distorted not only by the fog of war, but also by the blinding light of their own cultural arrogance, misperceptions, and predilections.

To understand the detrimental effects this caused, one must freeze-frame several snapshots of the Russian intelligence view taken through two lenses: *the urban battlespace environment* lens and the *threat* lens. The first lens describes the view gleaned through products provided to commanders, the Intelligence Preparation of the Battlespace (IPB) process, and the employment of reconnaissance. The second lens focuses on the role of Russian intelligence, especially their misperceptions of critical Order of Battle (OB) factors.

The Urban Battlespace Environment Lens

Russian commanders attacking Grozny lacked clarity of the urban battlespace lying before them. Three factors contributed to this situation. First, few commanders and leaders had access to detailed maps or overhead imagery of the city objectives. Second, Russian intelligence preparation of the battlefield failed to provide commanders with an accurate appreciation of the decisive terrain within and around Grozny. The IPB process also overlooked the effects of urban terrain on friendly and enemy courses of action. Finally, poor reconnaissance contributed to an incomplete picture of the threat facing Russian units entering the city.

Always considered "close-hold" commodities tightly guarded by Russian military leaders, maps and overhead imagery were in short supply during the planning and execution of operations against Grozny. Despite operating on home territory, Russian intelligence agencies could only provide assault commanders with 1:100,000 scale maps instead of the 1:25,000 or 1:12,500 scale products essential for urban missions. "Tactical maps," according to one observer, "were often made from plain blank paper by hand, with Russian soldiers filling in the sheet with the city vistas (streets, buildings, etc.) in front of them."[194] Overhead imagery was in equally short supply. As Russian military expert Lester Grau explains, "essential aerial photographs were not available for planning because Russian satellites had been turned off to save money and few aerial photograph missions were flown. Lower-level troop commanders never received vital aerial photographs."[195]

After the January 1995 debacle, Russian journalists pressed senior government officials for explanations of these obvious intelligence shortcomings. Defense Minister Pavel Grachev countered charges of incomplete intelligence support by claiming, "large scale maps, plans of the city, and photographs of the regions of expected conflict were prepared and provided for every assault detachment and assault group commander."[196] Likewise, Sergei Stepashin, head of the Russian Counterintelligence Service (FCS), when interviewed about his agency's map "miscalculations" in Grozny, had this to say: "Maps of the city communications, streets, air raid shelters, and bunkers—all this was provided to the military command by the Counterintelligence Service. The fact that these maps were not passed on in time to the field commanders represents, of course, a tremendous omission."[197] Yet, firsthand reports from journalists who interviewed soldiers and commanders in Grozny contradict the Russian national leadership's claims. Anatol Lieven's interview of a young Russian infantryman just hours after the battle provides one example. "The commanders," reported the soldier, "gave us no maps, no briefing, just told us to follow the BMP in front, but it got lost and ended up following us. By morning, we were completely lost and separated from the other units. I asked our officer where we were, he said he didn't know—somewhere near the railway station. No, he didn't have a map either."[198]

Unlike the Chechen defenders, Russian troops operated with inadequate knowledge of the city's sewers, subway and train systems, road networks, critical infrastructure, and back streets. Coordinating simple yet vital control measures like unit boundaries, fire coordination lines, objectives, axis of advance, checkpoints, and friendly and enemy locations became exceedingly difficult given the poor resolution of the smaller scale maps. In short, the failure to provide commanders and assault elements with adequate maps and imagery products represented a critical oversight on the part of Russian intelligence agencies.

Poor Intelligence Preparation of the Battlespace

Besides inadequate maps and imagery products, poor intelligence preparation of the battlespace also obscured the Russian operational view of Grozny. The initial plan of General Kvashnin, the commander of the operation, was quickly to seize Grozny on the march with attacks from the north, east, and west. After Chechen defenses desynchronized his converging elements, Kvashnin consolidated his forces along the same general axis of attack before delivering the main effort from the north. Like the original plan, this deviation left the southern portion of the city uncovered by Russian forces. Some suggest this was a deliberate omission designed to offer the rebels an escape route when presented with overwhelming Russian power. As one Russian journalist noted, "staff commanders maintain that the southern exit from Grozny is deliberately being held open. They hope that the rebels will leave for the mountainous areas of

Chechnya which will become a trap for them."[199] However, more plausible evidence indicates insufficient resources, poor planning, and Chechen resistance prevented Russian surveillance and interdiction of key terrain along the city's southern perimeter.[200] Covering the battle from within Grozny, journalist Sebastian Smith found "no effort being made [by the Russian forces] to blockade the southern end of the city, the hardest and most strategic end, because it linked up with the rebel-held countryside and villages of southern Chechnya."[201]

This failure to surround the city throughout the seven-week "siege" cost the Russians dearly. Chechen reinforcements and vital supplies flowed regularly into Grozny during the battle and casualty evacuations through the open corridor sustained Chechen morale. Moreover, when the military situation became hopeless by late February, Chechen fighters escaped southward in good order ready to fight again.

Perhaps just as importantly, not sealing off Grozny had unforeseen consequences that transcended the military aspects of the campaign. In one bewildering story, a Russian mother turned a search for her missing soldier-son into a saga closely followed by the Russian press—much to the chagrin of government leaders. After telegrams to Yeltsin and the Russian Parliament failed to yield results, the mother, Valentina Krayeva, began a search of her own. Traveling from her hometown of Volgodonsk, Krayeva slipped through Russian lines only to find her way to Dudayev's headquarters on January 17. Here, braving nearly 4,000 Russian artillery rounds per hour, she pleaded with Dudayev and his chief military commander Shamil Basayev for her son's release. Glad to comply, the Chechen leaders quickly turned the episode into a propaganda windfall. While covering the story, authors Carlotta Gall and Thomas de Wall reported:

> Krayeva was soon followed by dozens more soldiers' mothers looking for their sons who had fallen prisoner to the Chechens. Encountering indifference and helplessness from the Russian military, they ended up searching for their sons themselves. They were in an extraordinary situation, traveling behind Russian lines, under fire from their own armed forces, dependent on the assistance and hospitality of the Chechens who were supposed to be their enemy. They became a fixture at the gates of the Russian bases and at the doors of the Chechen leadership. Some lived in Chechnya for over a year, searching all over the republic for news about their sons.[202]

A plethora of smaller, yet nevertheless significant IPB-related shortcomings degraded the overall Russian performance in Grozny. For example, Russian intelligence officers and analysts overlooked urban terrain effects on tactical frequency modulated (FM) communications. Relying on FM radios to issue orders, Russian leaders soon found themselves unable to contact friendly units. Command and control, as well as situational awareness, became a nightmare.

Commanders also neglected the effects of Chechen defenders firing from basements and high-rise apartments. Templating probable Chechen defense position along avenues of approach into Grozny—and sharing this analysis on updated large-scale maps and overhead imagery—would have helped leaders select proper support by fire positions for BMP armored fighting vehicles and ZSU mobile anti-aircraft artillery. These vehicles, with main gun elevations of +74 and +85 degrees respectively, could have suppressed Chechen positions in the high-rise buildings better than the ineffective T-72 and T-80 tanks.[203] However, as Lester Grau maintains, the "planners failed to take elementary precautions or to forecast how the Chechens might defend the city. As Russian columns moved to Grozny, they were surprised by snipers, road blocks and other signs of Chechen determination to defend the city."[204]

Russian intelligence preparation of the battlespace, then, presented commanders with an incomplete understanding of the urban battlespace effects. Describing these deficiencies, Russian military expert Timothy Thomas argues, "the Russians did not do a proper intelligence preparation of the battlefield—indeed, there does not seem to be an established procedure for processing data for the intelligence preparation of the battlefield in the Russian armed forces. Commanders and troops tried to overcome this shortcoming in the course of combat actions, leading to delays in operations and reduced effectiveness."[205] Together with insufficient maps and imagery support, the IPB process thus shrouded Russian views of Chechen capabilities and intentions. These miscalculations, combined with poor reconnaissance and intelligence analysis, complicated Russian operations in and around Grozny throughout the battle.

Poor Reconnaissance

Russian reconnaissance activities at both the strategic-operational level and tactical level failed to support commanders with timely, accurate, and relevant intelligence during operations in Grozny. At the strategic-operational level, the Russian Counterintelligence Service (FCS)—not unlike its American counterparts—traditionally lacked sufficient human intelligence resources. In this instance, they were insufficient in number to uncover Dudayev's true capabilities and intentions. Although the FCS initially dispatched a general officer and twenty *Vympel* counterterrorist soldiers to Grozny to collect intelligence, FCS director Sergei Stepashin later admitted, "understandably, twenty people were unable to do anything serious."[206]

Moreover, special purpose *Spetsnaz* units—ideally suited for reconnaissance missions—were apparently underutilized or overlooked by conventional commanders. For example, after interviewing senior Defense Ministry officials about the need for "special troops" in Grozny, Russian journalist Vladimir Kartashkov gleaned "there is no need whatsoever to carry out reconnaissance during combat operations against an irregular army."[207] Perhaps more telling was Kartashkov's conclusion that "for all the seeming multitude of special-purpose subunits, the Defense Ministry does not have a single military unit trained to carry out combat operations in urban areas against a well-armed enemy. Nor do other power structures have such units."[208] Anecdotal evidence supports Kartashkov's view. In at least one case, a platoon-sized group of "elite" paratroopers inserted along the southern approaches to Grozny on New Year's Eve quickly ran into trouble. After just two days in the woods, the unit ran out of food and requested resupply. In response, higher headquarters dropped in 25 more paratroopers -- but no rations. Journalists Carlotta Gall and Thomas de Waal continue the story:

> The situation was growing serious when the paras ran into two Chechen hunters in the woods with their shotguns, and took them prisoner. When the hunters failed to return home, Zelimkhan Amadov, a karate expert and professional athlete, formed a search party of 37 villagers, mostly armed with hunting rifles. They came upon the Russians on the third day and a firefight broke out. After about twenty minutes, they heard someone shouting. 'It was one of the hunters, his elder brother was with us and recognized his voice,' Amadov recounted a few days after the incident. 'He came to us and said they wanted to talk.'
>
> The Chechens suggested the Russians surrender and three officers came out, agreed, and laid down their weapons. They sealed the agreement with a much-needed cigarette. Two Russians had been

> killed in the shooting and two more were wounded. The Chechens marched the Russians down the hill. 'For two days they had eaten nothing. When we gave them food they fell upon it like dogs,' Amadov recalled.[209]

Their mission compromised, the elite Russian prisoners were however allowed to telephone their mothers "to come and fetch them home."[210]

Russian tactical air and ground reconnaissance operations attained similar results. Poor weather conditions, smoke and haze from burning oil refineries, and the ever-present threat of Chechen small arms fire kept air reconnaissance assets from accurately finding enemy positions in Grozny. To minimize risky air reconnaissance missions Russian commanders deliberately avoided using those assets until late in the operation. By January 5, realizing that the value added outweighed the risks, the Russian Air Force stepped up air reconnaissance—albeit with meager resources amounting to "several planes and helicopters."[211] Yet, despite air superiority, Russian air reconnaissance added little to the overall picture of Chechen defensive dispositions.

Ground reconnaissance elements were equally hard pressed to provide assault units with accurate information. Normally a mainstay of Russian military planning, ground reconnaissance efforts in Grozny often occurred too late and with insufficient focus. Poor communications and inadequate maps further hampered reporting. More disquieting was the lack of aggressiveness displayed by typical reconnaissance elements. Instead of dismounting and searching for the enemy, scouts "did not dare step outside the protection of their armored vehicle[s] for snipers lurked everywhere, and they saw at every turn of the street what would happen to them if caught by the Chechens."[212]

Even debriefs of truck drivers—often a source of valuable information—yielded little intelligence. One driver returning from a nighttime Grozny mission offered this explanation: "It was essential not to stop, because they said if you ever stopped anyone could fire on you, from a grenade launcher or a sniper, so if I stopped I would be a dead man. And there was no way to avoid them, because if they saw a Russian they came running for you."[213]

In short, as authors Stasys Knezys and Romanas Sedlickas conclude in their book *The War in Chechnya*, "Reconnaissance was done only according to the rule 'What I see, I report,' though the purpose of intelligence is to gather and report sufficient information to ensure that the opponent's actions will not come as a surprise."[214] Lacking information normally provided by strong reconnaissance efforts, Russian assault elements all too often blindly encountered Chechen defenders who possessed a better view of the urban battlespace.

In summary, insufficient mapping and imagery products, inadequate IPB processes, and poor reconnaissance deeply distorted General Kvashnin's view of Grozny throughout the campaign. Shrouded behind these failures, the actual intentions and capabilities of the Chechen threat remained hidden from Russian Army commanders.

The Threat Lens

Evaluation of order of battle (OB) factors provides a basis to analyze the Russian assessment of Chechen capabilities and intentions during the 1995 Grozny operation. As delineated in FM 34-3, *Intelligence Analysis*, many factors contribute to the overall OB analysis.[215] Analyzed together, these factors help intelligence analysts and commanders develop accurate threat models "to piece together information, identify information gaps, speculate and predict, and do problem solving. Most importantly, the threat model allows some of the risk in a given situation to be quantified." For the purposes of this discussion, we will focus on five key OB factors: strength estimates, composition, disposition, tactics, and combat effectiveness.

Strength Estimates

Russian planners estimated the Chechen force in Grozny at about 5,000 to 7,000 fighters. In fact, the Chechen opposition numbered closer to 15,000 on the eve of the battle—nearly double the Russian estimate.[216] Poor reconnaissance and limited human intelligence sources in the city contributed to these inaccurate estimates. Chechen reinforcements flowing into Grozny's unsecured southern corridor also made timely and accurate strength computation more perplexing. The Russian High Command's underestimation of available reinforcements contributed further to the problem. As a 1996, Russian Duma committee charted to investigate the causes of the war concluded: "The military operation had been planned without considering the fact that on [Dudayev's] side stood a regular and well-armed army of up to 50,000 people."[217]

However, the FCS's method of estimating Chechen strength -- upheld by senior Defense Ministry officials -- represents the most grievous error in the order of battle strength equation. Indeed, according to Carlotta Gall, "the [FCS's] information was undoubtedly fatally flawed since its main source was the self-serving anti-Dudayev opposition. Grachev was a fool to trust it."[218] The anti-Dudayev opposition forces collaborating with covert Russian forces several months before the assault often underestimated Chechen rebel capabilities when reporting to the Kremlin. Using these reports as a primary basis for their planning, Russian commanders, as Timothy Thomas notes, failed to achieve "the 6:1 force ratio desired for attacking a city (a doctrinal norm derived from combat experience in World War II). . . . On the contrary, the correlation of forces was 1:2.5 *against* Russian forces at the start of combat."[219] [Original emphasis.]

Composition and Disposition

Besides miscalculating Chechen strength, Russian intelligence services also misjudged the enemy's composition and disposition. Even when initial contacts and assaults on critical facilities suggested otherwise, lower level staffs still pictured Chechen composition as "armed bandits" and criminal factions acting independent of clear command and control. Instead, Chechen leaders often maneuvered highly mobile elements numbering up to twenty fighters -- more akin to platoon-sized elements by Russian standards -- composed of cohesive, disciplined warriors with tremendous fighting experience.

Additionally, analysts overlooked larger battalion-sized formations such as the "Abkhaz" Battalion formed from veterans of the Chechen National Guard. These battle-hardened and well-organized soldiers played decisive roles throughout the battle. Kremlin intelligence services from the Defense, Internal Affairs, and Internal Security Ministries each disregarded still other Chechen units forming for the battle despite their acknowledgement in press reports. According to one author, these forces included:

- Volunteers arriving from Dagestan and other areas of the Caucasus on December 2;
- Local villagers forming their own battalions on December 2;
- Mercenaries from the North Caucasus republics, the Baltic States, Ukraine, and Afghan Mujahedin arriving from Azerbaijan on December 5;
- 300 fighters from the former Russian Republic of Georgia's arriving in Chechnya on December 22;
- A suicide regiment and the formation of a "women's" battalion on December 7.[220]

In short, actual Chechen composition remained a mystery unsolved by Russian intelligence staffs—from national to tactical level—until late in the battle.

Accurate portrayal of Chechen dispositions represents another miscalculated order of battle factor. As you recall, General Kvashnin's forces met unexpected stiff resistance along their approaches toward Grozny. Once breached or bypassed, frequent encounters with other unlocated enemy forces led to further delays and losses. Yet, failure to identify the Chechen deployment in three concentric defensive rings around the city proved the major blunder of Kvashnin's analysis of enemy dispositions. As Timothy Thomas again explains,

> The Russian leadership did not do a good job of preparing the 'theater' for warfare. . . One general, choosing anonymity, noted that after liberating several city districts, Russian forces realized that Dudayev had created numerous firing points, communication nets and underground command points, which made the job much more difficult. In this respect, the main military intelligence (GRU) and the federal counterintelligence services (FSK) did poor jobs of providing infor-mation on the illegal formations that the Russian forces faced, com-pounding the fate of the untrained soldiers.[221]

Not surprisingly, Kvashnin's failure to uncover Chechen dispositions short-circuited his ability to deduce Dudayev's intentions. Soldier debriefs and journalist reports pasted together after the battle disclose a much stronger and more integrated threat arrayed against the Russian forces than perceived beforehand. A more complete view of Chechen unit locations would have signaled to the Russians not only Chechen intentions to fight a protracted battle, but their determination and sophistication as well. Arguably, foreknowledge of Chechen dispositions would have motivated Kvashnin to modify either his assault plan or task organization allowing him to better leverage advantages in Russian firepower against gaps or weak points in the defenses. Unfortunately, by stumbling repeatedly into hidden enemy strong points, widely dispersed Russian forces became diluted and then hopelessly bogged down.

Tactics

Tactics, or the manner in which units conduct operations, was another OB factor overlooked by the Russian commanders. Given their predilections about Chechen strength, composition, and disposition, it is not difficult to understand why Russian commanders initially dismissed "bandit" tactics as irrelevant. Nonetheless, as described above, Chechen fighting methods proved very effective against Kvashnin's forces. One such tactic adopted by the Chechens was "hugging" Russian units. By interlocking with their foes, the Chechens negated Russian advantages in indirect and aerial firepower. Indeed, few Russian officers requested indirect fire at such risky distances. More motivated than their Russian counterparts, the *boyeviks* often gained the upper hand in the ensuing man-to-man battle.

Dudayev's design of a "defenseless defense" demonstrated another effective urban warfare tactic.[222] The Chechens realized early in the battle that superior Russian firepower made positional warfare a definite disadvantage. Thus, rather than using strong points as the main method of defense, the Chechens employed mobile hit and run forces to conduct ambushes against their foe. *Mayak* Radio reporter Vladimir Pasko summarized these tactics during a January 3, 1995 broadcast. "The commander of the federal troops has reported certain tactics being used by the fighters: small detachments using vehicles mounted with large-caliber machine guns, grenade launchers and light weapons appear in areas where Russian servicemen are located, fire at their positions, and withdraw among the housing blocks."[223]

Sometimes these mobile forces would simply harass Russian soldiers and convoys by firing several volleys and then quickly disengaging. In such cases, the Russians responded typically with massive artillery barrages that needlessly destroyed Grozny's infrastructure but seldom accomplished the aim of killing the provocateurs. Other times the Chechens executed well-orchestrated three-tiered ambushes simultaneously from basements, ground floors and roofs of high-rise structures. Hunter-killer teams equipped with RPGs, working closely with deadly snipers, attacked their targets with great effect. The destruction of the 131st "*Maikop*" MRB at the Presidential Palace on New Year's Eve exemplified these tactics. Here, General Kvashnin's decision to commit predominantly armored forces into the heart of Grozny demonstrated a complete misunderstanding of the tactics employed by his foes. In fact, "no one in the Russian military command" writes Stasys Knezys "had dared to imagine that Chechen fighters would forgo traditional tactics or that tank and armored columns would lose their efficacy and be lit on fire from close range under battle conditions where they could not maneuver."[224]

In sum, Russian intelligence analysts failed to provide their commanders with an accurate analysis of Chechen strength, composition, disposition, and tactics prior to the Battle of Grozny. An after action report written by a high ranking Russian general staff officer involved in the planning—and subsequently leaked to the Russian press on 25 January 1995—admitted as much. According to the report's author, "The enemy's situation, composition, and the probable character of its actions were not analyzed."[225] Yet, Russian analysis failed in at least one more critical OB factor: judging the *combat effectiveness* of the Chechen forces.

Combat Effectiveness

Combat effectiveness, according to FM 34-3, describes the abilities and fighting quality of a unit. Analyzing factors such as morale, belief in a cause, and the national characteristics and will of the people helps analysts deduce an enemy's effectiveness and predict their capabilities and intentions. Yet, Kvashnin's attack into Grozny shows no evidence of factoring these intangibles into his planning. Like the other OB factors, Russian intelligence analysts and commanders viewed Chechen combat effectiveness through a lens distorted by overconfidence, biases, and preconceptions.

Overconfidence permeated the Russian military staffs from the Defense Ministry down to tactical units. Defense Minister Grachev boasted on more than one occasion that a single paratroop regiment could defeat the Chechen criminal elements.[226] According to authors Carlotta Gall and Thomas de Waal, "it was a mixture of personal inexperience and racial arrogance that made Grachev overconfident."[227] At lower levels, a young Russian officer offered this view to western journalists just prior to the attack: "We need a new Stalin who would show us how to deal with these dark-skinned types."[228] Lulled into a false sense of security by their own propaganda machines, few Russian commanders really understood the fighting abilities of their opponents. It was not until two weeks into the heavy fighting that a senior Kremlin official, Deputy Defense Minister General Georgy Kondratyev, finally admitted, "It's not just the gangs which are fighting in Chechnya. It's the Chechen people. The men have taken up arms. They are fighting for their homes and for their land and for the graves of their forefathers."[229]

The Russians also misunderstood Chechen nationalism and their deep-seated hatred of Moscow's rule. Fiercely independent, Chechen culture was steeped in both long traditions of nationalism and martial spirit. "Their God is freedom, their law is war," wrote Russian poet Mikhail Lermontov in 1832. Indeed, "the bulk of the *boyeviks*," writes author Sebastian Smith, "were inspired not by politics but by their national mythology of the warrior and defense of freedom." They might be Dudayev supporters, but they might also despise him and his team's robbery of Chechnya. 'Protecting my home', more often than not, was what a fighter answered if asked why he'd taken up arms."[230] Certainly Russian callousness fanned the flames of Chechen nationalism. For example, in 1949 the Red Army in Grozny erected a statue of General Alexi Yermolov whom in 1816 "launched a scorched earth policy . . . treating the Chechens with extreme cruelty."[231] The inscription on the statue read: "There is no people under the sun more vile and deceitful than this one." Chechens attacked the statue repeatedly in the 1970s and 1980s.

The Stalin-era deportations further fueled Chechen nationalism. While some Russian nationalities remain indifferent to the suffering spawned by deportations, the Chechens only grew to hate the Russians more. Indeed, as one author explains, "Joseph Stalin earned the further enmity of the Chechen people by deporting the entire population to Central Asia in 1944. Many died during these deportations, which Chechens viewed as genocide."[232] Furthermore, regarding the deportations, Russian author Alexander Solzhenitsyn remarked:

> Only one nation refused to submit to the psychology of submission . . . the Chechens. The strange thing was that everybody feared them and no one prevented them from living as they liked. The authorities who had owned the country for 30 years could not force them to respect their laws . . . . No Chechen ever tried to be of service or to please the authorities. Their attitude towards them was proud and hostile.[233]

Ironically, the 1995 Russian Army commanders overlooked Chechen military service in the Red Army during the Great Patriotic War. Chechen soldiers received no less than 56 Hero of the Soviet Union medals during the war—a disproportionately large share of medals given their relatively small population at the time and the fact that many Chechens hid their true identities from the communists. Moreover, as one author observes, "even today, few Russians are aware that more than 300 of the men who perished during the suicidal defense of the fortress in Brest, Belarus, a battle of almost legendary symbolism in Soviet patriotic lore, were Chechens and Ingush."[234] Just as importantly, contemporary Russian soldiers disregarded the fact that many of the rebels had recently filled their ranks—departing with valuable insights into the way the Russian Army thinks and fights. Combining Chechen history with their current fighting experience, Russian analysts should have deduced the real warrior traits of the Chechen people. Unfortunately, weeks of terrible city fighting ensued before the Russian soldier would uncover the true capabilities of the *boyeviks* defending Grozny.

To review, Russian intelligence services failed to provide their commanders a clear view of the urban battlespace. Lack of sufficient maps and imagery products, poor reconnaissance, and improper IPB procedures shrouded the threat residing in Grozny. Poor analysis of enemy OB factors—most importantly Chechen tactics and combat cohesiveness—further obscured the Russian commanders' view of true rebel capabilities and intentions. General Kvashnin's *coup d'oeil*—his ability to see the situation in "the twinkling of an eye"—remained distorted throughout the battle.

The distorted view of Chechen capabilities and intentions led to serious flaws in the Russian plan. Rather than factoring the effects of modern urban warfare into their equation, Russian planners instead focused on their traditional "correlation of forces" paradigm. That paradigm failed to adequately gauge the response of the Chechen people, their deep hatred of Russia, or the fighting spirit of the *boyeviks*. By overlooking these factors and totally disregarding the complexities of the urban environment, Russian planners embraced techniques derived from Soviet urban warfare tactics traced to the Cold War. As Russian Army expert Lester Grau maintains:

> Soviet urban tactics . . . were designed to complement large-scale, high tempo offensive operations in foreign countries. These tactics called for capturing undefended enemy cities from the march and bypassing defended cities. The doctrine assumed the enemy to be foreign professional soldiers who prefer declaring an open city instead of seeing it reduced to ruble. The situation in Chechnya, however, didn't fit these Soviet assumptions about urban combat.[235]

Senior Russian Defense Ministry official Lieutenant General Leonid Isashov reinforces this view. Speaking to a reporter just five days after the 131st MRB defeat in Grozny, Isashov declared, "the troops, the command, and the staffs were trained for classic combat operations, they were not taught to fight on their own territory against their own people."[236] In short, flawed intelligence analysis contributed greatly to the battle plan formed by Russian commanders. As a senior officer from the 81st Motorized Rifle Regiment attacking into Grozny alongside the 131st MRB observed, "If the fools in the FSK had given us any idea of the kind of the kind of [*sic*] resistance we were going to meet, of course we wouldn't have driven into the town like that."[237] Deputy Defense Minister Gromov more succinctly quipped that the Chechnya campaign was "being handled by idiots."[238]

Doctrinal Implications

Military leaders from other armies can learn much from the Chechnya experience. "Doctrine," as defined in the U.S. Army's Field Manual 101-5-1, *Operational Terms and Graphics*, encompasses the "fundamental principles by which the military forces or elements thereof guide their action in support of national objectives. It is authoritative but requires judgment in application."[239] A strong doctrinal foundation provides commanders with an operational framework for tactics, techniques and procedures. Just as importantly, doctrine guides commanders toward accomplishing national interests.[240]

Given the complexity of urban warfare, commanders need sound doctrine for intelligence support to urban operations. Current Army intelligence doctrine inadequately addresses the full range of requirements in a modern urban environment. Three recommended improvements for intelligence doctrine could begin to remedy that situation.

First, capstone intelligence manuals—especially FM 34-130—require a rigorous and systematic methodology for city fighting. For example, defining the urban battlespace environment should include more than just general descriptions or building and street patterns. These factors, albeit important, too often receive the priority of initial analysis leaving critical nodes or "decisive points" within the urban area overlooked or disregarded. Indeed, as Russell Glenn again argues *in "We Band of Brothers:" The Call for Joint Urban Operations Doctrine*:

> Cities have additional nodes that may qualify as centers of gravity or decisive points. Power generation plants, police stations, and water-distribution facilities, for example, have an operational significance often not found in other environments. Early identification of what elements qualify for such status and subsequent determination of their location and other relevant information is essential to proper operational planning.[241]

As evidenced during the Russian campaign in Grozny, the Presidential Palace or other government facility, while symbolic, may not be the key to controlling the city or the enemy. Enemy lines of communications flowing through urban areas—both physically and electronically—require special attention. Detailed analysis must include synthesizing fragmented and disparate OB factors into a meaningful whole focusing on the "so what" or second and third order effects of controlling urban critical nodes. Just as important, identifying these critical nodes allows intelligence operators to focus limited collection capabilities on priority requirements.

Second, doctrine must address the specific types of intelligence products necessary to support commanders during urban operations and the ways to disseminate those products to users. Given the isolated and compartmented nature of the urban warfare environment, leaders down to squad level require special consideration for timely, accurate, and relevant intelligence products. Today, paper and electronic maps provide leaders a vital method to visualize the terrain, plan operations, navigate through cities, and record situational awareness. As such, detailed up-to-date mapping products with a scale of no greater than 1:25,000 remain essential, especially in Third World cities. Since urban sprawl, enemy preparations, and the effects of collateral damage from military operations can quickly change the urban geography, leaders will require current overhead imagery to supplement mapping products. Linking real time thermal, infrared, or electrical-optical imagery feeds from unmanned aerial and ground vehicles to manpackable receivers, offers one possible solution.

Finally, urban IPB doctrine must include a more deliberate and sophisticated analytical approach to evaluating the threat and determining its courses of action. Toward this end, analysis at lower levels needs to transcend the purely traditional—albeit indispensable—tactical IPB considerations and address the more profound effects of the opponents' will, combat cohesiveness, and cultural characteristics. Combining a clear view of the terrain with knowledge of OB factors such as strength, composition, disposition, and tactics provides the foundation for analyzing enemy capabilities. However, only by grasping fully the fighting spirit and political will of an adversary can we hope to discern his real intentions. Timothy Thomas' commentary on Russian operations in Chechnya reinforces this point:

> Any force considering an attack in an urban environment must evaluate both the type of opponent it is

> attacking (guerrillas, regular force, etc.) and its will. If the opposing force has deep and persistent antipathy towards the attackers, then it will be impossible to achieve victory without a decisive confrontation and military conquest. The local force has the advantage; if it can persevere, it can pick the attacker apart in both the short and long term, eventually wearing him out. In this sense, the moral-psychological orientation of the defenders adds an important element beyond mere weaponry to the "correlation of forces."[242]

As we explored above, Russian soldiers in Grozny paid a heavy price for miscalculations and oversights of the *boyeviks'* combat cohesiveness by intelligence analysts.

Besides emphasis on the opponents' combat cohesiveness and cultural characteristics as the dominant urban OB factor, future Army intelligence doctrine should address additional analytical considerations germane to cities. These areas might include:

- Intelligence support to Urban Information Operations: special em-phasis on denying enemy use of information systems and computer operations, identifying cultural vul-nerabilities and ways to exploit them, and understanding the threat environ-ment to support friendly courses of action.
- Intelligence support to civil affairs operations: plan to locate and care for non-

combatants to minimize casualties, understanding their concerns and needs, and tapping them for intelligence

- Less preoccupation with "Soviet-style" organization and tactics: prioritize and build data bases that include Third World and irregular force threats based on current theater operations plans; avoid "mirror imaging;" incorporate real world threats like *the Fuerzas Armadas Revolucionaries de Columbia* (FARC), Hezbollah in Lebanon, or tribal factions in Mogadishu into Army, Marine, and joint exercises.
- More attention to Third World city characteristics vice European urban operations
- Templating noncombatants and Non-governmental Organizations to minimize collateral losses
- Understanding enemy tactics, techniques, and procedures for negating U.S. strengths and advantages: improve analysis of asymmetric threats to U.S. and coalition forces

Materiel Implications

The functions discussed above demand renewed emphasis on materiel solutions to improve intelligence support to urban warfare. Cities present many challenges for intelligence collection. Camouflage and concealment provided by high-rise buildings, sprawling urban growth, or subsurface transportation or sewer systems often shroud enemy dispositions from the ever-present eyes of U.S. overhead reconnaissance platforms. Line of sight problems also degrade SIGINT operations designed to intercept, exploit, and locate enemy communications assets. Further, as one urban warfare expert maintains, "U.S. military technology, designed for large-scale war in open areas of central Europe of the dessert, is not well suited for urban operations."[243]

Unmanned ground vehicles (UGVs) offer one solution to fill the tactical commander's current intelligence collection demands. Although they are being designed in a number of sizes and configurations, many are lightweight, easily transportable by one soldier, and sturdy enough to be "hand tossed" over a 6-foot high fence or dropped through a manhole cover. UGVs typically use articulated tracks to negotiate stairs, climb curbs or stand upright to navigate through narrow twisting passageways. An operator uses a handheld computer to maneuver the UGV while head-mounted or handheld devices display information collected from a variety of infrared, thermal, Electro-optic or acoustic sensors.[244] While not a panacea to urban intelligence collection requirements, UGVs offer one innovative solution to improve situational awareness for tactical units and help commanders better understand their environment.

Besides improved collection capabilities, tactical commanders need improved tools to help them visualize the urban battlespace. While accurate, small-scale mapping products remain indispensable, developing technologies offer tremendous advantages especially during predeployment planning and mission rehearsal. A U. S. Army Topographic Engineering Center (TEC) initiative known as the Urban Tactical Planner (UTP) provides one example. The UTP exploits commercial imagery and other map and imagery products. The lightweight system allows commanders to zoom onto multiple perspectives of targets in both two- and three-dimensional views. Other planning and rehearsal tools are equally promising.

Conclusion

Timely, reliable, accurate, and relevant intelligence support to commanders remains a prerequisite for conducting successful urban operations. Russian operations during the 1994-1995 battle for Grozny offer a useful case study on intelligence support for military operations in cities.

Russian commanders and intelligence staffs failed to adequately *define the urban battlespace environment and describe its effects*, and *evaluate the Chechen threat*. Insufficient maps and imagery products, inadequate IPB processes, and poor reconnaissance shrouded Chechen capabilities. Faulty analysis of Chechen OB factors—most importantly the *boyeviks'* combat cohesiveness—prevented Russian commanders from truly gauging the enemy's intentions. As such, Russian commanders viewed their operational plan through an intelligence lens distorted not only by the fog of war but also by the blinding light of their own cultural arrogance, misperceptions, and predilections. This inaccurate view was perhaps the paramount reason for their operational and tactical failure in the first major battle for Grozny, a failure for which they would make amends, finally, only by the wholesale destruction of the city four years later.

CHAPTER NINE

BOSNIA, 1997

FIGHTING CROWDS IN CITIES

by Colonel Jim Greer

(Editor's note: This essay is a firsthand account)

When one usually thinks of military conflict in cities, one recalls Stalingrad or Leningrad, massive battles in World War II that consumed hundreds of thousands of troops and lasted for years. However, since the Cold War the U.S. military has often been asked to fight a different kind of fight in cities: the mostly nonlethal struggles that result from conducting stability operations around the globe.

This is not to say that stability operations are not often violent. In such operations conducted in Africa, Haiti, Bosnia, and Kosovo, the mind-numbing boredom of daily patrolling and checkpoint duty has frequently erupted, virtually without warning, into violent conflict with hundreds or thousands of civilians motivated by ethnic or religious hatred. Such conflict is almost impossible to avoid, since the mission of stability operations requires American troops to operate for long periods in contested urban areas.

For the foreseeable future, the United States will continue to engage in stability operations around the globe. Our national strategy and interests demand such engagement, and, thus, the U.S. military will continue to deploy, maintain and support armed forces in cities. While many of these operations will result in few, if any, deaths, the missions are still dangerous and difficult, and success remains a daunting prospect. One such operation is the subject of this chapter.

On August 28, 1997, forces belonging to Task Force 1-77 Armor, the Steel Tigers, were conducting peace enforcement operations in Bosnia-Herzegovina when they were attacked throughout their sector by large crowds of Bosnian Serb civilians. No uniformed soldiers opposed the Steel Tigers and no bullets were fired at U.S. troops; yet, the Americans endured a complex situation against opponents who were well led, armed, organized, and effective. By the end of the day, the Task Force had defended itself against approximately 2,000 civilians and learned a great deal about stability operations in the face of hostile crowds. Ultimately, the Americans' success was the product of their hard-won lessons learned conducting support and stability operations.

By late August 1997, the Steel Tigers had been operating for over five months in the critical region of the Posavina Corridor in northern Bosnia. As part of Allied Stabilization Forces (SFOR) in Bosnia, their mission was one of peace enforcement; specifically of the agreement brokered at the Dayton Peace Accords (DPA) in late 1995. The Posavina Corridor region had been the scene of some of the most intense fighting during the Bosnian War, as Serbs, Croats, and Muslims vied for control of its rich farmland and key industrial and transportation-hub cities. At the conclusion of the conflict, most of the key terrain comprising the Corridor had remained in the Republika Serpska (RS), the geographical area the Bosnian Serbs gained at the peace table, including the key cities of Brcko and Bjelina.

An aerial view of Camp Alicia, Bosnia-Herzegovina showing vehicles of the 16th Engineer Battalion from Bamberg, Germany, and other supporting units, during Operation Joint Endeavor. Even stability and support operations require prodigious quantities of military equipment and materiel and long-term commitment. (Photo Credit: Sgt. Alejandro Francisco, U.S. Army Combat Camera.)

For many reasons, Brcko was the most important city in Bosnia in terms of securing peace and bringing about the implementation of the DPA. The city sat astride a chokepoint where the Bosnian Serb controlled RS was only four kilometers wide. Loss of the city to the Bosniac and Croat Federation would effectively split the RS into two pieces. Further, road, rail, and river lines of communication in an east-west direction through the RS, and north-south between Bosnia and Central Europe, ran through the city. Much like Atlanta was the transportation hub of the Confederacy in the Civil War, Brcko served as the transportation hub of northern Bosnia. Because it was such a vital area to both the RS and the Muslim-Croat Federation, its fate was a specific issue in the November 1995

DPA, and ultimately its administration became the final sticking point preventing a peace agreement. For the time being, the people of Brcko remained unsure as to which entity they would eventually belong.

The city of Bjelina was almost equally important, but for reasons which pertain exclusively to the RS. Because it contained the headquarters of the Ministry of Police (MUP) and because, in the corrupt politics of the RS, power was invested in the police more than any other government institution, Bjelina comprised the seat of authority in the northern RS. Whoever controlled the police dominated the RS landscape. Additionally, just south of Bjelina the town of Janje housed the headquarters of the Special Police (Anti-terrorist) Brigade, the most capable armed force in the RS.

During August 1997, there were significant indications of unrest in the RS. Biljane Plavsic, the President of the RS, who supported implementation of the Peace Accords, challenged the hard-line RS leadership, still controlled by the indicted war criminal, Radovan Karadic. His henchmen and cronies tried to block cooperation with the Allies at every turn, while Plavsic's supporters sought ways to ensure a peaceful solution to their problems. Plavsic's challenge was manifested in a split of the RS police, with some police in each city favoring each faction. SFOR monitored such internal squabbling (common occurrences throughout Bosnia) and prepared to intervene as necessary to maintain stability.

On August 27, RS police challenged each other over control of key towns and radio transmission towers in the British and Nordic Brigade sectors that flanked U.S. forces. Indications of similar problems in Brcko, Bjelina, and several radio transmission sites caused TF 1-77 Armor to deploy and monitor events.

Early on the morning of August 28, a reinforced mechanized infantry company was in the city of Brcko; a mechanized infantry company was approaching Bjelina; a tank-heavy team and engineer company were observing the movements of Special Police Brigade (SBP) forces out of their main site in Janje; and a military police company was moving toward a large radio relay tower close to Lopare. A reserve mechanized-heavy team, along with a 155mm howitzer platoon, and combat trains (repair and logistics elements) were forward deployed under the control of the task force's Tactical Command Post (TAC), while the two Task Force base camps, McGovern and Colt, were protected by HMMWV-equipped cavalry troops attached from the 2d Armored Cavalry Regiment (ACR). Later in the day, a reinforcing company (HMMWV-mounted) and military police company were employed after a two-hour road march to arrive in sector.

SFOR forces were in Temporary Checkpoints (TCP), Observation Posts (OP), and blocking positions at 4:30 A.M. on the morning of August 28 when air raid sirens sounded in the cities of Brcko, Bjelina, and Janje. Almost immediately, crowds ranging from 500 to 800 civilians gathered in each city and began to attack SFOR forces throughout the sector. The remainder of the day was spent restoring order, extracting and protecting members of the international community, securing key sites, and protecting Soldiers. The situation in each city was significantly different, producing distinct outcomes at each location.

How Crowds Fight in Bosnia

As with any military contest, it is only possible to succeed if one knows the opponent. That simple observation is as true engaging crowds in a city as it is maneuvering an armored formation in the desert. Because crowds are not traditional military formations, doctrine, historical patterns of fighting and traditional military approaches are not applicable. Without prescribed methodology, learning how the crowds of a particular city or ethnic faction operate is a difficult military dilemma.

It is important to understand that the Yugoslavian crowds were not spontaneous formations of people with simple complaints. They were in fact a planned response to SFOR operations. Many of the people, by their own admission, earned up to 100 German marks to demonstrate against, or to attack SFOR troops. This pattern of paying crowds to fight SFOR was repeated so often throughout Bosnia that the peacekeeping forces coined the term, "Rent-a-Crowd." When a town might not have sufficient people willing to be paid to fight SFOR, criminals, hoodlums, and unemployed youth were often bussed into a city before a planned operation and hidden in apartments until needed. The use of Rent-a-Crowds in the cities reduced the SFOR advantages of firepower, range, and mobility and reinforced the crowd advantages of mass and momentum.

The Rent-a-Crowds employed by the Serbs were not simply mobs. In fact, they were led by hardcore leaders, wielding a simple and effective command and control system. The tactics employed by the crowds had been developed during many such engagements throughout the Balkans. The Serbs had thorough and timely reconnaissance, strong tactical control and mobility, flexible tactics, and good morale—in short, the best that DM 100 could buy.

Crowd Recon

Deliberate reconnaissance was an integral part of the crowds' operations. Local Serb police and civilians manned Observation Posts (OP) along the major routes that SFOR traveled between Base Camps and the cities. Because SFOR used only approved routes known to be clear of mines, their movements were reasonably predictable. Thus, an effective Serb OP could be comprised simply of a single man in a telephone booth or a civilian couple sitting in their front yard. Likewise, civilians in private cars moved about the sector, reporting on SFOR movements and observing SFOR columns. Within cities, OPs were set up to peer from apartment windows. These OPs reported primarily using either phones, and comprised a comprehensive network of human intelligence to give the Serbs excellent situational awareness, not only at the command level, but also at the crowd level.

Nonetheless, on August 28, Task Force 1-77 executed a deception plan that enabled three company teams to move into position near Bjelina largely unobserved. This was accomplished by initially moving into the Federation territory, giving the appearance of action against the Muslim-Croat entity. This served to place those companies out of Serb observation, since Serb movement into Muslim-Croat Federation territory was precluded by

Dayton. Then the companies reappeared and moved along routes never before used by U.S. forces, reaching their positions on the outskirts of Bjelina largely unobserved. However, since the peace enforcement operations of SFOR were overt, once the companies were set in position they were easily detected. Thus, the deception provided only a short-lived advantage to the Task Force.

Crowd Command and Control

For the Serbs, command and control of the crowds was extremely important and well executed. First, the crowds had to be assembled. This was accomplished by the simple expedient of turning on all the air raid sirens in the cities. This prearranged signal caused the crowds to leave their homes or hiding places and move to assembly points. The sirens were also the signal to turn on standard FM radios. The local radio stations, emanating from Radio BET in Brcko, passed instructions about where to assemble and what actions to take. Those people who did not have a radio simply went to the local police station and were told what to do. This effective process resulted in the assembly of crowds that began operating against SFOR within half of an hour of the first siren's alert.

For command and control within the crowd, several "instigators" were placed in each group, functioning as small unit leaders. The instigators were generally hard-line "toughs," minor cronies of the local Serb leadership. In some cases, they were police who had taken the day off from their normal duties in order to participate in the fight. Instigators were often marked by a Serb flag or had one nearby, so the crowd could easily recognize its leadership. They would pass the word verbally on what actions to take, whether throwing stones, rushing barbed wire, or backing off to rest and reorganize. Handheld Motorola radios were used by the instigators and their local OPs for communications. Cellular phones were deployed by reconnaissance elements and for connectivity back to the behind-the-scenes senior leaders. The final means of communication was music. Patriotic Serb songs were sung to rally the crowd when desired by the Serb leadership. Taken together, these means provided the Serbs with excellent crowd control and synchronized operations.

Crowd Mobility

Mobility is a problem for crowds, but one that was largely overcome by the Serbs. Tactically, of course, crowds move by foot, which in a city is often an advantage over mounted troops, as the crowds can easily flow around and even through buildings. Foot mobility did become a drawback for crowds when they attempted to engage mounted SFOR forces not tied down to a fixed point. Operationally, crowds were transported around the RS using buses and cars. For instance, a few days after August 28, buses hauled a crowd of approximately 400 Serbs to invest a radio transmission tower. In September of 1997, over 250 buses conveyed Serb crowds from all over the RS in an attempt to overthrow Biljana Plavsic in the city of Banja Luca. A key lesson learned was to keep track of the local bus companies for any use of buses beyond normal daily routes.

Crowd Tactics

The crowds that attacked SFOR on August 28 did so without using small arms or any other military weapons. Instead, they carried largely with sticks and stones, both of which were readily available in the rubble and refuse of the postwar cities of Bosnia. Later in the day, Molotov cocktails were used against SFOR forces defending the Brcko Bridge in attempts to set armored vehicles on fire. Crowds were composed of men and women of every age, including children and the elderly. Women and children often threw barrages of rocks at troops, based on the theory that SFOR Soldiers were unlikely to retaliate. Women and children usually took position nearest the SFOR troops, with the able-bodied men behind and to the flanks. Military-aged men were usually the instigators or would pass through the rock-throwers to engage in hand-to-hand fighting with Allied troops.

Frequently, the Serbs attempted to amass a crowd of several hundred against a single platoon, normally twenty SFOR Soldiers. Most periods of actual confrontation were less than an hour, at the end of which crowds would withdraw to extreme rock range. They would sit down, rest, eat, and await the next set of instructions from the instigators. Occasionally, some Serb would throw a rock just for continued harassment. Then, on order, the crowd would surge forward again.

Tactics against SFOR vehicles were also well considered. Men and women would lay down in front of vehicles, knowing that Allied soldiers would stop. In towns, barricades were quickly built out of junk, dumpsters, timbers, or destroyed cars. These barricades channeled SFOR vehicles into cul-de-sacs or directly into the crowds. This allowed other elements in the crowd to attack with stones or by climbing onto the vehicles. Once atop of vehicles, people would physically attack SFOR

Soldiers, steal equipment (antennas, individual equipment), or damage the vehicle.

Bjelina - Mobile SFOR vs. Stationary Crowds

Fights in three different cities took place virtually simultaneously during the day of August 28, 1997. One fight took place in Bjelina, where the Steel Tigers had deployed Charlie Company, 2d Battalion, 2d Infantry Regiment, nicknamed Cold Steel, and ably commanded by Captain Paul Finken. The mechanized infantry company, as the Task Force's main effort, had several critical tasks, among which were to support the United Nations International Police Task Force (IPTF) monitors as they attempted to enter the RS Ministry of Police Building (MUP) and conduct an inspection to locate illegal weapons and ensure the police were in compliance with the provisions of the DPA.

Charlie Company consisted of three platoons of mechanized infantry, mounted in Bradley Infantry Fighting Vehicles (BFVs), along with a platoon of military policemen mounted in HMMWVs. Unfortunately, the drawback of the mechanized infantry formation was that each company had relatively few Soldiers who could dismount and fight on foot. In fact, at full strength a mechanized infantry company could only dismount about 50 Soldiers. Against crowds of over 500 civilians, this inequity became a liability. However, Charlie Company was experienced at operating in the cities of Bosnia and understood their Serb opponent very well.

In order to support the IPTF, the men of Cold Steel both had to provide access to the MUP building in the center of Bjelina and to protect the international policemen as they entered the building to inspect. Bjelina is a town of approximately 40,000 Serbs. Before the war the city had been largely Islamic, but the infamous ethnic cleansing by the Serb paramilitary force known as Arkan's Tigers had killed or driven out nearly every Muslim. With the arrival of Serb refugees from other parts of Bosnia, the city was virtually 100 percent Serb by 1995.

Over 500 years old, Bjelina featured the typical medieval labyrinth of narrow, winding streets and bridges crisscrossing meandering streams. Doubtless, once a scenic hamlet, decades of communist neglect and four years of privation during war had changed it into a dreary, unhappy place. Having suffered through the war, the citizens of Bjelina were a bitter, anti-SFOR group. Thus, as soon as the Serbs had realized that an operation was going to be made against the MUP building, the air raid sirens in Bjelina sounded. Before the IPTF and SFOR even reached the center of the city, the entire MUP building was protected by approximately 800 civilians armed with rocks, bottles, and sticks. Additionally, large trucks blocked all roads leading to the MUP building. Instead of a normal day of checkpoints, patrols and inspections, the day turned into a struggle against overwhelming crowds.

The men of Cold Steel made two mounted attempts to reach the MUP building. The first attempt began before the SFOR and IPTF knew that they would face serious resistance. Thus, Charlie Company moved along a single route, resulting in the near entrapment of the entire company in the narrow streets surrounding the MUP building.
The Soldiers quickly found that not only was the way forward blocked, but as soon as SFOR vehicles penetrated the outer ring of crowds, trucks moved in

from side streets and obstructed the egress routes. On several occasions, BFVs were forced to cut through yards and parking lots to break contact.

After regrouping, a second attempt was made, this time with the Task Force Commander and the Chief of the IPTF approaching the MUP building from one direction, while the Bradleys of Cold Steel approached from two different directions. This multi-pronged effort forced the crowd to react in different directions simultaneously, enabling the IPTF to reach the MUP headquarters. Unfortunately, the crowd refused entrance to the IPTF and attacked the SFOR Soldiers and IPTF who had dismounted to approach the building. The mechanized infantry company, with fewer than fifty dismounts, had little chance to push through a crowd of 800 Bosnian Serbs without endangering the lives of many civilians, so the IPTF and SFOR broke contact and withdrew to holding positions.

On the east side of the MUP building, the task force commander, the military police squad that served as his personal security detachment, and approximately eight IPTF police had dismounted and moved unobserved to within fifty feet of the MUP building. Unfortunately, as the crowd returned from attacking the Bradleys and HMMWVs of Charlie Company, they caught sight of the advancing group. Attacking with a hail of rocks, they drove the SFOR and IPTF backwards, nearly surrounding the small party. Fortunately, Colonel Que Winfield, the Brigade Commander for the SFOR Soldiers, was overhead in a UH-60 Blackhawk helicopter supporting the operation on the ground. The pilot of the helicopter directed his rotor blast to drive the crowd away from the friendly force long enough for them to break contact and return to the IPTF headquarters in a quieter portion of the city. At that point, the IPTF Chief decided that further attempts to enter the MUP building were too great a risk.

Several key lessons emerged from the operation in Bjelina. The BFV proved to be an effective vehicle for operations in built-up areas. The ability to pivot steer, traverse low walls, and high mobility enabled the BFVs to extract themselves from tight spaces and difficult situations. The height of the BFV let Soldiers observe over the crowds and the traversing turret made it difficult for attacking civilians to climb up on the vehicle. In contrast, the HMMWV proved difficult to maneuver; it required significant jockeying to turn around in the narrow streets and remained vulnerable to attack by people on foot.

The limited numbers of dismounts available to mechanized task forces made it extremely difficult to conduct traditional riot control tactics, which are manpower intensive. This is particularly true in the case of the MUP building, a mission that required the task force to penetrate through a large, dense crowd of civilians. Although the infantrymen had been trained in the appropriate tasks and drills, there were so few SFOR soldiers on the ground they were easily surrounded and overrun.

At other locations within the city, the infantry company team was more successful in its secondary task of securing and guarding three radio towers. That success was largely due to careful planning and resolute action that enabled Soldiers to secure the towers swiftly, before the civilians could react, and with no casualties. Once SFOR was in control of the radio towers, the Bosnian Serbs made no attempt to attack the friendly forces.

In Bjelina, as throughout the sector, SFOR helicopters proved invaluable for assisting the ground elements. Adequate coordination had taken place at the task force level, but a key lesson learned was the value of face-to-face coordination between aircrews and the maneuver unit on the ground. The ability of the aircraft to recon routes through the city from the air and provide advance warning of crowd movements was enhanced if the aircrews had detailed knowledge of the company plan. Throughout the operations, SFOR Apache and Blackhawk helicopters provided critical observation down narrow streets. In addition, although not a preferred solution, on the one occasion, helicopter rotor wash proved to be an effective nonlethal tool to disperse a hostile crowd.

Janje - Mobile SFOR vs Mobile Crowds

The Special Police Brigade (SBP) Headquarters for the RS was located about five kilometers south of Bjelina in a compound on the outskirts of the town of Janje, along the Drina River. On the other side of the Drina was Serbia proper. The Special Police compound at Janje included not only the Headquarters of the SBP, but also its mechanized detachment (which included approximately ten T-55 tanks and several BOV armored personnel carriers), as well as the 4th Detachment of approximately 300 Special Police. The compound itself was a cluster of low barracks and office buildings with the river on the eastern edge and the town of Janje on the northern side. The SBP fought as light infantry during the war and were employed successfully to infiltrate and attack key targets.

The Serbian Special Police were generally well disciplined, well led, and committed to the hard-line leadership. They were totally committed to Karadzic's defiance of the Dayton Peace Accords. A specified task of the SBP, and more specifically the 4th Detachment at Janje, was to protect the MUP Headquarters in Bjelina. As the Steel Tigers deployed to Bjelina and Brcko, they were unsure as to how the Special Police would respond, since they possessed the assets to engage in limited combat and might do so.

As a preventive measure, Bravo Company, 1st Battalion, 77th Armor Regiment, nicknamed Team Bull, and the Steel Sappers of Bravo Company, 82d Engineer Battalion, were assigned the task of blocking any Special Police movement out of the Janje compound. Team Bull consisted of two tank platoons, a mechanized infantry platoon, and a military police platoon, with the engineer company in support.

Early on August 28, the two teams established a cordon around the compound with platoon blocking positions oriented not only on the two roads into Janje, but on the compound's perimeter. At approximately 4:30 A.M., a Special Police Major appeared and informed the SFOR soldiers that if they didn't leave immediately, "all the Serbs in the world" would come to the compound and force them to leave. A slight exaggeration, but at 5:00 A.M. the air raid sirens in the town of Janje sounded. At approximately 5:15 A.M., first contact was made with a crowd of between 300 and 500 Bosnian Serbs that attacked an engineer platoon blocking position. The Serbs attempted to climb onto the platoon's vehicles and attack the SFOR soldiers with bricks and sticks. In order to maintain the blocking position, the engineer platoon displaced, but the crowd followed it. For the next several hours the crowd continued to attempt to attack, overrun, and envelop each of the tanks, mechanized infantry and engineer platoons in turn. SFOR platoons used their mobility to reposition continually, avoiding injury to anyone in the crowds, while accomplishing their blocking mission. Unlike Bjelina, Janje was less dense. Thus, the SFOR vehicles were less constrained by narrow streets and were able to maneuver away from the crowds more easily.

As in Bjelina, there were several key lessons learned from mobile SFOR operations against mobile crowds. Eventually, Captain Dombrovskis, commanding Team Bull, made the decision to leave approved roads and go across yards, small gardens, and fields to continue the mission. This surprised the Serbs, since they counted on the standard SFOR use of routes known to be free of mines. In this case, the mine maps carried by each vehicle proved invaluable, since they showed no known minefields within twenty kilometers. Given that there had been no fighting in the Janje vicinity during the war, Captain Dombrovskis' prudent risk was both justified and the key to mission success.

Another lesson involved using the mobility of SFOR's vehicles to wear down the crowd. August 28 was a hot day and by noon, the Serbs had spent about six hours chasing the armored vehicles through the town and its surrounding areas. The crowd simply ran out of energy, and most of the Serbs simply sat down in the shade and stopped. Crowd leaders brought in buses and cars to restore some tactical mobility to the crowd, but again SFOR's ability to go cross-country defeated the road-bound buses.

Some specific techniques employed by Team Bull proved particularly effective. Setting out double strand concertina by itself was of little effect: the crowds simply pulled the wire out of the way. However, when the M-1 Abrams tanks, with their turbine engines, were reversed and used to heat the concertina with their exhaust, the wire was too hot to handle, and the crowds were slowed until they could find a bypass. Tanks also proved very difficult for individuals to climb on due to the heat of the exhaust and the ability to rapidly swing the gun tube, knocking the attackers to the ground. A technique that failed was the ruse of masking and throwing smoke to simulate CS tear gas; the smoke grenades were either thrown back by Serbs or simply ignored. Team Bull and the Steel Sappers persisted in their mission, and by the end of the day, the crowd, fatigued and frustrated, had dispersed.

Brcko - Stationary SFOR vs. a Mobile Crowd

Although not initially the main effort, the events in Brcko proved to be the most significant of the day. There are three separate incidents that warrant examination: first was the defense of the Brcko bridge by Team Dog (D Company, 2d Battalion, 2d Infantry Regiment, reinforced with military police and scouts); second was the evacuation of the SFOR Joint Commission Observer Team (JCO) by elements of the Steel Tigers; and third was the rescue of members of the IPTF who were trapped in downtown Brcko by the violent crowds. Each instance showed the adaptability and ingenuity of the SFOR Soldiers in the face of violent, though nonlethal, threats.

Team Dog initially deployed into OPs and checkpoints both in and around the city of Brcko to prevent the movement of long-barreled weapons into the city and to support IPTF in the performance of U.N. mandated inspections. As at Janje, around 4:30 in the morning, the city's air raid sirens sounded. Soon, angry crowds gathered and began to attack Team Dog throughout the city. As the various platoons were attacked and overrun by crowds of up to 800, they began to fall back toward the fixed position guarding the Brcko Bridge, one of only two SFOR lines of communication over the Sava River. For the next twelve hours, the bridge defenses were surrounded and almost continually attacked by crowds wielding bricks, railroad ties, and eventually Molotov cocktails. Direct attacks on the bridge came with little warning and consisted of attempts to penetrate the wire barrier and wall, as crowd members tried climbing on BFVs and HMMWVs to reach the SFOR Soldiers.

As at Janje, hand-thrown and M203 fired CS grenades had little effect on the crowds' actions. Throughout much of the day, SFOR Soldiers engaged in hand-to-hand altercations with the crowds. An important lesson was the value of physical training and conditioning. The SFOR Soldiers were generally stronger than the Serbs and able to hold their ground for a longer time without becoming tired. Key to this effort was the early realization by the commander of D/2-2 Infantry, Captain Kevin Hendricks, that the attacks on the bridge would last for an extended period. Thus, he periodically rotated his Soldiers across the bridge to the Croatian side of the Sava. This achieved the twin effects of letting them rest while keeping them out of sight of the action, thus enabling them to relax in a setting of lower tension.

Captain Hendricks' graduated response was masterful. Shortly after the siege began, he realized his unit was probably going to have to employ warning shots to break up attacks. He ordered that the graduated response from his Soldiers would consist first of firing pistols, then M16, then BFV coax and finally, if necessary, the 25mm main gun to deter crowd violence. Additionally, he designated specific Soldiers to fire warning shots, established signals for when to fire and targets they could shoot at that were safe for friendly forces and the crowd. As the day progressed so did the response. Eventually in the early afternoon, Team Dog fired 9mm and M16 warning shots, but the crowd continued to attack and penetrated the wire in several places. Based on their rehearsed actions, the designated gunner fired a burst of coax into a nearby deserted building. That machine gun warning had a quick and sure effect on the crowd, conditioned by war to the lethality and power of machine guns. The crowd quickly withdrew and further attacks were limited to stones and Molotov cocktails. Discipline, training, planning, and rehearsal had paid off.

The crowd did not limit its attacks to the bridge. Several thousand Bosnian Serbs roamed the city of Brcko attacking virtually any SFOR or UN personnel they found. Initially, they surrounded the JCO headquarters containing an eight-man team of Americans. The JCO team was evacuated by a BFV platoon from Camp McGovern. Key to success in the JCO evacuation was constant communications and use of a plan that had been pre-coordinated and rehearsed. Besides the JCO, the IPTF was also a key target in the Serbs' attacks. Over forty IPTF vehicles were destroyed and burned, and those IPTF members who could not escape were surrounded in their headquarters building. Late in the afternoon, Second Lieutenant White, commanding 2d platoon of Team Dog, took his four BFVs into the city to rescue the IPTF.

A military necessity reinforced in this operation was knowledge of the terrain. During their patrols during the six months prior, the platoon had memorized every road, corner, building, and alley in the city, enabling them to get in and out quickly.

A different lesson involved the vulnerability of combat camera teams. The Serbs were well aware of the threat of having their actions recorded by video and shown on TV. They attacked the SFOR camera crews, as well as civilian news teams, whenever possible. To protect the combat camera teams SFOR learned to position them under cover, but where they could continue to record, such as in a building or inside the back of a BFV or 5-ton truck.

Information Operations

Throughout, information operations (IO) in support of SFOR remained critical and challenging because safeguarding information was exceedingly difficult. Several techniques were employed to mitigate the risk of breach in security. First, planning groups were kept small. This avoided possible leaks through interpreters, local hire workers, or other non-SFOR individuals who were operating in the sector. Special staff officers—including the public affairs officer (PAO), psychological operations officer (PSYOPS), and civil affairs officers—were brought in early enough to integrate IO into SFOR missions. The risk was always present that IO efforts would breach security, but the payoff was being able to use the power of the media and civil-military interactions to control the crowds and limit misinformation. In addition, to avoid too much presence too soon, deployments were delayed until the last possible minute, and routes were used that were different from those habitually used by SFOR.

Maintaining positive command of rapidly changing situations on the ground also proved challenging. Mechanized and armor task forces conventionally operate in an expanse about 10 by 25 kilometers. In this case, the area of operations was 125 by 75 kilometers; far more than one command post with FM radios could cover. It therefore became necessary to divide the command and control facility into separate cells; the tactical operations center (TAC) and the main command post (TOC) and connect the two using TACSAT communications to expand the command and control footprint. By having each node run its own FM command net, command and control was possible and effective over a much larger area than traditionally accepted.

In Summary

August 28 was a tough day. Fortunately, through discipline, training, and motivation no casualties on either side occurred. By dawn on the 29th, order had been restored, and SFOR was continuing its mission of enforcing the military and civilian provisions of the DPA. It would be months before relations between the Steel Tigers and the Serbs in sector returned to "normal," but further violence was successfully avoided.

The effective techniques for handling adversarial crowds in stability operations in Bosnia remain applicable to cities around the globe where American forces continue to carry out national strategy.

CHAPTER TEN

AFGHANISTAN 2001-2002

FIGHTING IN COMPLEX TERRAIN

By Colonel Kevin W. Farrell

The insolence of the Afghan, however, is not the frustrated insolence of urbanized, dehumanized man in western society, but insolence without arrogance, the insolence of harsh freedoms set against a backdrop of rough mountains and deserts, the insolence of equality felt and practiced (with an occasional touch of superiority), the insolence of bravery past and bravery anticipated.[245] Louis Dupree

International observers, uniformed and civilian alike have drawn many conclusions about both recent and current military operations in Afghanistan. Some argue that the much-quicker-than-expected collapse of the Taliban provides evidence that special operations forces, supported by precision-guidance weapons and high-technology communications, can accomplish what once required massed field armies, signifying a new era in warfare. Others point out the opposite: the basic rules of warfare have not changed and, thus, the original principles of warfare remain valid.[246] In either case, Afghanistan offers a fresh case study in the application of Western military technology and doctrine against fanatical enemies in a harsh setting.

U.S. forces in Afghanistan found the setting unique. A poor nation, the country's rugged topography and extreme climatic conditions have served over the centuries as a brake on population growth, limiting the ability of the population to concentrate. There are cities, of course, just not of the size and sophisticated construction found in most regions of the world. So even here, cities remain important to the operation of society. They serve all of the political, cultural, and economic functions that cities the world over fulfill, if admittedly not on the same scale.

Western Kabul as it appears today, with its miles of ramshackle buildings and uncharted alleys. (Photo by Lt. Col. Kevin Farrell.)

In the last half century, Afghanistan's cities have fared badly. What the men and women of Afghanistan have managed to build has largely been destroyed by human agency.[247] Most built-up areas are often little more than clusters of adobe-built walled enclosures or similar primitive structures, with deteriorated services and infrastructure.

Despite the fact that most of Afghanistan is arid and unevenly populated, urban areas constituted key terrain for combatants during Operation Enduring Freedom, launched in October 2001. While Kabul, the capital and most important city of Afghanistan, was abandoned to the forces of the Northern Alliance without a fight and its other major cities, Herat and Kandahar, were not subject to extended urban combat, the lesser urban areas where combat did occur (and continues intermittently) offer some insight as to what the 21st century holds for urban combat.

Although the Soviets and previous invaders learned that occupation of Kabul was not synonymous with effective rule of Afghanistan, it is difficult to envision the successful management of the country without the control of it. In each attempt to control the country throughout Afghanistan's history, command of the cities has emerged as a key to the country itself. Mountain passes and key terrain might dictate the direction of combat operations, but control of cities and villages proved vital to securing the country.

While an extended discussion of the history of Afghanistan is well beyond the scope of this chapter, it is worth noting briefly the experiences of the two previous powers who vied for Afghanistan in the last 160 years: the United Kingdom and the Soviet Union. In the extensive combat experienced by various regiments of the British army in Afghanistan, cities were only infrequently the sites of decisive engagements.[248] In their three wars, the British encountered a pre-industrial Afghanistan, a land with scattered and minor urban areas.[249]

The Soviet experience was different. They viewed urban areas as essential for more than military reasons. Political and ideological considerations drove Soviet strategy and tactics. In the words of a contemporary commentator, "Of all the Marxist revolutions in the Third World, the Afghan revolution has been most conspicuously [driven] from above."[250] Simply put, occupation of Afghanistan's cities was an absolute prerequisite for a successful campaign; in the Soviet view, the cities served as a nexus from which they would carry the "revolution" to the countryside.

Although this was not the first Soviet invasion of its southern neighbor, the size and cost of the 1979 invasion dwarfed previous incursions.[251] With surprisingly few casualties, the Soviets secured Kabul and the major Afghan cities within days of launching their Christmas Eve attack. However, control of the majority of the countryside eluded the Soviets and their Afghan allies even at the peak of the Soviet military involvement.[252] Key cities and outposts often had to be resupplied by air since normal logistic routes were frequently targeted for ambushes.

The Soviet strategy was to concentrate on securing the key cities of Kabul, Kandahar, Herat, and the highways linking them to the Salang Pass and the Soviet Union and then to carry the war to the opponents of the Soviet-backed regime, the Democratic Republic of Afghanistan (DRA).[253] Although most of the fighting occurred in mountainous and remote regions rather than urban areas, there were major exceptions. The largest rebel attack of the war happened in 1985 when over 5,000 Mujahideen attacked the DRA garrison at Khost. Fierce street fighting also took place in Kandahar in 1985.[254] The intent of Soviet tactics was to separate enemy fighters from their means of support. This often meant that the civilian population bore the brunt of Soviet operations, either indirectly or purposefully. The result of Soviet strategy was the death of tens of thousands of civilians and the mass exodus of millions, both within Afghanistan's borders and to neighboring Pakistan and Iran.

Sprawling adobe homes on the outskirts of Kabul. The rugged terrain and intricate maze of buildings made Kabul a deathtrap for Soviet troops who tried to pacify the city. (Photo by Lt. Col. Kevin Farrell.)

Despite their determined efforts to enable the DRA (after 1987, the Republic of Afghanistan) to become a nationally accepted and legitimate government, the Soviets never succeeded; the vast majority of the country and its population remained outside the control of the Soviet army and the DRA.[255] Soviet tactics might have worked sometimes at the local level, but their strategy, despite significant adaptation throughout the war, ultimately failed.[256] The fate of Kabul after the withdrawal of the Soviets is emblematic of the civil war that ravaged Afghanistan as a whole.

With the pullout of the Soviets in 1989, the Republic of Afghanistan vainly struggled to survive against a broad array of rebel forces until it collapsed in 1992 when the Mujahideen finally captured Kabul. Anarchy soon followed as rival ethnic groups and religious factions fought each other for power. Over the next two years, western Kabul was flattened, and thousands of civilians were slaughtered by rival ethnic warlord leaders when they fired artillery and rockets indiscriminately into the city.[257]

During the 1990s, the United States paid little attention to Afghanistan. Within a dozen years of the Soviet withdrawal, however, Afghanistan would become the staging area for the deadliest foreign attack on American soil in the history of the United States.

Following the September 11, 2001 attacks, it became clear that the suicide missions had been planned and directed from within the largely governmentless country of Afghanistan. Al Qaeda irregulars and the Taliban led by Osama Bin Laden and Mullah Omar, respectively, had succeeded in conquering all of Afghanistan except for the twenty percent of the remotest territory in the mountainous northeastern portion of the country.

In the words of a former member of the Clinton administration: "When we looked at the Afghanistan situation, there was a sense we were going to bomb them *up* to the Stone Age. There is just so little to attack. It is the most target-impoverished environment conceivable."[258] Almost the size of the state of Texas and possessing a population of approximately 26 million people, Afghanistan's cities by this time were largely dilapidated, lacking even the most basic human services due to decades of war and neglect.

Prior to 2001, the only direct military action taken by the United States against Afghanistan had been an ineffectual strike by 72 cruise missiles launched during August of 1998. The event that prompted this U.S. strike was the bombing of American embassies in the capital cities of Kenya and Tanzania that cost 12 American and 212 African lives. Because the Central Intelligence Agency (CIA) traced these deadly acts of terrorism to the Al Qaeda terrorist network, President Clinton authorized the cruise missile strikes against training and operations bases of Osama Bin Laden. The missiles had no discernable impact when they detonated near Khost and Jalalabad.[259] Subsequent acts of terrorism between these strikes and September 2001 failed to incur additional retaliation; the Al Qaeda strike against the USS Cole, which resulted in the deaths of 17 U.S. sailors and wounded another 39, passed with impunity.

Although conventional U.S. military forces had no experience in Afghanistan, during the 1980s' Soviet-Afghan War the CIA had worked closely with resistance elements within Afghanistan and Pakistan. American agents provided large sums of money and ultimately supplied the Stinger missile system, often credited (perhaps erroneously) with being a decisive factor in convincing the Soviets to withdraw.[260] Following the airliner strikes on the World Trade Center and the Pentagon, U.S. intelligence agencies quickly confirmed the direct linkage between the attacks and Osama Bin Laden and his Al Qaeda network.[261]

As the Department of Defense began planning its response, the U.S. government demanded that Mullah Omar and his organization, the Taliban, turn over Osama Bin Laden to the United States. Despite attempts by Pakistan to convince Omar to see otherwise, the Taliban refused and the United States prepared to take military action in Afghanistan. On

September 20, 2001, President Bush presented perhaps the most significant speech of his presidency. With great conviction he stated that the United States would not back away from the challenge presented by Al Qaeda and related terrorist organizations. The United States was effectively in a state of war and prepared to harness its tremendous resources and worldwide network of naval bases, airfields, and staging areas to destroy the terrorist cells in Afghanistan and those connected to it throughout the world. The name of the American military operation in Afghanistan, "Enduring Freedom," was chosen after earlier selections were rejected because they might prove offensive to Muslims, or at least fuel the propaganda efforts of the Islamic terrorists.[262]

On October 7, 2001, land-based and carrier-based aircraft delivered bombs while American and British warships launched dozens of cruise missiles that struck Taliban targets throughout Afghanistan. As with the aforementioned strikes of the Clinton administration, the effect was again minimal, apart from the negative press reaction to the deaths of United Nations workers and innocent Afghans, but Operation Enduring Freedom had begun.[263] U.S. planners recognized that destruction of the Taliban in Afghanistan would require troops on the ground to close with and destroy the enemy. The issue would be synchronization: getting the right troops in the right numbers to the right places at the right time.

The initial American plan called for special operations forces to fly into Afghanistan in October and November of 2001 to link up with the hard-pressed Northern Alliance and help prepare them for a spring offensive.[264] In keeping with the traditional mission of the Army Special Forces, the Northern Alliance "soldiers" were to be trained and led by American advisors. What this plan could have achieved will never be known, however, because the Northern Alliance would soon receive far more resources than initially envisioned. The massive firepower of the U.S. military was to be made available to tip the balance squarely in favor of the Northern Alliance.

Two Northern Alliance leaders were crucial to the American-Northern Alliance success: Mohammed Fahim Khan, the successor to Massoud and later vice president of Afghanistan, and General Abdul Rashid Dostum, an experienced veteran of the Afghan-Soviet War who had fought on both sides of the struggle, finishing the war not surprisingly on the side of the anti-Soviet rebels. The Northern Alliance did not wish to wait for winter to pass before bringing the fight to Taliban; American and British forces, coupled with their comparatively limitless resources, hence brought about a swift conclusion to a civil war that had exhausted native warlord armies who had been fighting amongst themselves intermittently for more than two decades.[265]

The first major victory in the war in Afghanistan and perhaps the only one that came close to urban combat in the classic sense occurred at the city of Mazar-e-Sharif, one of the most populated areas in Afghanistan and located in the far northern center part of the country. On November 9, 2001, Northern Alliance forces under the leadership of General Dostum and General Osta Atta Mohammad, backed by U.S. airpower directed by U.S. Army Special Forces advisors, broke out of the Balkh Valley and captured the city of Mazar-e-Sharif.

Mounted patrol in Afghanistan during the summer of 2003. Security while moving is always paramount in restricted terrain. This Soldier mans a .50-caliber machine gun. (U.S. Army photo.)

Outside the city, several hundred Pakistani Taliban volunteers fortified a girls' school and prepared to offer stout resistance. Smart bombs guided by U.S. Army Special Forces advisors destroyed the school and killed the Pakistani defenders. Shortly thereafter, the remaining 3,000 Taliban fighters in the city surrendered to Northern Alliance forces.[266] On November 11, 2001, the city of Taliqan fell when its defenders came under siege by the Northern Alliance, prompting the defenders to switch sides and join their attackers.[267] In the weeks that followed, a familiar pattern developed. The Northern Alliance, when faced with organized Taliban resistance, would use American-delivered munitions to destroy exposed enemy positions. Often senior Afghan leaders negotiated with their opponents for surrender or even a change of allegiance. City after city fell to the Northern Alliance in rapid succession. Perhaps the most striking example was Kabul in December 2001.

Kabul itself had been an open city in the classic military sense; when it was threatened, the forces defending it simply abandoned it, leaving it to the coalition. Thus, by the start of 2002, Herat, Bagram, Kabul and Kandahar were all under the firm control of the Northern Alliance. Although skirmishes occurred on the outskirts of the major cities of the country, the general absence of prolonged urban combat in Afghanistan raises some intriguing issues.

Throughout the 1990s one of the great concerns of the U.S. military was how best to face the challenge of increasing worldwide urbanization. Strangely, Afghanistan offers some perspective on this challenge, because cities were important objectives even though major instances of urban combat failed to develop in them. This happened because the Taliban usually chose not to engage in bitter street-to-street, house-to-house fighting, opting instead to flee urban areas for the greater security they believed the mountains and ill-defined border areas with Pakistan offered. Mullah Omar and Osama Bin Laden explicitly urged Taliban defenders to retreat to remote mountain redoubts and caves. An additional factor complicating any assessment of urban operations in Afghanistan was the cultural readiness of opponents to change sides and allegiances, and this occurred frequently throughout the war.

In sum, the nature and extent of urban combat in Afghanistan offers a different—in contrast to the American experience in Mogadishu, for instance—example of what might be expected when Western armies confront indigenous forces in the developing world. Many observers concluded that the battle in Somalia, in which Americans fought for their lives amidst hordes of aggressive civilians, presented a harbinger of future war in the "Third World." Yet, urban operations did not occur in Afghanistan's cities on an appreciable scale. The relative apathy of urban populations, the firepower advantage of the Northern Alliance, and the gross military amateurism of the Taliban leadership meant that armed resistance did not develop inside of cities. While urban areas were decisive objectives, the contests for their control did not occur within their streets to the degree expected.

Nonetheless, cities remained key to the Northern Alliance and U.S. military plans. American civilian and military leaders suddenly found themselves in possession of extensive urban areas that were in deplorable condition. Initially, U.S. forces did not possess sufficient resources – personnel or materiel – to administrate them properly or even to establish secure conditions for the populace. The unexpectedly rapid seizure of the major cities of Afghanistan hampered the U.S.-led information and diplomatic campaign because the indigenous population expected a quick and consistent improvement in economic conditions. Now years on, U.S. forces on the ground are still proving incapable of significantly raising the living standard of the typical Afghani. Therefore, a lasting lesson pertaining to urban operations from the experience of the United States in Afghanistan must be the necessity to prepare immediately for urban management after victory.

CHAPTER ELEVEN

IRAQ 2003

CITIES IN THE DESERT – THE 101ST AIRBORNE (AIR ASSAULT) DIVISION

by Lieutenant Colonel Clayton Odie Sheffield

"There are some who would argue that the all-volunteer Army and especially "Generation X" lacks the spirit and resolution demonstrated by our forefathers who won previous American wars. Those who make such arguments are wrong. I have witnessed our Army's warrior ethos in Iraq—it is not lacking." Lieutenant Colonel Clayton Odie Sheffield

(Editor's note: This essay is a firsthand account.)

When I first set boots upon the sands of Iraq in late February 2003, I shared the beliefs of many Americans: Iraq consists of barren desert with no respite from the heat of day and the cold of night; a place where nomads live in adobe huts, and where except for the few cities that dot the vast coastline of the Persian Gulf, modernity is absent. I would eventually observe—and be tasked with the challenge of fighting within—Iraqi cities that are as densely constructed as any I had seen elsewhere in the world. High-rise buildings, four lane highways with clover leafs, streetlights, stoplights, road signs, and restaurants; all the characteristics of familiar Western cities are frequently evident. I learned that Baghdad has a population of over 5 million people, roughly the size of Baltimore. For the moment, however, that knowledge still lay in the future.

I became the Brigade S3 for the Third Brigade "Rakkasans," 101st Airborne Division (Air Assault) in August 2002, shortly after our unit's redeployment from Afghanistan. We spent that fall and winter like many other Army units: training hard. By the time our deployment arrived, I felt our battle staff was prepared.

Our training focus had been operations in a desert environment, and though we did review the ramifications of urban combat, it was not to the level of detail that subsequent events would warrant. At the time, I reasoned that we would certainly spend the majority of our days far out in the desert, as had happened during the Gulf War. We did plan air assault missions into the heart of large urban centers, but with little regard for details such as the potential for an enemy to launch surface to air missiles from windows or rooftops, or the ease that small arms could reach helicopters flying low-level over sprawling urban areas. The need to fight in or through Iraqi towns would confront somebody, I knew, but the extent of urban operations was not clear. A senior officer asked me at Fort Campbell prior to our deployment, "Do you think you are spending too much time on MOUT (military operations on urban terrain)"? My response had been "no," but later I wondered if it were possible to spend too much time on urban operations.

We crossed "the berm" at 2200 hrs. On March 21, 2003, headed north from Kuwait to Baghdad shrouded by the piercing desert darkness. As usual, the quality of the tactical intelligence we received varied between nothing at all and contradictory. We were told to expect everything from a chemical attack to fierce resistance to the surrender of "most" of Iraq's conventional forces. Adopting an attitude of resignation of the sort that Soldiers often make, we chose to believe in ourselves and assumed we would encounter the worst.

Our convoy consisted of over 500 vehicles, organized into serials and march units. Each serial had a different mission and was between 50 and 200 vehicles in length. There were no armored vehicles—all were wheeled and soft skinned. This lack of armor for protection against direct and indirect fires, as well as the threat of mines, weighed heavily on my mind as we moved across the western desert of Iraq.

Our mission was several-fold: Establish and secure two forward arming and refueling points (FARPs) to facilitate the attack of V Corps north, then establish a forward operating base southwest of the Karbala Gap for follow-on 101st Airborne Division operations. The FARPS in the western desert were to facilitate the operational reach of the Corps and allow deep targets to be struck with attack helicopters and air assaults.

The next morning the rising sun painted our ground assault convoy (GAC) pushing northward. I strained my tired eyes across the vast expanse of desert looking for the first sight of a T-72 barreling our way. The extent of the enemy fortifications was unclear. We knew the mechanized forces of the 3d Infantry Division had cleared the same crossing points that we had taken, but we also knew that as we continued to attack into Iraq, our paths would diverge. Situational reports from the progress of the 'Rock of the Marne' Division were sporadic at best. I sometimes resorted to asking our CNN correspondent what kind of communications he had gleaned. I also watched the forward line of troops in the form of icons on our computerized "Blue Force Tracker" (BFT) system. The BFT was installed in two vehicles within each battalion and three vehicles in the brigade headquarters. The BFT allowed us to see on a computer screen every unit in Iraq that had a BFT terminal. We could even send minimal text messages allowing us to keep in contact across hundreds of kilometers.

We drove north for over two days and 300 miles, rotating drivers and only stopping for fuel. The villages we passed were small, which reinforced my first assumption that Iraqi urban areas lacked the extensive development of "real" cities. Along the march, we launched several deep attacks with our attack helicopter battalions against the Medina and Hammurabi Divisions of the Iraqi Republican Guard. Although a very important mission in the operational context of the war, as ground Soldiers we felt far removed from the violence of air combat. The desert was unforgiving. The sun baked us during the day and the cold chilled us to the bone at night. A few nomads moved through the area who seemed to be unaware there was a war underway to the east. I did not sleep well when given the chance. Then, the specter of urban warfare suddenly appeared.

On April 6, we received the order to liberate the town of Al Hillah in south-central Iraq with only 48 hours to plan and execute. Crisis action planning and expedient mission analysis required us to begin immediate movement of troops and equipment to a central forward operating base in closer proximity to the front line of troops. During this juncture in the war, the 3d Infantry Division was maneuvering towards Baghdad, having bypassed the central corridor. *Fedayeen* forces were interdicting V Corps supply lines along the main supply route, Highway 8, from Kuwait to Baghdad. Our First Brigade liberated the town of An Najaf while our Second Brigade had isolated the town of Karbala and was prepared to begin combat operations to liberate that town. That left Al Hillah to us, a town of over 300,000 residents and the second holiest city in Iraq. Our first foray into urban combat was about to begin.

For the execution of this operation, the divisional cavalry unit (2d Squadron-17th Cavalry Regiment "Sabre") with their OH-58D scout helicopters and a battalion of AH-64 attack helicopters (3d Squadron-101st Cavalry Regiment (Attack)) were attached to our brigade along with another infantry battalion (2d Battalion-327th Infantry Regiment, 'No Slack' from First 'Bastogne' Brigade), a tank battalion (2d Battalion-70th Armor Regiment, 'Thunderbolt' from the 1st Armored Division), a reinforcing artillery battalion (1st Battalion-320th Field Artillery Regiment), and a battery of 155mm howitzers. The planning to ensure all these units were properly positioned for the impending attack was an organizational feat in itself. Thunderbolt was assisting with combat operations in Karbala as was Sabre. No Slack and 1-320 FA were south in the vicinity of An Najaf and one of our own organic infantry battalions, 2-187 IN, was still deploying north from their initial FARP security mission in the southern Iraqi desert. One of our organic infantry battalions, 3d Battalion, 187th Infantry Regiment, 'Iron Rakkasans,' had attacked north with the 3d Division and would soon attack Baghdad International Airport.

The 101st Airborne Division's Operations Order Briefing for the attack on Al Hillah, April 7, 2003, as the division made initial contact with Iraqi forces. The U.S. Army's deliberate mission analysis and staff processes enable Army units to maneuver effectively even under the most difficult conditions of terrain, distance, and enemy action. (Photo by Lt. Col. Odie Sheffield.)

We established tactical assembly area (TAA) Rakkasan above the An Najaf escarpment, an elevation increase of over 300 feet from the surrounding desert. The difference in elevation brought significant environmental change. Instead of the dust and wind we had battled for over two weeks, we now found a lush cropland of trees and small farms. The unwelcome side effect of the sudden change to our bodies was the vast increase in allergic reactions to the wheat, grass, trees, pollen, and whatever else was in the air. The threat of attack from the civilian population did not appear evident as we established our assembly areas. The local people were extremely friendly, albeit curious, and did not seem too anxious about our activities. The days of traveling the wastelands of the western desert had worn on our morale, but now a mission was at hand that focused our energies and raised spirits.

Our new mission was to destroy the enemy forces operating in the vicinity of Al Hillah who might try to obstruct V Corps' main supply route along Highway 8. We planned to execute this mission by isolating the city, then attacking along two avenues from the south and the west. We were to destroy the security zone forces to set the conditions for main attack the following day. After the security zone fight, we would identify key targets in the city, conduct deliberate preparatory fires using artillery, attack helicopters, and air interdiction sorties from the Air Force, and then assault to the heart of the city at first light using an armored battalion with an attached light infantry company to spearhead the advance. As the penetration attack secured key terrain in the heart of the town, the three infantry battalions with mechanized support would systematically clear their respective zones to ensure we obtained freedom of maneuver throughout the city.

Our task organization for the fight was critical to ensuring success in the urban environment. We were familiar with the Russian assaults on Grozny, as well as accounts of armored warfare from World War II. We understood that the urban fight must be a coordinated effort between heavy and light forces. Therefore, during our preparation for the attack, we ensured that each infantry battalion had at least a platoon of tracked vehicles whether it was a platoon of M2 Bradleys or M1A2 Abrams tanks. In addition, the tank battalion received a light infantry company to provide critical flank and close-in security.

Our intelligence information regarding enemy dispositions in Al Hillah was not detailed. During training exercises, we were accustomed to access to satellite imagery and data from unmanned aerial vehicles augmented by observations of special operations forces that passed information to us. However, now, "in the real world," none of that was available so we planned the attack as a movement to contact. We would trust our prewar maps that identified mosques, schools, hospitals, military installations, and some government buildings such as oil refineries, power plants, and water distribution centers. These 1:12,500 maps became the standard map for conducting combat operations in the urban areas.

A consideration that prompted extensive discussion was the matter of indirect fires. Should we use preparatory artillery fires? Our target list approached 100 targets for a town and surrounding area of over 300,000 people. First and foremost on my mind was the complete destruction of enemy forces in the area with minimal collateral damage. There never was a question of "if" we could destroy the enemy; the question was "by what means" we would destroy him.

At the same time, I felt a heavy burden and responsibility for any innocent family who might be caught in our fires while walking down the street, or playing in the neighborhood, or just sitting down at the table for their evening supper. I knew that the American people who were watching back home, to include my wife and family, expected us to be victorious, and honorable too.

While our staff and commanders worked through these issues, I considered another factor of urban warfare. We could not hide from our enemy.

Our command post presented an obvious target, and our units co-mingled with Iraqi neighborhoods. In a gesture to demonstrate that they were not hostile, Iraqi's began driving by our positions holding white sheets, towels, or shirts. This served as a small indicator that at least a part of our psychological operations campaign had been understood, as some of the flyers we distributed indicated that persons bearing a white flag of truce would not be fired on by American troops. Of course, our enemies had also received the flyer and could easily navigate our exterior positions and map our tactical operation center (TOC), with its large conglomeration of multi-antenna vehicles and frequent rotary wing activity. In response, we immediately increased our perimeter security posture and positioned military police units on the main road to interdict would-be intelligence gatherers.

The morning of our attack arrived with our plans not as complete as we would have liked, but it was time to go. We crossed the Euphrates River and began our attack on the Al Hillah security zone with Thunderbolt in the lead. The Thunderbolt tankers were not on the road long before their first contact. The enemy security zone stretched about ten miles west of Al Hillah. The road shoulders leading east into town were inundated with fighting positions. In some locations, there were fighting positions every ten to twenty yards, almost all abandoned. It appeared some had been prepared simply as a ruse to intrigue our satellites, as they were machine dug with no overhead cover and no signs of individual improvement.

The brigade commander moved forward in the tactical command post (TAC), consisting of four HMMWVs – the commander, the direct support artillery battalion commander for fire support, the Air Force liaison for air support, the cavalry and attack liaison officers, and a few other strap-hangers – commo expert, etc. We moved to the rear of Thunderbolt's column, the best location to exert command and control.

At one point, we suffered communication difficulties so I began to walk to the rear of the armor commander's tank to get his attention. We were on the right side of a four-lane divided road moving east towards Al Hillah. Residential buildings loomed on our right, farmland on the left, and a few trees dotted the median. Walking down the road I felt isolated, and then downright exposed when the tree line to my front left about 300 meters ahead, erupted in fire. I realized that I should return to the HMMWV, which I did quickly, trying to maintain an outward appearance of complete calm. A rocket-propelled grenade flew across the road to our front and clipped the antenna on a scout HMMWV, startling the exposed gunner in the hatch who never saw the round coming. Our response was immediate and impressive as the left side of the road was soon filled with lead and multiple explosions from tank fire, MK19s (HMMWV mounted grenade launchers), artillery rounds, and .50-caliber machine gun fire. After the devastating artillery barrage and direct fire ceased, aero scouts provided overwatch as several trucks of infantry dismounted and cleared enemy stragglers from the area.

The front of the tank column had been stopped at a very large trench dug across the road. The trench was over fifteen meters across and just as deep, connected on both sides by a water-filled ditch. As we moved engineers forward with earth moving equipment (the removed dirt had been deposited on our side of the trench for ease of filling in the crater), the Iraqi's sprung an ambush. Emerging from behind a large storage facility, the largest building at four stories in height, the enemy snipers fired hastily. Fortunately, in only a few minutes Thunderbolt dispatched the enemy, breached the crater, and continued to attack to the east.

We continued to move toward Al Hillah. When the column came to an abrupt stop a few miles farther down the road, I moved forward with the brigade command sergeant major to assess the situation. I could hear machine gun fire and could see that paramilitary forces had initiated an ambush—a more well disciplined ambush from what we had seen before. These fighters hid in positions on the side of the road and allowed the tank and Bradley columns to move past, waiting for the soft-skin trucks filled with infantry to appear. Two Iraqis within 20 meters of the road sprang the ambush with an RPG shot to the front of a 5-ton truck and threw a hand grenade as Soldiers were dismounting out of the back of another. Several Soldiers dropped immediately with wounds—none life threatening. Two had shrapnel wounds to the face and were bleeding profusely. Another had a shrapnel blast completely through one cheek while a third had taken shrapnel to the leg and arm. As I moved forward, it was difficult to determine incoming and outgoing rounds as the air was filled with the sounds of combat and the ground shook with explosions. Soldiers were crouching behind every available form of cover, returning fire to enemy positions across the road as well as towards a grain silo nearby. Kiowa Warrior helicopters contributed to the din by firing rockets at enemy targets both seen and suspected.

As I ambled forward, it was clear that our Soldiers were having difficulty determining enemy locations. Nonetheless, junior leaders rapidly responded by synchronizing fires from our available weapon systems. The Kiowa Warriors serviced targets in the upper floors of the storage buildings while direct fire assets struck targets on the bottom floors, and dismounted infantry secured the area from three different directions simultaneously.

The proliferation of small arms throughout Iraq makes pacification of urban areas remarkably difficult. Most Iraqi males have access to a wide variety of sidearms, machineguns, and rifles, frequently of Soviet-block design and construction. (Photo by Lt. Col. Odie Sheffield.)

While the suppressive fire continued, the company commander and his internal leadership prepared a platoon to assault through a small breach in the fence and into the grain silo complex to clear any enemy remnants. After the assault force had cleared away the last resistance, they uncovered several large caches of weapons and equipment. It was evident by the sheer number of abandoned fighting positions that included uniforms, stacks of weapons, and dispersed ammunition, that at one time the enemy force had been much larger than what we encountered. We found prepared ambush sites with RPG rounds carefully stacked and some camouflaged positions paralleling the road. A series of bunkers and fighting positions appeared to have once housed a command post.

The night of April 8, I sat on the hood of my HMMWV and listened as volleys of indirect fire screamed overhead. It was a beautiful night. The moon was about three-quarters, and other than our fires, it was very quiet. The townspeople were nowhere to be seen, lights were out, and there was a relaxed sense that we were extremely secure in the walled school compound we occupied. The day's activities were still fresh in my mind but I did not feel threatened. Thunderbolt was securing the highway and terrain to our east while Leader and Raider were to our west. Artillery positions virtually surrounded us and we had local security in small outposts all within small arms range. For thirty minutes, we lobbed shells into the town at targets we had so carefully chosen before sunset.

Then suddenly, shouts of "counterfire, counterfire, counterfire" shattered the stillness. I ran inside thinking that the enemy had finally decided to return the favor. A quick review, however, determined that we were not, in fact, under enemy indirect fire. Either his artillery or mortars assets were grossly inaccurate or we had received an erroneous indication.

After informing the night battle captain that we would not fire any counterfire missions without my approval, I moved back out to the HMMWV to grab a few hours of sleep before our morning attack. We would attack at 5:30, one half-hour prior to sunrise. As I lay on the hood of my HMMWV, thinking of the decisions I had made that day, another artillery barrage pierced the tranquil night. After a 30-minute barrage, there was a 30-minute lull to allow the Air Force to service targets with precision munitions, a mission of dubious utility.

As the JDAMs dropped on their intended targets not fifteen kilometers away, the ground rumbled and my mind drifted off to my kids back home. I wondered how they would they sleep if our town were under siege and there were forces on the outskirts lobbing shells into our buildings. I assured myself that our target selection was the best we could do given our information and the need to complete the mission. Still, I could not sleep.

In the morning, we isolated the town from the north and east by deploying an attack aviation battalion. The Apaches patrolled the main axis into the city from Highway 8 in the southeast, along the east side of the canal, then north to old Babylon. Their mission was to destroy any military vehicles moving in their area of operations, maintain observation on several military compounds, and provide early warning of vehicles moving into the city. Sabre would attack along the main axis and support Thunderbolt, Leader and Raider as needed. When Leader passed through Thunderbolt at the critical juncture and became the main effort, Sabre would continue east with Leader. From previous incidents, we realized that the helicopters were very susceptible to enemy fire when flying low over urban areas. The Kiowa Warrior was mobile, easily maneuverable, and allowed the pilot great flexibility, making it highly responsive to the infantry in the close fight on the ground. The Kiowas could place fires no more than 200 meters from friendly forces, and did so successfully on a number of occasions.

As the first rays of light crept over the horizon, Thunderbolt crossed their line of departure and began their attack into a very quiet town. Making only light contact, Thunderbolt quickly secured key intersections in the heart of Al Hillah and attacked north to establish security near the ancient ruins of Babylon. The Rakkasans followed Thunderbolt into the heart of the town then immediately struck east across the bridge over the Tigris Canal to the Ba'ath Party headquarters. This was the most dangerous of the battalion missions as they struck the very heart and soul of the enemy to include the Mayor's house, Ba'ath party headquarters, and several military compounds.

The dense, random construction we encountered downtown was very Western in design. The high-rises stood upwards of six stories with stores on the first level: a bakery on one corner, a jewelry shop across the street, and many restaurants and meat shops about. Avenues were of contemporary design; trees graced medians; and stoplights regulated major intersections. Sidewalks and streetlamps, school crossing signs, and playgrounds were familiar sights. Of course, the downtown area was a congested locale. Roads weaved around buildings and bent behind high-rises with back alleys that terminated in dead ends or hidden passages.

Most houses were self-contained, featuring individual walled compounds and were usually two or three stories tall. These compounds provided excellent cover for the enemy to observe our movements and to snipe at our Soldiers. Each structure connected to its neighbor's walls, so covered lateral movement down a block was impossible unless holes were blown in the walls. The requirement to provide 360-degree security took on a completely new meaning as Soldiers attempted to maintain surveillance on every rooftop, every window, and every piece of vegetation.

Most soldiers had trained in one of the Army's premier training centers, either the Joint Readiness Training Center at Fort Polk, Louisiana, the National Training Center at Fort Irwin, California, or even the Combat Maneuver Training Center in Hohenfels, Germany. The Army's MOUT sites are similar in nature, consisting of a cluster of buildings that are separated to allow the enemy excellent fields of fire. If an attack during training is not going well, one can sink back into the wood line and attempt to breach in another location. In contrast, the sheer size of the "real" urban environment with all the complexities of a genuine city proved a significant shock to many junior leaders.

Leader battalion proceeded to move through town. With the east side of the canal isolated, Leader systematically pushed forward to secure the bridge with tanks in the lead. Sporadic gunfire from across the canal resulted in a short delay as the commander deployed Soldiers from trucks and ordered the tanks to suppress the buildings on the far shore. Infantrymen dismounted to place their mortars in the midst of the sea of concrete. Wielding picks, sledgehammers, and shovels they crushed the pavement so they could settle their guns' baseplates. Once the mortars were ready, the attack across the bridge commenced.

The Leader battalion quickly seized critical government offices and buildings downtown while continuing to push east, coming across a very extensive military structure that appeared to be a training compound. It contained arms rooms that were still mostly intact featuring color-coded weapons, ammunition, and supplies. Since I had previously lost my canteen cup—the lifeblood of a deployed Soldier only second to his poncho liner—I gratefully liberated an Iraqi cup to do the job.

Aside from the Saddam Fedyaheen, most Iraqis welcomed the arrival of U.S. forces. Here, crowds gather in Al Hillah to greet the U.S. Army's 101st Airborne Division (Air Assault). (Photo by Lt. Col. Odie Sheffield.)

The Raider battalion followed Leader into town from the west, then pushed south to link up with No Slack. There were several smaller military compounds that Thunderbolt and Leader bypassed by design that Raider would need to clear. No Slack secured the southern portion of town and continued to encounter small pockets of resistance throughout the day. There were two large military compounds on the southern edge of town and a huge warehouse complex that housed substantial amounts of items that appeared to support the United Nations sponsored food-for-oil program.

An Iraqi cartoon painted on the wall of an Iraqi Army barracks. The boastful outcome predicted by the artist did not come to pass. (Photo by Lt. Col. Odie Sheffield.)

Within three hours of occupying Al Hillah, we began operations to restore power and water, while smaller elements continued to destroy pockets of *fedayeen*. We consolidated huge sums of small arms, ammunition, and military supplies from the military compounds we occupied. We turned over a number of gas trucks to the local water treatment authorities so they could transport gas to their generators. Saddam owned a beautiful hotel on the top of the hill overlooking the ruins for the pleasure of Ba'ath party officials and dignitaries. We decided the hotel belonged to the people of Iraq so we established our TOC in a maintenance area of the guest quarters at the base of the hill.

Within hours, the Division command net barked out our next orders. We were to leave the No Slack battalion in Al Hillah and attack north to Baghdad. The staff dove into the same processes they had completed for our current operation: crisis action planning, issue of a fragmentary order, and the positioning of assets for the attack. Just over 48 hours later, we were assaulting into southern Baghdad.

Lessons Learned

- American technological superiority is critical to synchronize overwhelming combat power onto the enemy and his suspected locations. We used TOW missiles to clear rooms, Air Force JDAMS to clear buildings, and overwhelming direct fire to clear snipers. The enemy was unorganized and fought in small teams that were quickly defeated after initial contact.
- Soldier kit and fieldcraft are essential when conducting prolonged combat operations. Our Brigade learned from Afghanistan what is important to carry and what is not. In Iraq, I wore the bare necessities. I stripped my kit to a few pouches and attached them to my interceptor body armor. I threw away my canteens and used my "Camelback"® and bottled water exclusively. Moreover, I never wore an LCE (load carrying equipment), LBV (load bearing vest), or new "Molle" vest, as my statement of charges can attest when I cleared Fort Campbell.
- The 101st Airborne Division by nature is a light force that relies on its helicopters for mobility and transportation. At the tactical level,

vehicle assets to transport Soldiers on the battlefield do not exist. Departing Kuwait, we stocked as much food, water, and ammunition we could carry aboard a ragtag fleet of 5-ton trucks provided by our higher echelons. These trucks became living quarters and moving bunkers for our Soldiers. Their floors were lined with MRE or water boxes. Other water boxes were stacked in rows two deep and two high, then sandwiched by plywood strapped together with ratchet straps. The original seats were discarded so Soldiers could sit facing outward to maintain observation. Each Soldier's rucksack was strapped to the outside of the cargo bed to provide protection against small arms. Since the brigade never received enough trucks to move the entire unit at the same time, each battalion "acquired" their own vehicle fleets to assist with the movement of their troops. These new assets varied in size and shape but all were turned into "war wagons." The sight of units traveling in this way conjured images of a strange cross between Mad Max and the Clampett's.

- Marksmanship is critical. Many leaders have a preferred method for configuring their weapons with close combat optics, laser designators, and tactical lights. The configuration is not nearly important as the time spent to ensure that the Soldier using that configuration is comfortable with his weapon.
- Every Soldier, regardless of duty specialty, must be an infantryman first. The Warrior Ethos must permeate branches and specialties of the entire Army. The enemy did not sit on the side of the road and wait to only attack combat arms formations. Every training school must

emphasize the basic fundamentals of Soldiering: shooting, moving, and communicating. Likewise, the Army's equipment fielding plan must incorporate all Soldiers equally.

- An unmanned aerial vehicle at battalion and brigade level capable of providing streaming media downloads to multiple servers would prove to be very beneficial to the ground commander. If Thunderbolt had been able to deploy a UAV to recon routes ahead with video, then plot waypoints using global positioning system technology and distribute this information throughout the unit, preparatory fires would be more accurate and we would eliminate much of the unknown during movement to contact operations.
- Operations in urban terrain present issues and problems not easily prepared for. In cities, communication ranges are diminished, artillery placement is difficult given the restricted angles of fire and height of buildings, attack aviation cannot hover for close-in support without becoming vulnerable, and Soldiers lack sufficient cover and concealment when moving down streets and alleys while danger lurks around every corner and dumpster. Extensive training is necessary to mitigate these conditions and ensure that American Soldiers can fight and win in any city.

CHAPTER TWELVE

BAGHDAD, 2004

FIGHTING AN URBAN INSURGENCY

by Major Seth Morgulas

(Ed. Note: This chapter is a firsthand account.)

It wasn't supposed to be this way. Forces in the second rotation of Operation Iraqi Freedom were supposed to be engaged in "stability and support" operations in the classic sense as called for by American doctrine of the late twentieth century. The city fight in Mogadishu had provided a stern warning of what could go wrong in such places, but in that contest, American forces simply withdrew. The battle initiated in Baghdad by various Iraqis, Iranians, Syrians and other fighters in Iraq, however, proved to be another matter entirely.

I was assigned as the commander of Bravo Battery, 1st Battalion, 258th Field Artillery, New York Army National Guard, just ten days before the battery flew to Iraq. Upon mobilization in late 2003, Bravo Battery's 90-man table of organization and equipment had been expanded to 182 to replicate the strength of a combat support military police company, the kind of organization whose mission we were tasked to assume. Approximately 120 Soldiers were assigned from Bravo Battery, Headquarters Battery and Alpha Battery. The remaining 60 Soldiers (and the first sergeant who arrived at about the same time I did) arrived from the 1st Battalion, 127th Armor and five or six other units. Most of the leadership was composed of recently promoted officers and NCOs from the 1-258 FA. The ad hoc nature of the unit's organization, and the challenges involved with the evolving conditions in Iraq meant that we needed to learn about the nature of urban military conflict – in a hurry -- and so we did.

What we encountered in Baghdad was an insurgency, a violent, "illegal" challenge to the existing American-sponsored government of Iraq, whose fighters drew support from actors beyond state sanction. Part criminal in nature and part military in its scope, the conflict smoothly migrated between the dialogues of law enforcement and war. The three doctrinal levels of war, so neatly stacked in the field manuals: tactical, operational, and strategic, were in the cities of Iraq flattened to the point that they were not any longer distinct. What did remain was the terror, and the fighting, and the killing.

American (Coalition) and Iraqi government technological superiority rendered friendly forces unbeatable in rural environments so insurgents adopted Iraq's cities as their battlefield. There, technology mattered less to the outcome of military contests. Insurgents viewed slums teeming with disillusioned people as rich environments for recruiting, and as safe havens for their organizations. Government forces could not fully employ kinetic weaponry such as artillery, mortars and bombs because they understood that inflicting mass casualties and substantial collateral damage only served the insurgents.

Baghdad's "Sadr City" was just such a breeding ground of insurgency and terror. A mere four kilometers by seven kilometers, Sadr City comprised less than one sixth of Baghdad's total area. Nevertheless, Sadr City's 2.5 million residents constituted about one-half of Baghdad's population. During its decades in power, Saddam Hussein's Sunni regime severely repressed the Shiite population of Iraq in general and of Sadr City (then known as Saddam City), in particular. Most of Sadr City's residents lived in abject poverty, were poorly educated, and suffered from corrupt and inefficient civic services. Sadr City lacked reliable electricity, and raw sewage often contaminated fresh water running into homes.

Many of the local Shiites expected their lot to change when Saddam's regime fell. It did, but not quickly or evenly. Expecting that within months they would benefit from a standard of living on par with the lifestyle they had seen Hussein's regime members enjoy, the residents of Sadr City were severely disappointed. In particular, young males suffered the worst dissatisfaction. As in many impoverished countries, males between the ages of 15 and 25 tended to have few prospects, and consequently the least to lose by joining an insurgent movement. It was no wonder then that radical clerics, Al-Qaeda terrorists, and former Baathists had little trouble recruiting from this abundant group. As local conditions remained grim, frustration turned to anger and then to violence.

American troops faced the challenge of establishing security and suppressing insurgents long enough to repair Iraq's economy and infrastructure was a Herculean task, a challenge not made easier by the lawlessness that followed in the wake of the decision of the Coalition Provisional Authority (CPA) to disband the Iraqi army and police force. Rebuilding these twin institutions of civil authority therefore, became a strategic priority for the Coalition forces in Iraq.

The Iraqi National Police Academy (sometimes also referred to as the Baghdad Public Services Academy) was a crucial component of the plan to build a credible police force for the new Iraq. It was there that I and my unit found ourselves in a small measure responsible for America's progress waging what has since become known as a campaign in the "Long War" against terrorism.

In the first seven months of our deployment, I relieved one platoon leader and replaced two out of four line platoon sergeants with more experienced NCOs from the 1-127 Armor. I found it necessary to replace over half of the staff sergeant squad leaders with more motivated junior sergeants as well. Although there were undoubtedly many success stories for field artillery batteries serving as "in lieu of" military police or "ILO-MPs," I observed that junior field artillery officers and NCOs lacked the skills required to train and lead platoons with law enforcement and mounted maneuver missions. Moreover, the composite company comprised of Soldiers from multiple units created innumerable leadership obstacles at all levels. Because many of the NCOs had been promoted upon mobilization, had not attended the NCO school associated with their new rank, and lacked experience in their new positions, they experienced substantial difficulties adapting to the demands made of them. The two ILO-MP companies from the 1-258 FA also mobilized as separate ILO-MP companies with minimal battalion support. Therefore, the batteries experienced substantial obstacles addressing personnel and logistical problems during mobilization.

The battery loitered at Fort Dix for eleven weeks (substantially longer then originally planned), training as ILO-MPs. In its eleven weeks there, the company received fewer than four days of military police individual task training and less then two weeks of collective training. MOUT (military operations on urban terrain) training, despite a Baghdad destination for the unit, was limited to a jumble of 2x4s posing as structures. Convoy training was limited to rural, wooded terrain. When we arrived at Camp Uidairi in Kuwait we conducted additional MOUT training under the watchful eye of three retired Special Forces Soldiers. Although well intentioned, few of these preparations adequately prepared us for our actual mission in Iraq. Nonetheless, the unit leadership was determined to care for our Soldiers and to do well at our mission. We would simply have to depend on ourselves and each other to remedy our training shortfalls.

Arriving in Baghdad I could see that war had wrought a terrible havoc on a once proud city. Shattered buildings, their rafters and beams exposed like horrible decayed skeletons, sat rotting in greenish ooze, others smoldered in the streets. Wide, modern highways, not dissimilar to those in the United States or Europe, their guard rails rent from their moorings and their pavement pocked with craters and lined with gargantuan piles of burning trash, terminated in barren fields and ruins. We passed power plants that had not seen maintenance in 30 years, their sole operating stack belching fetid black smoke and powering little more than a few square blocks. Coalition checkpoints, manned by a team or squad dismounted from HMMWVs (high mobility, multipurpose-wheeled vehicles) or Bradley Fighting Vehicles, with an occasional M1A2 tank to accompany them, completed the scene.

The Iraqi National Police Academy consisted of a sprawling, palm tree-filled compound built in the 1940s on the east side of the Tigris River, near the monument to the martyrs of the Iran-Iraq War, the Ministry of the Interior, and Uday Hussein's Olympic Headquarters. Its newly carved back gate spilled directly out onto Palestine Avenue at the southeast corner of Sadr City.

As I stepped out of my HMMWV, I could see that the compound had certainly seen better days. It was surrounded by a wall of "Alaska Barriers" (modular concrete barriers approximately 13 feet high) and "hescos" (dirt filled, felt lined wire baskets) in varying stages of disintegration—good fences make good neighbors. Tangles of concertina wire and garbage littered the exterior like giant tumbleweeds. A gutted building, once the home of Uday's torture machines, loomed at the end of a parking lot.

About one-half of the Academy had been commandeered as a patrol base by the First Cavalry Division's 1-162 IN (Oregon National Guard), a quarter had been laid waste by squatters, and the remainder was devoted to training the new Iraqi police force under the auspices of a joint team of U.S. and British civilian trainers and U.S. military police. Our mission, in conjunction with the 415th MP Detachment and a platoon of the 272d MP Company was to defend the compound; repair it, expand it, and train the police (as many as possible and as quickly as possible).

The Iraqi National Police Academy had not seen enemy activity for months. Not since the outbreak of violence in Baghdad's now infamous "Sadr City" in April 2004 had the Academy experienced even so much as one mortar round, although one or two had hit on Patrol Base Volunteer next door. The most excitement had been the "fireworks" celebration one night when Iraq trounced Saudi Arabia on the soccer pitch. That all changed in one salvo at approximately 1000 hours on August 6, 2004.

The day before, the Academy had conducted a graduation ceremony for nearly 500 new police officers (today the Academy conducts its graduations in secret to avoid potential security risks). Despite rumors of an impending attack we conducted the ceremony on the Academy's most prominent feature, the parade ground (often referred to jokingly as target reference point one), to honor the new Dean of the Academy. Although the towers of the Academy were manned by Iraqi Police, graduations required a more substantial armed presence. An outer cordon of HMMWV's and Armored Security Vehicles (ASV's) armed with MK-19's (grenade launchers) and M2 .50-caliber machine guns established a presence on the streets, while observation posts on prominent surrounding buildings remained alert for snipers, roving mortar attacks and vehicle-borne improvised explosive devices as OH-58D's (Kiowa scout helicopters) or AH-64's (Apache attack helicopters) circled overhead.

Moments before the conclusion of the ceremony, my first platoon leader reported that he had detained four pickup trucks near the Ministry of the Interior. Nearly 40 men were crammed into the trucks, bristling with AK-47's, AK-74's and, more ominously, RPG-7's (rocket launchers). It was these deadly weapons that piqued the curiosity of my platoon leader as they were prohibited in the confines of Baghdad. The rules of engagement at the time would have permitted him to open fire upon seeing the RPG's. That he did not was primarily attributable to the fact that many of the men of the platoon were familiar with the difficulties encountered by other Soldiers who had exercised such judgment in the heat of the moment. We periodically received emails from faceless generals asserting the need to follow TTP's (tactics, techniques and procedures), and not to hesitate to fire when an Iraqi ran a checkpoint or came too near to a convoy. Nevertheless, every Soldier knew that each time he pulled a trigger he would be filling out sworn statements and may subject himself to a "15-6" investigation or, worse.

That the Soldiers did not fire in this case may have been fortuitous. Although two of the vehicles were not marked, the last two bore the words "Babylon S.W.A.T." No one could explain what these men were really doing, armed to the teeth with RPG's and driving towards the Academy. One of my Soldiers later identified four of the men as students from a previous training class. Did we instruct a fifth column? Were they headed to Sadr City to engage our fellow Soldiers? We never found out.

The next morning, in the Academy's first week of a planned expansion, the sound of whistling 60mm and 81mm mortars broke the silence. To those who have lived through it, there is no more distinct sound than that high-pitched whistle (you will only hear this sound when the round has already past overhead, rounds landing on top or in front of you make no sound until they explode), ever increasing in volume until it terminates in a loud popping sound. Not the explosions of an action movie, but rather like a paper bag popping sound, only amplified: Three, then four, then six. The mortars impacted around the Academy headquarters. Amazingly, no one was injured and damage was limited to some broken windows.

Days later, a 60mm round struck between two Golf Company barracks buildings, throwing a Soldier through a doorway and inflicting minor shrapnel injuries. The next day a Soldier instructing police cadets suffered shrapnel wounds on both hands as a round crashed through the tin roof of his classroom. Then shrapnel struck another Soldier standing his post at the rear gate. At first, the attacks were relatively indiscriminate, revealing no pattern. Gradually they became increasingly more accurate, six rounds pummeling the pistol range, four striking the parade ground and eight bracketing an observation tower. Were they getting lucky or was it better aim?

We were kept guessing until we noticed someone on the balcony just below the roof of the Ministry of Water. As the rounds hit, a big fat man on the balcony placed his leg on the guardrail, raised his hand and, in an exaggerated manner, slapped his right knee or his left knee. Was he spotting for the mortar crews? Or was it just coincidence? Again, considerations of the bureaucratic consequences, particularly of firing on a government building, dissuaded my Soldiers from shooting. I dispatched two teams of MP's to the Ministry, but we were too late and found nothing. Yet, this state of affairs was hardly surprising. The Academy is surrounded by three tall buildings and any window overlooking the Academy might provide an observation post for an insurgent. Of course, plenty of danger lurked outside the boundaries of the Academy as well.

Despite the fact that G Company's primary missions were instructing cadets at the Academy and protecting the Academy, our logistical requirements required us to conduct, on average, two to three trips outside its boundaries every day. Although we were located at Patrol Base Volunteer, which housed the 1-162 IN, we did not receive any logistical support from the patrol base other than fuel. Our battalion headquarters was located at Camp Cuervo (recently renamed "Camp Rustamiyah"), our supply accounts were located at Camp Liberty (near Baghdad International Airport ("BIAP")), and our ammunition and clothing could only be obtained at Logistics Support Area Anaconda, a 90 minute drive north of Baghdad. Moreover, we had to transport Soldiers heading home on leave to BIAP and pick up returning Soldiers at least once, if not twice, every day. Of course, each excursion brought with it the potential of violence.

On June 19, 2004, we began a trip to LSA Anaconda just as we did any other mission outside of the Academy. Four armored HMMWVs lined up in our motor pool. The team leaders and squad leader conducted their pre-combat inspections under the watchful eye of their platoon leader. The convoy consisted of four vehicles and one trailer, with the trailer in the middle of the formation. The location of the trailer is a tactical toss up. If you put it at the rear of the convoy, the gunner cannot protect the back of the formation, but if it is in the middle then vehicles following cannot easily push it out of a kill zone. We had received some mild ribbing from the battalion operations officer because our convoys looked like they were ready for the Battle of the Bulge but I always figured it was better to be too careful than not careful enough. The lead and trail vehicle mounted both an M2 .50-caliber machinegun and an M249 squad automatic weapon while the two vehicles in the center carried MK-19 automatic grenade launchers and M249's. We also carried plenty of ammunition because we never knew how much we were going to need, particularly on a trip that was likely to take the entire day to accomplish. Today's Soldiers are no different then their predecessors of previous wars—if you can carry extra ammunition bring it. There was plenty of room in those HMMWVs so we did.

We drove out of the Academy and headed northwest on Route Pluto, past Sadr City. We kept to the center lane as much as possible, because even a few extra feet from a blast can make a difference. Every underpass required a drill. Trucks swerved and weaved randomly, exiting in a different lane than they entered, making it more difficult for the enemy to drop something or fire on us as we emerged from the underpass. Gunners scanned with their rifles or pistols to cover anyone on the overpass then quickly switched back to the road ahead. Drivers and "TCs" watched for the enemy and for IED's.

Our gunners directed traffic from their hatch, sometimes with their hands, sometimes shouting, sometimes they pointed their pistol at a recalcitrant driver who refused to move out of the way or appeared too aggressive. Sometimes it was not just vehicles that blocked our route, and such proved the case this day. While we were stopped in heavy traffic a gunner yelled "get that donkey out of the way, pull that fucking donkey cart over!" Then something hit my truck with a loud thud. I yelled at the gunner who informed me that it was only a head of lettuce lobbed by a teenager on the side of the road. Better salad then grenades!

About five kilometers north of Taji we encountered another traffic jam. This time it was caused by American Soldiers conducting an IED sweep. They found one. Unfortunately, the traffic was pressed up against their trail vehicle, a scant 50 meters from the site of the IED, which apparently consisted of two 155mm shells wired together. The senior NCO on site told us we needed to back up to a safe distance some 400 meters back. What about the civilians? The NCO stated that he did not know what to do to warn them, so we dismounted once again. A funny thing about that MP brassard was that it seemed to create an involuntary urge to direct traffic. Lacking the Arabic skills to impress upon the civilians the need to back up, we stuck our fingers in our ears, made explosion noises and gestured with our hands as we pointed ahead to where the EOD (explosive ordnance disposal) team worked. Fortunately, the Iraqis understood and all of us made it through the choke point. Eight hours later, after a hunt through the LSA Anaconda cannibalization point for a left rear break cable, a trip to the central issuing facility, and numerous other errands, we made it back to the Academy. All in a day's work.

One evening in August the sound of mortars and small arms fire broke the evening quiet from near our rear gate. Fortuitously, my team and I had just returned from a patrol. We drove to the back gate and found six of my Soldiers and ten Iraqi police beating the brush in the swamp behind the Academy. The force protection platoon sergeant and a team were actually in the swamp, farther out than prudence dictated so I ordered them to return. The quick reaction force arrived a few minutes later. With only three sets of PVS-7B's (night vision devices) we were hard pressed to mount an effective search of the area. The infantry refused to fire mortar or artillery illumination, so we fired a few rounds of 40mm illumination and some parachute flares. A shadow moved across the swamp into an abandoned building. For the first time in four months, our MOUT training came in handy. Two teams moved quickly across open ground to the building. Flashlights and PVS-7B's were some help, but again we found nothing. Like the weary denizens of a besieged castle, we returned through our sally port, secured the gates and waited for the next probe. We had only to wait several hours.

Three loud explosions shattered the calm. They sounded like mortars, but could have been RPG's; it is often hard to tell at a distance with the reverberation of the buildings. We popped off about ten more 40mm illumination rounds and stalked around for a few more minutes. Calming an angry lieutenant, who was ready to run headlong into the swamp looking for the enemy, took a bit longer. Once we roamed outside of our safe areas, we possessed technological and firepower advantages, but in the dark, in a swamp, the odds of being ambushed or blown up with an IED were high, so we refrained from venturing farther.

I returned to my company area and went to sleep fully dressed, only to be awakened around midnight once more by the sound of mortars. Over the radio came a call for medics. Who was injured? Soldiers? Civilians? Police? Two medics ran to their truck and took off to the back gate of the Academy. I arrived moments later. The back gate was locked but the medics and two teams were on the far side of the gate. The sound of AK-47's and M-16's crackled through the air. Having first sent a truck back to find the key for the gate I climbed over it with a platoon leader. One medic ran toward me and stumbled on the dark ground. Since he was exposed, I grabbed him by the collar. He had twisted his ankle, so I hauled him to a covered spot by a wall. Two teams were pinned. Perhaps ten Iraqi police, some 20 meters forward, huddled behind another wall. The Iraqi police had apparently run out of ammunition (the result of firing their ammunition to celebrate soccer victories) and had resorted to throwing their empty magazines at the insurgents.

By the time the infantry's quick reaction force arrived we had cordoned off the building in which we believed the insurgents to be hiding. So far, we had found no casualties. Where were the three dead that the Iraqi police claimed they had suffered? I began to believe that either something had been lost in the translation or that one of the police had lied in order to lure us out to be ambushed by the insurgents. Together with the infantry, we searched the empty warehouse. Nothing more than some muddy footprints remained as evidence that the attackers had been there. Before departing the scene, we questioned the Iraqi police. We knew we were unlikely to get the truth out of them. Most of them were too concerned about losing their jobs to talk. Our language assistant was unable to pry anything useful out of them other than that there were two or three attackers. Where were the wounded, we asked? No response- which was typical. Wearily we returned to our barracks. In the morning, we found several dried pools of blood in the abandoned warehouse, nothing more.

On another day, I gained a new respect for the power of indirect fire. I have had too many close calls with 60mm, 81mm mortars and 107mm rockets, and on September 26, 2004, I came about as close to 120mm mortar fire as I would like. The Iraqi Army was recruiting for a law and order (riot control) battalion in an open area at the north end of the Academy. At around 8:30 a.m., I went to check on my Soldiers and to ensure that they were keeping at a safe distance and letting the Iraqi police do their jobs. They were not. After a brief discussion with one of my platoon leaders, I ordered his Soldiers back toward to the protected area at the north gate. I remained behind with the platoon leader, a Department of Justice civilian and two other Soldiers. Less then three minutes later, the first round impacted some 300 meters to the north-west in Sadr City. The next round hit to the north of the parking lot some 50 meters away. The Iraqi recruits scattered and we ran toward the nearest bunker. An instinct told me I had been running too long (or maybe it was Sergeant Harvey yelling for me to get down) and when a round impacted, it felt close, very close. A platoon leader, some 15 meters away, yelled "sir, run! run! come on!" I felt for my throat protector and took off towards the bunker still some 50 meters away. Looking to my rear, I saw the cloud of dust kicked up by the last round. Finally reaching the bunker, we took a deep breath and checked each other for blood. One specialist sported a big gash in his Kevlar helmet but no one was wounded.

When the impacts ceased, we checked our equipment and took a head count, then returned to look for unexploded ordnance and Iraqi casualties. We found the fins of a 120mm round embedded in the pavement. Thank God for *hesco,* the round had struck not more than 12 feet from where I crouched. An Iraqi policeman pulled his hair and kicked his now ruined car, its windows blown out, tires torn to shreds and its body perforated with holes. If he sympathized with the insurgents before, he certainly did not now. In addition, the athletic facility sported some new rooftop ventilation. How many times had we used it as a staging area? Why had we chosen not to today? Nothing but luck. I later learned that a UAV had spotted the mortar crew and an A-10 had engaged them with its 40mm cannon, apparently to no effect, as they sped away in a white pickup truck.

Over time, the pattern to the mortar attacks became fairly routine and obvious. Typically, at 8:00 a.m. the first salvo would land near the back gate. The target was not really my Soldiers. Rather, the insurgents sought to discourage the police cadets, maybe even get lucky and hit a formation of them. For the most part, it became readily apparent that the insurgents knew they were out-classed when it came to direct confrontation with American troops, so they needed a softer target. Their consequent attacks on police stations, particularly those serving as recruiting stations for the police force and Iraqi National Guard, underscored the point.

The enemy's change of tactics prompted us to reevaluate how and where we formed the cadets for class and where we conducted graduation ceremonies. We began to stagger in-processing to limit the number of cadets milling about. Pistol qualification, conducted on two recently refurbished ranges, was organized carefully. The ranges were flanked by a set of bunkers, and the insurgents' mid-day barrage usually targeted the range. Although the cadets suffered numerous minor injuries, the mortar attacks were singularly ineffective in producing casualties. Furthermore, they did little to discourage recruiting.

Overall, force protection at the square mile sized Academy remained a difficult task. On any given day, nearly 5000 people and over 200 vehicles, including delivery and tanker trucks, entered and exited the facility. The police and my Soldiers had to search everything and everyone that entered and exited the Academy. With a maximum of sixteen Soldiers on a shift, it was difficult for the troops to search everyone. Therefore, we relied on the Iraqi police to perform the majority of the searches. This situation produced numerous security hazards. We prohibited the use of cellular phones on the Academy- we believed that they were being used to spot for mortar crews- and we permitted only the police who actually worked at the Academy to bring their weapons into the facility. However, the police at the gates were often reluctant to thoroughly search visitors. Frequently, they allowed friends or higher ranking police to enter freely. Moreover, a police constable earning only $300 a month is highly susceptible to bribery.

Since the fall of Saddam's regime, the vast majority of Coalition casualties have been the result of improvised explosive devices. Whether placed (PIEDs), Vehicle-Born (VBIEDs) or otherwise, IEDs pose the single largest threat to Coalition forces in Iraq. IEDs are nothing new in the history of human conflict; however, the insurgents appear to have elevated the use of IEDs to something of an art form. As a result, Coalition forces gradually adapted to the changing techniques and equipment employed by the bomb makers.

The training we received during mobilization encouraged us to view everything as a potential IED threat, and with good reason. Unfortunately, everything in Baghdad looked like the ideal location for an IED. There was garbage strewn everywhere. Piles of rubble littered the roads. Dead animals were ubiquitous. With its reasonably advanced highway system, every on- ramp, off-ramp, overpass and underpass in Baghdad looked like an ideal spot to hide a bomb. Filled potholes and unfilled potholes alike, seem to beckon the insurgent bomber. In the morning, and often throughout the day, patrols swept the MSR's (main supply routes) and the many of the ASR's (alternate supply routes) for IED's. However, there was no certainty they would find everything or that an insurgent would not emplace something between sweeps. It was also true that mechanical systems like the "Warlock" and "Compass Call" have reduced the effectiveness of IEDs. Moreover, the increased number of armored vehicles as well as add-ons to the Interceptor body-armor substantially increased the protection afforded to Coalition Soldiers. However, IEDs remain a significant threat. Every time I drove past a bloated animal on the side of the road, a suspicious pile of rubble or an abandoned car, I couldn't help but think either "this is going to hurt" or "chances are I won't even feel it."

Initially VBIED's were not overwhelmingly prevalent in Baghdad. However, since the summer of 2004, insurgents substantially increased their use of this tactic. Although PIEDs could be as large as two or more 155mm artillery shells wired together, or occasionally consist of complex multiple device systems designed to destroy multiple vehicles spread at substantial intervals, PIEDs more typically targeted specific military assets and were usually substantially smaller then VBIED's. Packed with hundreds, if not thousands of pounds of explosives, VBIED's produced an extraordinary amount of shrapnel. To identify VBIED's we routinely received "be on the lookout for" (BOLO) lists: a green Toyota, or a white Volkswagen, a license plate number in Hindi or maybe a location. These lists were rarely useful. Virtually every vehicle on the road looked like it could be a VBIED. Every parked car could hide a bomb. Even descriptions of enemy TTP's identifying aggressive drivers trying to get around convoys or getting close to vehicles were largely useless. Iraqis rarely observed any rules when driving and numerous shootings of innocent civilians testified to the large number of aggressive drivers whose desire to get from point A to point B quickly could readily be confused with malevolent intent.

On Sunday, October 11, 2004, I awoke at 7:20 a.m. to the sound of an enormous blast. The concussion rattled the entire building. At first, as I hastily donned my Kevlar, I thought a 120mm round had struck our motor pool right outside our barracks. When I arrived at my TOC (tactical operations center), I realized that the blast had actually occurred outside the Academy's north gate. In fact, there had had been not just one blast, but two. My Soldiers at the north gate reported that a VBIED had exploded on Palestine Road and that mortar round or rocket had struck the swamp behind FOB Volunteer. After gaining accountability of my men and ensuring that we had not sustained any casualties, we attempted to ascertain the exact location and cause of the blasts. As it turned out, the first blast at 7:19hrs was a PIED on Palestine Road to the north-east of the Academy. That blast caused minor injuries to one U.S. Soldier and some damage to several vehicles. The second blast, at 7:20 was a VBIED. Not more than five minutes after the blasts, CNN reported that a VBIED had entered the Academy and detonated. Our battalion commander, who had received numerous conflicting reports called and instructed the commander of the 415th to "get eyes on" and report. I joined him and we drove out to the scene of the blast.

The debris field was oval in shape, about 200 meters long by about 50 meters wide. As we walked to the crater, I looked down at the ground and narrowly avoided stepping on what appeared to be a human liver. Pieces of flesh and pools of blood littered the street, together with pieces of shredded metal and rubber. The chassis of a Daewoo sedan was over 150 meters east of the crate, the engine 200 meters to the north. We later found pieces over a mile away, including a piece of the alternator. The crater was at least five feet deep and ten feet by eight feet in shape. The 1-162 IN was still treating several of the wounded. The bodies of the dead, or what was left of them, were already gone. One man, we were told, was literally blown through the bars of a wrought iron fence on the side of the road. We found a few pieces still on the fence. Several body sized smears of blood lay on the road. The infantry told us that there had been little left to pick up.

The American combat Soldier of World War II certainly had many dangers to worry about: Enemy troops, artillery, tanks, planes, and grenades. However, on the linear battlefield, these dangers were readily identifiable and usually approached from one or a few, directions. In the non-contiguous battlespace created by urban insurgency, danger is literally everywhere. Moreover, the threats are typically difficult to identify and quantify. Nowhere was this reality more evident then in the city of Baghdad. Even in "safe areas" like forward operating bases and camps, threats lurk. If insurgents can emplace IEDs in the roads and drive VBIEDs around the city, then they can sneak them into "safe areas." If insurgents can cause casualties on the roads and in buildings, they can compromise security of any "safe area."

Traditional lessons of military security no longer apply. For instance, junior officers almost universally study the military classic, *The Defense of Duffer's Drift*. In that parable, a British soldier learns that allowing civilians into a military encampment only invites trouble. Yet, in Iraq, every FOB, camp and patrol base operated by Coalition forces employs local nationals and, frequently, foreign workers. Although Kellogg, Brown and Root conduct background checks on their employees and local contractors are searched when they enter coalition encampments, there is no guarantee that insurgents are not slipping in. Moreover, it is clear that coalition forces run substantial intelligence risks when they allow local nationals to enter their camps. Despite its obvious benefits and necessity, the Academy itself poses a great risk to both coalition forces stationed there and to friendly Iraqis attending the Academy. Because nearly 5000 Iraqis work on or attend classes at the Academy, it is nearly impossible to search them as carefully as is prudent, nor is it possible to prevent insurgent infiltration. As a result, cadets, police, language assistants and contractors are routinely identified by insurgents and threatened, harassed and occasionally murdered. Moreover, with over 500 contractors entering and leaving the Academy on a daily basis, insurgents have the opportunity to smuggle arms or explosives onto the campus. Furthermore, even the most thorough search of a vehicle may miss explosives. There is no reason to believe that insurgents cannot either smuggle an IED onto the Academy or assemble one out of smuggled components and place it in the midst of a large group of cadets or coalition troops. As a result, a walk around the Academy can be little different from a drive around Baghdad.

Although frequently described by the media as "another Vietnam," Iraq might be more similar to the U.S. Army's campaign in the Philippines in the wake of the Spanish American War. The doctrine of "winning hearts and minds" pioneered by the British during their Malay Emergency of 1948-60 has endured, despite its limited success in Vietnam and Somalia, as an accepted principle of waging a counterinsurgency. This appears to be our vaguely quixotic quest in Baghdad. Maintaining a military presence is not the end itself but rather, establishing and maintaining security as a necessary precondition to the establishment of functioning institutions of state and a growing economy. Somehow, disgruntled insurgents must be turned into productive citizens.

Intellectually, I understood that Golf Company, TF 759 MP, 89th MP Brigade, together with the 415th Military Police Detachment (Law and Order) and a platoon of the 272d MP Company were vital components of this plan. Day to day, however, I adopted a much more prosaic perspective. I learned to avoid large crowds of Iraqi police cadets, if possible. I avoided parked vehicles and clenched my jaw when I walked past any that looked particularly suspicious. I learned that an innocuous garbage can, or a vehicle barrier, or an air conditioning unit, could as easily contain a bomb as perform its intended function.

The terrorist and the insurgent work by instilling fear in everyday people doing everyday things. That is the nature of an urban insurgent campaign, and it is a deadly effective way to wage war.

CHAPTER THIRTEEN

IRAQ, 2006 A NEW WAY OF FIGHTING

STRYKERS IN IRAQ

by Major Douglas A. Sims, II

(ed. Note: This is a firsthand account.)

Most days in the city of Mosul, Iraq, dawned with great potential. The cool, clear mornings provided a sense of hope that the coming hours would not be stiflingly hot, the acrid smell of burning plastic would not invade every inch of your clothing, and that the quiet would not give way to the sounds of explosions and small-arms fire.

The early hours of November 10, 2004, were no different. As the city began to awaken, the "Lancers" of the 1st Brigade, 25th Infantry Division (1/25 Stryker) were already on patrol. What would turn into nearly two months of fighting erupted without warning when insurgent small-arms fire engulfed a convoy bound for a major Iraqi Army base west of the city. The convoy was contracted by American forces and operated by the security company Erinys.

Responding as they would hundreds of times over the next year, a Quick Reaction Force (QRF) from the 1st Battalion, 24th Infantry Regiment—nicknamed Deuce-Four—sped from Forward Operating Base Marez and darted north along Main Supply Route Tampa. Minutes later, they arrived on the scene of the ambush and immediately received fire from 15 to 20 insurgents. This was the Soldiers first substantial contact, but it would not be their last. After returning fire and recovering the members of the Erinys security team and other members of the convoy, the group broke contact with the enemy and sped their wounded to the Combat Surgical Hospital at the Mosul airfield. One member of the Erinys convoy was killed, three were wounded, and one of the vehicles was too damaged to recover. Of the evacuating force from 1/24 IN, one Soldier was wounded during the convoy's recovery.[268]

Viewed in isolation, the Erinys convoy incident was a minor action. The combat of that November morning, however, served as a catalyst for the insurgents as they dramatically increased their offensive efforts against U.S. and Iraqi forces. It provided a lesson for the American Soldiers about the nature of urban combat: In the constrained and complex environment of the city, every action is charged with consequences.

The troops of the Lancer Brigade, from Fort Lewis, Washington, were in the vanguard of the U.S. Army's transformation effort. As part of General Eric Shinseki's aggressive initiative to change the Army to meet 21st-century threats, the Stryker Brigade Combat Teams (SBCTs) were a leap ahead of traditional Army brigades. Named for the vehicle in which they rode into combat, the Stryker brigades brought extensive lethality and survivability to the fight. They did so with state-of-the-art digital and voice communications, greater organic intelligence capability, and most importantly, by fielding more combat Soldiers than a typical light or mechanized U.S. infantry brigade.[269]

Reflective of the spirit of ingenuity General Shinseki's transformation fostered, the eight-wheeled, light armored Stryker combat vehicle was selected as the new brigade's vehicular platform after competing against numerous other vehicle types and being fielded in record time through an accelerated acquisition process.[270] The initial focus of the competition had been to identify a vehicle light enough to be transported by a C-130, the Air Force's short-range aerial workhorse, but with enough protection to ensure Soldiers arrived at the battlefield unharmed. In the end, the Stryker used in Iraq, outfitted with additional armor and a full complement of ammunition and supplies, was never light enough to be lifted by a C-130, but it didn't matter. The Strykers that 1/25 rode to war were those already on the ground in Iraq. Rather than deploy the brigade's vehicles from Fort Lewis, Washington, 1/25 assumed control of the vehicles already in theater with a full year of combat under their hoods.

Within 1/25 were eight variants of the Stryker. The mainstay of the fleet was the infantry combat vehicle (ICV), featuring either a remotely operated .50-caliber machine gun or an MK-19 grenade launcher as the primary weapon system and capable of delivering a full squad of nine infantrymen to the battlefield. Variants included the reconnaissance vehicle (RV) with an extremely powerful laser range finder for long distance target acquisition and surveillance; the mortar carrier (MC), which carried mortarmen and their 60 mm, 81 mm, or 120 mm anywhere on the ground; the engineer squad vehicle (ESV) with either a mine roller or surface-laid mine plow; the medical evacuation vehicle (MEV), able to carry four patients on litters; the anti-tank guided missile vehicle (ATGM), able to launch TOW anti-tank missiles; and the fire support vehicle (FSV) and the command vehicle (CV), both with added command, control, and communications assets.[271] 1/25's nearly 4,000 Soldiers fought from more than 300 Stryker combat vehicles.[272]

Capable of cruising at speeds in excess of 60 miles per hour, the Stryker's eight wheels provided an incredibly smooth ride for its occupants, and the 350-horsepower engine was remarkably quiet. In fact, due to the vehicle's ability to seemingly appear out of thin air, the Stryker units from the 3d Brigade, 2d Infantry Division had earned from the Iraqis the moniker "Ghost Riders."[273] Unlike the original design, however, the Strykers in Iraq were modified with a birdcage-like armor system called SLAT. The SLAT armor fit around the exterior of the vehicle and provided additional protection from the rocket propelled grenades (RPG) preferred by the insurgents. In addition, Soldiers within the brigade improvised by building blast shields out of sand bags and steel plates to protect Stryker crewmembers pulling security from the top of the vehicle. The added armor and improvised protection increased the vehicles weight, but it was still quite maneuverable and allowed the Lancers to travel nearly everywhere in the city and the surrounding countryside.

Networking each Stryker vehicle and their headquarters was a digital system called Future Battle Command Brigade and Below (FBCB2). The FBCB2, contained not only in all Strykers but also in the majority of the 1/25's non-Stryker fleet, provided terrestrial-based, FM frequency transmitted locational data to all other systems.[274] The FBCB2 also allowed for digital message trafficking between vehicles, essentially providing e-mail capability in addition to the standard voice communications available throughout the brigade. The ability to monitor the "blue feed"—a picture that provided detail on all operating systems within the brigade's area of operations—allowed everyone within the brigade to view a standard common operating picture (COP). The automatically updating COP provided greater situational awareness than ever before seen on the battlefield. In addition to the "friendly" icons on the screen displaying current unit locations, "enemy" icons could also be populated into the system to indicate the enemy's location, allowing immediate awareness of ongoing or suspected activity. This digital picture helped operations and intelligence officers to predict the enemy's intentions and allowed forces to be moved within the area of operations as required.

The primary combat formations in the brigade were the three infantry battalions: 1st Battalion, 5th Infantry Regiment (1/5 IN), 1st Battalion, 24th Infantry Regiment (1/24 IN), and 3d Battalion, 21st Infantry Regiment (3/21 IN). Within each battalion were three infantry companies consisting of three infantry platoons and a mobile gun system platoon with four ICVs and three ATGMs, respectively.[275] Added to the company's strength was a mortar section of two MCs with the ability to fire either 60 mm or 120 mm mortars. Finally, each of the companies maximized precision fire capabilities with organic snipers at the company level and squad-designated marksmen within the platoons. In addition to the standard infantry companies, each battalion also consisted of one headquarters company, providing the battalion with the unit's staff personnel as well as a mortar platoon with 81 mm and 120 mm mortars and four additional MCs, a reconnaissance platoon with four RVs, and a medical platoon with four MEVs. All told, each infantry battalion consisted of approximately 700 men and 75 Strykers.[276]

Within the brigade structure were two additional combat battalions, a field artillery battalion, 2d Battalion, 8th Field Artillery Regiment (2/8 FA); and a reconnaissance, surveillance, targeting and acquisition (RSTA) squadron, 2d Squadron, 14th Cavalry Regiment (2/14 CAV). The field artillery battalion's three artillery batteries and one service battery lacked organic Stryker vehicles, instead possessing 155 mm towed howitzers. This artillery piece, old by SBCT standards, still provided on-demand combat power to the brigade and the ability to fire at targets over 18 kilometers away. The nature of the enemy in northern Iraq, however, most often required the artillerymen to fight and serve as infantry.

The RSTA squadron was designed to serve as the eyes and ears of the brigade. Originally envisioned as the true finders of the enemy, the squadron (the cavalry equivalent of an infantry battalion) possessed three reconnaissance troops and a surveillance troop. Each reconnaissance troop included three reconnaissance platoons of four RVs. In addition, the RSTA squadron also had an organic surveillance troop consisting of an unmanned aerial vehicle (UAV) platoon with four SHADOW tactical UAVs—an asset normally seen at division levels and above; a ground sensor platoon and multisensor platoon, both of which assisted with signals intelligence; and a nuclear, biological, chemical platoon with two FOX chemical recon vehicles. Combined with its headquarters company, the four troops gave the RSTA squadron a strength of approximately 430 troopers and 54 Stryker vehicles.[277]

One particularly advantageous aspect of the RSTA squadron was the presence of human intelligence specialists in each of the troops. As operations in Iraq proved time and again, human intelligence was fundamental to success. Similar to 2/8 FA's situation, the RSTA was needed in northern Iraq to perform missions not included in the original Stryker concept. Since most of the fighting was occurring inside the cities and towns, long-range detection, surveillance, and reconnaissance were less important than mounted and dismounted combat patrols inside the urban areas. As a result, 2/14 CAV and 1/5 IN exchanged a troop and company to provide a greater balance of capabilities to each formation. Because the brigade would be fighting in the constrained environment of urban areas, a further degree of centralized control was necessary for the RSTA squadron's surveillance assets. The UAV and two sensor platoons were assigned to brigade headquarters to work directly under brigade control, while the 2/14 CAV headquarters maintained only the NBC platoon.

Rounding out the brigade's organic organization and providing exceptional additional capabilities were the 73d Engineer Company, which consisted of 130 personnel, nine ESVs, and additional mobility, countermobility, and survivability engineering equipment; the anti-tank company, Delta Company, 52d Infantry Regiment (D/52) with 9 ATGMs and 54 Soldiers; the 176th Signal Company, which provided superb digital and voice communications support to the brigade; and the 184th Military Intelligence Company (MICO) with its tremendous intelligence gathering and analysis capabilities, including tactical level unmanned aerial vehicles and human intelligence (HUMINT) teams.[278]

Extensive and complex logistical efforts were required to support this extensive brigade structure. Although designed to support the SBCT in a 50 kilometer by 50 kilometer area of operations, the 25th Brigade Support Battalion (25 BSB) instead supported 1/25 in an area 20 times that size. With three companies specializing in the distribution of supplies and services, medical support and maintenance, the battalion called on more than 600 men and women to keep the brigade running.[279]

As they were a priority of Army transformation, the SBCT units were able to purchase the latest technological advances off the shelf for trial within the brigade. During a time when many units were constrained by limited budgets and the standard military supply system, the Stryker brigades enjoyed the advantage of a healthy transformation budget and were courted by the nation's top technology companies looking to advance their wares.

The Soldiers of 1/25 arrived in northern Iraq on October 21, 2004. They inherited a battle space of nearly 50,000 square kilometers with an Iraqi population of approximately 4.6 million people. The area of operations roughly followed Iraqi provincial boundaries, giving the Soldiers responsibility for the Ninewah Province. Within that province were the major population centers of Mosul and Tall Afar with 2.1 million and 150,000 people, respectively. Another population center extended along the banks of the Tigris River, which flowed through the battle space from north to south. Other small towns and villages dotted the landscape, further complicating the battle space environment.

Bordered by Syria to the west, Turkey to the north, and the Kurdish regions to the east, Ninewah—inhabited by Sunni and Shi'ite Arabs, Kurds, Christians, Turkomen, and Yezidis as well as smaller tribes—was more ethnically diverse than any other province in Iraq. These numerous ethnicities created a melting pot city but also led to civic tension. The Tigris River demarcated the city to an extent. Eastern Mosul consisted of primarily Kurds and Shi'ite Arabs while the western bank of the Tigris was predominantly Sunni.[280] The ease with which foreign fighters could transit the Syrian/Iraqi border from the west and enter Mosul added another element of instability and meant that conflict could spark quickly.

During the months leading up to 1/25's deployment to Iraq, the commander, Colonel Robert Brown, worked tirelessly on team building within his brigade. He did this through a number of events specifically designed to increase the unit cohesion and teamwork. In keeping with General Douglas MacArthur's quote, "On the field of friendly strife are sown the seeds that on other days and other fields will bear the fruits of victory," Colonel Brown brought all of his company-level commanders together for various physical fitness events.[281] Whether he was shooting baskets, conducting obstacles courses or leading staff rides, Colonel Brown created a group of leaders who knew they could count on one another when the shooting started.

One novel training technique he employed was to turn the brigade area at Fort Lewis into the fictional country of Kazar. The brigade's barracks and headquarters became FOBs, and leaving the FOB was treated as it would be in combat. Single vehicle convoys were forbidden, administrative movements were tracked by the battalion command posts, and security checkpoints were established on post. Garrison safety restrictions often limited the extent to which realism could be employed during such training exercises, but there was no mistaking Soldiers' change in attitude as they developed a combat-ready mentality. This ethos was tested almost the moment the Lancers arrived in northern Iraq.

The brigade's first challenge from the enemy came in the form of indirect fire. Insurgents, using both mortar and rocket fire, sent dozens of missiles into the American FOBs. In nearly all cases, the explosives landed without major injury. On November 9, 2004, indirect fire caused the brigade's first losses when Major Horst "Gary" Moore and Master Sergeant Steven Auchman were killed by mortar fire on the FOB housing the brigade's tactical operations center. The Soldiers of the brigade were determined to find and kill the mortar and rocket teams.

One particularly interesting pattern to the enemy's behavior was discovered by the brigade's digital topographic support team, a component of the Stryker brigade not found in other U.S. brigades.[282] As the brigade didn't possess the combat power to observe all potential indirect fire locations within and around Mosul, it was imperative that the pattern analysis reduce the locations to the most likely firing points. The team determined that the enemy was using the minarets from mosques as aiming stakes. In a large percentage of mortar and rocket attacks, the rounds came directly over the spires of the mosques.

To counter the mortars, the brigade launched Stryker ground patrols and employed its attached aviation battalion in an aerial countermortar role.[283] Unfortunately, the insurgents soon grew wise to the employment of aviation by watching the Americans' flight patterns around the city. When helicopters were aloft in one part of the city, mortar fire would come from another, uncovered area. To address this problem, the Lancers employed their aviation and Strykers in holding positions. When the brigade's countermortar radars identified mortar fire and the computers generated the firing point, aviation and Strykers were ready to pounce. Using rehearsed routes, the Strykers would move quickly to block the insurgents' exfiltration routes while the OH-58 Kiowas and AH-64 Apache helicopters interdicted the insurgents from the air. Working together, the aviation and ground forces were able to destroy several mortar teams and reduce the indirect fire threat from over 300 rounds fired against the FOBs in November 2004 to fewer than six rounds per month by the end of the deployment.[284]

The Erinys convoy ambush on November 10 initiated a chain reaction that significantly affected security in Mosul. Following the attack, and a near-simultaneous series of contacts on the east side of the river between insurgents and 3/21 IN, the insurgents assaulted three police stations on the west side of the city. By the day's end, only four of the 33 stations in Mosul were occupied by Iraqi police. In many cases, the stations were not actually attacked by insurgents, but when they were threatened, the police abandoned their posts. Following their departure, the buildings were looted of weapons, body armor, communications devices and other critical materials. In many cases, the structures were then burned or, as in some cases, the buildings were completely destroyed with explosives.[285]

In reaction to the police desertions, the Governor of Ninewah, Duraid Kashmoula, ordered a curfew of Mosul effective during the early afternoon and into the next day. In concert, Colonel Brown wasted no time deploying combat power to stem the flow of the insurgents in the city. In a technique that would be duplicated many times in the upcoming year, Soldiers of the 276th Engineer Battalion seized control of the five bridges crossing the Tigris River. Coupled with the bridge closures, 1/24 IN and 3/21 IN initiated a series of random tactical checkpoints to impede the insurgents' ability to move freely.

On Veterans' Day, November 11, 2004, elements of 1/24 IN departed on a planned cordon and search near the Yarmuk Traffic Circle, in northwest Mosul. Upon arriving at the scene, they came under immediate and heavy fire. Over the next three hours of contact, Lieutenant Colonel Erik Kurilla's men engaged insurgents using small arms, attack aviation, seven bunker busting TOW missiles, and two Joint Direct Attack Munitions (JDAM) dropped from fixed-wing aircraft. After killing, capturing, or forcing the withdrawal of all insurgents, the battalion resumed offensive patrolling activities on the west side of the city. The cost to the insurgents was nearly 40 killed in action.

1/24 IN also lost its first Soldier, Specialist Thomas Doerflinger.[286]

Across the river at nearly the same time, the Soldiers of 3/21 IN had their hands full with insurgents in the Palestine neighborhood southeast of the city. After receiving RPG fire during a movement to contact operation, Lieutenant Colonel Michael Gibler's 3/21 IN Gimlets initiated several cordon and search operations and engaged in fierce close combat with the enemy. Over several hours, the Gimlets traded fire with the insurgents before the insurgents finally broke contact. For their efforts, the Gimlets recorded 30 enemy killed and two captured at the cost of five friendly wounded.[287]

During the next two days, contact between U.S. forces and insurgents throughout Mosul remained steady. 3/21 IN fought another significant two-hour battle on November 12 in which RPGs and vehicle-borne improvised explosive devices (VBIED) were used in an attempt to destroy Strykers. In all cases, the Lancers proved ready for the insurgents' best punches, and the Stryker vehicles proved their worth. Strykers were hit numerous times by small-arms fire, RPGs and IEDs but damage was minimal. It was not uncommon for a Stryker to sustain IEDs damage and then roll back to the FOB with fewer than half of its tires in working order. The confidence the Soldiers gained in themselves and in their machines of war was monumental.

Another event of significance was the return of the brigade's third infantry battalion on November 12. Originally detached as the MNC-I operational reserve and then later as a part of the operations in Fallujah, Lieutenant Colonel Todd McCaffrey's 1/5 IN Bobcats had deployed from

Fort Lewis directly to Taji, Iraq, in the south. Events in Mosul in early November and the possibility that insurgents there had reinforced their forces led the MNC-I staff to return the Bobcats to 1/25. Capitalizing on the brigade's incredible digital architecture and the reliability and speed of the Stryker vehicle, 1/5 IN received its orders to return to 1/25 control and traveled the 300 mile distance from Fallujah to Mosul, in less than 24 hours. Highlighting the SBCT's abilities, the battalion, already on the road and out of voice communications range, received a digital fragmentary order to reroute one of its companies to reinforce operations in Hammam Al Alil, an insurgent-related town 20 miles south of Mosul. In stride, C Company moved to Hammam Al Alil while the remainder of the battalion continued their march.

By the time the Bobcats reached Mosul, an Iraqi security force was preparing to reestablish a presence in the police stations throughout the city. Arriving just after the brigade's transfer of authority in October, the 3d Iraqi Commando Battalion, part of the 1st Commando Brigade, was deployed to augment security in Mosul. An Iraqi Ministry of the Interior (MOI) organization, the Commandos had direct ties to the Iraqi Police, which was also an MOI organization. Commanded by the bold and daring Brigadier General Rashid, the Commandos were battle tested months before. Although their techniques were unsound by American standards, they were courageous to a fault.

The Lancer Brigade was new to Iraq and had only recently established ties to the Iraqi National Guard (ING) battalions in Mosul; therefore, it was unfamiliar with the Commando battalion.[288] When the battalion arrived, it had only two embedded American advisors: an active-duty Army Special Forces officer and a retired American officer. Further complicating matters, communications between the Commandos and U.S. forces was hampered by a lack of common operating equipment and a severe shortage of interpreters. The result was a well-intentioned but ill-fated operation in northern Mosul. In an attempt to overcome these shortfalls, a small element led by a sergeant first class and a military police squad was dispatched to provide liaison with the brigade. As fate would have it, the MP squad was called away on November 14 to evacuate a Commando seriously injured in an accidental shooting. This left the Commandos with only a staff sergeant from the brigade staff and the two embedded advisors.

While heading south on November 14 to reassert control at the Four-West Police Station, the Commandos were caught in an intense ambush of small arms and RPG fire almost as soon as they crossed the northernmost bridge. Traveling in U.S.-provided Dodge Ram pickup trucks, the Commandos had almost no protection from the insurgent attack. They fought their way to covered positions in the buildings opposite the insurgents and engaged in a hellish exchange of small-arms fire. Lacking established communications, the Stryker Brigade was unaware of the Commandos' plight.

Using a cellular phone to call for help, one of the American advisors contacted the battle captain on duty in the 1/25 tactical operations center. The brigade leadership immediately dispatched aviation support, UAVs, and a Stryker ground force to assist the Commandos. Once on station, the UAV provided real-time pictures to the leadership in the TOC, and through FM communications with the aviation element, cell phone contact with the Commandos, and the UAV feed to the TOC, the brigade was able to direct fires to assist the Commandos.

Meanwhile, Captain Robert Born's C Company from 3/21 IN and Lieutenant Colonel Gibler's battalion mobile command post—commonly referred to as the TAC—set off to assist with the ground fight, based on their relative proximity to the contact. Crossing over the bridge and into the normal 1/24 area of operations, the digital situational awareness allowed for cross-boundary support without fear of fratricide.[289] After an hour of continued contact, Captain Born's men and the Commandos ended the insurgents' attack, but not before three Commandos were killed and 38 wounded, in addition to one of the American advisers. The lessons regarding communications and coordination with Iraqi Security Forces and the need for better liaison between the two forces would stay with the Lancers throughout the next year. Future ISF actions would always be coordinated and conducted with the knowledge of all friendly units.

In the wake of the collapse of the Mosul police, the brigade reassessed its plans and refocused combat power. With the addition of 1/5 IN, another battalion's worth of combat power was now available in the city and surrounding area with more to follow in the form of three U.S. Infantry battalions—the 1st Battalion, 14th Infantry, the 2d Battalion, 325th Airborne Infantry Regiment and Task Force Tacoma, a mechanized task force with elements from both the 81st Brigade, Washington

National Guard and the 1st Infantry Division—by the time of the January 2005 elections.

October, November and December were marked by insufficient intelligence about the enemy. Without further knowledge, it was difficult to maximize the brigade's assets. Based on Iraqi culture, relationships and trust were built over time and were instrumental to information sharing. When 3/2 departed Iraq, the relationships they had established deteriorated quickly. Sources within the community who had in the past provided information on the insurgency now had to deal with Soldiers who were unfamiliar to them. Those Soldiers in turn, despite their cultural training prior to deployment, were still learning the ways of Arabic culture firsthand.[290] Furthermore, even as the handover from 3/2 and 1/25 was underway, the insurgent movement into Mosul from Fallujah was in full swing but had not yet been detected by Coalition forces.

With time, the Lancer Brigade gained experience. U.S-Iraqi relationships matured, and the amount and quality of intelligence about the enemy increased correspondingly. As a method to improve interaction with the local populace and simultaneously deny the enemy freedom of movement in the city, the brigade created combat outposts (COP) in areas frequented by insurgents. In some cases, Iraqi police stations were occupied and used as combat outposts; in other situations, buildings in key locations were acquired or were built. In all instances, the outposts offered local Iraqis the opportunity to interact with Soldiers from the Lancer Brigade and made it possible for locals to provide information to the Americans. The value of the COPs as a means to disrupt insurgent activities quickly became apparent, as they became flashpoints for enemy action.

In December, 1/24 IN established COP Tampa to provide overwatch on a portion of Main Supply Route (MSR) Tampa. Having paid the Iraqi owner for its use, 1/24 IN occupied a three-story apartment building that provided exceptional observation of the MSR and decent overwatch of Mosul's main neighborhoods. Employing one Stryker infantry platoon of four ICVs and approximately 40 Soldiers, 1/24 IN maintained 24-hour coverage on the road and immediately interrupted the insurgents. Once the COP was fully operational, the rate of IED emplacements fell dramatically.

Toward the end of December, 1/24 IN learned that an attack on COP Tampa was possibly in the works. On the evening of December 28, the unit increased force protection measures around the COP. Then on the afternoon of December 29, a large white dump truck approach COP Tampa from the south. As the truck neared the COP, it increased its speed and then crashed into the first set of concrete barriers. Private First Class Oscar Sanchez, on guard in the building, immediately opened fire, killing the driver and detonating the 2,000 pounds of explosives in the truck's bed. The massive explosion could be seen and heard throughout Mosul. In addition to the blast from the suicide vehicle, enemy small-arms and machine-gun fire erupted and struck the COP.

South of the COP along MSR Tampa, 1/24 IN's TAC was hit almost simultaneously when a suicide car bomb rammed one of the group's Strykers. Once that fire was put out, the TAC sped north and into the hail of projectiles engulfing COP

Tampa. Over the course of the next two hours, the men of 1/24 IN battled the insurgents, employing Maverick missiles from close-air support and other heavy weapons.

When the firing ceased, 1/24 IN was still in possession of COP Tampa. Private Sanchez's fire had forced the suicide bomber to detonate the explosive prematurely. Had the truck traveled another 20 feet, it is quite likely that the building would have been destroyed in the blast. In the event, the southwest face of the building was devastated. Private Sanchez gave his life to save the lives of his fellow platoon members.

The enemy's attempt to destroy COP Tampa cost them approximately 25 killed. It also demonstrated the importance of forward presence in the city.[291] This assault would mark the last time the Lancers faced a coordinated enemy attack of platoon size or larger.

Meanwhile, the brigade continued working a campaign plan designed to achieve peaceful elections to be held in January, 2005.The plan, based on four logical lines of operation—security, governance, economic development, and communications—provided a framework for efforts during the brigade's deployment. The overarching objective was the perception of security within the civilian population. The Lancers understood that simply killing insurgents was no guarantee—if the city was in a constant state of violence, the population would never feel secure, even if the insurgents were on the run. It was important that the civilians feel it was safe for them to participate in civic activities, that the Iraqi security forces were winning, and that elections were a visible indication of progress.

The insurgents knew how dangerous elections could be for their ideology; hence, they initiated an information operations campaign of their own. During November and December, they began a terror campaign of assassination, killing police and members of the Iraqi security forces—Commandos, soldiers on leave, ING members—and dumping their bodies with notes often pinned on them or written on the remains. These messages of intimidation filtered through the informal channels of the population and ensured the local citizenry was uncooperative with U.S. and Iraqi forces.

To counter the insurgents' terrorism, the Lancers' non-lethal effects cell—another Stryker Brigade organic asset—took center stage.[292] Although the lethal fight continued on a day-to-day basis, all violent confrontations were used as ammunition in the information operations battle. Iraqi newspapers, television, and radio became a priority for the brigade. If a car bomb exploded next to a Stryker, images of the inevitable civilian casualties were immediately provided to the local population through the various media sources. In addition, handbills and leaflets were created and distributed to show that the insurgency felt no remorse for killing the Iraqi people. Interaction between the locals and the Soldiers of the Lancer Brigade became a focused affair with coordinated messages designed to instill a perception of security.

At first, the face of the effort was decidedly American. For example, battalion commanders and other leaders conducted weekly radio interviews on the local Iraqi station. Soon, as security improved and Iraqi security and government personnel gained confidence in the situation, they too took to the airwaves. In a mutually supportive effort, civil affairs projects continued with renewed energy. Everything from building new schools to efforts to increase the availability of electricity and water received additional attention. Coupled with the strong themes of security and the upcoming elections, the non-lethal efforts of the brigade quickly became the unit's main focus.

By the middle of January 2005, change was in the air in Mosul. The insurgent attacks during November and December, which were numerous and often extremely violent, were portrayed by the information operations campaign as counter-productive to progress. In addition, the assassination campaign, portrayed to the people of the city as senseless acts of brutality, began to work against the insurgents. Slowly, the people of Mosul began to respond, and optimism for the January 30 elections was on the rise.[293]

The insurgents threatened to turn streets of Mosul red with the blood of the voters. However, the men and women of the Lancer Brigade worked tirelessly to prove the insurgents wrong. At 7 a.m. on January 30, the brigade established UAV coverage in the brigade tactical operations center and moved its eye in the sky to the Rashidiya neighborhood of northern Mosul. At first glance, the Lancers' instincts and three months of combat experience told them there was a problem. The screen showed hundreds of people milling about one of the 40 polling sites. Streaming toward the building was a line of individuals that went past the camera's viewing area.

Almost simultaneously, another report indicated that there were no voters at one of the polling sites that had just opened. Nevertheless, after several minutes, an elderly Iraqi woman crossed the street and walked through security to cast her vote. As if on cue, the remainder of the people watching from across the road mustered the courage to follow suit.

A Stryker patrol went out to investigate and gauge the mood of the populace. Soldiers observed thousands of people moving on foot toward a polling center—and these Iraqis were chanting, smiling and singing. Two months before, it had not seemed possible, but it was happening. Soldiers of the brigade spent the remainder of the day transiting the city, visiting one polling center after the other. At some sites, hundreds of people stood patiently in line; at others, perhaps only a hundred Iraqis filtered through during the entire day. Nevertheless, when the polling sites closed, the Lancers were ecstatic with the results—over 150,000 people braved the insurgent threats and exercised their civic rights.

In Mosul and Ninewah province, the Stryker formations demonstrated that their unique communications, mobility, direct fires, staff planning capabilities and non-lethal resources were well suited to modern urban warfare. While each echelon had to adapt to the particular threat environment of northern Iraq, the Stryker formations' ability to employ their technology in adaptive ways (integrated aviation and ground operations, focused information operations; net-worked ground and UAV sensors), their willingness to adopt new roles (cross training, cultural exchanges with local Iraqis), and their rigorous training, led to success in the most difficult kind of battlefield.

In the three months leading up to the provincial elections, 24 Lancers gave their lives so others might have a chance to experience freedom.[294] During that time and the nine months that followed, the men and women of the Lancer Brigade fostered liberty in a place where none had existed before, and they laid the first stones on the path to freedom for the deserving people of Iraq. The Stryker formations will likely be tested on other battlefields, but the lessons learned on the streets of Mosul, Tall Afar, and villages of the Tigris River Valley will surely enable American Soldiers to prevail again in tomorrow's forests of steel.

EPILOGUE

by Colonel John Antal, U.S. Army (Ret.)
and Lieutenant Colonel Bradley T. Gericke

As the authors of *Forests of Steel* remind us, some of the most difficult scenes of combat during the last 40 years have played out in the steel and concrete terrain of urban battlefields. Whether in cities located in the uplands of Vietnam, the arid plateaus of Afghanistan, the rugged mountains of Chechnya, or battle ravaged Somalia, city fights have pitted armies against one another under the most trying conditions.

Cities, as centers of human interaction, commerce, and political power, matter to people. In many cases, cities form the vital military objectives that will be fought over and through and cannot be avoided. The best that we can do today is to consider the lessons offered by these recent city fights and apply them to the development of our training, organization and equipment.

In 1968 at Hue, a city fight erupted as the North Vietnamese enemy and their Vietcong allies pursued an operational offensive in a bold stroke to win the war. The American Marines who opposed them employed combined arms techniques to deliver accurate direct and indirect fires, ultimately prevailing. Unfortunately, Hue, in a pattern that so often recurs, was largely destroyed.

Just over a decade later, the Soviet army invaded Afghanistan in 1979 and found controlling the cities in that complex land to be extraordinarily difficult. Unable to complement their military occupation with economic and diplomatic programs, the occupying forces were beleaguered by cells of Afghan fighters operating both within the urban sprawl and outside of it. The Afghans waged a persistent war of attrition that eventually compelled the Soviets to retreat.

In contrast to the Soviet experience, the U.S. executed a successful urban operation in Panama in 1989 that quickly overthrew a corrupt government, established stable political and econ-omic conditions, and demonstrated that a carefully defined tactical assault in a city was achievable and could accomplish decisive results.

The 1991 fight in Khafji occurred as a conventional contest between two armies in what was the opening skirmish of the Gulf War, but another battle in the region witnessed a very different sort of exchange. In 1995, Somali clans, jealous of their local power structures, staged an assault in Mogadishu against American peacekeeping forces that prompted the termination of the U.S. presence in that country.

A U.S. opportunity to demonstrate a more sophisticated ability at urban operations began with missions in the Balkans in 1997. There, U.S. and allied troops successfully negotiated competing local agendas to wage the peace and keep the use of force to a minimum. While American Soldiers and Marines were experiencing a variety of successes and defeats, Russian troops suffered much greater losses from their urban operations.

After invading Chechnya in 1994, the Russians assaulted Grozny on multiple occasions. Their attacks were bloody, slow, and destructive. What they lacked in their ability to employ combined arms, the Russians sought to make up for through firepower and sheer brutality. The Chechens responded in kind and the result is that the city of

Grozny ceased to exist as a functioning urban center. City fighting in Grozny looked much as it did in Hue -- a brutally tough, block-by-block battle in a forest of steel and concrete.

In Iraq, the U.S. military, its Allies and the new Iraqi Army have been able to take the cities, but has not has had the combat power to hold them. Unbeatable wherever they fight, the Americans and their allies move from fight to fight, putting out resistance in one region only to have it grow in another. It seems clear that the strategy of "Clear, Hold and Build" is correct – it is merely taking more forces that are currently available in Iraq.

Thus, contemporary city fighting is -- as city fighting has always been -- a perilous undertaking. The high numbers of casualties and tremendous expenditure of resources have made urban combat the option of last resort for American arms. While military doctrine, reinforced by the memory of difficult urban battles in past wars rightfully advocates the avoidance of urban combat, tomorrow's warfighters will not have the choice of refusing a city fight any more than today's Soldiers and Marines can avoid the ongoing and bloody contest for Iraq's cities.

Intelligent opponents have studied the American way of war and will be reluctant to subject themselves to the fury of U.S. precision-strike weaponry. They will not want to expose themselves to America's robust surveillance technologies and will seek refuge in places that allow them to continue to fight. Cities, then, are the best place for an enemy to resist. Moreover, cities, with all of their wealth, population, and power, must be possessed. Our enemies, therefore, will retreat into cities, and

Soldiers and Marines will pursue them there, seeking their destruction.

Forests of Steel foretells that urban warfare is with us to stay. We, the readers, are obligated to heed history's call and prepare.

EDITORS

Colonel John F. Antal, U.S. Army (Ret.) was commissioned as an Armor Officer in the U.S. Army in 1977 after graduating from the U.S. Military Academy at West Point. He served predominately in tank and infantry units for twenty-six years, culminating in an assignment as the G3 (Operations Officer) for the U.S. Army's III Corps at Fort Hood, Texas. Colonel Antal led the 2d Battalion, 72d Armor, the "Dragon Force," an M1A1 tank battalion stationed near the demilitarized zone in the Republic of Korea (1994-1996), served as a Special Assistant to the Chairman of the Joint Chiefs of Staff in Washington, D.C. from 1998-2000, and commanded the 16th Cavalry Regiment at Fort Knox, Kentucky (2000-2002). He earned a Bachelor of Science degree from the United States Military Academy, a Masters of Military Arts and Science degree from the Command and General Staff College and is a 1998 graduate of the Army War College. He is the Founding Editor of the Armchair General military history magazine and has published over 150 magazine articles in military history and military professional journals. He has authored six books: *Armor Attacks, the Tank Platoon*; *Infantry Combat, the Rifle Platoon*; *Combat Team, the Captain's War*; *Proud Legions, A Novel About America's Next War*; *TALON Force Thunderbolt*; and *City Fights, Selected Histories of Urban Combat from World War II.* He is currently a Vice President for Knowledge Operations for Gearbox Software, L.L.C.

Lieutenant Colonel Bradley T. Gericke earned a commission in armor 1988 from the United States Military Academy in 1988. He holds an M.A. and Ph.D. from Vanderbilt University in Early Modern European History and an M.M.A.S. (Strategy) from the U.S. Army Command and General Staff College. Lieutenant Colonel Gericke has published numerous essays regarding military affairs, several American history college texts, and most recently, *City Fights: Selected Histories of Urban Combat from World War II to Vietnam.* He is currently writing *Spearhead: America's Third Armored Division in Peace and War.* Lieutenant Colonel Gericke's assignments include duty in tank battalions of the 3d Armored Division in Germany and Southwest Asia, and the 2d Infantry Division in Korea. He has served as an assistant professor in the Department of History at West Point, as aide-de-camp and speechwriter for the Commanding General, U.S. Army Forces Command, and as an Army Fellow at the Institute of Defense Analyses in Alexandria, Virginia. His latest assignment is speechwriter and strategic policy analyst to the Vice Chief of Staff, Army.

AUTHORS

Lieutenant Colonel Kevin W. Farrell is a 1986 graduate of the United States Military Academy. He possesses the M.A., M.Phil. and Ph.D. in Modern European History from Columbia University, New York. He is a career armor officer who recently commanded 1-64 Armor, 3d Infantry Division, Fort Stewart, Georgia, in Iraq. His operational deployments include operations officer for Task Force 1-77 Armor in Kosovo in 1999 and as an advisor to the Afghan National Army in Kabul, Afghanistan in 2003. His military assignments include tank platoon leader, tank company commander, tank battalion operations officer, tank battalion executive officer and aide-de-camp to the commanding general, V Corps, Heidelberg, Germany. He most recently commanded 1-64 Armor in Iraq, and is now assigned to the faculty of the Department of History, USMA. Lieutenant Colonel Farrell is a graduate of the Armor Officer Basic Course, the Infantry Officer Advanced Course and the Command and General Staff Officers Course.

Lieutenant Colonel Lester W. Grau, **U.S. Army (Ret.)** U.S. Army, is a military analyst with the Foreign Military Studies Office, Fort Leavenworth, Kansas. He received a B.A. from the University of Texas, El Paso and an M.A. from Kent State University. He is a graduate of the U.S. Army Command and General Staff College, the U.S. Army Russian Institute, the Defense Language Institute and the U.S. Air Force War College. He fought in Vietnam and served in a variety of command and staff positions in the U.S., Europe and Korea as an infantry officer and Foreign Area Officer. He has written extensively on Russian and Soviet military topics.

Colonel James K. Greer is a career armor officer who has served in command and operations positions in Germany, the Middle East and the United States. In 1997, Colonel Greer commanded Task Force 1-77 Armor, of the 1st Infantry Division, in the Stabilization Force in Bosnia and Herzegovina. A 1977 graduate of the United States Military Academy, the U.S. Army's School of Advanced Military Studies and the National War College; Colonel Greer holds Masters Degrees in National Strategic Studies, Military Science, and Education.

Thomas Houlahan served in the 82d Airborne Division from 1981-1984 before receiving his commission and returning to the division as an armor platoon leader (Sheridans). He ended his second tour in 1989 as the Ft. Bragg Ammunition Officer. After leaving the service, he served one term in the New Hampshire House of Representatives. Mr. Houlahan holds a Bachelor's degree in History from Campbell University, a Master's degree in Government, also from Campbell, and a Juris Doctorate from Franklin Pierce Law Center. He is the author of *Gulf War: The Complete History*.

Lieutenant Colonel Evan A. Huelfer is a 1987 graduate of the United States Military Academy. He holds a Master's degree and Ph.D. in History from the University of North Carolina. He has led troops in combat as rifle platoon leader, commanded a

Long Range Surveillance Detachment, served as a staff officer at the battalion and brigade level, and taught Military History at West Point.

Jacob W. Kipp is a senior analyst with the Foreign Military Studies Office, Fort Leavenworth, Kansas. He graduated from Shippensburg State College and received a Ph.D. from Pennsylvania State University. He has published extensively in the fields of Russian and Soviet military history and serves as the American editor of the journal European Security. He is an Adjunct Professor of History with the University of Kansas and teaches in the Russian and European Studies Program.

Colonel Ali Ahmad Jalali is a former Afghan Army officer. A distinguished graduate of the Military University in Kabul, he has attended the U.S. Infantry Officers Advanced Course, the British Army Staff College, the U.S. Naval Postgraduate School, the Frunze Academy in Moscow, and the Institute of World Politics in Washington, DC. He has also taught in the Military Academy and advanced military schools in Kabul. Colonel Jalali joined the Mujahideen in 1980 and served as the top military planner on the directing staff of the Islamic Unity of Afghan Mujahideen (an alliance of three moderate Mujahideen factions) during the early 1980s before joining the Voice of America (VOA). As a journalist, he has covered Central Asia and Afghanistan for the past 15 years. He is the author of several books including works on the Soviet Military, works on Central Asia, and a three-volume Military History of Afghanistan. He is a co-author with Lester W. Grau of *The Other Side of the Mountain: Mujahideen Tactics in the Soviet-Afghan*

War, which is based on their interviews with eighty-five Mujahideen commanders.

Brigadier General Brian A. Keller is a 1980 University of Connecticut ROTC Distinguished Military Graduate who has served his nation for over twenty years as an Army tactical military intelligence officer. He has commanded intelligence units from company through brigade, and has served as the senior intelligence officer (S2/G2) for the 2d Squadron, 1st Cavalry Regiment, 10th Mountain Division (Light Infantry), and 1st Ranger Battalion, 75th Ranger Regiment, where he participated in Operation Just Cause. His recent assignments include Deputy Commanding General/Assistant Commandant, United States Army Intelligence Center and School, Fort Huachuca, Arizona, and Director of Intelligence, J-2, United States European Command, Germany. A graduate of the DIA's Post Graduate Intelligence Program and the U.S. Army's Command and General Staff College and War College, he also holds a Masters of Military Art and Science from the School of Advanced Military Studies.

Lieutenant Colonel Robert W. Lamont, U.S. Army (Ret.) USMC, is currently an Operations Analyst working for the Marine Corps Program Department in Fallbrook, California. His operational assignments include company-level tank billets, service afloat as a Guard Officer on the USS Constellation (CV-64) and Combat Cargo Officer on the USS Cleveland (LPD-7). He taught at the U.S. Army Armor School in both the Basic and Advanced Courses. He served as an exercise Action Officer responsible for Tandem Thrust in Australia and Cobra Gold in Thailand. As an analyst assigned to the Marine Corps Combat Development Command he was the lead Analyst for the Anti-Armor Force Structure Analysis, Joint Air Defense and Combat Identification Test, and the Advanced Amphibious Assault Vehicle Study.

Major Seth L. Morgulas was commissioned through the Reserve Officer Training Corps after graduating from the Johns Hopkins University. He served as a platoon leader in D Company, 2-72 Armor and C Troop 5-17 Cavalry in the Republic of Korea and in A Company 3-67 Armor where he also served as executive officer. Prior to leaving active duty Captain. Morgulas was a force modernization officer and division rear battle captain in the 4th Infantry Division. Captain Morgulas is a graduate of the University of Chicago Law School and has been in private practice for several years. Recently, Maj. Morgulas joined the 1-101 Cavalry, New York Army National Guard as the battalion maintenance officer and was then assigned as HHC commander prior to being reassigned to command B Battery 1-258 Field Artillery at Baghdad, Iraq.

Lieutenant Colonel Clayton Odie Sheffield served as the Brigade S3 for the 3d Brigade 'Rakkasans,' 101st Airborne Division (Air Assault) during OPERATION IRAQI FREEDOM. He also served as the Battalion XO and S3 of the 3d Battalion 187th Infantry Regiment, 101st Airborne Division (Air Assault) in Afghanistan during Operation Enduring Freedom. Previously he served as a company commander in IFOR during Operation Joint Endeavor. He has tactical assignments with the 25th Infantry Division (Light), 1st

Infantry Division, and the 3d Infantry Division. He earned a BS from the University of Florida, a MS from the Naval Postgraduate School, and an MMAS from the Command and General Staff College.

Major Douglas A. Sims, II, currently serves as the Executive Officer to the Director, U.S. Special Operations Command, Center of Knowledge and Futures (J7/J9). Prior to this assignment, he served in the 1st Brigade, 25th Infantry Division (Stryker) as the Executive Officer, 1st Battalion, 5th Infantry Regiment, and then as the Brigade Operations Officer (S3). During his position as the Brigade S3, 1/25 SBCT deployed to northern Iraq for Operation Iraqi Freedom. Prior to his assignment in the Stryker Brigade, Major Sims commanded companies in the 1st Battalion, 501st Parachute Infantry Regiment and in the 3d Infantry Regiment, and he led platoons in the 2d Ranger Battalion and 82d Airborne Division. He holds a BS from the United States Military Academy, a MA from Webster University, and is a graduate of the U.S. Army's Command and General Staff College.

NOTES

Preface

[1] United Nations Centre for Human Settlements (Habitat), *An Urbanizing World: Global Report on Human Settlements 1996* (Oxford: Oxford University Press, 1996), 1, 27. For other trends in world urbanization, see also World Resources Institute, *World Resources 1996-97: A Guide to the Global Environment* (Washington, DC, 1996).

[2] The dissonance between political ideals and the military costs in the Vietnam War continues to resonate in the popular press. See Colonel (Ret.) Bruce B. G. Clarke, "What We Should Have Learned From The Vietnam Experience," *Baltimore Sun*, April 16, 2000.

Chapter One

[3] Russell W. Glenn, *Combat in Hell: A Consideration of Constrained Urban Warfare* (Santa Monica, CA: Rand, 1996), 1.

[4] Max Weber, *The City* translated and edited by Don Martindale and Gertrud Neuwirth, (New York: The Free Press, 1958), 65-90.

[5] After Warsaw (1939) but before Stalingrad (1942), Hitler was very reluctant to commit his troops to prepared assaults on cities.

[6] Jacqueline Beaujeu-Garnier, "Conclusion," in Jacqueline Beaujeu-Garnier and Bernard Dezert, eds., *La Grande Ville: enjeu du XXIe Siecle* (Paris: Presse Universitaires de France, 1991), 619.

[7] Paul K. Van Riper, "A Concept for Future Military Operations on Urbanized Terrain", *Marine Corps Gazette*, (October 1997), insert, A-1.

[8] For a discussion of the Los Angeles and Rio de Janeiro operations, see William W. Mendel, "Combat in Cities: The Los Angeles Riots and Operation Rio", *Low Intensity Conflict & Law Enforcement*, Volume 6, Number 1 (Summer 1997), 184-204.

[9] For a discussion of Afghan urban guerrillas, see Lester W. Grau, *The Other Side of the Mountain: Mujahideen Tactics in the Soviet-Afghan War*, (Quantico: USMC Study DM-980701, 1998), Chapter 14.

[10] For a discussion of the battle for Grozny, see Timothy L. Thomas, "The Caucasus Conflict and Russian Security: The Russian Armed Forces Confront Chechnya. Military-Political Aspects and Military Activities, 11-31 December 1994", *The Journal of Slavic Military Studies*, Volume 8, Number 2 (June 1995), 233-256; "The Caucasus Conflict and Russian Security: The Russian Armed Forces Confront Chechnya. Military Activities 11-31 December 1994", *The Journal of Slavic Military Studies*, Volume 8, Number 2 (June 1995), 257-290; and "The Caucasus Conflict and Russian Security: The Russian Armed Forces Confront Chechnya. The Battle for Grozny, 1-26 January 1995", *The Journal of Slavic Military Studies*, Volume 10, Number 1 (March 1997), 50-108.

[11] A prime example is the U.S. intervention in Mogadishu, Somalia, which began as a mission to feed a starving populace and then switched to taking an active side in a civil war. A U.S. Army ranger battalion was sent into the United Nations area with a purely combat mission. In an unprecedented development, after President Clinton's emissary (former-President Carter) had met with Aideed, the United States State Department was engaged in diplomatic overtures with Aideed at the same time that the rangers were sent to capture him. A complicated coalition and U.S. chain of command further contributed to the ensuing debacle.

[12] Randolph A. Gangle, "The Foundation for Urban Warrior," *Marine Corps Gazette*, (July 1998): 52.

[13] The Chechens made an exception of the presidential palace and held this as a permanent strong point for its symbolic value.

[14] Gangle, 53.

[15] Ibid.

[16] Robert H. Scales, Jr., "The Indirect Approach: How U.S. Military Forces Can Avoid the Pitfalls of Future Urban Warfare," *Armed Forces Journal International*, (October 1998), 74.

[17] Blockades do not always achieve their intended purpose. The on-going blockades and embargos of Cuba, Libya, Iran and Iraq have not resulted in dramatic policy shifts by the leaders of these states. The people have learned to adjust to economic hardship. They can also learn to adjust to the demands of war.

[18] See Lester W. Grau and Jacob W. Kipp, "Chistilishche" [Purgatory], *The Journal of Slavic Military Studies*, (March 2000), 238-249.

[19] See Timothy L. Thomas and Lester W. Grau, "Russian Lessons Learned from the Battles for Grozny," *Marine Corps Gazette*, (April 2000), 45-48.

[20] Lester W. Grau and William A. Jorgensen, "Viral Hepatitis and the Russian War in Chechnya," *U.S. Army Medical Department Journal*, (May/June 1997), 4.

[21] For a look at Russian communications work-arounds during the battle for Grozny, see Lester W. Grau, "Urban Warfare Communications: A Contemporary Russian View," *Red Thrust Star*, (July 1996), 5-10.

[22] Lester W. Grau, "Russian Urban Tactics: Lessons from the Battle for Grozny," *Strategic Forum*, (July 1995), 3.

[23] Lester W. Grau, *The Bear Went Over the Mountain: Soviet Combat Tactics in Afghanistan*, (London: Frank Cass Publishers, 1998), 50-51.

[24] Grau, "Russian Urban Tactics", 3.

[25] Ibid, 3-4.

[26] For a look at the logistics side of urban combat, see Lester W. Grau and Timothy L. Thomas, "'Soft Log' and Concrete Canyons: Russian Urban Combat Logistics in Grozny," *Marine Corps Gazette*, (October 1999), 67-75.

[27] Grau, "Russian Urban Tactics", 3.

Chapter Two

[28] Keith William Nolan, *Battle for Hue, Tet 1968*, (New York: Dell Publishing Company, Inc., 1983), 75-76.

[29] Ibid., 32.

[30] Ibid., 38.

[31] FM 31-50, *Combat in Fortified and Built-up Areas,* (Headquarters, Department of the Army, 1964), 46.

[32] General Van Tein Dung, *Our Great Spring Victory*, (Monthly Review Press, London, England, 1977), 31.

[33] Nolan, 3.

[34] Ibid., xiii.

[35] Ibid., 13.

[36] Ibid., 16.

[37] Ibid., 42. The Ontos is a light tracked vehicle, weighing about seven tons, with a crew of two. It mounted six 106mm recoilless rifles, three on each side, on the outside of the vehicle. The vehicle commander could fire a .50 cal spotting round and once these rounds were on target he would follow-up with the 106mm anti-armor round. The six tubes could be fired one at a time or in a single six-gun volley. The armor of the Ontos was too light to provide any head-to-head anti-armor capability but the ability to fire six 106mm canister

rounds at one time proved to be a very effective anti-infantry weapon for the battlefields of Vietnam.

[38] Ibid., 42-3.

[39] Ibid., 43.

[40] Ibid., 44-5.

[41] Ibid., 69.

[42] John Hill, *Tet Offensive, 1968*, (Conflict , Simulations Design Corporation, San Diego Calif. 1973), 39.

[43] Ibid., 40.

[44] Nolan, 113.

[45] Ibid., 123.

[46] Ibid., 141.

[47] First Lieutenant Scott Nelson, *Lessons Learned Company C, 1st Battalion, 5th Marines, Operation Hue City, 31 January to 5 March 1968*, (www.ditc.mil/ndia/infantry/warr.pdf), 11.

[48] Nolan, 167.

[49] Nolan, 184-185.

[50] Marine Corps Combat Development Command, *Analysis of the Antiarmor Force Mix and Operational Methodology*, (Marine Corps Combat Development Command, Quantico, Virginia, 1993), B-2.

[51] Ibid., 4.

[52] Ibid.

Chapter Three

[53] The bulk of this chapter is based on Chapter 14 of Ali Ahmad Jalali and Lester W. Grau, The Other Side of the Mountain: Mujahideen Tactics in the Soviet-Afghanistan War (Quantico: USMC Study DM-980701, December, 1998).

[54] Based on Ali Jalali's interviews with Mohammad Amin Modaqeq, an HIH Mujahideen commander from Mazar-e Sharif, and Commander Didar Khan of NLFA from Kabul. Both interviews were conducted in Peshawar in September 1996

[55] The Soviets attempted to separate the rural guerrillas from the populace by bombing the rural populace and forcing some 5.5 million (one/third of the pre-war populace) to flee to Pakistan and Iran as refugees.

[56] Two million Afghan refugees fled from the countryside to the Afghan cities. They built their own refugee camps on the city periphery and in the suburbs.

[57] There were three rings around the capital city of Kabul.

[58] A description and sketch of one of these outposts is in Lester W. Grau, *The Bear Went Over the Mountain: Soviet Combat Tactics in the War in Afghanistan* (London: Frank Cass Publishers, 1998), 112-114.

[59] For an account of Soviet artillery use in Herat, see Grau, *The Bear Went Over the Mountain,* 48-51.

[60] Jalali and Grau, *The Other Side....*, pp. 369-370

[61] Ibid, 366-367.

[62] Ibid, 373-374.

[63] Ibid, 387.

[64] Ibid, 105 and 115.

Chapter Four

[65] Caleb Baker, Thomas Donnelly, and Margaret Roth, *Operation Just Cause: The Storming of Panama* (New York: Lexington Books, 1991), 43-47.

[66] Ibid., 247.

[67] Ibid., 93-96.

[68] Ibid., 96-101.

[69] Ibid.

[70] Robert D. Murphy, Written Interview, April 1992.

[71] The 3rd Battalion-504th Parachute Infantry Regiment from the 82nd Airborne Division at Fort Bragg, North Carolina, trained at the Jungle Operations Training Center at Fort Sherman, Panama at the time of *Operation Just Cause*. The battalion was divided up to conduct various combat missions during *Just Cause*. One platoon from that battalion was attached to our company for the mission at Coco Solo.

[72] Christopher J. Rizzo, Written Interview, March 1992.

[73] Daniel K. Kirk, Personal Interview, March 1992.

[74] Baker, Donnelley and Roth, 247-248.

[75] Major Tom Ryan, 4-17's Operations Officer, refutes Gray's story. "He didn't have an order. He didn't have a mission to take anything down, simply to block," clarified Ryan.

[76] Ibid., 240-242.

[77] Jimmie C. Mahana, Personal Interview, March 1992.

[78] Johnny W. Brooks, Written Interview, March 1992.

[79] Rizzo Interview.

[80] Mahana Interview.

[81] Walter Burke, Personal Interview, January 1998, and Baker, 246.

[82] David Rainer, Written Interview, April 1992.

[83] Ibid.

[84] Ibid.

[85] Baker, Donnelley and Roth, 251.

[86] Kirk Interview.

[87] United States Army, 4th Battalion, 17th Infantry, Operations Log, December 1989.

[88] Kirk Interview.

[89] Baker, Donnelley and Roth, 248.

[90] Richard M. Mowatt, Written Interview, April 1992.

[91] Baker, Donnelley and Roth, 249.

[92] Mowatt Interview.

[93] Mowatt and Burke Interviews.

[94] Burke Interview.

[95] Rizzo Interview.

[96] Burke Interview.

[97] Mowatt Interview.

[98] Burke and Mahana Interviews.

[99] Rizzo Interview.

[100] Clarence L. Wolfe Personal Interview, December 1991.

[101] Mowatt Interview.

[102] Rizzo Interview.

[103] Baker, Donnelley and Roth, 253.

[104] Mowatt Interview.

[105] United States Army, 4th Battalion, 17th Infantry, Intelligence Log, December 1989.

[106] United States Army, 4th Battalion, 17th Infantry, Operations Log, December 1989.

[107] Brooks Interview.

[108] United States Army, 4th Battalion, 17th Infantry, Operations Log, December 1989.

[109] Burke and Mowatt Interviews.

[110] United States Army, 4th Battalion, 17th Infantry, Operations Log, December 1989.

[111] Brooks Interview.

[112] Rizzo Interview.

[113] George Wilson, *If You Survive* (New York: Ivy Books, 1987), 41.

[114] Burke Interview.

[115] Murphy Interview.

Chapter Five

[116]http://www.pbs.org/wgbh/pages/frontline/gulf/oral/schwarzkopf

[117] The Battle of Khafji was actually a number of separate engagements involving U.S. Marines and Saudi and Qatari forces from 29 January to 1 February 1991. My Thanks to Colonel Martin Stanton, a senior U.S. Army advisor to the Saudi National Guard during the Battle of Khafji, who wrote a detailed account of the battle in Armor (March–April 1996, pp. 6–11) and answered dozens of my questions in a series of interviews. I also owe a debt to U.S. Marine officers and U.S. Army Special Forces advisors for information they provided.

[118] Abu Bakr, Othman and Omar were the three successors to the prophet Mohammed as leader of Islam. Tariq bin Ziyad was the Moorish conqueror of Spain.

[119] Though tons of bombs were dropped, little damage was done by the B-52s. They dropped their bombs from extremely high altitude, and accuracy suffered. In addition, many of the bombs were dropped on false targets picked up by JSTARS (Joint Target Attack Radar System). For example, in one instance, the reported destruction of a column of 80 armored vehicles during this period was found after G-Day to have been a raid on a long stretch of densely packed concertina wire.

[120] Whether the Iraqi company was forming to launch a counterattack or leave Khafji remains unclear.

Chapter Six

[121] A wealth of information is at the PBS *Frontline*, "Ambush in Mogadishu" website. Information is also available online at the various pages of the United Nations web sites.

[122] "Islamist fighters declare victory in Somali capital." *TimesOnline*, June 5, 2006.

[123] During the 1990s, it became somewhat trendy to disparage Clausewitz's writings. For a summary of contemporary theorists' wanderings as well as a robust explication of *On War,* see Colin S. Gray, "Clausewitz,

history, and the future strategic world," in *The Past as Prologue: The Importance of History to the Military Profession*, ed. Williamson Murray and Richard Hart Sinnreich (Cambridge University Press, 2006) 111-132.

[124] The French in Algeria and the Americans in Vietnam are two other examples of Western armies misunderstanding their foes. Western forces in each case erringly assumed that temperate responses could eliminate challenges to order.

[125] U.S. Army Field Manual 3-0, *Operations*, (June 2001), categorizes the types of military engagement that may confront American ground forces. It is a product of experiences like Somalia. According to this new doctrine, intervention in Somalia would have been termed a "foreign humanitarian assistance" (FHA) mission, a specific type of "support" operation. An FHA in a hostile environment may also be a "peace enforcement" operation that in turn is a sub-category of a "peace" operation, which is a component of a "stability" operation. p. 9-7. This hierarchy of classification hints at the complexity confronting Soldiers on the ground. See chapters 9 and 10.

[126] Unless noted otherwise, geographic and demographic statistics regarding Somalia come from Defense Language Institute, *Somalia: An Area Study*, January 1993.

[127] Before the recent civil war, education was free and compulsory, and the literacy rate had grown from about 5 percent in the early 1970s to 24 percent in 1990. Since war resumed in the late 1980s, however, most schools closed.

[128] The vegetation is primarily coarse grass and stunted thorn, acacia, eucalyptus, and mahogany trees Wildlife includes crocodiles, elephants, giraffes, leopards, lions, and zebras. Somalia has few natural resources, although mineral deposits await development. Before the most recent round of civil war, Somalia's economy was based on raising livestock. Crop farming was important only in the south. Principal crops were maize (corn), sorghum, bananas, and sugarcane.

[129] For information regarding the physical challenges of Somalia in military terms, see the following: Preventive Medicine Consultants Division, Office of the Surgeon General of the Army, *Staying Healthy in Somalia: Preliminary Recommendations*, December 3, 1992.; Defense Language Institute, *Surviving in Somalia #2*, December 1992.; Third U.S. Army, *Central Region Area Orientation*, Misc. Pub. 600-1, September 15, 1989; Professional Services Directorate, Office of the Surgeon General of the Army, *Diagnosis and Treatment of Diseases of Importance in Somalia*, 1st Edition, December, 1992.; Fort Drum Division Mental Health Section, *Combat Stress Control Handbook*, (not dated).; U.S. Army Corps of Engineers, *Manual of Environmental Effects: The Horn of Africa*, TEC-SR-4, December 1992.; U.S. Army Medical Research and Development Command, *Sustaining Soldier Health and Performance in Somalia: Guidance for Small Unit Leaders*, U.S.ARIEM Technical Note 93-1, December 1992.; The Defense Intelligence Agency and Armed Forces Medical Intelligence Center, *Operation Restore Hope: Health Risks and Countermeasures in Somalia*, AFMIC-1810R-058-92, December, 1992.; United States Army Intelligence and Threat Analysis Center, *Restore Hope: Soldier Handbook*, ATC-RM-1100-065-93.; The Economist Intelligence Unit Limited, *EIU Country Profile: Somalia*, (1993-1994), 49-70.

[130] Technological amenities to connect Somalis were not widespread. Only one in 434 Somalis own a telephone, and one in 22 possess radios. There were only less than 11,000 passenger cars and about 12,000 commercial vehicles in the country.

[131] Allard, 10-12.

[132] Principal trading partners are Italy and Saudi Arabia. Per Capita Gross Domestic Product averages about $500.

[133] The ancient Egyptians knew the region of Somalia as Punt. From the 2nd to the 7th Century A.D., the area belonged to the Ethiopian kingdom of Aksum. Arab tribes created a sultanate along the northern coast in the 7th century, and the Cushitic Somali began to migrate from Yemen in the 13th

Century. During the 16th Century, the sultanate disintegrated into small independent states. Great Britain colonized the nearby Arabian coast in 1839, and in 1875, Egypt occupied parts of Somalia. When Egypt withdrew, the British moved in to protect the Suez Canal route to their empire in India. Italy also acquired a foothold along Somalia's Indian Ocean coast. The British withdrew to the coastal regions in 1910, and Italy extended its control inland. In 1936, Italy merged Italian Somaliland, Eritrea, and Ethiopia into Italian East Africa, but after World War II (1939-1945), Italy gave up all its possessions in Africa. In 1949, the United Nations adopted a plan that granted Somalia independence in 1960. Major General Muhammad Siad Barre seized power in 1967 and declared Somalia a socialist state. In 1977, Somalia began fighting Ethiopia over Ethiopia's Ogaden region, and in 1982 insurgent groups clashed with government troops. The hostilities with Ethiopia ended in 1988, but the civil war intensified and precipitated U.N. involvement.

[134] Center for Army Lessons Learned (CALL), *Operations Other Than War: Operation Restore Hope Lessons Learned Report* (Fort Leavenworth, KS: U.S. Army Combined Arms Command, 1993), 2.

[135] A summary of the implementing U.N. Security Resolutions for Somalia operations:

-UNOSOM: #751, April 24, 1992

-UNITAF: #794, December 3, 1992

-UNOSOM II: #814, March 26, 1993

[136] Kenneth Allard, *Somalia Operations: Lessons Learned*. (Washington D.C.: National Defense University Press, 1995), 3-4.

[137] CALL, *Operation Restore Hope Lessons Learned Report*, 2. During its six months of execution, *Provide Relief* shipments averaged about 150 metric tons of supplies daily for a total of 28,000 tons overall. Allard, 15.

[138] Allard, 17.

[139] Ibid., 18.

[140] A significant literature has already been published concerning the intricacies of U.S.-UN and joint command relationships and deployment-related issues that confronted U.S. armed forces in Somalia. It is not the purpose of this short paper to review such subjects in any detail. Interested readers may consult works fully referenced elsewhere in these notes to include Kenneth Allard's *Somalia Operations*, which includes a bibliography with a number of relevant joint publications; the Center for Army Lessons Learned *Operation Restore Hope: Lessons Learned Report* contains numerous organizational charts in its appendices.

[141] In one case, American troops destroyed several "technicals" (pickup trucks sporting heavy weapons) with attack helicopters. U.S. Soldiers likewise became targets of snipers.

[142] Task Force Ranger consisted of U.S. Army special operations forces and helicopters, U.S. Air Force special tactics troops, and U.S. Navy SEALS. See Richard W. Stewart, *The United States Army in Somalia, 1992-1994* (Arlington, Virginia: Association of the United States Army, Institute of Land Warfare Commemorative Edition, 2002), p. 14.

[143] Accounts of the operation in Somalia and the fight in Mogadishu are plentiful. The most substantial book about the fight itself is Mark Bowden's, *Black Hawk Down: A Story of Modern War* (New York: Atlantic Monthly Press, 1999). Other works include: Charles P. Ferry, "Mogadishu, October 1993: Personal Account Of A Rifle Company XO," *Infantry* (September-October, 1994): 23-31, and "Mogadishu, October 1993: A Company XO's Notes On Lessons Learned," *Infantry* (November-December, 1994): 31-38; Michael Elliot, "The Making of A Fiasco," *Newsweek*, October 18, 1993, 34-38 and Tom Post et. al., "Fire Fight From Hell," *Newsweek*, October 18, 1993, 39-43; Kent DeLong and Steven Tuckey, *Mogadishu: Heroism and Tragedy* (Westport, CT: Praeger,

1994); Phil Parker, Center for Army Lessons Learned (CALL), *QRF Summary of Combat Operations* (Falcon

Brigade, 10th Mountain Division), October 3, 1993; Mark Walsh, "Managing Peace Operations in The Field," *Parameters*, (Summer 1996): 32-49.; Vernon Loeb, "Deadly Assets: The CIA's Failure in Somalia," *Washington Post*, February 27, 2000.; Patrick J. Sloyan, "Somalia Mission Control; Clinton Called The Shots In Failed Policy Targeting Aidid," *Newsday*, December 5, 1993 (4 parts).

[144] For examinations of urban warfighting and how the urban context affects military operations see GJ. Ashworth, *War And The City* (London: Routledge, 1991), and Russell W. Glenn, *Combat In Hell: A Consideration of Constrained Urban Warfare* (Rand, 1996). Interestingly, as the war in Vietnam was winding down the U.S. Army published a lengthy manual that outlines how American Soldiers should fight in an urban setting: U.S. Army Infantry School, *Combat In Cities Report*. 3 vols. Ft. Benning, GA, 1972.

[145] Ralph Peters presents the interesting notion that the "human terrain" of a city ought to be of equal interest to the military professional. He demonstrates his point by offering that cities might be classified as either "hierarchical," "multicultural," or "tribal." Such definitions are not ironclad, but serve to represent the kinds of human interaction, organization, and civic institutions that may be found in each type of city. Military ramifications thus depend in part in the type of human arrangements are ongoing in the city. Mogadishu would probably fall into the "tribal" category. See Ralph Peters, "The Human Terrain of Urban Operations" *Parameters* Vol. XXX, No. 1 (Spring 2000), 4-12.

[146] The following references present various aspects of UNOSOM II's mission and the fight of October 3 - 4: Elroy Garcia, "Hoping For the Best, Expecting the Worst," *Soldiers*, February, 1994, 13-16.; "We Did Right That Night," *Soldiers*, February, 1994, 17-20.; Lawrence Casper, "The Aviation Brigade As A Maneuver Headquarters," *ARMY*, March, 1995, 21-23.; Chester A. Crocker, "The Lessons of Somalia," *Foreign Affairs*, 74 (May/June 1995), 2-9.; Kent DeLong, and

Steven Tuckey, *Mogadishu!: Heroism and Tragedy.* Westport, Connecticut: Praeger, 1994, Center for Army Lessons Learned. *U.S. Army Operations in Support of UNOSOM II Lessons Learned Report, 4 May 93—31 March 94.* Fort

Leavenworth, Kansas; U.S. Army Combined Arms Command, (undated).; Major Phil Parker, *Summary of Combat Operations, 3-4 October 1993, Mogadishu, Somalia.* Quick Reaction Force, Falcon Brigade, 10th Mountain Division.; Captain Charles P Ferry, "Mogadishu, October 1993: Personal Account of a Rifle Company XO." *Infantry,* September-October 1994, 23-31, and "Mogadishu, October 1993: A Company XO's Notes on Lessons Learned." *Infantry,* November-December 1994, 31-38.

[147] During August and September, Task Force Ranger conducted six missions in Mogadishu. Stewart, 14.

[148] The pilot of the aircraft, CWO Michael Durant, was later taken captive from this site.

[149] Stewart, 17.

[150] "Humvee" is a shorthand term for the Army's High Mobility Multipurpose Wheeled Vehicle, the modern-day "Jeep."

[151] Chronologies vary from account to account. The times mentioned here are drawn from PBS, *Frontline: Ambush In Mogadishu.*

[152] Sixteen fatalities were from Task Force Ranger and two from 2-14 Infantry. The Malaysian force lost two killed and seven wounded, while the Pakistanis suffered two wounded. See Stewart, 19.

[153] Bowden, 329, 333. Aidid survived, only to die August 1, 1996, of gunshot wounds inflicted by rivals.

[154] Other battles have likewise caused politicians to act decisively. Bunker Hill in 1775 prompted a reluctant Continental Congress to action; First Bull Run caused

Abraham Lincoln to accelerate Union war preparations and Antietam prompted his issue of the Emancipation Proclamation; in this century, the Japanese attack on Pearl Harbor galvanized American support for World War II, while the attack by North Vietnamese forces during the "Tet" Offensive shook U.S. confidence. The difference between these cases and the fight in Mogadishu lies in both the resources involved and in their context. Each of the former were events within large-scale conflicts and each involved many times the number of troops engaged in the fight in Somalia. The fight in Mogadishu was in terms of numbers, a minor tactical contest that nonetheless contained significant strategic implications. In addition, conventional military forces fought it in a conventional manner. Hence, it was not merely a "political" action or event.

[155] Anthony Loyd, "Clouds Bring More Misery For Somalis," *London Times*, April 19, 2000.

[156] The dissonance between political ideals and the military costs in the Vietnam War continues to resonate in the popular press. See Colonel (Ret.) Bruce B. G. Clarke, "What We Should Have Learned From The Vietnam Experience," *Baltimore Sun*, April 16, 2000 from http://ebird.dtic.mil/Apr2000/s20000419what.htm

[157] Association of The United States Army, Institute of Land Warfare, *AUSA Torchbearer Issue: The Fiscal Year 2000 Defense Budget—Path To Unpreparedness*, (March 1999): 1.

[158] Emily Wax, "Dying for Water in Somalia's Drought." *WashingtonPost.com*, April 14, 2006.

Chapter Seven

[159] Russian Defense Minister Pavel Grachev in December 1994, before any Russian ground troops entered Chechnya, cited in Christopher Pancio, *Conflicts in the Caucasus, Russia's War in Chechnya* (London: Research Institute for the Study of Conflict and Terrorism, July 1995) 14.

[160] John B. Donlop, *Russia Confronts Chechnya, Roots of a Separatist Conflict* (Cambridge: Cambridge University Press, 1998) 167.

[161] "Kvashnin Describes Chechnya Operation," *Krasnya Zvezda*, (March 2, 1995) 3.

[162] Carl van Dyke, "From Kabul to Grozny," in *The Journal of Slavic Military Studies, Volume 9s* (London: Frank Cass Publisher, December 1996) 698.

[163] Carlotta Gall and Thomas de Wall, *Chechnya: Calamity in the Caucasus* (New York: New York University Press, 1998) 179.

[164] *Ibid.*, 180.

[165] "Kvashnin Describes Chechnya Operation," 2.

[166] Pavel Grachev as quoted in Thomas, 8.

[167] Spetsnaz are Russian Federal Force Special Forces units. Spetsnaz were highly effective in the Soviet Union's fighting in Afghanistan in the 1980s.

[168] "Kvashnin Describes Chechnya Operation," 5.

[169] Chechen leader Sheikh Mansur Ushurma led an uprising that reached from north Dagestan to the Kuban and lasted from 1785-1789. In 1785, Sheikh Mansur's forces destroyed an entire Tsarist army. He was finally captured and died in prison in 1793. Additional Chechen wars of revolt against Czarist rule broke out in 1830s, 1877-88 and again in 1922. The name of the capital of Chechnya, which means "menacing" in Russian, was the result of a fort built by Russian General Yermolov, Governor of the Georgia and the Caucasus (1816-26) who subdued the Chechens with terror and military might.

[170] Ian MacWilliam, "Russian Forces Face Long Haul," *Newsday*(January 22, 1995) A17.

[171] There are reported to be over separate 150 Chechen clans.

[172] General Pavel Grachev, "We Must Proceed from the Fact that This Was a Special Operation," *Krasnaya Zvezda* (March 2, 1995) 2.

[173] The *Maikop* Brigade gets its name from the capital of Adygheya, another autonomous republic in the foothills of the Greater Caucasus. The soldiers of Group *Sever* were virtual strangers to each other as the 131st *Maikop* Brigade was hastily filled with new recruits; some were not even issued ammunition for fear that they might shoot friendly civilians.

[174] Anatol Lieven, "The Meaning of the Chechen War," unpublished article. (Spring, 1996) 7.

[175] Carlotta Gall and Thomas de Waal, *Chechnya, Calamity in the Caucasus* (New York: New York University Press) 9.

[176] Yuri Zarakhovich, "Just Look at What They Have Done to Us," *TIME Magazine*. (New York: Time Inc., January 16, 1995) 46.

[177] "Kvashnin Describes Chechnya Operation," 8.

[178] Ibid., 8.

[179] Mariya Dementyeva, "The Lessons of the Last Phase of the Chechen Operation," *Segodnya*, (February 15, 1995) 9.

[180] Anatol Lieven, *Chechnya, Tombstone of Russian Power* (New Haven: Yale University Press, 1998) 112.

[181] Captain Second Rank Andrey Antipov, "Not a Matter of a Decoration. If Only There Were a Motherland" (Moscow: VOIN for ROSSIYSKAYA GAZETA, September 6, 1995), 3.

[182] Charles Blandly, David Isby, David Markov and

Steven Zaloga, "The Chechen Conflict A Microcosm of the Russian Army's Past, Present and Future," *Jane's Intelligence Review, Special Report Number 1*, 1994, 8. Hereafter cited simply as *Jane's*.

[183] Ken Fireman, "It's Not Over Yet; Chechens say they will keep on fighting," *Newsday* (February 12, 1995) A15.

[184] *Jane's*, 17.

[185] Anatol Lieven, *Chechnya: Tombstone of Russian Power* (New Haven: Yale University Press, 1998), 111.

[186] Lee Hockstaer, "Not All Quiet on the Chechen Front," *Washington Post*, May 6, 1995.

[187] Alexander Lebed, John Kohan, Yuri Zarakhovich, "For Better, For Worse: Awaiting His Nation's Call," *TIME Magazine* (New York: Time Inc., February 27, 1995) 26.

[188] *Jane's*, 20.

[189] Gall and De Waal, 350.

[190] "The first days of the fighting for control of Grozny required a buildup of the grouping. The 165th Regiment of Marines of the Pacific Fleet and an infantry battalion from each of the Northern and Baltic Fleets were sent in, and they gave an exceptionally good account of themselves." Grachev, 14.

[191]Marine Corps Intelligence Activity, "Russia's War in Chechnya: Urban Warfare Lessons Learned 1994-1996," 2.

[192]Robert R. Leonhard, *The Principles of War for the Information Age* (Novato, CA: Presidio Press, 1998) 20.

Chapter Eight

[193] Sebastian Smith, *Allah's Mountains: Politics and War in the Russian Caucasus* (London: I. B Tauris, 1998), 158.

[194] Timothy Thomas, "The Battle for Grozny: Deadly Classroom for Urban Combat," 91.

[195] Lester W. Grau, "Russian Urban Tactics: Lessons from the Battle of Grozny," *Strategic Forum* 38 (July 1995): 2-3.

[196] Thomas, "The Caucasus Conflict and Russian Security: The Russian Armed Forces Confront Chechnya III: The Battle for Grozny, 1-26 January 1995," 56.

[197] Vladimir Georgiyev, "The Chechen People Are for a Peaceful Life," *Rossiykiye Vesti*, 24 January 95, pgs 1-2, as reported in FBIS-SOV-95-015, 24 January 95, 22-24.

[198] Anatol Lieven, *Chechnya: Tombstone of Russian Power*, 110

[199] Pavel Felgengauer, "Russia on the Brink of a Catastrophe: The Russian Subdivisions Which Entered Grozny Have Been Routed," *Segodnya*, 5 January 95, p. 1, as reported in FBIS-SOV-95-003, 5 January 95, 25.

[200] Lieven, *Chechnya: Tombstone of Russian Power*, 109.

[201] Sebastian Smith, *Allah's Mountains: Politics and War in the Russian Caucasus*, 148.

[202] Carlotta Gall and Thomas de Wall, *Chechnya: Calamity in the Caucasus* (New York: New York University Press, 1998), 216-217.

[203] Adam Geibel, "Lessons in Urban Combat: Grozny, New Year's Eve, 1994," *Infantry* 85 (November-December 1995): 25.

[204] Grau, "Russian Urban Tactics: Lessons from the Battle of Grozny," 3.

[205] Thomas, "The Battle for Grozny: Deadly Classroom for Urban Combat," 93.

[206] Georgiyev, "The Chechen People Are for a Peaceful Life," 23.

[207] Vladimir Kartashkov, "There Are No Special Troops in Russia to Assault Grozny," *Moskovskiy Komsomolets*, 5 January 1995, p. 1, as reported in FBIS-SOV-95-003, 5 January 1995, 22.

[208] Ibid.

[209] Gall, *Chechnya: Calamity in the Caucasus*, 225-226.

[210] Ibid., 226.

[211] *INTERFAX*, "Task Force to Reinforce Federal Troops in Chechnya, 4 January 1995, as reported in FBIS-SOV-95-003, 5 January 1995, 12.

[212] Gall, *Chechnya: Calamity in the Caucasus,* 210.

[213] Ibid.

[214] Stasys Knezys and Romanas Sedlickas, *The War in Chechnya* (College Station: Texas A&M University Press, 1999), 80.

[215] U. S. Department of the Army, *Intelligence Analysis,* Field Manual 34-3 (Washington, D.C.: U. S. Department of the Army, 15 March 1990), 3-1. FM 34-3 lists nine specific order of battle factors: composition, disposition, strength, tactics, training, logistics, combat effectiveness, electronic technical data, and miscellaneous data.

[216] Thomas, "The Battle of Grozny: Deadly Classroom for Urban Combat," 89.

[217] Knezys, *The War in Chechnya*, 69.

[218] Gall, *Chechnya: Calamity in the Caucasus*, 208.

[219] Thomas, "The Battle of Grozny: Deadly Classroom for Urban Combat," 89.

[220] Thomas, *The Caucasus Conflict and Russian Security: The Russian Armed Forces Confront Chechnya: (Parts One and Two of a Three Part Study. Actions from 11-31 December 1994)*, 30.

[221] Thomas, *The Russian Armed Forces Confront Chechnya: The Battle for Grozny, 1-26 January 1995 (Part I)*, 412-413.

[222] Thomas, "The Battle of Grozny: Deadly Classroom for Urban Combat," 95.

[223] Vladimir Pasko, *Mayak* Radio, 3 January 1995, as reported in FBIS-SOV-95-001, 3 January 1995, p. 24.

[224] Knezys, *The War in Chechnya*, 68.

[225] Ibid., 82.

[226] Ibid., 50, and Thomas, *The Caucasus Conflict and Russian Security: The Russian Armed Forces Confront Chechnya: (Parts One and Two of a Three Part Study. Actions from 11-31 December 1994)*, 34.

[227] Gall, *Chechnya: Calamity in the Caucasus*, 202.

[228] Thomas, *The Caucasus Conflict and Russian Security: The Russian Armed Forces Confront Chechnya: (Parts One and Two of a Three Part Study. Actions from 11-31 December 1994)*, 26.

[229] Smith, *Allah's Mountains: Politics and War in the Russian Caucasus*, 161-162.

[230] Ibid., 153.

[231] Thomas, "The Battle of Grozny: Deadly Classroom for Urban Combat," 90.

[232] Ibid.

[233] Smith, *Allah's Mountains: Politics and War in the Russian Caucasus*, 121.

[234] Ibid., 63.

[235] Grau, "Russian Urban Tactics: Lessons from the Battle for Grozny," 1.

[236] Livia Klingl, "Idiots Are Responsible for the Organization," Vienna *Kurier*, 5 January 1995, p. 5, as reported in FBIS-SOV-95-003, 5 January 1995, 10.

[237] Lieven, *Chechnya: Tombstone of Russian Power*, 110.

[238] Klingl, "Idiots Are Responsible for the Organization," 10.

[239] U. S. Department of the Army, *Operational Terms and Graphics,* Field Manual 101-1-5 (Washington, D.C.: U. S. Department of the Army, 20 September 1997), 1-55.

[240] Russell Glenn, *"We Band of Brothers:" The Call for Joint Urban Operations Doctrine*, 17.

[241] Ibid., 30.

[242] Thomas, "The Battle for Grozny: Deadly Classroom for Urban Combat," 91.

[243] Rosenau, "Every Room is a New Battle: The Lessons of Modern Urban Warfare," 385.

[244] John A. Hadam, Sales Manager, IS Robotics, to Lt. Col. Brian A. Keller, Carlisle Barracks, PA, 21 December 1999, letter in the hand of Lt. Col. Brian A. Keller; additional information on "Urban Robot" is available at www.isr.com.

Chapter Ten

[245] Louis Dupree, *Afghanistan* (Princeton: Princeton University Press, 1973), xvii. Although now some three decades old, Dupree's work remains the single most important volume on the history and culture of Afghanistan and should be the starting point for anyone trying to understand the region.

[246] Two recent examples represent the diversity of interpretations: Stephen Biddle, *Afghanistan and the Future of Warfare* (Carlisle, Pennsylvania: Strategic Studies Institute, 2002) and Charles H. Briscoe *et al.*, *Weapon of Choice: U.S. Army Special Operations Forces in Afghanistan* (Fort Leavenworth, Kansas: Combat Studies Institute Press, 2003). Biddle attempts to present a balanced, if early, analysis of lessons to be drawn from military operations there during the first year of U.S. military involvement and essentially states that advocates proposing that U.S. and allied actions in Afghanistan herald a new era in warfare have it wrong – the old, time proven rules still apply. Precision weapons alone cannot win wars on their own, troops on the ground (in this case, Northern Alliance) supported by indirect fires remain essential to winning land campaigns. Briscoe argues, essentially, that the Afghanistan operation is proof that Special Operations Forces can cover the full spectrum of operations and Afghanistan is in fact proof of a new era in warfare.

[247] Fortunately, this situation might be changing. Despite the enormous obstacles blocking the development of Afghanistan, Kabul in particular appears to be poised for economic growth. The United Nations, the North Atlantic Treaty Organization and the United States as of this writing are investing large sums of money and effort

[248] For an insightful and brief account of British experience in this regard see Michael Barthorp, *Afghan Wars and the North-West Frontier 1839-1947* (London: Cassell, 2002).

[249] For a superb account of how parts of Afghanistan, especially the capital city of Kabul, did modernize relatively quickly, see Part IV., "The Present," Dupree, 415-666.

[250] Bhapani Sen Gupta, *Afghanistan: Politics, Economics and Society* (Boulder, Colorado: Lynne Rienner Publishers, Inc., 1986), v.

[251] Thomas T. Hammond, *Red Flag Over Afghanistan: The Communist Coup, the Soviet Invasion, and the Consequences* (Boulder, Colorado: Westview Press, 1984), 9.

The three previous invasions or incursions took place in 1925, 1929 and 1930.

[252] David C. Isby, *War in a Distant Country: Afghanistan: Invasion and Resistance* (London: Arms and Armour Press, 1989), 56.

[253] Robert F. Bauman, *Russian-Soviet Unconventional Wars in the Caucasus, Central Asia, and Afghanistan*, Leavenworth Paper Number 20 (Fort Leavenworth, Kansas: Combat Studies Institute, 1993), 136.

[254] Ibid., 145.

[255] The official Soviet withdrawal from Afghanistan began in May of 1988, but significant Soviet involvement – and casualties – in Afghanistan began well before the December 1979 invasion and continued well into 1989.

[256] A superb and concise analysis of the Soviet-Afghan War can be found in Bauman, Chapter 4, "The Soviet-Afghan War," 129-210. This should be required reading for anyone interested in understanding the Soviet experience or involved with current U.S. operations there today.

[257] Tom Heneghan, "The Tormented State," in Reuters, ed., *Afghanistan: Lifting the Veil* (Upper Saddle River, New Jersey: Prentice Hall, 2002), 7-9. For students of urban combat, the seizure of Kabul and its subsequent destruction in 1992 and 1993 offers little relevant information other than modern weapons can wreak enormous destruction against a helpless population. To this day western Kabul remains nothing more than dozens of square miles of rubble.

[258] Stephen Tanner, *Afghanistan: A Military History from Alexander the Great to the Fall of the Taliban* (New York: Da Capo Press, 2002), 293.

[259] Ibid., 286.

[260] A riveting, but by no means perfect account of these operations is provided in the recent release, George Crile,

Charlie Wilson's War The Extraordinary Story of the Largest Covert Operation in History (New York: Atlantic Monthly Press, 2003). For a more scholarly account of some of these same operations, but viewed in the larger international and strategic perspective, see Diego Cordovez and Selig S. Harrison, *Out of Afghanistan: The Inside Story of the Soviet Withdrawal* (New York: Oxford University Press, 1995).

[261] Tanner, 291.

[262] The original operational name of "Infinite Justice" was scrapped because it evoked, according to some, imagery of the Crusades.

[263] Tanner, 295-6.

[264] Briscoe, 94.

[265] Of course, air-delivered ordnance, even when guided by laser designators, was not always perfect and the deaths of allied soldiers was still an unfortunate fact of the war. The most notorious example of this occurred on December 5, 2001 when a 2,000-pound precision-delivered bomb killed three American and five Afghan soldiers and wounded dozens of others, including the president of Afghanistan, Hamid Karzai. Tanner, 308.

[266] Briscoe, 101-102.

[267] Tanner, 301.

[268] Daragahi, Borzou, "Insurgent Violence Mounting in the North," *San Francisco Chronicle*, 12 November 2004, A1.

[269] United States Army White Paper. "Concepts for the Objective Force," http://www.army.mil/features/WhitePaper/ObjectiveForceWhitePaper.pdf (accessed October 10, 2006).

[270] The acquisition process to purchase the Interim Armored Vehicle, later named the Stryker, began in 1999 with the first vehicle delivered for use in 2002. That timeline is a

major departure from the standard acquisition process, which typically takes 8-30 years for the delivery of a major mechanical system or platform.

[271] Each Stryker variant had either a .50 caliber machine gun or an MK-19 grenade launcher, with the exception of the MEV and ATGM. The MEV, as a medical vehicle, did not have an associated weapon system. The ATGM had M-240 machine gun in addition to the TOW launcher.

[272] The Department of the Army, *FM 3-21.31: The Stryker Brigade Combat Team* (Washington, DC: 13 March 2003), 1-17.

[273] Gilbert, Michael, "Troops Bask in Bush's Praise," *The Tacoma-News Tribune*, 21 June 2004, http://www.strykernews.com/archives/2004/06/21/troops_bask_in_bushs_praise.html (accessed October 10, 2006).

[274] 1/25's non-Stryker fleet included in excess of 700 other vehicles including HMMWV's, 5-ton trucks, recovery vehicles, fuel trucks, et al.

[275] Based on continued testing of the Stryker Mobile Gun System variant, ATGMs were used in- lieu of MGS in the infantry battalions.

[276] The Department of the Army, *FM 3-21.21: The Stryker Brigade Combat Team Infantry Battalion* (Washington, DC: 08 April 2003), 1-12.

[277] The Department of the Army, *FM 3-20.96: Reconnaissance Squadron* (Washington, DC: 20 September 2006), 1-43.

[278] Based on the lack of Strykers within 2-/8 Field Artillery, D/52 was task organized to the battalion prior to deployment from home station. Non-organic units were attached to 1/25 to provide additional combat power and support to the brigade. Included in these attachments at various points in the deployment were 1st Battalion, 151st Aviation Brigade (South Carolina National Guard); 2nd2d

Battalion, 101st Aviation Regiment; 139th Field Artillery Detachment; 113th Engineer Battalion (Heavy); and the 276th Engineer Battalion (Heavy)

Further task organization involved expanding the brigade's HUMINT capabilities. The MICO, with four organic human intelligence (HUMINT) teams, was complemented by reorganizing HUMINT trained Soldiers from the RSTA and several nonorganic assets to create 12 HUMINT teams .

[279] The Department of the Army, *FM 3-21.31: The Stryker Brigade Combat Team* (Washington, DC: 13 March 2003), 1-25.

[280] Although extensive operations were conducted in both Tall Afar and the Tigris River Valley, this work focuses specifically in Mosul. The efforts of 2-/14 in Tall Afar, 2-/8 in the lower Tigris River Valley, and 1-/5 in the upper Tigris River Valley offer many of the same lessons presented in this document.

[281] United States Military Academy Prospectus, "The West Point Experience," http://admissions.usma.edu/prospectus/wpe_physical.cfm (accessed October 10, 2004).

[282] The Department of the Army, *FM 3-21.31: The Stryker Brigade Combat Team* (Washington, DC: 13 March 2003), 1-28 c. (4) (a).

[283] The type of aircraft under brigade control changed slightly throughout the 1/25 deployment. Upon arrival, OH-58's were the sole aircraft. That changed to AH-64s with the arrival of 1-/151 Aviation. 2-/101 assumed aviation responsibilities later in the deployment and employed both OH-58s and AH-64s.

[284] U.S Department of Defense, "News Transcript: Colonel Robert B. Brown Interview, September 14, 2005."

[285] Wong, Edward, "Insurgents Attack Fiercely in North, Storming Police Stations in Mosul," *New York Times*, 12 November 2004.

[286] U.S. Department of Defense, "News Release: DOD Identifies Army Casualty," 12 November 2004.

[287] Task Force Olympia Press Release, "On-going Operations to Stabilize the Situation in Mosul and Northern Iraq," 14 November 2004.

[288] When 1/25 transferred authority with 3/2, it inherited responsibility for the 101st and 106th ING in Mosul, the 109th ING in Tall Afar, and the 102nd102d and 107th ING in the Tigris River Valley. At the onset of 1/25 operations each ING battalion was paired with a 1/25 battalion for operations, training, and logistical support. That pairing would increase with proficiency and effort as the brigade increased in experience and understanding of the situation. The term ING was replaced with Iraqi Army (IA) in 2005.

[289] Although TACs differed some within each battalion and brigade, typically the TAC consisted of at least three Strykers. It was normally led by the unit commander and manned by key staff leaders including the operations officer, and representatives from the intelligence and fire support staff sections. Brigade and battalion command sergeants major, the units' senior noncommissioned officers, were also normal members of the TAC. TAC elements typically provided their own security but often worked in conjunction with other maneuver elements from their respective units.

[290] 1/25 learned that face-to-face interaction was essential to success in northern Iraq. In an effort to facilitate the continued development of personal relationships, the brigade made only minor adjustments to unit boundaries throughout the deployment. With the exception of additional territory ceded to 1-/5 following the elections, there were no other significant changes throughout the deployment. Constant boundaries and areas of operations allowed company and battalion commanders to develop strong relationships with the local populace. Similar to "beat" policemen in the United

States, this made it possible for leaders and Soldiers to notice small changes within their respective areas.

[291] Searcey, Donna, "U.S. Shoots Back at Insurgents," *Newsday*, December 30, 2004, http://www.newsday.com/news/nationworld/world/ny-woiraq1230,0,4433709.story?coll=ny-world-big-pix (accessed October 10, 2006).

[292] The Non-Lethal Effects Cell consisted of the Brigade Information Operations Officer, the Civil Affairs officer, the brigade public affairs officer, the brigade's staff judge advocate, and representatives from the 1290 Psychological Operations Detachment and 448th Civil Affairs Detachment, both working directly for 1/25 in northern Iraq (the 1290th was later replaced by the 3611th Psychological Operations Detachment).

[293] The Joint Coordination Center housed an operations center with representatives from all portions of Mosul security and first responder organizations. In October 2004, the JCC was not fully manned. Although the ING, Mosul Police, ambulance services, and government representatives were part of the center's organization, there were seldom representatives from each organization present. Initially, 1/25 conducted routine visits to and weekly meetings at the JCC to ensure combined activities were being pursued appropriately. Unfortunately, internal disputes often kept key Iraqi stakeholders from attending weekly coordination meetings. After the police collapse in November 2004, attendance at the weekly meetings dropped dramatically. Colonel Brown realized the potential and importance of the JCC to future operations and installed a 24-hour 1/25 liaison cell at the JCC. That connectivity ensured mutual support throughout the brigade's deployment. At the beginning of the brigade's deployment, the JCC received an average of 40 calls per month, reporting insurgent activity or emergency-related information. By the summer of 2005, that number surpassed 400 calls per month.

[294] Of the 24 Lancers killed in action, nine died on a single day when a suicide bomber breeched the security of the FOB Marez dining facility by posing as a member of the Iraqi National Guard and detonating his explosive vest in the

middle of the lunch meal. 1/25 SBCT lost 44 soldiers during the yearlong deployment, including Soldiers of units killed while attached to the Lancer Brigade. For its sacrifices and efforts surrounding the Iraqi Provincial Elections on January 30, 2005, the brigade was awarded the Valorous Unit Award, presented to the unit for extraordinary heroism in combat.

Back Cover Photo:
Soldiers from the Future Combat Systems, Evaluation Brigade Combat Team, employ an unmanned vehicle to clear a road during an exercise and live demonstration Feb. 1 at Oro Grande Range, Fort Bliss, Texas. Photo by Maj. Deanna Bague February 2, 2007.